THE GHOST BRIDE

THE GHOST BRIDE

Yangsze Choo

ωm

WILLIAM MORROW

An Imprint of HarperCollins*Publishers*

THE GHOST BRIDE. Copyright © 2013 by Yangsze Choo. All rights reserved. Printed in the United States of America. No part of this book may be used or reproduced in any manner whatsoever without written permission except in the case of brief quotations embodied in critical articles and reviews. For information address HarperCollins Publishers, 195 Broadway, New York, NY 10007.

HarperCollins books may be purchased for educational, business, or sales promotional use. For information please e-mail the Special Markets Department at SPsales@harpercollins.com.

A hardcover edition of this book was published in 2013 by William Morrow, an imprint of HarperCollins Publishers.

FIRST WILLIAM MORROW PAPERBACK EDITION PUBLISHED 2014.

Designed by Lisa Stokes

Library of Congress Cataloging-in-Publication Data has been applied for.

ISBN 978-0-06-222733-1

23 24 25 26 27 LBC 15 14 13 12 11

This book is for James

THE GHOST BRIDE

PART ONE

Malaya 1893

CHAPTER 1

O NE EVENING, MY father asked me whether I would like to become a ghost bride. *Asked* is perhaps not the right word. We were in his study. I was leafing through a newspaper, my father lying on his rattan daybed. It was very hot and still. The oil lamp was lit and moths fluttered through the humid air in lazy swirls.

"What did you say?"

My father was smoking opium. It was his first pipe of the evening, so I presumed he was relatively lucid. My father, with his sad eyes and skin pitted like an apricot kernel, was a scholar of sorts. Our family used to be quite well off, but in recent years we had slipped until we were just hanging on to middle-class respectability.

"A ghost bride, Li Lan."

I held my breath as I turned a page. It was hard to tell when my father was joking. Sometimes I wasn't sure even he was entirely certain. He made light of serious matters, such as our dwindling income, claiming that he didn't mind wearing a threadbare shirt in this heat. But at other times, when the opium enveloped him in its hazy embrace, he was silent and distracted.

"It was put to me today," he said quickly. "I thought you might like to know."

"Who asked?"

"The Lim family."

The Lim family was among the wealthiest households in our town of Malacca. Malacca was a port, one of the oldest trading settlements in the East. In the past few hundred years, it had passed through Portuguese, Dutch, and finally British rule. A long, low cluster of red-tiled houses, it straggled along the bay, flanked by groves of coconut trees and backed inland by the dense jungle that covered Malaya like a rolling green ocean. The town of Malacca was very still, dreaming under the tropical sun of its past glories, when it was the pearl of port cities along the Straits. With the advent of steamships, however, it had fallen into graceful decline.

Yet compared to the villages in the jungle, Malacca remained the epitome of civilization. Despite the destruction of the Portuguese fort, we had a post office, the Stadthuys city hall, two markets, and a hospital. We were in fact the seat of British administration for the state. Still, when I compared it to what I had read of the great cities of Shanghai, Calcutta, or London, I was sure it was quite insignificant. London, as the District Office once told our cook's sister, was the center of the world. The heart of a great and glittering empire that stretched so far from east to west that the sun never set on it. From that far-off island (very damp and cold, I heard), we in Malaya were ruled.

But though many races—Malay, Chinese, and Indian, with a sprinkling of Arab and Jewish traders—had settled here for generations, we kept our own practices and dress. And though my father could speak Malay and some English, he still looked to China for his books and papers. Never mind that it was my grandfather who left his native soil to make his fortune trading here. It was too bad that the money had dwindled under my father's hands. Otherwise I don't think he would even have considered the Lim family's offer.

"They had a son who died a few months ago. A young man named Lim Tian Ching—do you remember him?"

Lim Tian Ching was someone I had seen perhaps once or twice at some festival. Apart from the name of his wealthy clan, he had left no impression at all. "Surely he was very young?"

"Not much older than you, I believe."

"What did he die of?"

"A fever, they say. In any case, he is the bridegroom." My father spoke carefully, as though he was already regretting his words.

"And they want me to marry him?"

Distracted, I knocked over the inkstone on his desk, its contents spilling onto the newspaper in an ominous black stain. This practice of arranging the marriage of a dead person was uncommon, usually held in order to placate a spirit. A deceased concubine who had produced a son might be officially married to elevate her status to a wife. Or two lovers who died tragically might be united after death. That much I knew. But to marry the living to the dead was a rare and, indeed, dreadful occurrence.

My father rubbed his face. He was once, so I was told, a very handsome man until he contracted smallpox. Within two weeks his skin became as thick as a crocodile's hide and scarred with a thousand craters. Once gregarious, he retired from the world, let the family business be run by outsiders, and immersed himself in books and poems. Perhaps things might have been better had my mother not died during the same outbreak, leaving me behind at the tender age of four. The smallpox passed me by with only one scar behind my left ear. At the time, a fortune-teller predicted that I would be lucky, but perhaps he was simply being optimistic.

"Yes, it is you that they want."

"Why me?"

"All I know is that they asked if I had a daughter named Li Lan and if you were married yet."

"Well, I don't think it would suit me at all." I scrubbed fiercely at the ink on the table, as though I could wipe away the topic of conversation. And how had they known my name?

I was about to ask when my father said, "What, you don't want to be a widow at almost eighteen? Spend your life in the Lim mansion wearing silk? But you probably wouldn't be allowed any bright colors." He broke into his melancholy smile. "Of course I didn't accept. How would I dare? Though if you didn't care for love or children, it might not be so bad. You would be housed and clothed all the days of your life."

"Are we so poor now?" I asked. Poverty had been looming over our household for years, like a wave that threatened to break.

"Well, as of today we can no longer buy ice."

You could buy a block of ice from the British store, packed tightly in sawdust and wrapped in brown paper. It was a cargo remnant, having come by steamer all the way from halfway round the world, where clean ice was stowed in the hold to preserve fresh food. Afterward, the blocks were sold off to anyone who wanted a piece of the frozen West. My amah told me how in earlier days, my father had bought a few exotic fruits for my mother. A handful of apples and pears grown under temperate skies. I had no recollection of such events, although I loved to chip at our occasional purchases of ice, imagining that I too had journeyed to the frigid wastes.

I left him to the rest of his opium pipe. As a child, I spent hours standing in his study, memorizing poetry or grinding ink for him to practice his calligraphy, but my embroidery skills were poor and I had little idea of how to run a household, all things that would make me a better wife. My amah did what she could, but there were limits to her knowledge. I often used to fantasize about what life would have been like had my mother lived.

As I left the room, Amah pounced on me. She had been waiting outside and gave me quite a fright. "What was it your father wanted to ask you?"

My amah was very tiny and old. She was so small that she was almost like a child—a very opinionated and despotic one who nonetheless loved me with all her heart. She was my mother's nurse before me and by right should have retired long ago, but still she puttered around the house in her black trousers and white blouse like a clockwork toy.

"Nothing," I said.

"Was it a marriage offer?" For someone who claimed to be old and deaf she had surprisingly sharp hearing. A cockroach couldn't skitter across a dark room without her stamping it out.

"Not really." As she looked unconvinced, I said, "It was more like a joke."

"A joke? Since when has your marriage been a joke? Marriage is very important to a woman. It determines her whole future, her life, her children . . . "

"But this wasn't a real marriage."

"A concubine? Someone wants you to be his concubine?" She shook her head. "No, no, Little Miss. You must be a wife. Number one wife if possible."

"It was not to be a concubine."

"Then who was it from?"

"The Lim family."

Her eyes widened until she resembled one of those saucer-eyed jungle lemurs. "The Lim family! Oh! Little Miss, it was not for nothing that you were born as beautiful as a butterfly," and so on and so forth. I listened with some amusement and irritation as she continued to list many good qualities that she had never bothered to mention to me before, until she came to an abrupt halt. "Didn't the son of the Lim family die? There is a nephew, though. He will inherit, I suppose."

"No, it was a proposal for the son," I said with some reluctance, feeling as though I was betraying my father by admitting he had even entertained such an outrageous thought. Her reaction was just as expected. What could my father be thinking of? How dare the Lims insult our family!

"Don't worry, Amah. He's not going to accept."

"You don't understand! This is very unlucky. Don't you know what it means?" Her small frame quivered. "Your father should never have mentioned this to you, even as a joke."

"I'm not upset." I crossed my arms.

"*Aiya*, if only your mother were here! Your father has gone too far this time."

Despite my attempts to reassure Amah, I felt uneasy as I went to bed, shielding my lamp against the flickering shadows. Our house was large and old, and since our financial decline had not had one-tenth of the servants needed to fully staff it. In my grandfather's day it was filled with people. He had a wife, two concubines, and several daughters. The only surviving son,

however, was my father. Now the wives were dead and gone. My aunts were
married off long ago, and my cousins, whom I had played with as children,
had moved to Penang when that side of the family relocated. As our fortunes
dwindled, more and more rooms were shuttered up. I seemed to recall the bus-
tle of guests and servants, but that must have been before my father withdrew
from the world and allowed himself to be cheated by his business partners.
Amah occasionally talked about those times, but she always ended up cursing
my father's folly, his wicked friends, and ultimately the god of smallpox who
allowed all this to happen.

I was not sure that I believed in a god of smallpox. It didn't seem right to
me that a god should stoop himself to go around blowing smallpox in through
windows and doors at people. The foreign doctors at the hospital talked about
disease and quarantining outbreaks, an explanation that seemed far more
reasonable to me. Sometimes I thought I would become a Christian, like the
English ladies who went to the Anglican Church every Sunday. I had never
been, but it looked so peaceful from the outside. And their graveyard, with its
neat green sward and tidy gravestones under the frangipani trees, seemed a far
more comfortable place than the wild Chinese cemeteries perched on hillsides.

We went to the cemetery on Qing Ming, the festival of the dead, to sweep
the graves, honor our ancestors, and offer food and incense. The graves were
made like small houses or very large armchairs, with wings on either side to
encompass a central tablet and small altar. The paths up the hills were overgrown with weeds and *lalang*, the sharp elephant grass that cuts you if you ran
your finger along it. All around were abandoned graves that people had forgotten or which had no more descendants to care for them. The thought of having
to pay my respects as the widow to a stranger made me shudder. And what
exactly did marrying a ghost entail? My father had treated it as a joke. Amah
had not wanted to say—she was so superstitious that naming something was
as good as making it come true. As for myself, I could only hope that I would
never need to know.

CHAPTER 2

I TRIED MY best to put the Lim's disturbing overture out of my mind. After all, it wasn't really what one would hope for in a first proposal. I knew I ought to be married some day—a day that was drawing ever closer—but life was not yet too restrictive. Compared to how things are done in China, we were fairly casual in Malaya. Locally born Chinese women didn't bind their feet. Indeed, the other races looked upon foot binding as strange and ugly, crippling a woman and making her useless for work in the home. When the Portuguese first landed in Malacca more than three hundred years ago, there were already Chinese here, though the earliest Chinese who came to seek their fortunes brought no women. Some took Malay wives and the resulting mix of cultures was known as Peranakan. Later, settlers sent for women from home who were often older, divorced, or widowed, for who else would undertake such a long and perilous voyage? So we were less rigid here, and even an unmarried girl of good family might walk in the streets, accompanied, of course, by a chaperone. In any case, despite my father's eternal interest in all things cultural from China, the reality was that the British were the ruling class here. They set the laws and precedents, established government offices, and opened English schools for natives. Our bright young men aspired to be government clerks under them.

I wondered what had happened to the unfortunate Lim Tian Ching and if he had hoped to rise to such a clerkship, or whether such things were beneath him as the son of a rich man. His father was well known as the owner of tin mining concessions, as well as coffee and rubber plantations. I also wondered why the family had approached my father, for it wasn't as though I had any kind of personal history with their son.

Over the next few days I tried to badger my father into revealing more of their conversation but he refused to answer, retreating to his study and, I am sure, smoking more opium than he ought. He had a vaguely sheepish air as though he was sorry he had ever mentioned it. Amah also got on his nerves. Not daring to berate him openly, she wandered around with a feather duster, addressing various inanimate objects with a stream of muttered complaints. Unable to escape her onslaught, my father eventually placed the newspaper over his face and pretended to be asleep.

In this way, I thought the matter settled. However, a few days later a message came from the Lim family. It was an invitation from Madam Lim herself to play mahjong.

"Oh, I don't play," I said, before I could stop myself.

The servant who had been sent merely smiled and said it didn't matter; I should still come and watch. Indeed, I was very curious to see the interior of the Lim mansion, and despite pulling a sour face, Amah could not help fussing over my clothes and hair. Meddling was always her second nature and since I was much raised by her, I feared that it was also one of my own qualities.

"Well, if you must go, at least they will see that you are nothing to be ashamed of!" she said as she laid out my second-best dress. I had two good dresses: one of thin lilac silk with morning glories embroidered on the collar and sleeves, and another of pale green with butterflies. Both belonged to my mother, as I hadn't had new silk clothing for a while. Most of the time I wore loose cotton *cheong sam*, which is a long gown, or *sam foo*, the blouse and trousers used by working girls. As it was, when these dresses wore out, we would probably unpick the embroidered collar and cuffs to reuse on another garment.

"What shall we do with your hair?" asked Amah, forgetting that she had disapproved of this visit only moments ago. My hair was usually kept in two neat plaits, though for special occasions it was skewered up with long hairpins. These gave me a headache, particularly when wielded by Amah, who was determined that not one strand should stray. Stepping back, she surveyed her handiwork and stuck in a couple of gold pins with jade butterflies. The hairpins were also my mother's. After that, she clasped no less than five necklaces around my neck: two of gold; one of garnets; another of small freshwater pearls; and the last with a heavy jade disk. I felt quite burdened by this largesse, but it was nothing compared to what wealthier people wore. Women had little security other than jewelry, so even the poorest among us sported gold chains, earrings, and rings as their insurance. As for the rich—well, I would soon see how Madam Lim was attired.

The Lim mansion was farther out of town, away from the close quarters of Jonker and Heeren Streets, where wealthy Chinese merchants had taken over old Dutch shop houses. I heard that the Lims too had such property, but they had moved their main residence to where the rich were building new estates in Klebang. It wasn't too far from our house, though I had heard it was nothing like the European quarter's villas and bungalows. Those were very grand, indeed, with many servants, stables, and great expanses of green lawn. The Lim mansion was in the Chinese style and said to be quite imposing in its own right. Amah had called for a rickshaw to take us there, although I thought it wasteful when we could have walked. She pointed out, however, that it was still a fair distance and it would do no good to appear covered in sweat and dust.

The afternoon sun had begun to abate when we set off. Waves of heat rose from the road along with clouds of fine white dust. Our rickshaw puller moved at a steady trot, rivulets of sweat streaking his back. I felt sorry for those coolies who hired themselves out in this manner. It was a hard way to make a living, although better than working in the tin mines, where I had heard the mortality rate was almost one in two. The rickshaw pullers were very thin, with concave rib cages, leathery skin, and bare feet so calloused that they resembled hooves. Still, the scrutiny of these strange men made me uneasy. Of course, I was not supposed to go out unaccompanied and when I did, must shade my face with an oiled-paper parasol. Before I could muse much further, however, we had drawn up to the Lim mansion. While Amah gave the rickshaw puller stern instructions to wait for us outside, I gazed at the heavy ironwood doors, which swung open noiselessly to reveal an equally silent servant.

We passed through a courtyard lined with large porcelain pots planted with bougainvillea. The pots alone were worth a small fortune and had been shipped from China, nestled in chests of tea leaves to protect against breakage. The blue-and-white glaze had the limpid quality that I had seen on the few small pieces that my father still possessed. If such costly ceramics were left out in the sun and rain, then I was certainly impressed. Perhaps that was the point. We waited in a grand foyer while the servant went ahead to announce us. The floor was a black-and-white checkerboard and the sweeping teak staircase had carved balustrades. And all around there were clocks.

Such clocks! The walls were covered with dozens of clocks in every style imaginable. Large ones stood on the floor and smaller examples nestled on side tables. There were cuckoo clocks, porcelain clocks, delicate ormolu clocks, and a tiny clock no larger than a quail's egg. Their glass faces shone and the brass ornaments winked. All about us rose the hum of their works. Time, it seemed, could scarcely go unmarked in this house.

While I was admiring this sight, the servant reappeared and we were ushered through a further sequence of rooms. The house, like many Chinese mansions, was built in a series of courtyards and connecting corridors. We passed through stone gardens arranged like miniature landscapes and parlors stiff with antique furniture, until I heard the raised chatter of women's voices and the sharp clack of mahjong tiles. Five tables had been set up and I had an impression of well-dressed ladies who put my own attire to shame. But my eyes were fixed on the head table, where the servant muttered something to a woman who could only have been Madam Lim.

At first glance I was disappointed. I had penetrated so far into this domain that I was expecting, perhaps naively, nothing less than the Queen of Heaven.

Instead, she was a middle-aged woman with a figure that had thickened at the waist. She was dressed beautifully but severely in an inky-hued *baju panjang* to signify mourning. Her son had died nine months ago but she would mourn him at least a year. She was almost overshadowed by the woman who sat next to her. She too wore blue and white mourning colors, but her stylish *kebaya* had a waspish cut, and her jeweled hairpins gave her an insect-like glitter. I would have thought that she was the lady of the house except for the fact that she, like the other women at the table, couldn't help but glance at Madam Lim as though to take their cue from her. I learned later that she was the Third Wife.

"I'm glad you could come," said Madam Lim. She had a soft voice, strangely youthful and much like the purring of a dove. I had to strain to hear her over the surrounding chatter.

"Thank you, Auntie," I replied, for that was how we addressed older women as a mark of respect. I wasn't sure whether to bob my head or bow. How I wished I had paid more attention to such niceties!

"I knew your mother before she was married, when we were children," she said. "She never mentioned it?" Seeing my surprise, Madam Lim showed her teeth briefly in a smile. "Your mother and I are distantly related." This I had never heard of either. "I should have asked after you earlier," said Madam Lim, "It was very remiss of me." Around her the mahjong game started up again with a brisk clatter. She gestured to a servant, who pulled up a marble-topped stool beside her. "Come, Li Lan. I hear that you don't play, but perhaps you'd like to watch."

So I sat next to her, looking at her tiles while she made bids, and nibbling sweetmeats that issued in a never-ending stream from the kitchens. They had all my favorite kinds of *kuih*—the soft steamed *nyonya* cakes made of glutinous rice flour stuffed with palm sugar or shredded coconut. There were delicate rolled biscuits called love letters and pineapple tarts pressed out of rich pastry. Bowls of toasted watermelon seeds were passed around, along with fanned slices of mango and papaya. It had been a long time since we had had such an assortment of treats at home, and I couldn't help indulging myself like a child. From the corner of my eye I saw Amah shake her head, but here she was powerless to stop me. At length Amah disappeared to the kitchen to help out, and without her disapproving eye, I continued eating.

From time to time, Madam Lim murmured something to me. Her voice was so soft, however, that I scarcely understood her. I smiled and nodded, all the while gazing around with undisguised curiosity. I rarely had the chance to go out in society. Had my mother lived, I might have sat beside her just like this, peering over her shoulder at the ivory tiles and soaking up gossip. These women peppered their conversation with sly references to important people and places. With nonchalance, they mentioned what seemed to me astounding gambling debts.

Madam Lim must have thought me simple or at the very least unsophisticated. I caught her sharp pigeon eyes studying me from time to time. Strangely enough, this seemed to relieve her. Only much later did I understand why she was so pleased with my gauche performance. Around us, the ladies chattered and made bets, jade bangles ringing as the tiles clattered. The Third Wife had moved to another table, which was a pity since I would have liked to study her a little more. She was certainly handsome, though she had a reputation for being difficult, as Amah had earlier found out through servants' chatter. I saw no sign of a Second Wife, although I was told that Lim himself, as a rich man's prerogative, kept other minor concubines whom he had not bothered to marry. There were four daughters from the different wives but no surviving sons. Two had died in infancy and the last, Lim Tian Ching, had been buried less than a year ago. I had wanted to ask Amah how he died but she was unwilling to discuss it, claiming there was no use having any interest in him since I would never be married to him. As it was, the only heir was Lim's nephew.

"Actually he is the rightful heir," Amah had said on our way there.

"What do you mean?"

"He's Lim's older brother's son. Lim himself is the second son. He took over the estate when his older brother died, but promised to bring up his nephew as his heir. As time went on, however, people said that maybe he didn't want to overlook his own children. But what's there to talk about anyway? Lim has no more sons of his own now."

As I considered this web of relationships, I couldn't help feeling a frisson of excitement. It was a world of wealth and intrigue, much like the crudely printed romances that my father was so dismissive of. Of course Amah disapproved. I knew, however, that she too was secretly enthralled. It was so different from our own penurious household. How depressing it was to think of how we scraped along year by year, always trying to stretch things and never buying anything pretty or new! The worst was that my father never did anything. He no longer went out to make contracts or run his business. He had given all that up and was walled up in his study, endlessly copying his favorite poems and writing obscure treatises. Lately, I felt that we were all penned up with him too.

"You look sad." Madam Lim's voice broke in on me. Nothing seemed to escape her gaze. Her eyes were light for a Chinese, and the pupils small and round, like the eyes of a bird.

I colored. "This house is so lively compared with my own home."

"You like it here?" she asked.

I nodded.

"Tell me," she said, "do you have a sweetheart?"

"No." I stared fixedly at my hands.

"Well," she said, "a young girl shouldn't be too worldly." She gave me one of her abbreviated smiles. "My dear, I hope you're not offended that I ask you so many questions. You remind me so much of your mother, and also myself when I was younger."

I refrained from asking her about her own daughters. There were a few young women at the other tables, but everyone had been introduced to me in such a cursory manner that I had a hard time keeping track of who was a cousin, friend, or daughter.

The mahjong game continued but as I wasn't a player, I began to feel restless after a while. When I excused myself to use the washroom, Madam Lim beckoned a servant to escort me. She was in the middle of an exciting hand and I hoped she would stay that way for a while. The servant led me along various passages to a heavy *chengal* wood door. When I was done, I opened it a crack. My guide was still waiting patiently outside. But there was a call down the hallway and, casting a quick glance at the door, she left to answer it.

With a thrill, I slipped out. The house was built in a series of courtyards with rooms looking into them. I passed a small sitting room, and then one with a marble table, half laid for a meal. Hearing voices, I turned hastily down yet another passageway into a courtyard with a small pond, where lotus flowers tilted their creamy heads amid green stalks. A sultry, dreamlike stillness settled over everything. I knew I ought to go back before I was missed, but still I lingered.

While I was examining the lotus seedpods, which resembled the nozzles of watering cans, I heard a faint silvery chime. Perhaps I was near the clock room after all. Wandering over, I peered into what looked like a study. One door was thrown open to the courtyard, but the interior was dark and cool. Momentarily blinded by the difference in the light, I stumbled against someone working at a low table. It was a young man, dressed in shabby indigo cotton. Cogs and gears scattered on the table and floor, rolling away into the corners.

"I'm sorry, miss. . . . " He glanced up with an apologetic air.

"I heard the chiming," I said awkwardly, helping him gather the pieces as best I could.

"You like clocks?"

"I don't know much about them."

"Well, without this gear, and this one, the clock stops completely," he said, collecting the shining innards of a brass pocket watch. With a pair of tweezers, he picked up two tiny cogs and laid them together.

"Can you fix it?" I really shouldn't be having this conversation with a young man, even if he was a servant, but he bent over his work, which put me at ease.

"I'm not an expert but I can put it back together. My grandfather taught me."

"It's a useful skill," I said. "You should open your own shop."

At that he looked up quizzically at me, then smiled. When he smiled, his thick eyebrows drew together and his eyes crinkled at the corners. I felt my cheeks grow hot.

"Do you clean all the clocks?"

"Sometimes. I also do a little accounting and I run errands." He was looking directly at me. "I saw you beside the pond earlier."

"Oh." To hide my discomfort I asked, "Why are there so many clocks in this house?"

"Some say it was a hobby, perhaps even an obsession with the old master. He was the one who collected all of them. He could never rest until he had acquired a new specimen."

"Why was he so interested in them?"

"Well, mechanical clocks are far more precise than water clocks that tell time by dripping water, or candles where you burn tallow to mark hours. These Western clocks are so accurate that you can use them to sail with longitude, not just latitude. Do you know what that is?"

I did, as a matter of fact. My father had explained to me once how the sea charts were marked both horizontally and vertically. "Couldn't we sail with longitude before?"

"No, in the past the great sea routes were all latitude. That's because it's the easiest way to plot a course. But imagine you're far out at sea. All you have is a sextant and a compass. You need to know exactly what time it is so you can reckon the relative position of the sun. That's why these clocks are so wonderful. With them, the Portuguese sailed all the way from the other side of the world."

"Why didn't we do that too?" I asked. "We should have conquered them before they came to Malaya."

"Ah, Malaya is just a backwater. But China could have done it. The Ming sea captains sailed as far as Africa, using only latitude and pilots who knew the local waters."

"Yes," I said eagerly. "I read that they brought back a giraffe for the emperor. But he wasn't interested in barbarian lands."

"And now China is in decline, and Malaya just another European colony."

His words had a faint tinge of bitterness, which made me curious because his hair was cut short with no shaved pate or long hanging queue, the braided hair that many men still maintained even after leaving China. This was either a sign of extreme low class, or rebellion against traditional practices. But he merely smiled. "Still, there's a lot to learn from the British."

There were many other questions I wanted to ask him, but with a start I realized I had been gone too long. And no matter how polite he seemed, it was still improper to talk to a strange young man even if he was only a servant.

"I must go."

"Wait, miss. Do you know where you're going?"

"I came from the mahjong party."

"Should I escort you back?" He half rose from the desk and I couldn't help noticing the ease of his clean-limbed movements.

"No, no." The more I thought about my behavior, the more embarrassed I felt and the more certain I was that I had been missed. I practically ran out of the room. Darting down several passages, I found myself in yet another part of the house. Luck was with me, however. While I was standing there undecided, the same servant who had escorted me to the washroom reappeared.

"Oh, miss," she said. "I just stepped away and when I came back you were gone."

"I'm sorry," I said, smoothing my dress. "I went astray."

WHEN WE GOT BACK to the mahjong room the game was still underway. I slipped into my seat, but Madam Lim hardly seemed to notice. From the number of tokens piled in front of her, she had been on a winning streak. After a while, I made my polite good-byes, but to my surprise Madam Lim rose to see me out.

On our way back to the front door, we passed a servant arranging funeral goods to be burned in one of the courtyards. These were miniature effigies of wire and brightly colored paper that were burned for the dead to receive in the underworld: paper horses for the dead to ride on, grand paper mansions, servants, food, stacks of hell currency, carriages, and even paper furniture. It was a little unusual to see these goods laid out now, as they were usually only prepared for funerals and Qing Ming, the festival of the dead. The devout could, however, also burn them at any time for the use of their ancestors, for without such offerings, the dead were mere paupers in the afterworld, and without descendants or proper burial, they wandered unceasingly as hungry ghosts and were unable to be reborn. It was only at Qing Ming, when general offerings were burned to ward off evil, that these unfortunates received a little sustenance. I had always thought it a frightening idea and looked askance at the funeral goods, despite the gay-colored paper and beautifully detailed models.

As we walked, I studied Madam Lim covertly. The brightness of the courtyard revealed shadows under her eyes and the loose flesh of her cheeks. She looked unutterably weary, although her posture denied such weakness.

"And how is your father?" she said.

"He is well, thank you."

"Has he made any plans for you?"

I ducked my head. "Not that I know of."

"But you are of marriageable age. A girl like you must already have many offers."

"No, Auntie. My father lives quite a retired life." And we're not rich anymore, I added to myself.

She sighed. "I would like to ask you a favor." My ears pricked up, but it was strangely innocuous. "Do you think you could spare me that ribbon in your hair? I was thinking of matching it to make a new *baju*."

"Of course." I pulled the ribbon loose. It was nothing special. The color was a common pink, but who was I to gainsay her? She grasped it with a hand that trembled.

"Are you well, Auntie?" I dared to ask her.

"I've had trouble sleeping," she said in her small, feathery voice. "But I think it will soon pass."

AS SOON AS WE were ensconced in the rickshaw, Amah began to scold me. "How could you behave like that? Eating so much and mooning around—I couldn't tell which was larger, your eyes or your mouth! They must have thought you a goose. Why didn't you charm her, tell her clever stories and flatter her? *Cheh*, you behaved like a *kampung* girl, not the daughter of the Pan family!"

"You never said I was charming before!" I said, stung by her remarks, though I was secretly relieved she had been helping in the kitchen when I took my extended walk-around.

"Charming? Of course you're charming. You could cut paper butterflies and recite poems before any of the other children on our street. I didn't tell you before because I didn't want you to be spoiled."

This was typical Amah logic. But she was bursting with gossip from the kitchen and easily distracted, particularly when I told her about Madam Lim's request for my ribbon. "Well, it's a funny thing to ask. She hasn't had new clothes made for months. Maybe when the period of mourning is over, they'll arrange a marriage for the nephew."

"He's not married yet?"

"Not even betrothed. They said that the master should have arranged an alliance for him earlier, but he held back because he wanted to make a better marriage for his own son."

"How unfair."

"*Aiya*, that's the way of this world! Now the son is dead, they feel guilty for not doing so. Also they probably want to get another heir quickly. If the nephew dies there'll be no one left to inherit."

I was somewhat interested in this story, but my thoughts roamed back over the afternoon. "Amah, who looks after the clocks in that house?"

"The clocks? One of the servants, I should think. Why do you want to know?"

"I was just curious."

"You know, the servants say that Madam Lim is very interested in you," she said. "She's been asking lots of questions lately about you and our household."

"Could it be about the ghost marriage?" For some reason, the piles of funeral effigies rose to my mind and I shuddered.

"Nobody knows about that!" Amah was indignant. "It was a private conversation with your father. Maybe he even misunderstood. All that opium he smokes!"

However much Father smoked, I doubted that it had clouded his understanding that day, but I merely said, "Madam Lim has been asking me questions too."

"What sort of questions?"

"Whether I have a sweetheart, whether I'm betrothed yet."

Amah looked as pleased as a cat that has caught a lizard. "Well! The Lim family has so much money that perhaps a good upbringing matters more than family fortune."

I tried to point out to her that it seemed unlikely they would pass up this chance to acquire a rich daughter-in-law in favor of me. It also didn't explain the unease I felt around Madam Lim. But Amah was happily off in her own daydreams.

"We should show you off more. If people know that the Lim family is interested in you, you may get other marriage offers." Amah was so shrewd in some ways. She would have made an excellent poultry dealer.

"We'll buy some cloth tomorrow to make you new clothes."

CHAPTER 3

T HAT NIGHT, I went to bed early feeling tired and overexcited. It was hot and I tugged at the wooden shutters. Amah did not like me to open the windows too wide at night. Something about the night air being unwholesome, but when there was no monsoon it could be stifling.

When the oil lamp was blown out, the moonlight slowly strengthened until the room was filled with a pale, cold radiance. The Chinese considered the moon to be *yin*, feminine and full of negative energy, as opposed to the sun that was *yang* and exemplified masculinity. I liked the moon, with its soft silver beams. It was at once elusive and filled with trickery, so that lost objects that had rolled into the crevices of a room were rarely found, and books read in its light seemed to contain all sorts of fanciful stories that were never there the next morning. Amah said I must not sew by moonlight; it might ruin my eyesight, thus jeopardizing the chance of a good marriage.

If I were married, I wouldn't mind if my husband was like the young man I'd met that day. Endlessly, I replayed our brief conversation, remembering the tones of his voice, the quick confidence of his remarks. I liked how seriously he had spoken to me, without the avuncular condescension of my father's few friends. The thought that he might share my interests or even understand my concerns caused a strange flutter in my chest. If I were a man and found a serving girl who pleased me, no one would stop me from buying her if she was indentured. Men did so every day. It was far more difficult for women. There were stories of unfaithful concubines who had been strangled, or who'd had their ears and noses sliced off and were then left to roam the streets as beggars. I didn't know anybody personally to whom these atrocities had happened, but I could not meet this young man or, worse still, fall in love with him. Even my father, lax as he was, was unlikely to allow a match with a servant.

I sighed. I barely knew him, it was all hope and conjecture. Though if I did marry, my husband was likely to be a stranger to me as well. It was not necessarily so for all girls of good family. Some families had an early betrothal, others entertained often enough that young people could meet and even fall in love. Not our household, however. My father's withdrawal from the world meant that he had sought out no friends with sons and had arranged no match for me. For the first time I began to fully comprehend why Amah was continually angry with him on this subject. The contrast between the realization of his neglect and the fondness I had for my father was painful. I had few marriage prospects, and would be doomed to the half-life of spinsterhood. Without a husband, I would sink further into genteel poverty, bereft of even the comfort and respect of being a mother. Faced with these depressing thoughts, I buried my face in my thin cotton pillow and cried myself to sleep.

THAT NIGHT I HAD a curious dream. I wandered through the Lim mansion though all was still and silent. It was bright, but there was no sun, merely the whiteness that comes from a fog at midday. And like a fog, parts of the house seemed to vanish as I passed, so that the way behind was shrouded in a thin white film. Just as I had that very day, I passed through artfully planted courtyards, dim corridors, and echoing reception rooms, although this time there was no distant murmur of voices nor servants moving about. Presently,

I became aware that I was not alone. Someone was following me, watching from behind a door or peering through the balustrades of the upper level. I began to hurry, turning down passage after passage as they began to resemble one another with a dreadful sameness.

At last, I came into a courtyard with a lotus pond, very much like the one I had visited that day, although the flowers here had an artificial air, as though they had been stuck into the mud like so many sticks of incense. As I stood wondering what to do, someone sidled up beside me. Turning, I saw a strange young man. He was grandly dressed in old-fashioned formal robes that came down to his ankles. On his feet, curiously short and broad, he wore black court shoes with pointed toes. His clothing was dyed in lurid hues, but his face was quite undistinguished, being plump with a weak chin and a smattering of acne scars. He gazed at me with a solicitous smile.

"Li Lan!" he said, "How I've longed to see you again!"

"Who are you?" I asked.

"You don't remember me, do you? It was too long ago. But I remember you. How could I forget?" he said with a flourish. "Your beautiful eyebrows, like moths. Your lips, like hibiscus petals."

As he beamed, I was struck by a lurch of nausea. "I want to go home."

"Oh no, Li Lan," he said. "Please, sit down. You don't know how long I've been waiting for this moment."

As he gestured, a table appeared laden with all kinds of food. Boiled chickens, melons, candied coconut, cakes of all possible varieties. Like his clothes, they were intensely and unappetizingly pigmented. The oranges looked like daubs of paint, while a platter of *pandan* cakes were the sickly hue of the sea before a typhoon. Piled up in rigid pyramids, this largesse looked uncomfortably like funeral offerings. He pressed me to have a cup of tea.

"I'm not thirsty," I said.

"I know you're shy," said this maddening creature, "but I'll pour myself a cup. See? Isn't it delicious?" He drank with every evidence of enjoyment.

"Li Lan, my dear. Don't you know who I am? I'm Lim Tian Ching!" he said. "The heir of the Lim family. I've come to court you."

The queasiness continued to build until I felt light-headed.

"Aren't you dead?"

As soon as I said that, the world contracted as though it had wrinkled. The colors muted, the outline of the chairs blurred. Then, like the snap of a gutta-percha string, everything was back the way it had been. The white light shone and the food on the table positively glowed. Lim Tian Ching closed his eyes as though pained.

"My dear," he said, "I know this is a shock to you, but let's not dwell on that."

I shook my head doggedly.

"I know you're a delicate creature," he said. "I don't wish to distress you. We'll try again another time."

He tried to smile as he faded away. I was forcing myself awake with all the will I could muster. It was like struggling through a mangrove swamp, but slowly the colors bled away until, gasping, I was aware of the moonlight spilling over my pillow and a numbness in my hands from where I had pressed my forehead.

I could hardly sleep the rest of the night. My body was covered in sweat, my heart racing. What I really wanted to do was to go down the hallway and crawl, like a child, into Amah's bed. I used to sleep next to her when I was small, and the pungent smell of the White Flower Oil she daubed on her temples against headaches comforted me. If I went now, however, Amah would be worried. I would get a scolding and she would force all sorts of nostrums on me. Still, the loneliness and terror I felt almost drove me to disturb her until I remembered that she was an incorrigibly superstitious woman and any mention of Lim Tian Ching would upset her for days. Toward dawn, I finally fell into an uneasy torpor.

I MEANT TO TELL Amah about the dream, but my fears seemed less consequential in bright sunlight. It was a result of dwelling on the Lim family, I told myself. Or eating too much rich food. I also didn't want to admit to Amah that

I had been thinking about husbands before I went to bed. The whole encounter with the young man who fixed clocks made me feel guilty.

The next evening, I went to bed with trepidation, but there were no dreams and so when a few more uneventful nights passed, I put it behind me. My thoughts were, in any case, more concerned with another. Try as I might, they kept drifting back to my conversation with the clock cleaner. I thought about how knowledgeable he had seemed, and what a pity that such a man should be a servant. I wondered how it would feel to run my hands through his cropped hair. When I had a free moment, I studied the angles of my face in the small lacquer mirror that had been my mother's. Growing up, my father took little notice of my appearance. He was more interested in my opinions on paintings and the liveliness of my brush calligraphy. Occasionally, he mentioned that I resembled my mother, but the observation seemed to give more pain than pleasure and afterward, he would withdraw. My amah seldom praised and often found fault, yet I knew she would throw herself under an oxcart for me.

"Amah," I asked her some days later. "How was my mother related to Madam Lin?"

We were walking home after buying material for a new dress. Somehow Amah had found the money for it. Embarrassed, I couldn't bring myself to ask from what private store she had scrimped this unnecessary luxury. All amahs put aside their wages for their retirement. They were a special class of servant sometimes known as "black and white" because of the clothes they wore: a white Chinese blouse over black cotton trousers. Some were single women who refused to marry, others childless widows with no other means of support. When they became amahs, they cut their hair into a short bob and joined a special sisterhood. They paid their dues and banked their money there, and in return after a lifetime of working for others, passed their old age in the Association House where they were fed and clothed until the end of their days. It was one of the few options for a woman with no family and no children to take care of her in her dotage.

I suspected that Amah had been raiding her own savings for me. It was shameful. If our family really ran out of money, then she ought to look for another position. Or she could simply retire. She was old enough to do so. If I married well she might come with me as my personal maid, just as she had come with my mother upon her marriage. Now as I glanced at her tiny form trotting beside me, I felt a surge of affection. Despite her exasperating strictures, which often made me wish to escape her control, she was fiercely loyal.

"Your mother and Madam Lim were second or third cousins, I believe," she said.

"But Madam Lim talked as though she knew my mother."

"Perhaps. But I don't think they were close. I would have remembered," she said. "Madam Lim was a daughter of the Ong family. They made their money building roads for the British."

"She said they played together as children."

"Did she? Maybe a couple of times, but she wasn't one of your mother's close friends. That's for sure."

"Why would she say such a thing, then?"

"Who knows what a rich *tai tai* thinks?" Amah smiled suddenly, her face wrinkling like a tortoise. "I'm sure she has her reasons, though. The servants say it isn't a bad household. Of course, they're still in mourning for the son. It was a great loss for them when he died last year."

"Does she have other children?"

"Two other sons died in infancy. There are daughters by the second and third wives, though."

"I saw the third wife, but not the second one."

"She died four years ago of malaria." Malaria was a scourge for us in Malaya, a constant fever in people's veins. The Malays burned smoky fires to keep the disease away, and the Hindus garlanded their many gods with wreaths of jasmine and marigold to protect them. The British said, however, that it was borne by mosquitoes. Thinking about insects reminded me of the Third Wife and her glittering jeweled pins.

"The Third Wife looks difficult," I said.

"That woman! She was nobody when the master married her. No one even knows where she came from. Some town far south, maybe Johore or even Singapore."

"Do the wives get along?"

Only rich men could afford many wives and the custom was becoming infrequent. The British frowned on it. From what I heard, it was the women-folk, the *mems*, who were most against it. Naturally they disapproved of their men acquiring mistresses and going native. I couldn't say that I blamed them for it. I too would hate to be a second wife. Or a third, or fourth. If that were the case, I would rather run away and pledge my life to the Amah Association.

"As well as you could expect. And then there's all that vying to see who can produce an heir. Fortunately for Madam Lim, she seems to have been the only one."

"And the son, Lim Tian Ching, what was he like?" I shivered despite the heat of the day, remembering my dream. Amah usually avoided speaking of him, but I thought I would see what I could worm out of her today.

"Spoiled, I heard."

"I think so too." I blurted this out without thinking, but she didn't notice.

"They said he wasn't as capable as the nephew. *Aiya*, no point discussing him. Better not speak ill of the dead."

CHAPTER 4

AMAH'S FORESIGHT IN preparing a new dress was proven right when a few days later I received another invitation to the Lim mansion. This time my father was invited as well. In honor of the upcoming Double Seventh Festival, it was to be a musical gathering with a private performance for family and friends. There were not many public venues for entertainment that women of good family could repair to, so from time to time soirees were held at home. Amah had often told me about how the main courtyard in our house would be cleared and how my grandfather hired men to build a temporary stage. Needless to say, such occasions had been nonexistent in recent years, so I was much excited at this prospect. My father had consented to go. Master Lim had been part of his previous circle of business contacts, and their relationship, though sporadic, was still cordial. Truly, I wasn't very certain with whom my father was still in touch. Sometimes he surprised me.

The seventh day of the seventh month was a festival to celebrate two heavenly lovers—the cowherd and the weaving maid. Amah told me this tale when I was small. A long time ago, there was a cowherd with nothing but an old ox to keep him company. One day, the ox suddenly spoke and told him that he might win himself a wife if he hid beside a pool and waited for the heavenly weaving maidens. As they bathed, the cowherd hid one set of clothes and when one of the maidens was left behind searching for her garments, he accosted her and asked her to be his wife. Eventually, the magic ox died. At this point, I always burst in with questions. Amah would brush aside my protests, continuing her well-worn tale. She was a pedantic storyteller who repeated her stories in exactly the same words each time.

When the magic ox died, it told the cowherd to keep its skin for a time of great need. And soon enough, the Queen of Heaven was angered that one of her best weavers had married a mortal and commanded that she be brought back to heaven. In despair, the cowherd followed his wife on the magic ox skin, bearing their two children in baskets at the end of a pole. To prevent him from catching up, the Queen of Heaven took her hairpin and drew a river, the Milky Way, between them in the heavens. On one day each year, however, the magpies of the earth took pity on the lovers and made a bridge so they could cross to see each other. This was the conjunction of the two stars Altair and Vega on the seventh day of the seventh month.

When Amah told me this story, I couldn't understand why such a tragedy was considered a festival for lovers. There was no happy ending, only endless waiting on each side of a river. It seemed like a miserable way to spend eternity. Instead, I was most interested in the ox. How did the ox know that the heavenly maidens were coming? Why could it speak? And most of all, why did the ox have to die? Amah never gave me very satisfactory answers to these questions. "The point of the story is the lovers, you silly child," she said, and, indeed, the festival was particularly suited for young girls who took part in competitions to thread a needle by moonlight, bathed their faces with flower water, and sang songs to celebrate needlework. I had never had a chance to take part in these maidenly activities, however, because the other thing that was celebrated on the Double Seventh Festival was the sunning of the books.

The seventh day of the seventh month was also considered a particularly fortuitous time to air old books and scrolls; and as my father had vast quantities of both, this was our major activity during the festival. Tables were placed in the courtyard and his collection was laid out in the sun, papers turned to ensure even drying. A careful watch must be kept to ensure the ink would not fade. I still remembered the smooth, hot feeling of the paper beneath my palms, and the brilliance of the colors intensified by the sun. Our climate was hot and damp, an adverse environment for libraries. Many times I would find that silverfish or bookworms had begun to consume the paper, and I would be set to tracing the wormholes to get rid of the pests. That was why my memories of the Double Seventh Festival were inextricably linked to the smell of moldy paper. This year would be different, though. I suspected that the Lims would celebrate in a far grander fashion.

THE PERFORMANCE WAS IN the afternoon, to be followed by a dinner afterward. I spent the morning laying out what few pieces of good jewelry I had. Amah pressed the new dress with a heavy charcoal iron until it was smooth and crisp. I rarely wore a *kebaya*, but I wished I did so more often because it was very flattering. The *baju*, or shirt, was fitted at the waist and made of sheer white cotton with cutwork embroidery down the front and edges. The front of the *baju* was fastened with three gold brooches shaped like flowers and attached to one another by fine gold chains, while the ankle-length sarong was made of fine batik in a curling pattern of green leaves and pink and yellow flowers. When I had bathed and dressed, and Amah put my hair up, I barely recognized myself. But as I gazed at my reflection, it seemed as though there was someone in the corner of the room watching me. Glancing round, I saw nothing out of the ordinary. Yet in the mirror I had the distinct impression of a figure standing near the large wardrobe. Uneasily, I continued to stare into its depths. Amah came in as I was doing so and caught my anxious looks.

"Why so sour? No one will marry you if you pull a face like that!"

I didn't have the heart to tell her that I thought I had seen someone in the mirror so I put on a smile, although my pleasure in my appearance was quite dampened after that.

At the entrance hall of the Lim mansion, I had my first glimpse of the master of the house. Lim Teck Kiong was short and inclined to a certain porky affluence, but he had an imposing personality. He greeted my father warmly and studied me with interest.

"So this is your daughter!" he said. "Where have you been hiding her?"

My father smiled and murmured something noncommittal, glancing around the reception room with an air of familiarity. He must have been here many times before while my mother was alive, I realized.

I didn't have much time to observe however before I was sent off for refreshment with the ladies. In accordance with Islam, the upper-class Malays kept their ladies in purdah and no men other than immediate family members were allowed to glimpse them unveiled. The local Chinese did not observe such strict segregation of the sexes, though too much intimacy between young people was discouraged.

The house was full of people. Children ran underfoot with an air of excitement, reminding me of my own childhood, when my cousins and I had raced around the courtyards of our house. But my cousins had long gone to Penang, together with my two aunts when their husbands had relocated. I had only sporadic letters from them, especially since three of them had already married. Servants passed swiftly bearing trays. I looked around to see whether I recognized any of them, but the one I sought wasn't there. A stage had been set up in the main courtyard. "I heard a famous opera singer will give a private performance today," one young matron told me. She had a face like a floured dumpling, but it bore a kind expression. I had been introduced to her before but could not remember her name.

"You're Pan Li Lan, aren't you?" she said. "I'm Yan Hong, the eldest daughter of the house." As I stammered my apologies for forgetting her name, she smiled. "Now that I'm married I don't live here anymore, but I come back from time to time to help out and show off the grandchildren."

"How many children do you have?" I asked.

"Three," she said, rubbing the small of her back. "My eldest is already seven, but the younger two are barely walking."

Just then Madam Lim passed us. "The performance won't start for a little while," she said. "Why don't you get some refreshments?" She still looked ill to me, although she had applied a little rouge to her sallow complexion.

"Is your mother all right?" I asked Yan Hong.

Yan Hong laughed. "She's not my mother. My mother was the Second Wife."

"It's hard for me to get used to a household with so many people."

"Your father has only one wife?" she asked.

"Yes, he never remarried."

"You're lucky."

I supposed it would have been strange to have a stepmother or two. But then Yan Hong didn't know my father and how the god of smallpox had stripped him of almost everything he had. "My father lost interest in life after my mother died," I said. "We'd never have as many people over as this."

Yan Hong grimaced. "It's a good show, isn't it? But I'd never want to be a second wife. If my husband thought about remarrying, I would leave him."

"Would you?" Silently I wondered at her confidence. But then she was from a rich and powerful family. Presumably that gave her a certain amount of clout with her husband.

"Ah, I'm frightening you. Marriage isn't so bad, and my husband is a good man. If you can believe it, I was madly in love with him." She laughed. "They didn't want me to marry him because he was too poor, but I knew he was clever. He got a scholarship from his Clan Association and went to Hong Kong to study with my cousin."

I looked at her with new interest. I knew that some of the sons of rich men went abroad to Hong Kong and even England to study, and came back as doctors or lawyers. Had I been a boy, I would have liked to do so too, and I said as much to her.

"Oh, I don't know," she said. "The voyage can be dangerous because of the typhoons. And once you're there life can be difficult." She looked as though she was about to say something further, but pressed her lips together. I had heard about the unrest in Hong Kong, despite its British rule, and was curious as to what she meant, but she merely said that her husband had studied at the new Hong Kong College of Medicine, founded by the London Missionary Society.

"Come," said Yan Hong. "Let's find something to eat."

We wandered toward a large inner room from which issued the sounds of musicians playing. I was transfixed by the music. The *er hu* was a two-stringed Chinese violin played with a horsehair bow. The strings were steel and the resonator cover made of python skin. It had a peculiarly haunting quality, like a voice singing. The small ensemble here was playing folk music, and the tunes were traditional and lively.

"You like *er hu* music?" asked Yan Hong.

"Yes, I do." A blind musician used to play in the street near our house and the melancholy sound of his instrument had always exemplified dusk and yearning to me. The performers today were two *er hu* players and one *yang qin* player who accompanied them on the hammered dulcimer. To my surprise, one of the *er hu* players was none other than the young man who had been repairing clocks. Seated on a low stool with the instrument held vertically before him, his fingers flew over the neck while his other arm plied the horsehair bow. Despite his loose-fitting cotton gown, I could see the square breadth of his shoulders as he leaned over the instrument and how his torso tapered to narrow hips. I must have been staring for quite a while when I realized that Yan Hong had asked me a question.

"I'm sorry," I said. "I was listening to the music."

She looked amused. "Listening, or looking?"

I flushed. "They're quite good, don't you think?"

"Yes, for amateurs. My father enjoys music and encourages his household to play."

"Who are they?"

"The older *er hu* player is my third uncle, and that's his son on the *yang qin*. The other player is my cousin."

Cousin! I looked down to hide my confusion. My heart was beating like a drum. The music ended, but I could still hear the blood rushing through my ears. Embarrassed, I selected a large and sticky *kuih angku*, a steamed red cake stuffed with yellow bean paste, and bit into it. When I looked up again he was standing next to Yan Hong.

"Li Lan, this is my cousin Tian Bai."

We did not shake hands as I had heard the British do, but under his gaze, I felt a flicker run through my veins.

"In addition to cleaning the clocks, I also play a little music," he said.

Yan Hong looked at him with amusement. "What are you talking about?" Turning to me, she said, "Li Lan is the daughter of the Pan family."

I tried to swallow my *kuih*, but it was sticky and clung to my throat.

"Are you all right?" he asked.

"I'm fine," I said with as much dignity as I could muster.

"I'll get you some water," said Yan Hong, darting after a passing servant.

There was a little crease at the corners of his eyes, exactly like the fold in a freshly laundered sheet. "I had a hard time finding out who you were," he said. "You just ran off the other day."

"I was away too long." I was too embarrassed to admit I had thought he was a servant, but had a horrible feeling that he knew anyway.

"You don't like mahjong?"

"I never learned to play well. It seems like a waste of time."

"It is. You have no idea how much money some of these women can gamble away."

"What would you rather they spent their time on?"

"I don't know. Books, maps, maybe clocks?"

I hardly dared to look him in the eye, yet I was drawn to his gaze like a moth to a flame. It wouldn't do to appear silly and empty-headed. A man who had traveled across the ocean must surely be bored by small talk. He gave no sign of it, though, asking me what books I had read and why I knew about the sea charts.

"The world is almost mapped," he said. "There are a few places still unknown: the depths of the African continent, the poles. But the vast landmasses are charted now."

"You sound more like an explorer than a doctor."

He laughed. "Did Yan Hong tell you that? I'm afraid that I never finished my medical degree, although her husband did. My uncle called me back before I was done. But it's true I would have preferred to be an explorer."

"That's not a very Chinese sentiment."

China had eschewed sea voyages in the past, disdaining contact with barbarian peoples and only interested in her own affairs. China was the center of the universe, as even we overseas Chinese were taught. The British were amazed at the speed at which news of China's affairs reached us in this far-off colony. The clan associations had couriers on fast junks, and they regularly exchanged information before the British, with their spies and settlements in Canton and Peking, could do so.

"Maybe I'm not filial enough," he said with a smile. "People have often complained about that."

"Complained about what?" Yan Hong reappeared with a cup of water for me.

"About my disobedience," he said.

She knit her brows in mock annoyance. "You've been talking to Miss Pan for far too long. The performance is beginning and Father is looking for you. Hurry up or he'll never be able to arrange the seating properly."

I WISH I COULD remember more of the operatic performance. I'm told it was quite good. A well-known troupe was in town and had been hired to give a private performance. They did a few scenes from the opera about the Cowherd and the Weaving Maid, but I hardly paid attention. From where I sat among the women, I tried surreptitiously to catch a glimpse of Tian Bai. I could see his uncle, Lim Teck Kiong, seated in front with a number of important-looking gentlemen, but he wasn't with them. Finally I caught sight of him in the back, arranging additional seating for some late guests. No wonder he was considered useful in the household. Had his life changed since Lim Tian Ching, the son of the house, had died the past year?

Thinking about the dead man gave me an oppressive feeling, as though the air had curdled in my lungs. My father was very dismissive about things like ghosts and dreams. He would often quote Confucius, who had said it was better not to know about ghosts and gods, but rather to focus on the world we lived in. Still, thoughts of Lim Tian Ching cast a pall over the proceedings. I hardly saw the actors as they leapt and postured before me, faces elaborately painted and embroidered costumes quivering with feathers. When I raised my head again, I caught Tian Bai's eye from across the courtyard. He gave me an unreadable look.

The dinner that followed the performance was of the first quality. Even the rice was this year's new crop, the grains chewy and tender. At home we bought only old rice because it was drier and you could get more rice per *kati*. I would have been content eating only the white rice, but there were many other delicacies to sample. Steamed pomfret, the silvery sides of the fish veiled in soy sauce and shallot oil. Fried pigeons. Tender strips of jellyfish quivered under a sprinkling of sesame seeds; and I was delighted to see my favorite *kerabu*, a dish of fiddlehead ferns dressed with shallots, chilies, and tiny dried shrimp in coconut milk.

After dinner, there were games for the young ladies in the courtyard. The daughters of the house, together with their innumerable cousins, displayed their needlework, which was exquisite, and were complimented on their fair complexions. I stood shyly on the side. No one had told me about this so I had brought nothing to show. In any case, my own sewing was very poor and mostly restricted to mending things nowadays. There were so many people that I was sure that no one would care if I did not participate, but soon I heard Yan Hong calling.

"Li Lan, come! Join the needle-threading competition!"

The lamps were blown out and the silvery radiance of the moon permeated the courtyard, bathing everyone in its pale glow. A table was set up with several stations of needles and thread. The unmarried girls would compete to see who could thread all their needles the fastest. As I took my place, I was jostled by my neighbor, a large-boned girl with horsey good looks. She gave me a cold glance, her eyes sliding over me dismissively.

"Ready?" cried Yan Hong. "Ladies, start!"

There were five needles in front of me in varying thicknesses from large to very fine. I quickly threaded the first three but the last two were more difficult. Girls sighed and complained coquettishly. In the wavering moonlight, the harder I squinted, the less I could see; so I used the tips of my fingers to feel for the holes, just as I had traced the pathways of insects and bookworms in my father's manuscripts. The thread slipped through and I waved my hand in excitement. "I'm done!"

There were congratulations from the other girls. My horse-faced neighbor sighed and shrugged. I wondered what I had done to offend her, but soon forgot in the excitement. There were other games as well, lantern decorating and singing, and by the end of the evening I could not remember when I had enjoyed myself so thoroughly in recent times. As we were leaving the Lim mansion, my father glanced at my bright face.

"Did you enjoy yourself?" he said.

"Yes, Father. Indeed, I did."

He smiled sadly. "I forgot how quickly you've grown up. In my mind you're still a little girl. I should have arranged for you to mix more after your cousins left for Penang."

I did not like to see the shadow pass over his face again. Tonight he had seemed quite cheerful and appeared to have enjoyed the performance. I once overheard Amah telling the cook that when my mother died, part of my father died too. She had spoken, no doubt, in a slightly theatrical manner, but when I was younger I took her words literally. No wonder he sometimes drifted, as though the thin line that anchored him to the present was fraying away. When I was younger I often felt guilty when he seemed troubled. Of course, sons were better. Everyone said so. But I suspected that even if I had been a boy, I would not have been enough to console him for the loss of my mother.

CHAPTER 5

THOUGHTS OF MY parents put me in a melancholy mood before I went to bed. Amah always said too much thinking made me pale and peaky. Of course, she was perfectly capable in the next breath of scolding me for going into the sun and ruining my complexion. She never seemed bothered by her ability to embrace two opposing things at once. I sometimes wished that I had that blithe assurance. My father made the dry observation that Amah had no difficulty reconciling her viewpoints because she had learned everything as custom dictated, and that was both her bondage and her solace. I felt this was a little harsh. Amah did think about things—just not the same sorts that Father did. Her mind ricocheted between practicality and superstition. Somehow, I had managed to exist between both Amah's world and Father's, but what did I really think? These thoughts drifted through my mind until I fell into an uneasy slumber.

I WAS IN AN orchard of peach trees. The leaves were dazzlingly green and the fruit that hung from the branches was pink and white, gleaming like alabaster. The trees themselves were monotonously similar, as though they had been copied from a painting. This was unsurprising as there were no peach trees in Malaya, though I had seen them depicted in scrolls from China. With a mounting feeling of dread, I saw how they stretched ahead in all directions, each broad vista looking exactly the same. From behind the trees came the wavering sound of an opera aria, the same that had been sung that evening by the actors in the Lim mansion. The sound was muted and scratchy, as though heard from a great distance. There was no depth or liveliness to it. As the music announced his presence, Lim Tian Ching emerged from between the trees, a spray of peach blossoms in his hand.

"Li Lan, my dear!" he said. "May I present you with this floral token?"

He held the branch out to me but I was suddenly stricken with suffocation, as though the air had curdled.

"What? No word to greet me?" he asked. "You don't know how impatiently I've been waiting to see you again. After all, the Double Seventh Festival is for lovers."

Unwillingly, I found myself walking with him beneath the trees. He floated beside me with a curiously inhuman gait, and it was only by a great effort of will that I managed to halt.

"How do you even know me?" I asked.

"I saw you last year at the Dragon Boat Festival. You were down on the quay throwing rice dumplings into the water. How elegant, how graceful you were!"

Taken aback, I recalled that I had, indeed, gone with my father to celebrate that festival, which commemorated the suicide of a poet. In their grief, the common people threw dumplings into the water to persuade the fish not to eat his body.

Lim Tian Ching continued, "Oh, my dear, don't frown so. It spoils your features. Really, I was very impressed by you. Of course, I'd seen my share of pretty girls," he tittered, "but there was something about you that was different. So refined. That must come from your father. I heard he was a good-looking man before the smallpox."

Taking my silence as assent, he continued with his grotesque flirtation.

"I asked everyone who you were. They said you were the daughter of the Pan family. If circumstances hadn't overtaken me"—and here he looked suitably melancholy—"I would have wooed you a long time ago. But don't despair, now we have all the time in the world to make up for it."

I shook my head.

"Li Lan, I'm a man of simple words," he said. "Won't you be my bride?"

"No!" It took all my strength to form the word.

He looked hurt. "Now, now," he said. "Don't be so hasty. I know that I should have approached you through your father. In fact, I asked my mother to do so for me, and to get an article of your clothing so we could meet like this."

My thoughts flew to the ribbon that Madam Lim had requested from me. I gagged, my throat as dry as if it had been filled with *kapok*, the silky fibrous seed coverings that were used to stuff cushions and mattresses.

"I can't marry you."

He frowned. "I know, it is a little difficult with my being . . . " He waved his hands as though he didn't want to say it, then continued, "but it's not a problem. Many lovers have managed to surmount this obstacle."

"No!"

"What do you mean, no?" He sounded peevish. "We'll have a grand wedding. And afterward we'll be together." He stopped and smiled. It was a terrible, fatuous smile. Air was being crushed out of my rib cage. The peach trees swam together in a haze of green and pink. Dimly I heard Lim Tian Ching shouting, but I forced myself awake with every ounce of willpower until I sat up in bed, trembling and sweating.

I wanted to vomit, to spit up the bile of that unwholesome encounter. I, who had been so carefully schooled by my father not to believe in spirits, confessed to myself in the dead of night that Amah was right. The ghost of Lim Tian Ching had passed through my dreams. His unwelcome presence had violated the recesses of my soul. I was so terrified that I curled up on my bed and wrapped the covers around myself, despite the sweltering heat, until dawn came.

. . . .

THAT MORNING, I LAY abed for a long time, wondering if I was going mad. There was a lunatic who sometimes wandered our street, his emaciated body barely clothed in rags. He muttered to himself constantly; the pupils of his eyes constricted till he resembled a crazed bird. I had given him a few coins before. Sometimes he pocketed them, other times he licked them or cast them away. Amah said he conversed with the dead. Was I destined to become like him? Yet I had never heard of madness in our family, only whispers of the sad collapse of our house. True, Amah and Old Wong, our cook, had odd dislikes, such as the main staircase of our house. But I had grown up with their superstitions and was used to them. I had never yet heard talk of madness. Yet I felt oppressed by shadows. It seemed to me that the dead were all around us. Of course this was foolish. Life was followed by death in the endless cycle of rebirth, if one believed the Buddhists. We were all nominally Buddhist I supposed, although my father, as a strict Confucianist, reserved a certain contempt toward them. I told myself that it was a dream, nothing more.

Downstairs, Amah clucked over me but seemed to think that my lassitude stemmed from too much excitement the night before. I felt obliged to be cheerful as she quizzed me about the festivities. At length, I asked her about Yan Hong.

"The daughter of the Second Wife?" said Amah. "She's the one whose marriage was a love match, though it was a big scandal. I heard it from the servants. And luckily the young man came from a good family although they had no money of course."

"How did she manage to marry him?"

"*Aiya!* The oldest way of course. She got pregnant. How they managed it I don't know, but they blamed her mother for it. They said that was why Second Wife died."

"I thought it was malaria."

"Well, that was what they said. But if you ask me, it sounds like she was so ashamed that she lost the will to live. And after she died they felt guilty, so the marriage went ahead. The boy went to Hong Kong after the marriage to study and she had the first child at home. When he returned, she had the other two."

So Yan Hong's mother had bought her daughter's happiness with her life. It was a sad story but also explained the age gap between her children. I thought back to last night. Yan Hong had seemed cheerful, busy, and fulfilled. How I had envied her fortunate marriage. Nothing was as it seemed, after all.

I SPENT THE AFTERNOON lying on a rattan daybed downstairs. The tiled floor in the study remained cool even during the burning heat of the day. I could not imagine how the coolies managed to work the tin mines. The mortality rate was very high but still they came by the boatload from China, along with Indians who disembarked from Madras and Chennai to work the rubber and coffee plantations. I had often wondered what it would be like to set sail from here to other lands. Tian Bai had done so, and I would have liked to go east to see the Moluccas, and then onward to Hong Kong and even Japan. But such voyages were not for me.

I was ruminating over this when a parcel arrived from the Lim household. "What is it?" I asked when Amah brought it in. It was wrapped in brown paper and tied with string. I picked it up with both hands and frowned. After my frightening dream the night before, I felt suspicious of anything that came from that family. But it turned out to be a length of batik, beautifully printed with floral motifs of indigo and pale pink. There was a note enclosed from Yan Hong.

> *You forgot to collect your prize for winning the needle-threading competition. I hope to see you again. Best wishes, etc., etc.*

"Very nice," said Amah approvingly.

For her, the best part of the evening had been the fact that I had won the competition. I had been forced to tell it several times for her benefit and had even overheard her boasting about it to our cook, Old Wong. I had never done well in the feminine arts and I suspected that Amah felt bad about it. "Reading, reading!" she would grunt, and snatch away whatever book I had. "Spoil your eyes, you will!" I once pointed out to her that needlework would have done the same thing, but she never listened to me. This piece of cloth was the best thing I could have brought home, short of a marriage proposal.

Although I didn't want to admit it, I was pleased too. I shook out the cloth and something shiny fell out of the folds.

"What's that?" asked Amah. Her sharp eyes never missed anything.

"It's a pocket watch."

"Was it part of your prize?" It was a brass men's watch with a round face and delicate hands. "That's very strange. It doesn't even look new. And why would Yan Hong give you a watch? It's so unlucky."

She looked fretful. We Chinese did not like to give or receive certain gifts for superstitious reasons: knives, because they could sever a relationship; handkerchiefs, for they portended weeping; and clocks, as they were thought to measure out the days of your life. If any of these were presented, the recipient usually paid a token amount to symbolize that it was a purchase and not a gift. My heart was beating so loudly, however, that I was afraid that Amah would hear it. I was almost certain that I had seen this watch before.

"It could have slipped in by accident," I said.

"Careless!" she said. "If it isn't your property you shouldn't keep it."

"I'll ask Yan Hong if I see her again."

I left Amah shaking her head and escaped to my room, where I examined my find. Amah was right; it was not a new watch. There were scratches on the brass case and the chain was missing. The more I looked at it, however, the more certain I was that it was the same watch that Tian Bai had been repairing the first time we met.

In the novels that I read, the heroines were continually exclaiming over some love token they exchanged, whether it was a hairpin, inkstone, or more daringly, a tiny shoe from a bound-foot girl. I had always discounted them as ridiculous. But now, as I cupped the watch in my hands, the soft ticking was like the heartbeat of a small bird. I slipped it into the pocket of my dress. This unexpected gift filled me with secret delight for the rest of the day, and my spirits only began to sink as dusk fell and I remembered my dreams. After dinner, I lingered so late in the kitchen that Old Wong shooed me out with his dustpan.

I was on the point of going to Amah's room for comfort and gossip when I remembered that this was her evening off. Once in a while she would go out to visit her friends and play mahjong. When I was very small, I sometimes tagged along to this fascinating parallel world of amahs, where much gossip and information exchanged hands. We slipped in through back doors to the servants' quarters and listened until, lulled by the conversation, I fell asleep and Amah carried me home on her back. I'm sure my father never knew about these excursions. Now as I climbed the stairs, I wished that I could sleep like a child again, safe in a warm circle of friends. As it was, I opened the windows. The night was cooling and the air smelled like rain. Somberly I climbed into bed. I was afraid.

CHAPTER 6

Y FEARS WERE well founded, for this marked the beginning of many nights when it felt as though all I did was dream. Despite my resistance, I couldn't help falling asleep. Pricking my fingers with needles, biting my tongue, or even standing and pacing were of no use to me at all. Night after night, I found myself in that strange world I had come to associate with Lim Tian Ching. Once I attended a grand feast where I was the only guest at a long table laden with heaps of oranges, bowls of rice, boiled and quartered chickens, and pyramids of mangoes. Displayed like funeral offerings, the food had a distasteful quality to it, despite its splendor.

Another time I found myself in a stable filled with horses. Some were dappled, others white, brown, or black. Despite their varied coloring, they were all exactly the same size and had the same ears and tail. Each stood in its stall, ears pricked forward and eyes fixed obediently ahead. When they moved, there was no sound other than the loud rustling of paper. As I walked farther into the shadowy building, there were carriages, phaetons, and sedan chairs, all gleaming with polish and lacquer. But the most fearful sight was a rickshaw equipped with a man standing silently between the poles, his grip frozen on the shafts as he stared blankly ahead. Though I passed my hand before his eyes, he didn't blink. I shrank back, seized by the sudden fear that he would snatch at my wrist. From his attitude of readiness, I suspected that he would respond to a command. Perhaps the horses were the same way if one chose to ride them, though I dared not try. This shadowy world filled me with unease; my skin prickled, morbid fancies filled my mind, and my spirits sank until I barely had the energy to keep moving.

The greatest mercy was that Lim Tian Ching did not appear in these dreams. I was alone as I wandered through vast halls, echoing court-yards, and landscaped gardens. There was an enormous kitchen filled with pots and pans and heaps of food piled on the tables, and even a scholar's study, complete with reams of paper and graduated sets of wolf-hair writing brushes. When I examined the books and scrolls, however, they were blank inside. Everything was staged as though for a grand performance; and though nothing ever seemed to happen, I felt a constant knot of tension in my stomach.

Occasionally, I came across servants of the same type as the rickshaw puller. Sometimes they moved involuntarily with a sharp rustling sound, which alarmed me. The houses and landscapes were cheerless despite their grandeur, and I found the puppet servants grotesque and frightening. I was thankful that I didn't meet Lim Tian Ching, though I suspected he was some-where around. Sometimes I sensed his presence in the next room or behind a copse of trees. Then I would hurry along, my heart beating faster and an inner voice shrieking to wake up.

I didn't tell anyone about the dreams, though many times I was on the verge of going into my father's study to unburden myself. I realized, however, that he was unlikely to believe me. He would soothe what he considered child-ish fears and tell me not to worry about such things. After all, if he who had longed for my mother so much was unable to see her, or grasp any essence of her spirit, why then surely the afterlife must not exist. It was a repository of folk beliefs. He was a devout Confucianist, and Confucius had specifically spoken against such things. I knew him too well to expect him to change his mind on the basis of a few dreams. Instead, he would blame himself for ever mentioning that unlucky marriage proposal to me.

If I told Amah, I would have the opposite problem. She would be only too ready to believe me. She would get an exorcist, burn chicken feathers, instruct me to drink the blood of a dog or suggest splashing it around the room to unmask ghosts. She might drag me off to visit a medium. And certainly she would work herself into a frenzy of superstitious fear.

Sometimes, I wondered whether this immersion in a dead world was the beginning of lunacy. I tested my memory and checked the pupils of my eyes for madness, but I didn't like to look in the mirror too long. There were too many shadows. The only thing that comforted me was Tian Bai's watch. I kept it with me at all times, fingering the brass case in my pocket. Each time I wrenched myself awake from the dreams, I was comforted by its soft ticking. In fact, the person I really wanted to talk to was Tian Bai, but I had no way of contacting him. I sent a message back to Yan Hong, thanking her for the cloth and I wondered whether she had known about the watch. Somehow I doubted it. Yet if I sent a letter to her, he might see it.

In the end the note I wrote was simple.

Thank you for the beautiful gift. It was entirely unexpected, but I will certainly treasure it and think of some good use for it to pass the time.

A little awkward, but it was the best I could manage. Or perhaps someone had accidentally dropped the watch into the bundle of cloth. Maybe a child had done it. Between my nightmares and my waking preoccupation I lost weight, spending my days in listless withdrawal. Amah noticed, of course.

"What's wrong with you?" she asked. "Are you sick?"

When I confessed to not feeling well, she administered a series of brews. Boiled radish soup with pork bones to flush out poisons. Mung beans and yellow sugar to cleanse. Chicken soup and cordyceps for stamina. Her soups had helped me recover from many childhood illnesses in the past. This time, however, they had a limited effect. One afternoon when I was lying on the rattan daybed downstairs, I joked that I felt like Lin Daiyu, the tragic heroine of the classic *Dream of the Red Chamber*. She was a consumptive and spent a great deal of time in the book coughing up blood and looking wan and interesting.

"Don't talk about such things!" Amah's sharp response surprised me.

"I was only joking, Amah."

"Sickness is nothing to joke about."

She was always at her most belligerent when worried. It was true that the dreams were wearing me down, but I still hoped that they were something that I could surmount if I had enough willpower. Didn't I prove that night after night when I woke myself up? Just how illusory that was would soon be proved to me.

I HADN'T SEEN MUCH of my father since the Double Seventh Festival at the Lim mansion. He spent a surprising amount of time out of the house and when he returned, shut himself up with his books. When he emerged for meals he looked haggard, his pupils dilated. Normally, I would have been more alert to his condition, but I had been too preoccupied with thoughts of Tian Bai and the dreams that plagued me nightly. Thus I was surprised when one afternoon he called me into his study.

"What is it, Father?" I asked him. It was very hot. The bamboo *chiks* were drawn against the sun and wetted down for coolness, but his study was still stifling.

He passed a hand over his face. "Li Lan, I realize that I haven't been doing my duty by you."

"Why do you say that?"

"You're almost eighteen. Most girls your age are already married or at least betrothed."

I kept silent. When I was younger I had sometimes teased my father and asked him about my marriage. He had replied that I was not to worry about it and he was sure that I would be happy. I had somehow come to assume that he meant to allow me to choose. After all, my parents' marriage had been by all accounts very happy. Maybe too happy, in retrospect.

"As you know, our finances haven't been good," he said. "But I thought that there would be enough for you to live modestly on, even if something should happen to me. I'm afraid, though, that we're now in worse straits. In addition to that, a marriage alliance I had in mind for you since you were a child has fallen through."

"What marriage? Why didn't you tell me about this before?"

"I didn't want you to worry about such things. I also thought, and maybe this was a romantic notion of mine, that you would be well suited to the young man and might naturally be drawn together without being burdened by expectations. It was, after all, what happened with your mother and myself." He sighed. "If anyone is to blame it is myself. I've been too unworldly about such things. I expected—"

"What marriage?" I asked again.

"It was never formal, but I had an understanding with an old friend. We were not, of course, an equal alliance with his family as the economic disparity was too great." He laughed bitterly. "My friend, however, had a nephew, a bright young man with no family of his own. Years ago when you were young, he proposed a marriage with our family as we still had a good name and a modest income. I had seen the young man and felt it would be a good match. A better match, perhaps, than with the main family as there would be less family pressure on you."

I was in a fever of curiosity and agitation. This sounded horribly familiar to me. "What happened?"

"My friend's own son died and his nephew became the heir. For a while I thought our arrangement still stood. In fact until very recently . . ." His voice trailed off.

"Who is the family?" I felt like shaking him.

"The Lim family."

Blood was rushing in my ears. I felt dizzy and short of breath. My father continued. "Until very recently, I thought it was still settled. After all, they had asked you to the house and showed you signs of favor. But there was that strange request from Madam Lim."

"The ghost marriage." My heart sank.

"She approached me about it one day. I wasn't sure whether she was serious or if she had somehow confused the betrothal arrangements of her nephew and her son."

Everything was falling into place, even Lim Tian Ching's mention, in my dream, of using his mother to ask my father about the marriage. "So now what happens?"

"Lim Teck Kiong, my supposed friend, spoke to me a week ago. He said that given his nephew's new status as the family heir, it was impossible to marry a penniless girl. He did, however, once again broach the subject of you becoming his son's spirit wife."

"And what did you say?"

"I said I would think it over and talk to you." My father stopped me. "Wait! I know it's distasteful, but you should at least know that it means you would be well provided for in their household, which is more than I can say right now about our own. We've lost a great deal of capital, and unfortunately the person who holds my debts is none other than Lim. He offered to buy up our debts and I thought he meant to do me a favor."

"I will not! I will never marry his dead son!"

"Hush," said my father. "Don't fret so. Whatever else I've failed to do, I won't force you into this ghost marriage. I thought that the best thing would be to betroth you to someone else. Then everyone would save some face. I've been asking around discreetly, but have had no luck. It's my fault. I didn't cultivate new or useful friendships since your mother died. Those old friends I approached were under the impression, no doubt from Lim, that you were always betrothed to his son. But we'll think of something."

Tears filled my eyes. If I started to cry, I would be unable to stop. My father stared at his desk, guilt and shame written across his countenance. Then he glanced involuntarily at his opium pipe. I felt a stinging rebuke rise to my lips. No wonder Amah had grumbled at him so often. I had always defended him, feeling that my father doted on me and was sweetly unworldly. But now I began to comprehend the true cost of his failure. I bit my lips until they bled. The hours, days, and years that had bled away in his opium haze demanded a payment from my future. In his apathetic way he had squandered my chance at happiness. The storm of tears overtook me and I ran from the room.

CHAPTER 7

T IAN BAI'S WIFE! That was all I could think of. All this time I had been promised to him. I shut myself up in my room, crying. It was a tragedy to be sure, but there were some horribly comic elements to it. I heard Amah rattle the door anxiously, and then my father's voice. I wished I had never seen Tian Bai. Then I wished that my father had married me off to him sooner, before Lim Tian Ching had managed to die. As upset as I was, I had to admit that my father had good taste. He was right, I would have liked—I did like—Tian Bai. Very much.

Did Tian Bai know about this arrangement? Was that why he had sent me the pocket watch? If so, then presumably he had not been informed that it was terminated. I wondered whether he had merely been polite to me because custom demanded it. But his eyes had lingered too long. Remembering his steady gaze, I felt weak. Was this love? It was like a consuming flame, licking through my defenses at a slow burn.

My father's second instinct to betroth me to someone else was also astute. That was my father: clever but no will, no impetus to follow through, so his plans had little chance of realization. When it came down to it, there was no one in his limited circle who could or would make such a marriage arrangement in haste, and frankly I could scarcely blame them. But presumably he had only looked at good families. If I really wanted to get married, there must be some poor man who would welcome a bride. But I didn't think I could bring myself to marry anyone else. I suppressed a shudder as I thought about Lim Tian Ching. This was all his doing, I was sure of it. Well, I would not bow to him. I would rather run away. Cut my hair, become a nun, or an amah. Anything rather than be a bride to his shade.

My eyes were red and sore. As I peered into the watery depths of my mother's mirror, I caught a glimpse of a dim form standing behind me. In a fit of anger, I caught up the nearest object and flung it at the shadows. Too late, after it had left my fingers, did I realize that it was Tian Bai's watch. Well, what did it matter anymore? I burst into tears again; and having exhausted myself, fell asleep.

BUT SLEEP WAS NO aid to me. I should have known that by now. Part of me tried to swim back to the waking world but instead I felt myself sinking downward into mist, as though I was drawn along a ribbon or a string. The fog parted and gave way to a dazzling brightness. I was in a magnificent hall, lit with hundreds of red candles. Red satin runners lay on the tables and large rosettes of scarlet ribbons were garlanded from the ceiling. I looked around with unease. The darkness outside the brightly lit hall was oppressively flat. The other thing that made me uncomfortable was the obvious preparations for a feast. Red is the celebratory color for auspicious occasions such as New Year's. And weddings.

As was always the case in that world, the great hall was empty. It could have held scores of guests but there were only rows of vacant seats. Not a breath of air stirred. It was as silent as the grave. My skin prickled at the thought that anyone, or anything, could be watching from outside those blank, dark windows. No sooner had that crossed my mind than the gay red ribbons began to flutter. Someone was coming. Desperately I tried to wake up. To make this world dissolve away as I had done so many times before. But while I was summoning up my willpower, Lim Tian Ching stepped out from behind a screen. His silent entrance, as though he had been waiting there all along, filled me with terror.

"So you've come, Li Lan."

I took an involuntary step back.

"My dear," he said, "I have to admit that I'm disappointed in you."

He sighed and twirled a paper fan. "I thought I would be patient, show you some of the things that we would share together. You did like them, didn't you?" Seeing that I was speechless, he allowed a smile to steal across his face. "There are so many wonderful things that I have. Houses, horses, servants. Really, I don't see how any girl could be unhappy here. But what do I find?" His eyes became opaque. "I find you mooning over another man! And who is this man?"

I tried to gather my strength but he kept advancing.

"My own cousin, that's who! Oh, it's bad enough that he had to outshine me in life but even in death . . . " As Lim Tian Ching said the word *death*, I noticed something strange. His figure blurred for an instant, but it was merely a flicker, for he continued, "Tian Bai has to compete with me. Don't think I didn't know you were promised to him! That was one of the first things I discovered after I saw you at the Dragon Boat Festival. Imagine how I felt when I found out that there was some kind of prior arrangement with him." An expression of distaste crossed his face.

"Why him, of all people? My mother said it had been arranged because your family was poor and they didn't want his marriage to outshine mine. Well, I told her, why did you have to pick such a girl for him and she said she had no idea; no one had ever seen you." His face suffused with color, like a fat schoolboy complaining about the theft of his sweets.

"You should forget about me," I said. "I'm not worthy of your family."

"That's for me to decide. Although I commend your modesty." He bestowed a smile on me again. "My dear, I'm willing to overlook your momentary weakness. After all, you did throw it away."

"Throw what away?"

"That clock, that watch. I hate those things," he muttered. "When I saw that, I knew that you couldn't possibly be interested in him. Now, Li Lan, shall we drink to our union?" Lim Tian Ching held out a wine cup in a grotesque parody of a wedding toast.

"How is it even possible? After all, you're dead."

He winced. "Please don't mention it. But I suppose you have a right to know. There will be a ceremony. I've already instructed my father as to how it must be held. You'll have a magnificent wedding, everything a girl might want. There'll be bride presents and jewelry, even a kingfisher feather headdress, if you want. We'll send a sedan chair and a band of musicians to your house, though a rooster will ride with you instead of me."

I shuddered at this image, but he pressed on, pleased with himself. "For the actual ceremony, you'll exchange bridal cups with my soul tablet in front of the altar. Then after the formal marriage, you'll enter the Lim household as my wife. You'll have all the material things that you need. My mother will take care of it. And every night we shall be together." He stopped and gave me a roguish smile.

Despite my terror, I felt a slow burning in my stomach. Why should I be married to this autocratic buffoon, alive or dead?

"I don't think so."

"What?"

"I said, 'I don't think so.' I don't want to marry you!"

Lim Tian Ching's eyes narrowed into slits. Despite my bold words, my heart quailed. "You don't have a choice in this matter. I'll ruin your father."

"Then I'll become a nun."

"You don't know the extent of my influence! I'll haunt you; I'll haunt your father; I'll haunt that meddling amah of yours." He was raging now. "The border officials are on my side, and they said I have a right to you!"

"Well, you are dead! Dead, dead, dead!" I shrieked.

With each iteration of the word his figure began to shiver and shake. The opulent hall with its hundreds of red candles wavered and began to disappear. The last glimpse I had was of Lim Tian Ching's face dissolving, his form smearing as though a giant hand was rubbing it out.

I WAS VERY ILL after this experience. Amah found me lying on the floor, curled up like a crayfish without a shell. The doctor looked at my tongue, felt my pulse, and shook his head gravely. He had said he had rarely seen a case of someone so young with so little *qi*, or life force. It was as though someone had drained me of half my vital energy. For that he prescribed a course of heating foods. Ginseng, wine, longan, and ginger. On the third day when I had recovered enough to sit up in bed, Amah brought me a bowl of chicken soup laced with sesame oil to strengthen the heart and nerves. In the morning light she looked shriveled, as though a puff of wind would blow her away.

I gave her the ghost of a smile. "I'm all right, Amah."

"I don't know what happened to you. The doctor thought it was brain fever. Your father blames himself."

"Where is he?"

"He was at your bedside the past few days. I made him rest. There's no sense everyone in the household getting sick."

I sipped the scalding soup. Amah had an arsenal of brews in her battery, but she said we would start with chicken soup as I was so weak. Later I should have ginseng.

"That's expensive," I said.

"What's the point of saving when things have got this far? Don't worry about the money."

She made an angry face and turned away. I was too tired to argue with her. The doctor came again and prescribed a course of moxibustion and more herbs to warm my blood. He seemed pleasantly surprised at my progress but I knew the real reason. During the past week I had had no dreams.

I had no illusions about this state of affairs, however. If it was madness, the situation seemed hopeless. But if the spirit of Lim Tian Ching was really haunting me, there might be something I could do about it. Presumably I had to consent to the marriage, judging from his insistence on a ceremony. But his wild talk about border officials, whomever they were, and his assertion that he had a right to me was disturbing, even terrifying. I wished I still had Tian Bai's pocket watch. When I had flung it, it had fallen behind the heavy *almirah*, or cupboard; and while I was so weak in bed, there were no means to move the furniture and retrieve it. I asked Amah to find it for me but she refused. She had been set against the gift of a clock as bad luck in any event, and I quickly realized it was better not to mention it again in case she decided to get rid of it for me.

A few days later, there was a commotion in the house. Noises floated up—people talking and doors banging in the courtyard below. I came out of my room and asked our maid, Ah Chun. Besides Amah, she and the cook, Old Wong, were the only servants in our large and empty house.

"Oh, miss!" she said. "Your father has a visitor."

My father occasionally had visitors, but they were old friends; mild, retiring people like himself who came and went with little ceremony.

"Who is it?" I asked.

"It's a handsome young man!"

This was clearly the most exciting event that had happened in a long time; and I could imagine that Ah Chun would be pressed against the courtyard wall gossiping with next door's maid before nightfall. But my heart was pounding. The hope that rose in my throat almost choked me.

I made my way slowly down the stairs. The front stairs in our house were finely carved of *chengal* wood in my grandfather's time. Visitors always exclaimed over the exquisite handiwork, but for some reason neither Amah nor Old Wong liked the staircase. They would never say why but preferred to come and go by the cramped back stairway. When I reached the bottom, Amah found me.

"What are you doing?" she cried, shaking her dust cloth at me. "Go back to your room at once!"

"Who is it, Amah?"

"I don't know, but don't stand here. You'll catch a chill."

Never mind that it was a warm afternoon. Amah was always darkly muttering about drafts and cooling elements. I started back up the stairs slowly when my father's study door opened and Tian Bai came out. He stood in the courtyard taking leave of my father while I clung to the railing. I wished I didn't look so disheveled, yet hoped desperately that he would see me. As I hesitated over the impropriety of calling his name, he exchanged a few more words with my father and took his leave.

When Amah had thought me safely upstairs, I made my way hastily to the front door. At the very least, I wanted to gaze upon his retreating back. There used to be a porter to man the great doors of our house and announce visitors, but now his post lay derelict. There was no one to see as I opened the heavy wooden door. To my surprise Tian Bai was still there, standing irresolutely under the eaves of the great gate. He started at the cracking sound of the hinges.

"Li Lan!" he said.

A wave of happiness washed over me. For a moment, I could not speak.

"I brought some medicine from Yan Hong. She heard you were ill." The warmth of his gaze seemed to penetrate my skin.

"Thank you," I said. The urge to touch him, to place my hands on his chest and lean against him was overwhelming, but that would never do.

After a pause, he said, "Did you get the watch I sent you?"

"Yes."

"I suppose it wasn't a very appropriate gift."

"My amah disapproved. She said it was unlucky to give a clock."

"You should tell her that I don't believe in such traditions." When he smiled, a dimple appeared briefly in his left cheek.

"Why not?"

"Didn't Yan Hong tell you? I'm a Catholic."

"I thought the English were Anglicans," I said, thinking of his education in Hong Kong's missionary medical college.

"They are. But as a boy I had a Portuguese priest as my tutor."

There were a hundred things I wished to say, a hundred more to ask him. But time had already run out for us. Tian Bai raised a hand to my face. I dared not breathe as he ran a finger lightly down my cheek. The look in his eyes was serious, almost intense. My face burned. I was seized by an urge to press my lips against the back of his hand, to bite the tips of his fingers, but I could only drop my eyes in confusion.

Tian Bai smiled faintly. "This is probably not the best time to discuss religious convictions. I really came to send my apologies."

"About what?"

He started to speak, but just then I heard voices from behind. "My amah is coming!" I said. I began to pull the door closed when a thought struck me. Swiftly, I wrenched an ornament from my hair. It was a plain oxhorn comb, but I thrust it into his hand. "Take this. Consider it payment for the watch."

AS SOON AS I could, I cornered my father to ask about Tian Bai's visit. Since the day that he had dashed my marriage hopes, he seemed to have aged. Our financial woes and my illness had weighed him down so that fresh lines creased his face like new-turned furrows. Indeed, he seemed so guilty that I could hardly bear to reprove him.

"What was the visit for?" I asked.

"He brought some medicine for you from the Lim family." My father was ill at ease, unsure whether or not to mention Tian Bai's name.

"I know who he is, Father. I met him at the Lim mansion. Did he have a message for me?"

My father hung his head. "He told me that he had heard from his uncle that the arrangement between the two of you was dissolved. He said he was sorry, but it was possible that his uncle might still change his mind."

"Oh." My heart gave a lurch.

"Don't get your hopes up, Li Lan. Tian Bai is not the one who will make these decisions. The family will have a great deal of say in it; and as far as I know from Lim Teck Kiong, he has made up his mind quite firmly."

I nodded but hardly heard a word that he said. I could only recall the slight pressure of Tian Bai's finger as it had traced the curve of my cheek.

CHAPTER 8

SINCE MY ILLNESS, Amah had taken to sleeping in my room on a thin pallet on the floor. I protested at this, as she was old and the wooden planks were hard, but she insisted. In truth, it made me feel much better. Every night Amah securely fastened the wooden shutters, no matter how hot and still the air was.

"You mustn't catch a chill," she said. "That would set you back."

I suspected that Amah kept the windows shut for other reasons. When I was a little girl, I had heard many tales of terror not only from Amah but also from her friends. Malaya was full of the ghosts and superstitions of the many races that people it. There were stories of spirits, such as the tiny leaf-sized *pelesit* that was kept by a sorcerer in a bottle and fed on blood through a hole in the foot. Or the *pontianak*, which were the ghosts of women who died in childbirth. These were particularly gruesome as they flew through the night, trailing placentas behind their disembodied heads. When my father discovered my childhood terrors, he forbade Amah to speak about spirits or the dead to me. Superstition was a sore subject for him, and Amah had grudgingly acquiesced. But now I thought I must try again.

"Amah, where do people go when they die?"

As expected, she clucked her tongue, grumbling that we shouldn't talk about such things, then contradicting herself by saying, didn't I know all about it anyway? But finally she relented. "When someone dies, the spirit leaves the body and after the hundred days of mourning are over, passes through the ten Courts of Hell. The First Court is the arrival gate. There the souls are sorted. The good ones go straight to rebirth, or if they are really saintly they escape the Wheel of Life and go to paradise."

"What about the not-so-good ones?" I asked.

"Well, if you were moderately good, you might be able to skip some of the Courts of Hell by crossing the gold or silver bridges. But if you committed some sin, you have to pass through the courts. The Second Court has the judges where they read out your good and bad deeds. Depending on that, you might be sent on to different punishments."

I had seen some of the painted hell scrolls that depicted the gruesome fates awaiting sinners. There were people being boiled in oil or sawed in half by horse and ox-headed demons. Others were forced to climb mountains of knives or were pounded into powder by enormous mallets. Gossips had their tongues ripped out, hypocrites and tomb robbers were disemboweled. Unfilial children were frozen in ice. The worst was the lake of blood into which suicides and women who had died in childbirth or aborted their children were consigned.

"But what about ghosts?" I asked.

"Most are hungry ghosts. If they die without children, or their bones are scattered, they are unable to even journey to the First Court. That's why we leave those offerings out at Qing Ming."

But Lim Tian Ching was not a hungry ghost. At least, not as far as I could judge from the pile of funeral offerings his mother had burned for him. So why was he haunting me?

"Amah, I need to tell you something," I said at last.

She turned. The expression on her face was strained, almost fearful. "Are you pregnant?"

THE GHOST BRIDE   67

"What?" The surprise on my face seemed to reassure her.

"You've been behaving so strangely!" she said. "I saw you at the gate with that young man the other day. He touched your face. And then I was sorry I told you that story about how Yan Hong managed to get married."

"Oh, Amah!" I felt like laughing hysterically. "If only it were so straightforward. Then we'd be forced to get married."

"Don't count on that!" said Amah sharply. "Yan Hong was the daughter of a rich man. Her mother died to ensure her marriage. You have no such clout."

"I thought you said her mother died of shame."

"No, I didn't tell you the real story." She pinched the bridge of her nose between her fingers. "Of course, they didn't want anyone to know that such an unlucky thing happened. The servants told me that Yan Hong's mother hanged herself, leaving a letter saying that if her daughter was not allowed to marry her lover, she would come back to haunt the family. That's why the marriage happened. Otherwise Madam Lim might have turned the girl out or forced her to get rid of the baby."

The more I heard about the Lims, the less surprised I was that the ghost of their son behaved the way he had. "Well, I'm not pregnant. But in some ways, it's worse. Lim Tian Ching is haunting me."

Amah was increasingly upset as I told her about my dreams, interrupting with cries of consternation. "This is bad, very bad!" she said. "Why didn't you tell me earlier? I could have got an amulet for you; we could have had you blessed in the temple or brought an exorcist in."

Although I quailed before the storm of her scolding, I felt an indefinable relief at sharing my burden. I wasn't mad, just cursed. The distinction gave me little pleasure.

"But I don't understand why he can haunt me. He said something about the border officials."

"The border officials of hell? *Dai gut lai see!*" Amah crossed off bad luck.

"Do we need an exorcist?"

"If an exorcist comes to the house, people will suspect we have ghost trouble." Amah frowned uneasily.

We already had ghost trouble, I thought, feeling a bubble of hysterical laughter rise in my throat. But if word got around that our family was ill fated, then I might as well forget about ever getting another marriage offer. Old Wong, our cook, was a taciturn fellow. Our maid, Ah Chun, on the other hand, was a different matter. She could scarcely hold her tongue about what we had for dinner.

"There is no help for it," said Amah. "We must go and see a medium."

THERE WAS A FAMOUS medium who lived next to the Sam Poh Kong temple at the foot of Bukit China. Bukit China meant China Hill in Malay, and in 1460 when Sultan Mansur Shah married the Chinese princess Hang Li Poh in order to cement trading ties with China, the hill was given to her as a residence. Because of the excellent feng shui, it later became the site of a huge graveyard. Some said it was the largest Chinese cemetery outside China itself. I didn't know how many people had been buried on its slopes, now overgrown with *lalang*, the wild elephant grass, and twining creepers of morning glory, but rumor had it that there were almost twelve thousand graves there. It was a veritable city of the dead.

We made our way there by rickshaw; and as I sat squeezed up against Amah, I shivered at the memory of Lim Tian Ching's stables and the puppet-like rickshaw puller I had seen there.

"What is it?" Amah was fearful of a recurrence of fever, but I told her it was nothing.

"Tell me, have I been to this temple before?" I asked.

"A long time ago your mother and I took you on a feast day. You were just a little girl at the time, barely three years old."

"Did Father come?"

"Him? You know your father! Anything that isn't Confucian he's bound to avoid."

"Confucius venerated the ancestors. I don't see that the Taoists would quibble with that."

"Yes, but the Taoists also believe in tree spirits, mountain spirits, and ghosts. *Aiya!* Didn't you study that, with all your father's book learning?"

"He made me read the classics."

I remembered copying a passage from Zhuang-Zi's dream of a butterfly. Zhuang-Zi, a Taoist sage, woke up from sleep and said that he didn't know whether he was a man who dreamed he was a butterfly or a butterfly who dreamed he was a man. Father had a rather lofty interpretation of Zhuang-Zi, preferring to concentrate on his philosophical ideas of man's place in the universe rather than the literal Taoist beliefs in immortality, shape-changing, and magic potions. He complained that the common people had corrupted these existential musings into all sorts of folk religion and mumbo jumbo. As a result I had never paid too much attention to their beliefs. Perhaps I should have.

The Sam Poh Kong temple was famous in Malacca. Even though I couldn't remember visiting it, I knew something of its history. The Sam Poh Kong temple was dedicated to the famous Ming admiral Zheng He. He was the one who, from 1405 to 1433, sailed from China around the Horn of Africa almost up to Spain. I had loved hearing about the exploits of Zheng He when I was a child, made all the more exciting since Malacca had been one of his ports of call. The accounts of his enormous treasure ships and the sheer numbers of war junks and seamen who accompanied him on his mission were amazing. In life, the admiral had been a eunuch who rose to his position by sheer ability. In death, he had become a god.

We climbed the temple steps and passed beneath the glazed roof tiles that had been brought from Chinese kilns. The deep eaves were hung with red silk lanterns and a red cloth was tied around the open door. Crowds of people moved through a haze of incense smoke from the hundreds of burning joss sticks. Amah bought a bundle and lit them at the main altar, mumbling prayers. I stood silently by while she bowed. Although I ought to do the same, I felt unable to. Years of my father's resistance prevented me. Instead I stared blindly at the statues of gods and demons that were fearfully and intricately carved around the huge altar. The muttering of the devoted filled the air, broken occasionally by the sharp clatter of bamboo fortune sticks being shaken.

This was the consultation of the oracle. A tube of sticks, each with a few cryptic words written on it, was shaken vigorously until one or two sticks fell out. For a fee, a meaning would be deduced by the priests.

I wondered whether Amah would have my fortune read in such a manner, but after she had completed her obeisance, she caught me by the sleeve and we went out of the temple into the dazzling sunlight again. Outside the gate containing Hang Li Po's well, poisoned twice but said to never run dry, she turned left and followed the wall until we came upon a makeshift stall set up against it. It was nothing more than an *attap* leaf shelter against the sun and rain. There was a mat on the ground and an enormously fat middle-aged woman was seated upon it. She leaned against a wooden box with multiple small drawers, such as peddlers carry, and flicked a palm-leaf fan against the heat.

"Is this the medium?" I whispered.

Amah nodded. Somehow this wasn't what I had expected. I thought that she might have a house near the temple or some other kind of more professional arrangement. This woman looked like a beggar. Amah had warned me earlier that the medium preferred payment not in the Straits dollars minted by the British but in the older tin currency of small ingots shaped fancifully like fish, crickets, or crocodiles. These were increasingly rare, and as we had none at such short notice, I could only hope that the copper half-cent coins in my purse would suffice.

There was a young man consulting her. He wore a broad-brimmed bamboo hat that completely concealed his face, though not his lean figure. The hem of his old-fashioned robe, though furred with dust from the road, was curiously embroidered with silver thread. Amah and I stood farther back, waiting our turn. She held an oiled-paper parasol to shield us from the merciless sun. Trickles of sweat crept down my collar, and the rice powder dusted over my face became damp and sticky. I stared at the man's clothes, wondering what was taking him so long and why he bothered to hide his face when his dress was so distinctive. The embroidery was worked in a pattern of clouds and mist, and I thought if I should ever see it again, I would certainly remember it.

At last the man finished. I noted that he had given her a small tin ingot, charmingly shaped like a tortoise. Some said that the tin animal money was cast during religious ceremonies, that spells were said over it, and that the animal shapes were sacrificial proxies; but I saw only that it shone as though it had just been minted, despite the fact that most tin-animal money was at least a few centuries old.

After the money was handed over, he hung back, asking yet another question. I suppressed a sigh of impatience. Perhaps he had ghost troubles of his own. Critically, I compared his figure with Tian Bai's. This stranger was slim with a sinuous grace. Though I could not see his face, I wondered what he looked like. It would be a pity if he were ugly, though I couldn't think of any other reason to hide a face unless it was hideously scarred, like my father's. I dropped my gaze, embarrassed at how quickly I had learned to eye men. I could only blame my brief association with Tian Bai, which had sensitized me to the sound of a man's voice, the touch of his hand. When the stranger finally left, he deliberately attempted to peer beneath my parasol as he passed. Amah forestalled him by lowering it so that he wouldn't catch a glimpse of my face, but he shrugged and walked on insolently, jingling the copper coins in his belt.

The medium turned toward us. One eye was clouded over with a hazy bloom while the other fixed us with a bright malicious stare.

"In a hurry, are you?" she said. She had a low voice for a woman, with a wheeze at the end of her sentences. Amah hastened to apologize, but the medium cut her off. "I don't mind," she said. "It's my fate to tell fortunes and see ghosts."

"See ghosts!" I said. Though the sun blazed down, I felt a chill as though someone had dipped my heart in cold water.

"Yes, I can see ghosts," said the medium. "It's no comfort to me, but I'm used to them now. Not like you—eh, Little Miss?"

Amah asked, "What can you see?"

"Sit down," she said, pulling out a couple of rickety bamboo footstools. Once seated, I had the sensation of having literally and socially come down in the world. Only coolies and other rough people squatted or sat on the street like this.

"How much?" asked Amah, always practical, but the medium paid no attention to her. She stared at me, her cloudy right eye roaming beyond my frame to sights unseen. At length she closed her eyes and gave a long drawn-out hiss. Amah and I glanced at each other. Skeptically I wondered whether this was merely some act to intimidate clients, when her eyes snapped open again and she began muttering charms under her breath. She then took out a pinch of gray powder and, placing it on the palm of her hand, blew it at me.

I coughed violently. The powder was gritty and felt like ashes. It stuck to my face and clung perniciously to the front of my dress. I groped for my handkerchief, but Amah was already cleaning my face with hers. As I blinked my eyes open, the medium chuckled. I stood abruptly.

"You give up too easily," she said. "If you go now, that young man will follow you forever."

"What man?"

"Ah, young lady. You think I couldn't see him? I gave him a taste of some medicine. He won't be back for a while."

I sat down again. "He's following me?"

"I'm sure he'll be back. But at least we can talk without him spying on you, eh?"

"What does he look like?"

She cocked her head to one side, favoring the clouded eye. "A fine well-fed fellow. Only recently dead, isn't he?"

"Less than a year," I whispered. "I thought he could only come into my dreams."

"In your dreams, yes. He talks to you?"

"He says he wants to marry me."

"And were you betrothed?"

"No!"

"He seems to have some hold on you. The dead don't usually do this to strangers."

I flushed. "Well, he said . . .   He said he had seen me at a festival before he died."

"That's possible. Some who die of love can come back as revenants."

I couldn't stop myself from snorting. "Him? Die of love? I don't believe it."

"Then did you walk through a cemetery at night? Make a vow to something, even a god or a tree or a river? Did you cast a spell on someone? Do you have a secret enemy?"

I shook my head. "Isn't he dead? Why hasn't he gone somewhere else? The Courts of Hell, or wherever the next passing is?"

She smiled. "Don't we all want to know that! Some stay because of their attachments to this world. Others have no one to bury them so they become hungry ghosts. But this one looks well provided for."

I shuddered, remembering the vast empty halls and endless corridors of Lim Tian Ching's mansions.

"He wants something from you."

"I can't marry him. Can you help me get rid of him?"

The medium rocked to and fro. "It depends, it depends."

"I have a little money," I said stiffly.

"Money? Ah, your money isn't worth that much here." Her sharp smile revealed a single canine tooth. "Not that I'll say no to it."

"But you just got rid of him!"

"So I did, so I did. But that was just for a while. I can give you something that will keep him away. But it won't last forever. You want to be completely free of him, you may have to do more."

"Like what?"

"Now, that I can't tell you right now."

I felt indignant, which was, I suppose in retrospect, rather foolish for I had come all this way in disbelief; and at the merest sign of help from this woman, pinned all my hopes on her.

"Take this powder." She took out another pouch and poured a coarse black dust into a paper cone. "Mix it in three parts of water and drink it every night before you go to bed. If it doesn't work, you can decrease the water to two parts. But it's very strong, so be careful. And wear this amulet." It was a grubby thing sewn of cloth and stuffed with pungent herbs. Finally she took out a fistful of yellow papers stamped with vermilion characters. "Paste these on your doors and windows. That will be five cents."

That was all? She had spoken at much greater length to the young man.

"Surely there must be more I can do!" I burst out. "Should I go to a temple, give alms, pray to a god? Should I cut my hair off and make a vow?"

She regarded me almost pityingly. "Of course, if you want to. Won't do you any harm. But as for cutting off that pretty hair and making vows ... well, why don't you wait first. Don't do anything rash."

Silently, I handed over ten copper half-cent coins, wondering whether I would have received better advice if we had, in fact, offered her tin-animal money. As I leaned over she suddenly grasped my hand.

"Listen," she whispered harshly. "I'll tell you one more thing, though it may get me into trouble. Burn hell banknotes for yourself!"

Taken aback by her grip, I said, "The money for the dead?"

"If you can't do it yourself, ask someone to do it for you." Turning, she said in a louder voice, "You want promises of success, assurances that all will be well? I don't do that. Ask your amah here. That's why I'm the real deal." She chortled again. "It's not a gift, my dear young lady. No, no it isn't. Those feng shui masters, those ghost hunters and face readers. They like to tell people that they can do what they do because they're so talented and blessed by heaven."

"And aren't they?"

She leaned close to me. Her breath was pungent with a yeasty odor. "Tell me, do you think it a blessing to see the dead?"

When we left, she was still laughing.

OUR JOURNEY BACK WAS subdued. I could see that Amah wanted to ask me what the medium had whispered, but she was too proud to speak of our private affairs in front of the rickshaw puller. Instead, I thought over the medium's words. Burn cash for yourself, she had told me. Did that mean funeral offerings? Was I fated for death? I lifted up my hands and pressed them against my eyes. Against the brilliant sunlight I could see the flush of blood pulsing through them. To die seemed impossible, unbelievable.

Out of the corner of my eye I caught Amah looking at me anxiously, and decided against telling her the medium's last instructions, disturbing as they were. I gazed out of the rickshaw, overcome by a flat sense of depression. We were descending the slope of Bukit China, past the enormous cemetery with its rows of Chinese graves. Some still bore traces of wilted flowers and burned joss sticks, but by and large they were neglected.

Most people were terrified of ghosts and would not go near a tomb unless it was Qing Ming. Indeed, some of the graves were so overgrown that you could barely make out the carved characters that proclaimed their occupants' names. The oldest had collapsed into themselves so that the slope was dotted here and there with gaping holes, like the empty tooth sockets of some giant creature. How different it was from the quiet Malay cemeteries, whose pawn-shaped Islamic tombstones are shaded by the frangipani tree, which the Malays call the graveyard flower. Amah would never let me pluck the fragrant, creamy blossoms when I was a child. It seemed to me that in this confluence of cultures, we had acquired one another's superstitions without necessarily any of their comforts.

CHAPTER 9

THE MEDICINE TASTED like ashes. Like bitter herbs and burned dreams. That evening I watched as Amah prepared it, using hot water poured from a small kettle that she kept for herbal infusions. To Amah all medicine must be taken hot. We had carefully pasted the yellow spell papers on the inside of every window and on the front door. When we finished, it was as though a host of small flags waved from each aperture. Uneasily, I noted how they seemed to flutter even when there was no draft. I hesitated, however, over the medium's instructions to burn funeral money for myself, not wanting to mention it to Amah. Instead, I passed her a small oilcloth packet. "Can you help me sell this?"

She shook out some gold hairpins. They were old-fashioned and ornate and I had forgotten who had bequeathed them to me. "Why do you do this?"

"Because we need more money and you can't keep dipping into your savings."

She protested, but in the end promised to ask her amah sisterhood if any lady wished to buy jewelry. That was the way it was always done. Discreet inquiries, the exchange of gold pieces or jade pendants for ready cash. No wonder every concubine and mistress asked for her favors to be returned in cold metal and gleaming gems. Surely, if I were a courtesan I would demand no less. As it was, the thought that we had come down to selling jewelry scraped at my conscience like a little claw.

I WENT STRAIGHT TO bed after imbibing the medium's draught. As I swirled the dark gritty powder in the bowl, I had some misgivings about whether I would be poisoned. In the end, however, I swallowed it and with a feeling of surprise, woke almost ten hours later to brilliant morning light. Amah was hovering anxiously over me, and as I sat up she managed a watery smile.

"What time is it?"

"Almost the hour of the snake," she said. "Did you sleep well?"

It had been a deep, almost smothering sleep, but mercifully uninterrupted by any dreams. I wondered whether the medium's secret ingredient was merely a sleeping powder. Looking at Amah's eager face, however, I couldn't help but smile back at her.

I made my way downstairs to my father's study, feeling a pressing need to talk to him about our finances, the marriage negotiations, and all kinds of things that we had not had the occasion to discuss for a while. I even longed to copy poems under his critical eye again. But his study door was closed and when I prised it open, the room was empty. All that remained was the musty smell of books and the heavy sweet odor of opium.

"Where has my father gone?" I asked Ah Chun.

"He went out early."

"Did he say where he was going?"

"No, miss."

Dissatisfied, I closed the study door and leaned against it. What was happening out in the world of men? Had Tian Bai talked to his uncle again? What were we to do with our debts? How I wished I could go out and make inquiries by myself. If only I had a brother or a cousin to rely on. Despite the fact that my feet were not bound, I was confined to domestic quarters as though a rope tethered my ankle to our front door. Even Amah, with her sisterhood placed in the employ of many families, had greater recourse than myself. I had heard nothing further from Yan Hong. Maybe she too had forgotten me. I wondered what Tian Bai was doing, and whether he even thought about me anymore. Disconsolate, I took up my sewing basket and attempted to finish a pair of panels intended as sleeve borders for a new dress. The work kept my hands busy as my thoughts churned incessantly.

I didn't see my father the next day either, which was worrisome. My father was not the kind of person who liked to go out, partly because of his smallpox scars. I was used to my father's looks and the few old friends who still frequented our house did not seem to care, but strangers would often stop and stare. When I was younger, I sometimes wondered whether my father would remarry. He had loved my mother, though, and perhaps no second wife, chosen from the dutiful ranks of impoverished spinsters, could have compared to her. She, he had once told me in an unguarded moment, looked like a houri from paradise. Our house was a shrine to my dead mother. My father still worshipped her in his study, and Amah could not help recalling her girlhood even as she helped me grow through mine. I sighed, wondering if Tian Bai would think so fondly of me if we were married. Despite the absence of dreams, I felt weary. There was an ominous heaviness, like the air roiling before a thunderstorm.

TWO DAYS LATER, THE front door flew open with a crash. It was early in the morning and the sound reverberated through the house like a crack of thunder. I ran downstairs as fast as I could. In the entrance hall, Ah Chun was white-faced, hands pressed against her mouth. A great stain showed wetly on the door, trickling into a dark pool. It was as though some creature had been slaughtered on our front step. I looked out but the street was empty. Dread filled me, as though I had swallowed a cold and heavy toad, for surely this was unlucky, very unlucky, indeed.

"What happened?" I asked Ah Chun. "Did you see anyone?"

"No . . . there was no one."

"But why did you open the door?"

She burst out crying. "It opened by itself."

"Surely you must have seen someone running away?" There had not been enough time, I thought, for the perpetrator to vanish.

"There was no one," she repeated. "The door was locked."

"Maybe you forgot to lock the door last night." Amah appeared anxiously behind her.

Ah Chun shook her head mulishly. "The bolts hadn't been drawn yet."

She started to cry again and talked about leaving.

"What do you mean, you foolish girl?" said Amah.

"It was ghosts. Ghosts did this."

THE REST OF THE day passed gloomily. Ah Chun wept and repeated she wanted to go home. She said she had heard of such things happening in her village before and it always ended in disaster for the household. I looked at the doorstep again after Old Wong had washed it. He was a lean old man, his sparse hair turning gray, but I had never been more grateful for his taciturn presence.

"What do you think it was?" I asked.

"Blood," he replied tersely.

"But what kind of blood?"

"Pig maybe. Get a lot of blood when you slaughter a pig."

"You don't think it was human?"

He scowled. "Little Miss, I've known you since you were as high as my knee. How many times have I made you steamed-blood pudding? Smells like pig, I'm guessing pig."

I looked down at my feet. "Ah Chun says ghosts did this. Do you believe her?"

He snorted. "Ah Chun also says that spirits ate the leftover rice dumplings in the pantry." With a curt nod, he stumped off.

"Could it be that some thugs mistook our house?" asked Amah hopelessly. Her words sent new fears snaking into my heart. Moneylenders. What had my father been doing? Miraculously he was home. He had been home all morning, in fact, and had slept through the entire incident. When he opened the door of his study, the room reeked of opium.

"Father!" I was torn between relief and fear at his appearance. He looked wild-eyed, his face unshaven and his rumpled clothes hanging off his gaunt frame. When I told him about the morning's incident, he seemed to barely register it.

"Is it gone?" he asked.

"Old Wong washed it off."

"Good, good . . . "

"Father. Have you borrowed money from anyone?"

He rubbed his red eyes. "The only man who holds my debts is the master of the Lim family, Lim Teck Kiong," he said slowly. "And I don't think he would resort to such tactics. Why should he? When all he wants . . . " His voice trailed off as he looked shamefaced.

"He wants me to marry his son. Did you say yes?" For an instant, a dreadful suspicion entered my heart.

"No, no. I said I would think about it."

"Did you talk to him again?"

"Yesterday. Or maybe the day before." He turned and went back into his study.

LATER I TOLD AMAH what my father had said and asked her if she thought the Lim family would do such a thing. She shook her head. "I wouldn't have thought it of them. But who knows?" Between us lay an unspoken dread. Amah would not give voice to it in case it strengthened any evil spirits, but I wondered if the ghost of Lim Tian Ching had become more powerful. Or perhaps the Lim family, living or dead, meant to drive me to madness.

I took Amah's thin hand in mine. This hand had dried my tears and spanked me as a child. It had combed my hair and spoon-fed me. Now it was spotted with liver marks, and the knuckles and joints swollen. I wasn't sure how old she was, but I felt a surge of melancholy affection. Sooner than later she would need someone to care for her. I wondered whether rich and fortunate young ladies ever had to think of such things. In a household such as the Lim family, I had seen so much abundance that even the senior servants had underlings to fetch and carry for them. If I married Lim Tian Ching in a spirit wedding, it would satisfy almost everyone, I thought. Amah would have a better old age; my father's debts would be canceled. But to live in that household as a widow and be forever separated from Tian Bai! To watch him marry someone else while I was visited nightly by a ghost. I couldn't bear it.

"I would rather die," I said.

"What?"

I had spoken aloud without thinking. Amah looked at me with concern. "Don't worry so much about what happened today," she said, thinking that I must be frightened.

"I'm not worried," I lied. "I know what to do." I took out a purse and counted the money inside. Amah had managed to sell the gold hairpins and for once the little purse was heavy with cash.

"Amah, will you do something for me? Can you buy some funeral offerings?"

She looked at me in surprise. "What kind of offerings?"

"Cash. Hell banknotes."

"How much?"

"As much as you think is necessary."

"But surely his family has burned plenty of money for him?" she asked. I realized that she thought we were to bribe Lim Tian Ching to leave us alone.

"The medium said to burn some," I replied evasively. Amah looked irresolute, but in the end she agreed to go. In the meantime, I had preparations of my own to make.

WHEN AMAH CAME BACK, she showed me a paper parcel containing printed stacks of hell banknotes, their colors garish with the seal of Yama, the god of hell. In addition to this, she had also bought gold paper to be folded into the shape of ingots, another favorite currency of the underworld. The numbers of the banknotes were in tens and hundreds of Malayan dollars. Hell must surely have seen inflation, given the recklessly high amounts of currency that were regularly burned. What of the poor ghosts who had died long before such large notes were printed?

Later that afternoon, when Amah had retired for a rest, I brought the funeral goods to the courtyard where we burned family offerings to the ancestors. I folded the paper ingots into the proper shape and now they sat, neatly stacked like small boats, on a large tray. I wanted to do the burning on my own without Amah, because it was better if she continued to believe the offerings were for Lim Tian Ching, and not me.

In the past, I had simply followed along with Amah at the appropriate festivals. She was the one who arranged everything at New Year's, or at Qing Ming, piling the paper funeral offerings to one side and laying out a tray of food for the ancestors. This was an elaborate affair, consisting of a boiled chicken complete with head and feet, cups of rice wine, a head of green lettuce tied with red paper, and pyramids of fruit. After the offering had been made, the family consumed the food. Apparently, the ancestors only needed to partake of the spiritual part of the offering. I had always thought this a practical way to approach things, though it didn't seem to entail too much sacrifice for the living. The paper grave-goods and funeral money were burned afterward. This was the part, I decided, that I needed to do.

Amah burned incense facing the ancestral tablets upon which the names of the deceased were written. I wasn't sure what to do about the lack of such a tablet for myself, but while she was out, I had prepared a makeshift one of wood and paper. My hand had trembled when I inked my own name on it, the pigment sinking into the paper like a dismal stain, but I had gone so far that I might as well try everything.

Long ago, I once saw my father burn handwritten poems. It was late one evening, and a blue dusk filled the air. When I asked him why he was destroying his calligraphy, he merely shook his head.

"I sent them," he said.

"Where?" I asked. I must have been very small at the time, for I had to peer up at his face.

"To your mother. If I burn them, perhaps she'll read these poems in the spirit world." His breath was heavy with the sweet reek of rice wine. "Now run along. You should be in bed by now."

I climbed the stairs slowly, watching as he stood in the dark courtyard. He seemed to have forgotten my presence as he lit yet another poem and watched the paper spark up then dwindle to nothing. After that incident I had asked Amah if I too could burn things for my mother, such as my drawings or my first tentative embroidery stitches. She had seemed unduly cross, snapping that we didn't do such things out of the right time and where did I get such ideas from? Amah was always a stickler about the correctness of worship and feast days.

Now I wondered whether my father still indulged himself by writing letters to my mother and burning them. Somehow, I doubted it. It was hard to imagine him still having the energy to execute such projects. And what of my mother? Was she still in the spirit world? Amah had always said my mother had surely already been reborn somewhere else. I hoped so. Otherwise I would have to pray that she would take pity on the daughter she had left behind. I had not been taught to pray directly to my mother, even though her death had remained a central, unspoken part of our lives. Amah clung to her belief that my mother had been spared the torments of hell and long since passed on to rebirth. Other than that odd incident from my childhood, Father did not acknowledge it either. I thought of Tian Bai—if I died, would he write letters to me?

Taking a deep breath, I arranged a sheaf of notes into a fan. Muttering a brief prayer to Zheng He, the admiral who had sailed so far around the world, I hoped it would do, though my heart was full of doubt. Then I faced my own name and bowed, saying, "May this money be of use to me somehow." It sounded weak and rather pathetic, but I dipped the notes into the brazier and they caught fire instantly. I was just about to arrange another fan of cash when Amah came into the courtyard.

"Started already?" she said, her eyes darting to the hell banknotes in my hand. Hastily, I cast them into the brazier and tried to hide the makeshift soul tablet with my name on it, but it was too late.

"What are you doing? You're not dead yet!" With surprising speed, she snatched away the paper tablet and tore it up.

"Amah," I said, but she was crying and scolding me.

"Unlucky! So unlucky! How could you do such a thing?"

"The medium told me to."

"She did?" Amah glared at me. "Then she's a liar. You're not going to die. You're too young to die!" As she wept, distraught, I clung to her like a child again, feeling the slightness of her frame and the frailty of her bones.

"I didn't mean it, I'm sorry."

How many times had she held me thus when I was small? After a while, she wiped her face with the backs of her hands.

"Don't ever do that again," she said.

"Why?"

"Because nobody ever burns offerings to a living person!"

"But this might be a special case."

Though I didn't wish to upset her, I couldn't help arguing my point. All that preparation wasted if I couldn't burn the money!

"Are you sure she didn't want you to burn them for him?"

"No. She said it was for me."

Amah sat down heavily. "It's as good as saying you're dead already. She doesn't know what she's talking about."

"But, Amah, you told me to see her!"

"She has some talent, to be sure, but she's not a god. How does she know what fate has in store for you?"

Two faint spots of color appeared on Amah's face. I knew that look. It meant that there was to be no more discussion over this, however rationally one might argue. I thought about insisting. After all, I was the mistress of the house now. Had probably been for years, in fact, though I had never thought of things that way. As though she could read my mind, Amah cast her eyes down.

"Li Lan, I'm just an old woman now. You can do what you want. But please, don't do this. It's very unlucky."

To my dismay, she began to cry again. I crouched down to look up at her. "I won't do it."

Tears slipped into the wrinkles on her face. "You don't understand. I raised your mother. I carried her when she was a baby, and held her hand when she learned to walk. And then she died so suddenly, poor creature. At her funeral you clung to me, your sweet baby arms holding on to my neck. I swore to her that I would never leave you. If you die young too, I can't bear it!"

I was amazed at this outpouring. Amah was usually so unsentimental, so unwilling to talk about the past. "Was she that young then?" I had always imagined my mother as being much older than me, looking like other people's mothers or my aunts.

"Not much older than you are now. She was like my own child."

Unconsciously, Amah's hand smoothed my hair, falling back into the old rhythms of childhood as though I were really only knee-high and had come to seek solace in her lap. "And now you. You are my little girl too." We clung to each other like two shipwrecked survivors.

CHAPTER 10

THAT NIGHT I had terrible dreams, despite the medium's medicine. My eyes were swollen from crying and I was in low spirits. Amah's fear had infected me. Death had already stolen from her once and she believed that it could easily happen again, whether from the god of smallpox or as a ghostly affliction. Not wanting to think about it, I went to bed early. The dreams began almost immediately, as though they had been pent up for days. From my drugged sleep, dark shapes wavered, pressing shadowy hands and faces against an invisible barrier. Everything was blurred and slow. I caught glimpses of Lim Tian Ching's face fading in and out. The mouth moved and the eyes rolled alarmingly. I didn't want to listen but eventually he swam into focus.

"Li Lan, my dear," he said. The distortions pulled his mouth into a strange rictus. "You've been so unfriendly lately. Surely this is no way to treat your betrothed?"

"Go away!" I shouted, though the words emerged with terrible effort. "I'm not your betrothed! I have no relation to you at all."

"I came to give you a warning," he said. "A little willfulness in a wife isn't too bad, but outright disobedience . . . Well, Li Lan, as your fiancé I do feel it is my duty to correct you, don't you think?"

"Did you put blood on our door?"

He giggled. "Wasn't it impressive? Even I was surprised."

"You did it yourself?"

"Now, now, I can't give away all my secrets. But suffice it to say that I have others at my command. I am a person of some prestige, which you may come to appreciate soon."

"How is it that you can command spirits?"

He laughed. "It was nothing really," he said. "I just told them to give you a fright. I would never have thought of blood myself, but I have to say it looked good. That maid of yours couldn't stop screaming. Really, I haven't enjoyed myself so much since . . . since . . . " He frowned and broke off.

I knew better now than to steer him onto the topic of his death. "And they did this for you? Who are they?"

"The border officials. Oh yes, they listen to me. They've been seconded to my command."

"By whom?"

"One of the Nine Judges of Hell, of course." He positively smirked at this, his shoulders hunching so that the thick pad of fat where his neck met his back shifted. It was a shame that dying had done so little for his physique.

"Does everyone get demons to command?" I asked.

"Of course not! As a special case, I received resources for my task. You don't think they would let people just do whatever they like! There are procedures, the proper people to know." He stroked his chin, fondling the ghost of a goatee. "But enough of that. I came to see if you had changed your mind. You didn't exactly make it very pleasant for me to visit you lately. Consulting that old witch."

"So the powder worked."

Too late, I realized I had said the wrong thing. Rage flitted across his face; his eyes flattened dangerously. This was the frightening thing about Lim Tian Ching. Living in our tranquil, slightly gloomy household, I had never experienced such tantrums.

"No powder can hold me!" he said. "It was a minor inconvenience. But I've come for my answer tonight."

"But why do you want to marry me?"

"Li Lan, Li Lan, you ask too many questions. Surely you don't mean to weary your bridegroom already." But he was still smiling, as though the game pleased him in some manner. "There will be plenty of time for our love to become intimate."

"Love? You hardly know me."

"Oh, but I know you very well, Li Lan." I shrank away as he approached. "And it was agreed, you would be part of my reward."

"For what?"

"I suppose I can tell you since we're to be married anyway. Someone important has granted me special restitution for the crime committed against me. I need only complete a few trifling tasks for them. And in return, the perpetrator shall be mine."

"What crime?" I asked, although my skin was prickling.

"Surely you don't think a strong young man like me could die suddenly of a fever, do you?" he said. "I was murdered."

I blinked nervously. "And are you trying to discover who did it?"

"But I already know. It was my dear cousin, Tian Bai."

AMAH WAS THE ONE who woke me, weeping and screaming as I thrashed about. For a long time afterward, she held me as I sobbed incoherently about Lim Tian Ching while she stroked the sweat-soaked hair back from my face. At last I fell into a fitful sleep. When I finally rose, it was almost noon and Amah was tapping on the door.

"What is it?" I asked. I was still preoccupied with Lim Tian Ching's revelations. My hair was wild, my eyelids swollen. I looked like a madwoman.

"Your father wants to see you." Amah seemed smaller than ever, a clock-work toy that had begun to run down. "Downstairs, in his study."

I looked at Amah but she merely shrugged. "Who knows what he wants?

But you! You're too ill to get out of bed. I'll tell him to wait until later."

"I'll go."

For some reason I felt profoundly uneasy about this summons and I suspected Amah did too, even as she tried to detain me by fussing and scolding. When I had washed my face and plaited my hair, I went downstairs. For the first time in days, the door to my father's study stood ajar. I knocked tentatively, even though I had never been in the habit of doing so.

"Come in," said my father.

He was standing behind his desk holding a painted scroll. The bones protruded from his emaciated cheeks and it struck me that the ghost of Lim Tian Ching was eating our household alive. I wondered what pressures he had brought to bear in the Lim mansion, and for the first time, felt a twinge of pity for his parents.

"A fine painting, don't you think? This has always been one of my favorites." It was a black-and-white study of mountains, the brushstrokes fierce as though the artist could barely control his impatience to bring the scene to life. "I tried to keep it out of the light and heat," said my father. "This is by a very famous painter. Can you guess who it is?"

Surely my father had not summoned me down to continue my neglected classical education. Or was he losing his reason after all? He twisted his lips in a grimace. "It will get a good price," he said. "And there are more. These old things that I've collected, perhaps they may be of some use after all."

"How much?" I said.

"Not enough. But I plan to declare bankruptcy. These are for you. We'll convert them into gold and cash so you'll have something to live on."

"And you? What about you?" I asked in sudden fear. Scenes flashed across my mind. My father in debtor's prison, or lying broken in the street.

"Don't worry about me." Seeing that I was becoming agitated, he said, "Li Lan, I actually wanted to give you some news. I thought it would be better that you heard it from me, rather than from some gossiping servant."

My heart sank. "What is it?"

"Tian Bai is to be married. The betrothal is official, the contracts have been signed and he will marry the daughter of the Quah family."

I STOOD THERE DUMBLY, his words ringing in my ears like the wash of distant waves. "The Quah family?" I said through stiff and clumsy lips.

"You may have seen her that night at the Festival of the Cowherd and the Weaving Maiden. She stood next to you at the needle-threading competition."

Of course I remembered her. That tall, horse-faced girl who had been so unfriendly to me. I was falling, drowning in dark water. I could barely hear my father. Numb, I watched as he grasped my cold hands.

"Li Lan!" he said. "I'm so sorry. That day when he came to talk to me, I was afraid he would raise your hopes."

I turned and walked away. Dimly, I was aware of my father calling me, of Amah running up to catch my sleeve, but all was underwater. A roaring filled my ears and my vision blurred. Tian Bai! Wrapped up as I had been in my struggles with Lim Tian Ching, I had taken it for granted that he was, in his own world, fighting his uncle to ensure that we could still be together. And now he had failed me. Had failed for quite some time, since the marriage contracts were already signed. What a fool I had been! Taken in by a charming smile and an old brass watch. I had indulged in daydreams while the Quah girl probably sewed her trousseau. Perhaps she too had received a length of cloth as a prize from Yan Hong. I felt sick.

I lay on my bed with unseeing eyes. I was exhausted, but could not rest. Lim Tian Ching's accusations. Tian Bai's marriage. They churned together in a nauseating morass. If Tian Bai was a murderer, then I was well rid of him. Yet I could not bring myself to trust Lim Tian Ching, nor even my own dreams. That way led to madness. I didn't know how long I lay there, but the sun moved from one window to the other as the day waned. Amah came in and lit the lamps. She brought soup, even as I turned my face away. She wept aloud and cursed Tian Bai, saying all the things that I wished I could say. As the light faded, the yellow spell papers over the windows shivered in an unseen wind.

I knew what that meant. My unwanted suitor would come again that night.

When Amah left, I sat up and fumbled for the pouch of powder that the medium had given me. With shaking fingers I poured a generous amount into a cup and sloshed some water in. She had said I could increase the dose if it didn't work. Well, it had certainly not worked last night. I told myself that all I wanted was oblivion, to sleep and forget. I told myself this even as I gulped it down, gasping at the bitter taste. Now, in retrospect, I asked myself why did I do that? Why didn't I wait for Amah to come back, to prepare it for me as carefully as she would surely have done? I was angry, despairing, and careless. But I truly don't think that I meant to die.

PART TWO

Afterworld

CHAPTER 11

S OMEONE WAS CRYING, the harsh sobs like the wheezing of an animal in pain. I opened my eyes to a bedchamber with windows half shuttered against the strong sunshine. Though they must have once been of good quality, there was an indefinable shabbiness about the furniture despite the scoured floorboards and neatly mended linens. All these things I saw with a hawk-like sharpness I had never experienced before. Every whorl on the wooden beams stood out in relief. Each mote of dust hung in the air like a star.

An old woman was huddled against the side of the bed but it was hard to concentrate on her. My mind seemed to wander, as though it was constantly being drawn away. The bed was a three-sided box and on it was a single cotton mattress, worn to a concave meagerness. I spent a long time examining the stitches that held it together. All this time, the sobbing continued until almost in irritation, I turned my attention back to the old woman. She crouched on the floor, her face buried in the side of the mattress. As she rocked back and forth, she exposed the thin soles of her cloth shoes.

As I studied her, I became aware of a girl lying in the bed. She lay unnaturally still, her eyelids furled tight as flower buds. The extreme pallor of her complexion made the gently curving brows and thick lashes stand out in stark contrast, as though they had been painted with a heavy hand. I wondered what she looked like when she opened her eyes. If she ever opened them, indeed, for it was apparent even from a distance that something was wrong with her.

The door opened and a maidservant entered. When she saw the girl on the bed she began to shriek. Her cries drew an older man with pockmarked skin. From his long robe I guessed he was the master of the house, though he seemed pitiably feeble. He grasped the girl's hands and called her name. Distracted, I was about to turn toward the windows, but the sound of her name arrested me and kept me where I was, watching almost disinterestedly as they tried to revive her. All the while the people in the room kept exclaiming "Li Lan! Li Lan!" as though that would bring her back.

At length a doctor arrived. Shooing away the hysterical maid, he listened to the girl's pulse, prised open her mouth, and examined her tongue. He felt the palms of her hands and the soles of her feet, pausing to turn up her eyelids.

Then he said, "She's not dead." The old woman, who had not left her post by the bed, burst into fresh weeping. "What has she taken?" he asked.

Painfully, she rose and brought a paper packet of powder to the doctor, along with the dregs of an earthenware cup. He sniffed it, put in his finger and licked it briefly. "Opium," he pronounced, "Along with a lot of other things, some of which I don't know. Who gave this to her?"

The old woman began some muddled explanation about a medium and other events that I barely paid attention to. Instead, fascinated by the fact that the girl was still alive, I drew closer. If I had paused to reflect, perhaps I should have found it strange that no one appeared to notice me but it didn't occur to me then.

The doctor was delivering his diagnostic. "Keep her warm and feed her plain chicken broth if you can. She may revive but you should also prepare for the worst."

"Are you saying she might die?" asked the master of the house.

In answer the doctor wiped his fingers fastidiously on his sleeve, then using the second and third fingers of his right hand, pressed hard on the girl's upper lip, beneath the nose. Surprisingly, her eyelids gave the merest flicker. At the same instant, I became aware of a tug at the very fibers of my being. If I were a kite blowing on some errant wind, that feeling would be the sudden jerk of the string catching up to me.

"You see?" said the doctor. "This is the acupuncture point to revive fainting and nosebleeds. She's taken an overdose that has slowed her life force drastically, yet there's still some *qi* circulating in her body."

"Will she recover?"

"She's young and her body may eventually break down the poison, so keep her warm and massage her. Try to see if she can take a little liquid."

"Please, Doctor. Tell me truly, what are her chances?" The older man looked haggard, his eyes wide and glassy. I could see his pupils were dilated as though he himself were taking stimulants. The doctor must have noticed too, for he paused to look at him with a faint expression of distaste.

"Let her rest and tomorrow I'll come back with acupuncture needles. I don't want to stimulate the *qi* until her condition stabilizes. But she may be in this state for a while." As the doctor prepared to leave, he took the old woman aside and muttered, "He's smoking too much opium."

She nodded, though I could see her heart wasn't in it. Her gaze kept straying back to the girl on the bed, and after the doctor left, she immediately began to massage her limbs. At first the girl lay motionless like a beautiful doll, but after about twenty minutes I began to perceive a hint of color in her face. It was so faint that I wondered whether the old woman could detect it, but an expression of relief crossed her face. Tenderly, she smoothed the girl's hair.

"I'll make you some soup, my little one," she said. "Don't worry, Amah will come back soon."

As soon as the door had closed behind her I went over to the girl. I felt intensely curious about her. When I gazed into her face I had the nagging feeling that there was something important that I couldn't remember. Close up, I could detect the barely perceptible pulse in her throat, the sluggish meandering of blood through her body, and the faint lift of her rib cage. Drawn by some unknown fascination, I placed my hand on her chest. A jolt of lightning ran through my body, burning its way with a rush of memories, images, and feelings. In a flash, I remembered who I was, who all those people were. That was my body lying on the bed.

For some moments I stayed there, frozen in fear and amazement. Was I a spirit now? Frantically, I circled the body. My body, I reminded myself. It was said that when the soul was parted from the body it could be enticed back. I walked round, peering at it and wondering whether I could enter through a nostril or an ear, but I didn't seem to have that ability. Frustrated at last, I lay down on it, my phantom form slowly sinking until it was completely engulfed by my unconscious self. I fit perfectly, yet there was a separation that couldn't be reconciled. But despite my anxiety, I no longer felt as distracted. My spirit must have remembered the cradle of my flesh, the soft murmurings of blood in my veins, and it quieted down like a nervous horse in a familiar stall.

WHEN I OPENED MY eyes again, Amah's familiar face hovered anxiously over me. For an instant I thought I was a child again, sick in bed, but then I remembered. She passed a hand over my forehead, but I felt nothing. It was a crushing disappointment. I called Amah, but she continued to gaze down at me sadly.

"Li Lan," she said. "Can you hear me? I brought some broth for you."

"I'm here!" I cried, but to her eyes there was no change.

When she propped my body up, I sat up in it as well. Amah brought a spoonful to my lips. "Just a little," she said. The fragrance was savory and enticing, but my body slumped forward and the broth dribbled out. Tears gathered in Amah's eyes but she kept trying. In desperation, I took up my place inside my body and pretended to swallow whenever she spooned the broth in. At first it seemed to make no difference, but eventually my body swallowed weakly. Amah was beside herself with delight, and so was I. She cleaned my face with a warm damp towel, dressed me in fresh clothes, and tucked me in. All this I observed while standing at her shoulder, though she paid no heed to my piteous entreaties.

When she left again, I followed her out. Contrary to my expectations of the spirit world, movement was not difficult. The only change was that I seemed to have less substance. Soft filmy things, like curtains, were no barrier to my passing, but denser objects required a struggle. I didn't even attempt the walls, not wishing to get stuck somewhere. Other people were impermeable to me. When Ah Chun brushed past, the movement of her shoulder pushed me back against the wall. Only my own body seemed to accept my passage easily.

Ghosts, it was widely believed, had the greatest difficulty turning corners and could be easily flummoxed by odd angles and mirrors. But they could also slip through cracks and dwindle like candle flames. None of these rules seemed to apply to me, and I wondered whether the fact that I was not quite dead had anything to do with it. Or worse, perhaps soon I would lose this ability to move purposefully and I would fade away, becoming no more than a wraith blown by the wind.

At the top of the stairs, I leaped impulsively, floating feather-soft down to the floor below. I was so pleased with this discovery that I was on the verge of running upstairs to repeat it when I heard voices in the courtyard. The air was beginning to cool and the smell of burning charcoal rose as stoves were lit for the evening meal. I could almost taste the food that was cooking, just as I had tasted the broth Amah had spooned into my body. While that had strengthened me, however, these aromas merely tantalized, leaving me unsatisfied.

I made my way slowly into the courtyard where Old Wong was talking to Ah Chun. Judging from her red nose and swollen eyes, she had either just stopped crying or was about to start again.

"The little mistress dead," she said. "And she so young—I'm sure this house is cursed!"

Old Wong made a sharp sound of annoyance. "She's not dead. Didn't you hear the doctor?"

"I mean to give my notice tomorrow," said Ah Chun. "I won't work here anymore."

"Go ahead, then," said Old Wong. "Try and see if you can find another job right away. At least you're still fed and housed here."

"What about you?" she asked. "Will you leave at the end of the month?"

"Don't know," he said. "They need the help."

"I heard the master is bankrupt." Ah Chun blew her nose.

"Still paying us, aren't they?"

I listened to them anxiously, wondering how our household would fare if Ah Chun and Old Wong should leave us. At that moment, Old Wong turned his head and looked directly at me. A spasm of emotion crossed his face, like a lizard skittering on hot stones. I was astonished. No one else had noticed me at all. I called his name but he turned away.

"Be off with you!" he said. "Go back to where you belong."

Obediently, Ah Chun picked up her pan of vegetable peelings and made her way indoors. I lingered, thinking about the words he had used. They almost seemed intended for me, but he didn't acknowledge me at all, even when I stood in front of him calling plaintively. Instead, he marched back to the kitchen, leaving me to doubt that instant of recognition.

FOR THE NEXT FEW days I stayed close to my body, often lying in it in the hopes that I could rekindle a connection. Compared to when I had first seen it, my body now looked as though it were merely sleeping. The waxen, lifeless cast was gone, and it could now eat a little and swallow involuntarily. When helped to the chamber pot, it would obediently void itself. This last I worked very hard on, for I didn't want Amah to be burdened as though I were an infant again. At first I was flushed with this success, but when improvement halted at this basic level, I began to despair.

The doctor came every day. I shuddered to think at how we were paying him, but thankfully there was still some cash from the jewelry I had sold. I hoped Amah would have the sense to sell more, if need be. He administered acupuncture and pronounced himself pleasantly surprised at the signs of progress, which he attributed entirely to his own devices.

"I've seldom seen such a marked improvement in a patient," he declared to my father.

"But what about her mind? She still doesn't respond to anything."

"It's an unusual case to be sure. Usually the spirit returns first, prompting the physical recovery."

"What do you think?" my father broke in. There were stains on his blue robe, which he had not changed for days.

"You need to call her spirit back. Who knows where it is wandering now?"

Since I was standing right beside him, I felt the horrible irony of his remarks. Wandering, indeed!

"And if her spirit can find its way back?"

"Then it should naturally join to the body. There is a strong attraction between the two."

This conversation made me more certain than ever that I must do something. Anything. The disaster of my disembodiment had overshadowed all else, but now I feared that in my current form I might be easier prey for Lim Tian Ching and his schemes. And what of his other accusations? I found it hard to believe Tian Bai was a murderer, but I tore my thoughts from him. Even if he was innocent, he was marrying another. I had enough troubles of my own.

I had not yet dared to pass beyond the barrier of yellow spell papers that Amah and I had pasted on the windows and entrances. Whenever I drew close, they fluttered wildly though there was no breeze. I feared that they might trap me, as their purpose was to block spirits. I had noticed that my spirit form wore the same clothes my physical body did, and the food Amah gave my body seemed to strengthen it. That seemed a good sign; in some indefinable way, my spirit was still tied to my body. But I wasn't sure what would happen to this bond if I left the house.

As I gazed at my body, wishing I had appreciated it more, I noticed a thin thread hanging in the air. At first I thought it was a strand of spider silk, but it glistened in the sunshine and in contrast to how solid objects had become for me in my new state, appeared strangely translucent. I put my finger out and felt a tingling hum, like the vibrating string of an instrument.

Startled, I drew my hand back. The thread emerged from a corner of the room and by kneeling on the floor, I saw the glint of brass that was Tian Bai's watch behind the heavy *almirah*. I had been unable to retrieve it since I had flung it at Lim Tian Ching's shade that evening, so long ago it seemed. The fine filament originated from the watch, drifting up to span the room until it was lost in the dazzling sunlight outside. I couldn't understand how I had missed seeing it before, and wondered with dread whether I had become closer to the spirit world.

Yet, the thread drew me. It held a strange attraction so that I couldn't help sliding my hand along it, following its path out of the window. On an impulse, I climbed onto the sill. The thread hummed like a captured bee in my palm. I glanced back at the girl on the bed, her eyes closed and her breathing regular. I knew that Amah would take good care of my body. Then I jumped.

CHAPTER 12

D ESPITE MY FEARS, the spell paper on the window didn't hinder my
exit. Instead, I drifted slowly down until I stood in the side alley looking back at our house, the glistening thread still clasped in my hand. When I
released my grip it floated up a little, blowing with the wind like spider silk as
it stretched on out of sight. Without it, I might well have lost my nerve and
returned home, for never in my life had I been alone outside like this.

I started to walk, passing the familiar houses of the neighborhood. There
was hardly anyone about; it was too hot to go visiting and too late in the morning for the peddlers who went from door to door, selling fresh tofu in buckets of water and live chickens. Now that I could wander around freely, I felt a
great curiosity to explore other people's houses and see how they lived, but the
thread in my hand reminded me that I had other things to do. I didn't know
where it was leading me, but it was all I had to go on.

I walked a long way, tracing the thread as it wended its way into a more
commercial district. There were rows of shop houses bright with signboards
and banners, so closely built that each one shared walls with its neighbors;
a *kaki lima*, or five-foot way—the cool, shaded walkway created by the over-

hanging second story of each shop house—ran in front. Here pedestrians haggled, old men dozed in rattan chairs, and stray dogs sprawled, their sides heaving in the heat. There were various sundry shops: an ironmonger; a *kopi tiam*; an Indian moneylender girdled in his white cotton *puggree* with three wavy caste lines painted on his forehead. When I was a child, Amah would bring me here during the Moon Festival to choose from the ranks of celluloid paper-and-wire lanterns, bent cunningly into the shapes of butterflies and goldfish. Afterward, I would wait while she pored over packets of needles and wooden clogs.

As I stood there surrounded by people hurrying about their business, I could almost pretend that I was merely another passerby. That I was still safe in my body. Tears filled my eyes. I felt utterly desolate, far from our familiar house and anyone who knew and cared about me.

I had been sobbing for some time when I gradually became aware of a beggar approaching me. Beggars were a common sight, but there was an unnatural air about this one. He dragged himself along, so broken down that his ribs protruded through his leathery skin. Even as I watched, a man walked unseeingly through him as though he were no more than a shadow. I shrank back in horror, but the beggar was now so close that I couldn't avoid him. When he lifted his face from beneath a tattered hat, I saw little more than dried skin and exposed bone, the eyes like shriveled fruits in their deep sockets.

"Who are you?" His voice was thin and weak, as though there were not enough air to pump through that collapsed rib cage.

He seemed so frail that I plucked up my courage. "Can you see me?"

His head lolled on his withered neck. "Only from certain angles." His gaze wandered. "You have no smell of death. Are you from heaven?"

"You are mistaken," I said. "I'm not a deity."

"Give me food, then." His mouth yawed like a grave. "I am starving!"

"What are you?" I whispered, but I think I already knew.

He was groveling now, making weak grabs at the hem of my clothes. "I don't remember. Nobody buried me. Nobody knows my name. Now give!" the wretched creature moaned. "Give me but a string of cash to buy something to eat."

Overcome with pity and horror, I fumbled blindly at my pockets and found myself clutching a few strings of antique copper coins strung together through holes in their centers. This must have been part of the funeral money that I had burned for myself, but I had no time to think about it, for he pounced on the money with surprising swiftness. Clutching it with skeletal hands, he began to drift dispiritedly away. To my dismay, I saw other shadowy forms begin to gather about him with interest. Even as I watched, two more hungry ghosts appeared behind me. One was even more tattered and demented-looking than the beggar I had spoken to. It moved in slow fits and jerks, and I wondered whether in time such creatures simply wore away into nothingness. The other, however, must have been more recently dead for he pushed forward.

"A girl was here, giving money!"

I shrank from his furious, unseeing gaze. In life he must have been a corpulent man for he was only just beginning to show signs of starvation. But when I moved, he gave a shout. "There she is!"

I fled down endless alleyways, plunging through the warren of shops. Hungry ghosts seemed to appear from all directions, detaching themselves from walls and fluttering out of passageways. Too late, I realized that I shouldn't have run. If the dead could only see me from certain angles, then it would have been better to stay still. As it was, I found myself far from where I had started. The sun was high in the sky when I stopped at a dreadful realization. In my flight I had let go of the gauzy strand that had led me out of the house.

For a second time that day, I stood in the road with tears in my eyes. This time, however, I dared not make a sound for fear of drawing attention to myself. The salt stung my cheeks and my swollen eyelids throbbed. Exhausted, I sat on a stone and wiped my face with my sleeve. My feet were sore and I checked them for blisters. It seemed utterly unfair that the spirit should suffer the torments of flesh without having any. But perhaps that was the whole point of the afterlife.

Well, there was no point crying. After a while, I began to look around, realizing that the road seemed familiar. I had passed this way before in a rickshaw, when I wore my best clothes to visit the Lim mansion. And from here, I could also find my way home. For a long moment, I struggled with temptation. It would be so easy to return, to slip back into our house. But there was another option, even without the strange thread that had guided me. Since Lim Tian Ching had come uninvited to my house, I might as well return the favor. Perhaps I might discover something to my advantage; anything was better than meekly waiting for him to come for me.

Although I had been tired, my steps were light and I found I could walk more swiftly than in my physical body. There were a few advantages of my spirit form, though I dreaded to think what price I was paying. Was I hastening my starvation like a hungry ghost? I dared not think too much about it.

The great gates of the Lim mansion were closed, though I could see the winding carriage drive through the ornate ironwork. I tested myself against it and was relieved to find that I could pass through with some effort. A porter dozed in the noon heat and the hibiscus blossoms by the gate barely quivered as I went by, as though I was merely some errant breeze. As I approached the house, I was struck anew by its old-fashioned air. Many of the rich were now building mansions in the British colonial style, with wide verandas and open ballrooms like the great houses in India and Ceylon. But the Lim mansion was uncompromisingly Chinese, its walls concealing warrens of rooms and courtyards. I wondered if Tian Bai's new bride would demand renovations, but shied away from such thoughts.

The heavy ironwood front door was mercifully ajar, no doubt to admit a cool breeze. I entered with some trepidation as I was no longer a guest but a trespasser and, even worse, a spirit. Averting my eyes from the looming family altar decked with offerings and wreathed with incense in the front room, I walked hastily to the inner courtyards. There, amid the cool marble tiles and glossy leaves of potted plants, I came upon two servants. One was the woman who had escorted me to the washroom before. She and a young girl were busy watering the plants and wiping the dust off their leaves. I meant to pass them, but as I approached, the girl started and dropped her pitcher.

"Look what you've done!" said the woman. The girl was only ten or eleven and she bit her lip with consternation. Instinctively, I made a movement to help with the broken pieces, forgetting I had no physical presence.

"I felt something," she said. "Like someone passed me!"

The older woman looked at her sharply. "You know that Madam Lim doesn't like talk about ghosts."

The little maid bent over the broken pieces. "But she's always burning funeral goods, isn't she? Maybe it's her son's spirit come back."

"*Tch!* Who would want him to come back?" Intrigued, I hung closer. "You've only been here three months. You never met the young master."

"Was he nice, like Master Tian Bai?"

The woman couldn't resist gossiping. "Oh no! There were times when we could do nothing right. But the mistress doted on him. She couldn't accept it when he died."

"Was it sudden?" The girl paused, enjoying this respite from work.

"He had a fever, to be sure, but he was just as demanding as ever. And then in the morning he was dead. The doctor couldn't believe it. He even wanted to know what he had eaten the night before, but there was nothing amiss. He ate from the same dishes as everyone at the table, which was a good thing."

"For who?"

"For all of us, you goose. We might have been blamed for it. Madam was very upset. She wanted to know if anyone had served the young master tea before bedtime, but nobody had. And all because his teacup was missing. He had a celadon cup, a family heirloom, but we couldn't find it anywhere. The mistress had all sorts of odd notions after his death."

"How strange." I could see the little girl's fancy was taken by this morbid tale.

"What's strange?"

Both servants started guiltily. It was Yan Hong. She frowned at the older woman. "My half brother died of a fever. I don't like to hear you repeating such gossip." I had never seen Yan Hong look so fierce, so different from the gracious, smiling hostess I remembered. When she turned on her heel, I hurried after her.

For the rest of the day, I shadowed Yan Hong as she moved purposefully about the house, at ease in both the grand drawing rooms as well as the cavernous kitchen. Although she was only the daughter of the second wife, she seemed to command a great deal of respect, often making decisions that should have fallen to Madam Lim. She had mentioned to me that she was merely visiting for a while, but she seemed so at home that I couldn't imagine how they would manage without her. Of Madam Lim, I saw little. She looked more ill than before, her feathery voice scarcely audible and her listless manner a great change from a mere few weeks ago.

I dared not approach her too closely, afraid that Lim Tian Ching would somehow sense my presence. In fact, I was terrified that he might return at any moment. Despite my earlier resolve, I no longer felt up to confronting him. The rooms with their tiled floors and stiff rosewood furniture, the long dark corridors and hurrying servants, reminded me at every turn that I was an intruder. Yet I couldn't quite tear myself away, for I noticed that in contrast to my own home, my presence here seemed to exert some influence. Remembering the oppressive atmosphere during my earlier visits, I wondered whether the Lim household had, in fact, been sensitized by Lim Tian Ching's ghost, for more than one person flinched if I stood too close, and the conversation invariably turned to spirits. This was not a particularly happy realization for me, but there was no doubt that it provided some useful information.

I had been following Yan Hong with no reason other than that she was the most familiar person to me. And she had been kind before. She seemed to take her duties as the eldest daughter of the house seriously, despite her marriage, and was firm with the servants, friendly with the other women, and solicitous of her stepmother. I remembered Amah's tale of how Yan Hong's mother had died to ensure her daughter's marriage, and was surprised that she could be so cordial to Madam Lim. There was no sign at all of Tian Bai. I had to admit that I had been half hoping to see him again. No matter how many times I told myself that he cared little for me, and was possibly even a murderer, I couldn't help but think about him. The sight of the lotus pond where we had first met produced a painful sensation, and the sudden chiming of a clock made my heart leap.

The more I observed Yan Hong, the more I began to feel that she was under some strain. She was careful to maintain her calm manner in front of others, but when alone she gnawed her lips, an anxious expression stealing over her face. She could scarcely sit still, jumping up to do one task after another. I wondered whether Yan Hong had always been this way, or whether it was a new development.

The afternoon whittled away until the shadows lengthened in the long passageways, stealing into rooms and dimming the gay patterns of the Dutch tiles on the floors. My spirits seemed to fail with the dying light and I was weighing what I should do that evening, when the porter came in and murmured something to Yan Hong.

"A man outside the house?" she asked. "What does he want?"

The porter ducked his head. "He didn't come close, but he's been standing there for some time."

"Why didn't you ask him?"

"I thought he might leave if I approached him. But you did say to tell you if anything unusual happened."

Yan Hong frowned. "Let me see." As she made her way down the curving drive, her pale *kebaya* fluttered ahead of me like a moth in the fading light.

"He's gone," said the porter as they reached the gate. Yan Hong peered out and shrugged in exasperation. But with my new sharp sight, I glimpsed a figure standing deep in the shadow of a tree. I could make out a bamboo hat and the glint of silver embroidery on the hem of his robe. With a start, I recalled the stranger who had consulted the medium at such length while Amah and I had waited. Even as I considered this, however, the man turned abruptly and disappeared into the dusk.

As we headed back to the house, my heart sank. I didn't want to meet Lim Tian Ching here, when I felt so weak and defenseless. Even as I hesitated, Yan Hong entered the house, which was now ablaze with lamps. Madam Lim was in the entrance hall.

"Where did you go?" she asked querulously.

Yan Hong patted her arm. "It was nothing," she said. "I'll join you for dinner in a moment."

Madam Lim nodded absently, but as she turned away, Yan Hong shot her a look of pure, unguarded hatred. Surprised, I followed her upstairs into a bedroom, despite my anxiety about leaving. Bolting the door, she lifted the heavy lid of a wooden chest. It was filled with clothing that she hastily set on the floor. At the very bottom of the chest was a cloth-wrapped bundle. Yan Hong wavered for a moment, then untied the knots as though she felt compelled to check something. She unrolled a corner and paused with a sigh of relief. Swiftly she wrapped it up again, but not before I had glimpsed the discolored rim of a celadon teacup.

CHAPTER 13

I WAS SO surprised that I could hardly gather my thoughts. Why did Yan Hong have what looked suspiciously like Lim Tian Ching's missing cup? There might be an innocent explanation, I thought, for surely only a fool would keep such a thing and Yan Hong didn't strike me as stupid. But the servant had said it was a family heirloom and perhaps she couldn't bear to throw it away. I was struck as well by the discoloration of the rim. Celadon was prized for its translucency, and from what I had glimpsed, the cup itself had a fine clear glaze.

Even as I speculated, however, I felt an increasing sense of oppression, like an ominous fog rolling into the room. Something was coming; I was sure of it. Fearful, I thought of Lim Tian Ching or even the border officials he had spoken of. The air became weighty and my chest constricted. It was the same choking sensation I experienced whenever Lim Tian Ching strayed too long in my dreams. My mouth was dry; I could barely draw breath, feeling that the house itself deeply resented my intrusion. With growing unease, I went to the window. In the deepening twilight, I saw a strange procession of dim green lights. They bobbed eerily as they passed the porter at the gate, though he did not appear to see them. It was then that I knew they were spirit lights.

I raced down the stairs, cutting through the servants' quarters and out through a side gate. My side ached, my lungs burned, but still I ran on, trying desperately to increase the distance between myself and those spectral lights. Terrified, I took turn after turn through a maze of back lanes until at last the suffocating sensation lifted and I could think clearly again. My heart was racing, my thoughts in turmoil. Yan Hong had just as much of a motive for murdering Lim Tian Ching if it meant depriving Madam Lim of her son, to avenge her own mother's death. And her husband was a doctor. It would have been easy enough for her to procure drugs or poison. Even as I considered this, however, I recalled with a sinking feeling that Tian Bai had also studied medicine. He had mentioned that his studies were interrupted, but I had never found out why.

A breeze sprang up with a tang of the sea that was never far from Malacca. Opposite, lamps were lit in the small row of shop houses. Drawn to the comforting clank of pots, I peered disconsolately at the enclosed backyards of these houses, eventually choosing a wooden gate that seemed less sturdy. I struggled to force myself through the tight grain of the wood, emerging finally in a stone courtyard. Large glazed jars held drinking water, and a girl my own age was drawing some into a jug. Balancing it against her hip, she carried it inside.

I followed her through a dingy kitchen into a tiny dining area. This was the living quarters of a typical shop house that was built extremely long and narrow so that each lay next to its neighbors like an eel in an eel bed. A family sat around a marble table. There was a father, mother, an old grandfather, two little boys, and the girl I had followed. But I was drawn to the aroma of food that rose like a mist from the table. It was a plain meal: soup and pickles, tofu, and a platter of fried fish, the *ikan kembong* that are no larger than a child's hand. I was so hungry, however, that it seemed like a feast. But despite my best attempts, the fragrance of the food left me gnawingly unsatisfied. It seemed that I would starve unless someone made a spirit offering to me. Miserably, I crouched in a corner of the room as they ate, envying their chatter and every mouthful of food they ingested. I had been hungry before, but never like this. Old Wong always had a few peanuts or a pinch of melon seeds for me. I missed him right now and our familiar kitchen with a fierceness that frightened me.

After a while, the old man motioned to the girl. "Did you make the ancestor's offering today?"

She pouted. "Of course I did, Grandfather."

He turned and squinted at the family altar. "How about the hungry ghosts?"

"Those creatures! It's not even Qing Ming."

The old man shook his head from side to side as though there was something in his ears. "Put a little rice out for them."

Sighing, the girl got up and scooped some rice into a bowl, setting it on the altar with a brief mumble. As soon as she was done, I ran to the altar, inhaling sharply so that the fragrance filled my nostrils and, thankfully, my stomach. I placed my hands together to thank the old man, though he was absorbed in his own meal. Eventually, lulled by their conversation and the events of the day, I closed my eyes. How strange it was that the spirit could sleep, eat, and rest, yet how else could one account for the quantities of paper funeral food and furniture that were burned to accompany the houses and carriages of the dead?

I WOKE SUDDENLY TO silent darkness. The family had retired to bed but some noise had startled me awake. Straining my ears, I heard a skittering rustle again. The darkness was gradually broken by a faint greenish light from the corridor, much like the ones I had seen approaching the Lim mansion. Nearer and nearer it drifted till I felt the hairs on my neck tingling. Petrified, I pressed myself half into a great chest of drawers, hoping for the semi-visibility that had aided my escape from the hungry ghosts.

The dim light entered the room and paused. At first, all I saw was the back of a figure clad in old-fashioned garments, the hair elaborately dressed with dangling ornaments. It was a young woman, not as thin as the poor hungry ghost who had spoken to me. When she turned, however, I saw the slight shriveling of her features, as though a slow process of mummification had begun. She began to wander around the empty dining room, pausing for a moment at the old man's chair. At the rice bowl offering, she stopped.

"Who has eaten this?" The corpse light that enveloped her rippled in agitation. "How dare you trespass here?"

Her sharp eyes roved around the room like needles. I raised my hand before my face and was horrified to see that it too emitted a faint glow. Not the eerie green that bathed the woman, but a pale shine like moonlight. Enraged, she swept around the room, finally catching sight of me the second time.

Her eyes widened as she examined me. "I thought you were a hungry ghost, but now I see that you're not of the dead. Are you here to call me back?"

Perhaps it was only natural, I thought, that each ghost's thoughts instantly flew to his own situation. After all, I myself could scarcely forget my disembodiment.

"What are you, demon or fairy?" she demanded.

Not knowing how to reply I said, "I'm sorry I took your rice. The old man said it was an offering."

"It was on the altar. But for years it has been mine."

Despite her initial hostility, she seemed eager to talk. Perhaps it had been a long time since there had been anyone to communicate with. I couldn't tell when she had died, as the fashion in funeral garments remained antique and unchanging. Still, I might learn something from her.

"Were you waiting for a messenger?" I hazarded.

Glancing doubtfully at me, she said, "So you were looking for me! I'm not yet ready to go, though."

"I'm not sure," I began, but she cut me off.

"My name is Fan, of the Liew family. I can explain why I'm still here."

"You're not a hungry ghost."

"Of course not! By rights I should have gone on to the courts already. Did the border officials send you?"

"My business isn't with you." I felt I ought to put her straight before I floundered into deeper waters.

She sighed. "I suppose it's silly to expect them to send someone like you. Are you a fairy maiden, then? I've always wanted to meet one. I know they sometimes come from paradise. Yet—" She broke off, studying my pajamas.

"I've lost my way."

"Did you lose your steed too?"

"My steed?"

"Don't you have a carriage or a horse? Or maybe your rank is too low," she said dismissively. "It's just that your clothes . . . I mean, you're very pretty of course. That's how I knew you were a fairy."

Stalling, I said, "I am but a humble handmaid on an errand."

"Oh!" she said. "Is it a love affair? Because that's why I'm here too!" Once she started, it was as though she couldn't stop talking. "I died for love, did you know that?"

"YES," SAID THE GHOST as she folded herself on one of the dining chairs. Unlike myself, she had far less mass, for her sleeves trailed through the wood of the chair and she was so light that a puff of air would have dislodged her from her perch. "It was really very romantic. I still remember when I first saw him. He was already married, of course, but she was much older than him. Anyway, it didn't bother me."

"You didn't mind being a second wife?"

She waved a hand negligently. "I was the one he loved. My father refused, of course. He was only a petty shopkeeper, not good enough for me, whereas my family owned a lodging house near Jonker Street. So when I locked myself in my room and refused to eat, my father said he would ship me back to relatives in China. He bought me passage on a junk through the Straits of Malacca. I think he really intended to marry me off to a business acquaintance in Singapore, but there was a terrible typhoon and our ship capsized. Never having learned to swim, I quickly drowned." Fan shook her long sleeves out with a sigh. "If I had known how easy it is to lose your life, I would have treasured mine better."

If she only knew how heartily I agreed with her. But I was desperate to discover as much as possible about this afterlife and how things worked. "If you drowned, why are you here in this house?"

She turned to me in astonishment. "Didn't I tell you? This is my lover's house."

"The old man?"

"He stayed with his wife and had more children. Still, he dreams of me every night. My father of course gave me a funeral and burned offerings, though my lover was never told of this. For all he knew I had been disowned and become a hungry ghost. That's why he puts out rice every evening. He means it for me."

With sudden anxiety, I wondered whether I would even realize it if my own physical body stopped breathing. "What was it like when you died?"

"I saw other souls streaming toward the gateway of the Courts of Judgment. I was supposed to go too, except I wanted to see my beloved again. Oh, his wife was relieved when I died, I tell you! But I made sure that he still loved me in his dreams." Her laughter was a thin tinkle. "Though I've always been afraid that they'll send someone to fetch me. But the time is almost at hand anyway."

"What time is that?"

"Why, I've been waiting for him to die, of course! He almost did several times. He fell off a ladder once and another time he contracted typhoid. But now I think the end is near."

"Do you wish him dead, then?" Repulsed by her cheer, I was reminded of the negative influence ghosts were said to be on the living.

"No!" she said in alarm. "Oh, you mustn't report me to the authorities! I thought that if he died then I would wait for him to go together. After all, we're linked by this." She held out an invisible object pinched together between her fingers. Try as I might, however, I could discern nothing.

"How odd," she said. "For I can see it clearly. It's a shining thread."

My heart gave a leap. "I've been searching for something like that. What is it?"

"It shows the intensity of your feelings," she said. "When I was alive we exchanged tokens. I gave him a hairpin and he gave me a jade thumb ring that had belonged to his father. Once I was dead, I found that if I followed this thread it led me straight to him. He still has my hairpin in a wooden chest upstairs."

I thought about Tian Bai's watch and the comb that I had slipped him the day he had come to our house. But how was it that my thread hadn't gone toward the Lim mansion?

"Perhaps your task is difficult because only lovers can find their own thread," said Fan.

"Does your thread float in the air?"

She frowned. "The other end is probably at the bottom of the sea with the ring that he gave me. But I manage quite well with this end. If I leave the house I hold on to it. It's so hard to get around as a ghost, you know! Corners, mirrors. Such things make me lose my way. And I'm so light now, I would blow away down the street if I didn't have this thread to hold on to."

Her words confirmed my suspicions that I was, indeed, different from the dead in the manner that I could move easily from place to place. Even the hungry ghosts that had chased me had fluttered wildly and dispersed.

"I don't go out much anyway," Fan continued. "It's so much of a bother. I'm sure I don't know what ordinary ghosts without a thread like mine do." She looked pointedly at me again. "You don't seem to know much about anything."

"We led a sheltered existence," I said, realizing that I had to come up with something to satisfy her curiosity. "My job was to pick fruit in the Blessed Peach Orchard." Though I felt guilty lying to her, she was enthralled.

"How very boring! Heaven must be overrated."

"It was marvelous fruit," I said cautiously.

"Then it must surely have been the fruit of longevity. If I only had one, I'm sure I could bribe the border officials to be lenient with me!"

Lim Tian Ching had also mentioned border officials. "Where can I find them?" I asked.

"At the gateway, of course. I can see it as soon as I go out."

"Why don't the hungry ghosts go there?"

"They can't find it," she said contemptuously. "What do you expect? They had no proper burial, no prayers or offerings. They're hopeless." I listened to her with a sinking heart.

In the end, I persuaded Fan to show me the gateway. She was reluctant to do so at first, coming up with a number of excuses. Eventually I managed to winkle out of her the fact that she had not left the house for almost three years. "I've just been keeping him company," she said with a sly glance.

I was suddenly reminded of something she had mentioned earlier. "Dreams," I said, thinking about Lim Tian Ching's access to my own dreams. She gave a guilty start. "You said he wouldn't forget you in his dreams. How did you manage that?"

Fan began to pleat her sleeves again. "If I tell you, you must put in a good word for me."

"I can't promise you that. But I'll try." Uneasily, I thought that if only she knew how desperately I was groping for information, barely even knowing who or what the border officials were, she would hardly bother to waste her time on me. But Fan looked satisfied.

"Well, I found that if I press this thread into his body while he's sleeping, sometimes I can make my way into his dreams. There he's young again, and we're together. Lately, though, his dreams have been getting stronger than reality, which is why I think he's going to die soon."

I shuddered. This was almost exactly what happened to itinerant scholars in the novels I had read. A beautiful ghost enticed them into a world of dreams until they wasted away in search of phantom pleasures. I didn't really understand the rules of this afterworld, but I was certain that they must exist from my conversations with Lim Tian Ching. No wonder Fan seemed fearful of the authorities. But she was already leading the way through the long shop house, passing through the front door with no resistance at all. With my greater mass, it took me longer to catch up. When I emerged onto the street, I stopped in wonder. The dark night was lit up with spirit lights.

SOME WERE GREEN, LIKE Fan's corpse light; others were different colors, like strange flowers that bloomed in the night. Among the crowds of hungry ghosts and other human phantoms were carriages and sedan chairs lit with swaying lanterns, and drawn by horses and other scaled creatures I had never seen before. There were tiger-headed men and tiny birds with female faces. Women with backward-pointing feet mingled with lizards dressed in court robes. The walking trees and enormous glowing flowers must be the plant spirits and minor deities that Fan had mentioned. In amazement, I stared at this parade of otherworldly creatures. Dimly, I could hear the sounds of a busy street but the noise was muffled, as though it had traveled a great distance. And at the same time, I was assailed by the same suffocating sensation that I had encountered at the Lim mansion. Retching, I gasped for breath.

"What is this?" I asked.

"Don't you know? It's the spirits. This is nothing, you should see how many come out on feast days."

"But I can hardly breathe."

She peered at me. "That's spiritual pressure, caused by the congregation of yin from the ghosts. I don't know what heaven is like, but the longer you mingle with the dead, the less it will bother you."

With horror, I realized that she was right. After all, when Lim Tian Ching had begun to haunt me, I had suffered from this choking sensation in my dreams. Earlier that day, when I had first seen such lights at the Lim mansion, I had been so overcome that I had been forced to leave. But now I was able to talk to Fan without any particular effect, though perhaps her long-dead spirit was more insubstantial. I braced myself against a wall until the intensity began to subside. This in itself was probably a bad sign, but there was nothing I could do about it.

"And there is the gate," she said, pointing upward to a brightness in the sky. Faintly, I could make out a great arch through which a host of spirits streamed in like an endless river of lights. But it was so far away.

"How do you get there?" I asked.

"You float," she said. "Can't you feel the pull it exerts? I'm sure that if I climbed on a roof and let go, I would drift there."

"I don't think I can float like you."

"Fly, then," she said. "Isn't that how you came from the heavenly realm?"
I was saved from having to reply by a sudden commotion.

"MAKE WAY! MAKE WAY!" Driven by these cries, the crowd surged like
a wave. Beating them back were four monstrous creatures with the heads of
belligerent oxen joined to the bodies of men. Each carried a halberd and wore
a black uniform with scarlet edging. With snorts and fearful bellows, they
parted the crowd easily. Beside me, Fan gave a convulsive shudder.

"Who are they?" I asked.

Frantically she motioned me to be silent. Behind this escort came a blood
red palanquin. There was something about the ostentatious trappings that
seemed familiar to me and I pressed forward, hoping for a closer look. The
shutters were drawn but an errant gust of wind blew them inward. Impatiently, a plump hand batted them back but not before I had seen its owner.
There, sitting at ease within, was Lim Tian Ching.

I cried out in amazement and started forward. In that instant, though,
my voice was lost in the roaring of the escort, Lim Tian Ching's eyes turned
toward me as though he alone had heard my cry. Instinctively, I ducked behind
a beast with curling antlers. A frown creased his features. In another moment,
the entire procession had passed.

"Who was that?" I asked Fan. She had been creeping back toward the
shop house, but I forestalled her.

"Those were the border officials!" she said. I blanched. I had been hoping
to find some sort of bureaucrat to appeal to, but these monstrous creatures
were beyond my comprehension. Fan looked queasy. "Well, those were only
foot soldiers, but the border officials are the same type of ox-headed demon.
We ghosts try to avoid them as much as possible."

"But there was a human ghost in the palanquin," I said.

"Then he's probably someone important. Or has plenty of money. The
authorities can be bribed to extend all sorts of privileges. Don't you know
that this part of the afterlife is ruled by the judges of hell? Before entering

the courts for judgment and reincarnation, there's a place called the Plains of the Dead, where you're allowed to enjoy the funeral offerings that your family burned for you. It's only for human ghosts, though; you can't stay forever. I have a little house there and a couple of servants. But I haven't gone back in a while." Despite herself, a shiver ran through Fan's frame.

"Why not?"

"I told you! My time is up. I was supposed to report to the gateway and have my case processed for judgment a long time ago." A stubborn look crossed her face. "If my father had only burned more funeral money for me then I could bribe the border officials. I hope that when my lover dies his family will burn a great deal of cash for him. I've been watching them for years and they're very fond of him."

"Won't you need to report to the courts eventually?"

"Well, certainly. But that may not have to be for a long time. Centuries, if we have enough money." I looked doubtfully at Fan.

"Don't look at me like that!" she said. "Didn't you see that ghost in the palanquin? He's proof that you can do what you like if you have the resources. Now, are we done?"

I watched as she slipped back through the shop house door. I hadn't particularly liked her, yet she had a pathos that made me pity her scheming. Still, something she'd mentioned stirred me. Studying the darkened doorway, I had the impression that Fan was still waiting, pressed against the other side. I walked over and addressed the silent facade.

"Just one more thing," I said. "How do I find the Plains of the Dead?"

There was a faint gasp, then Fan's pale face reappeared, floating upon the surface of the wooden door. It would have frightened me badly before but I had become accustomed to such sights. "How did you know I was there? You really are a fairy maiden after all!"

"Where are the Plains of the Dead?" I repeated. Somehow the place seemed to draw me. My thoughts flew, unaccountably, to my mother. Amah had always been so certain that she had been spared the torments of judgment and long since been reborn, but I could not help wondering if she was still there.

"There are entrances all over the place, like the gateway. The hungry ghosts can't go there either. They have no clothes and no money for the journey. They can't even steal, as spirit goods must be given freely."

"How do you go?"

"I told you, I have a couple of servants. When I reach the plains, I call them and they come and carry me."

"Could I go there?"

She gave me a long look, suspicion struggling with curiosity again. "Why do you need to go, and how will you cross the plains?"

"Perhaps you could give me a ride?"

"Certainly not! My servants are frail and rather rickety. They're beginning to fall apart after so many years. But if you have money, you can purchase your passage." She looked hard at me. I turned out my pockets, revealing a few strings of cash and a couple of small ingots.

"You'll need more than that," she said with a barely concealed snort. Inwardly, I cursed the fact that I hadn't finished burning all the funeral money before Amah had stopped me that day.

"I tell you what," said Fan. "If you wish to go to the Plains of the Dead, I'll show you the way. For a price."

"I thought you were provided for."

"Just barely. I don't want to meet my lover looking like a beggar when the time comes."

"Don't you see him in dreams already?"

"Dreams! I can manipulate the setting a little, but when he dies he'll see me as I am. Come, don't you think this is a good bargain?"

I thought it over and nodded.

"But you need more money. Ask your Heavenly Authorities. Remember, we'll have to buy horses, wagons, and clothing."

"And how will I find you when I need you?"

She shrugged. "I'm always here. But hurry! I'm afraid that he won't live much longer."

CHAPTER 14

I HAD ASKED Fan about the Plains of the Dead on an impulse, thinking of my mother and also that if I were really desperate it would be one place that I could surely find Lim Tian Ching, hopefully without a demon escort. After all, Fan had said the Plains of the Dead were for human ghosts and had I not witnessed firsthand his mansions and parklands, horses and stables in my dreams? Now that I had an alternate theory of his murder, with Yan Hong as a suspect, I might be able to persuade him to abandon his vendetta, though, to be honest, my prospects seemed bleak. I wasn't even sure how to persuade anyone to burn funeral money on my behalf.

As I went farther away from the shop houses, the number of spirit lights began to decrease. I wondered whether there was any significance to the roads most utilized by ghosts, some underlying meaning or ancient penchant for certain areas. In the meantime, I took care to avoid being seen by other spiritual denizens. The tales I had heard as a child suggested that there were far more terrifying things abroad than what I had just witnessed.

Before I realized it, I came upon the old Stadthuys. Squat and square, painted a deep red with heavy masonry walls and a sloping European roof, it was a reminder of the times when the Dutch ruled Malacca. I had never been inside but I knew the British still used it as government quarters. The locals said it was haunted and despite myself, I drew back with a prickle of fear. I looked around for spirit lights, but in this quarter there were none. Perhaps they were all inside, those stolid Dutch burghers and their wives in ancient crinolined splendor, still pacing the massive beamed floors and fretting over the trading prices of pepper and nutmeg, cinnamon and cloves. The town square lay in front, rigidly planted with flower beds in the Dutch tradition, and punctuated by a fountain. Water gleamed in its still basin and reminded me of my sore feet. I went cautiously over to look into it.

As I bent over the basin, I became aware of another image reflected next to mine, a hazy shape that resolved into an old man wearing a rumpled blouse. He was worn so thin that in the moonlight he was a creature stitched out of fine white lace.

"Who are you?" I whispered at last.

The old man stirred. "Ah, I see you now." The pale light illuminated a nose like a parrot's beak and deep eye sockets. A foreigner, I thought. I had never been so close to one before.

"You are not dead, but neither are you truly living. You poor creature." He was the first spirit who had seen clearly what I was and I drew back, frightened. "I won't bite. No, no, I won't. What are you doing here? You should go back to your home." Although his accent and appearance were strange to me, he spoke in a kindly manner and it was this, coupled with exhaustion, which brought tears to my eyes.

"There, there," he said. "Stop crying. You can hear me, can't you?"

Mutely, I nodded.

"A little Chinese girl, I see," he said. "Begging your pardon, a young lady."

"Who are you?"

"Me? Old Willem Ganesvoort, that's who. Just sitting by the fountain as is my wont."

"You are a Dutchman," I said excitedly.

"I *was* a Dutchman," he corrected. "Now I am, what? A spirit, a soul."

"Why are you here?"

"I should ask you the same question," he said in mild reproof, "but there, ladies will have their way." He gave me a stiff but courtly bow. As he did so I noticed that one of his arms was crippled, clutched to his chest like a fledgling's wing. "I shipped out to the Orient when I was a young man. Trained as an architect, that was my profession. Ah yes, my arm," he said, noticing my gaze. "Born with it, died with it. Nobody thought I could ship out from Rotterdam with this arm, though it was good enough to see the world with. But I always loved Malacca the best. And so when my time was up, I stayed a little longer. I like to look at my handiwork, I suppose."

"And what was that? The Stadthuys?"

"Oh no! Bless me, how old do you think I am? The Stadthuys was built in 1650. I am not quite of that vintage. I helped to make that small addition, however."

I peered at the darkened building but couldn't make out what he was pointing at. "Very nice," I said at last.

"You think so? Of all the buildings I designed, I like it the best. That little addition was nothing much, but I was very pleased at the way it came together. But where might you be off to?"

I opened my mouth, then stopped. I was tired of talking, tired of walking and finding no rest. I wasn't even sure of this Dutchman, though he seemed harmless enough and so insubstantial that I was quite convinced of his great age.

A faint smile broke across his face. "You don't trust me. I suppose I can hardly blame you. I myself didn't speak to another ghost for quite fifty years. But that was my own prejudice. We did not mix so much with the natives in my time, you see; and the only other Dutchman around was that lunatic who killed himself by jumping off the clock tower. Time has mellowed me, however. Besides, it is lonely not to have anyone to talk to."

The idea of lingering for centuries induced a state of near panic. "I'm looking for the Plains of the Dead," I said.

"The Plains of the Dead?" he said. "I cannot help you. I cannot find such a place at all, although I have often heard it mentioned. Those are not my beliefs, my child. That is not my afterworld."

I was silent for a moment. "But you can see me! You can talk to me!"

"Yes, yes. Of course, we are still very much in the living plane. And you also see these cobblestones beneath our feet, and the moonlight shining on this fountain. This is not really the afterlife, my dear. It is merely the very tail end of living. From here we all go on."

"So what happens to your kind when you die?" I asked.

"Do you know, I am not entirely sure? But my dear mother taught me that there is a merciful God and that is what I choose to believe. Either that, or I shall simply fade away."

"How did you know what I am?"

"Because I saw one such as you a long time ago. An Indian boy who fell from a tree. The fall didn't kill him so he lingered for a while."

"How long?"

"Only a few days. He couldn't eat, you see, and when his heart stopped beating, he finally became a ghost. Poor creature, he was so frightened."

"Does that mean that I have only a few days too?" My voice shook.

"I don't know. But you seem stronger than he was. Your body must be stable. But take good care of it. Unless, of course, you are ready to journey on."

Despite his kindly manner, his words frightened me more than anything I had encountered that night. "Is there no way for me to return to the living?" I asked.

"There may be. There! Don't fret. Pray that all will be well, and I will pray for you too." He sighed and for a time we were silent. A faint line of light appeared on the horizon. "Perhaps you should return to take care of your body," said the Dutchman at last.

"I'm not sure how to get there from here."

"That I may be able to help you with," he said. Hesitantly, I described our neighborhood.

"Ah, the merchant quarter," he said. "It has been a long time since I ventured there. But it is not so difficult to find. Here is how you go." He knelt, using his good arm to trace a map on a patch of earth. None of his gestures made the slightest mark, but by the faint afterimage left by his ghostly hand, I was able to understand his directions.

"And if I take this road instead?" I asked.

The fresh light of dawn began to flood the town square. I turned to look beside me but the old Dutchman was gone. I did not know what had happened to him; whether he had finally disappeared, his fragile form evaporating under the bright gaze of the sun, or whether he was so ancient that he could only be seen by moonlight. As it was, I sat there disconsolately for a while. Birds were chirping and mist lay above the night-chilled water in the fountain basin. I found that I was weary, so weary and heartsick that I went and lay down beside the Stadthuys, like any beggar on the streets.

WHEN I GOT UP again, the sun was high in the sky. I set off hastily, suddenly full of anxiety for my body. The Dutchman's directions had been good. Clear and concise, he had somehow impressed the overall pattern of the town upon me and soon I found myself on familiar streets. My steps quickened as I drew near our house, then I stopped short. Standing squarely in front of the door was an ox-headed demon.

Head lowered, it stood with folded arms. The heavy bovine head lolled forward in an attitude of boredom that would have been laughable in a less ferocious creature. Frantically, I pushed back into the wall, feeling the resistance as I forced myself into the brick. My thoughts were whirling like a storm of paper fragments. Why was it here? And why hadn't I felt the same warning sense of oppression I had experienced before? I could make the excuse that it was only one demon whereas last night the street had been full of spirits, but I couldn't fool myself. My awareness was dimming; every encounter with the dead drew me closer to them. I felt sick.

The demon stood motionless, like a figure carved from a massive tree trunk. There is a kind of wild ox called the *seladang* in the Malayan jungles, which stands taller at the shoulders than the height of a man and weighs more than a ton. A *seladang* is one of the few creatures that can kill a tiger. I had never seen a live one, but once, at the Chinese apothecary's, there had been a set of sweeping horns brought in by a hunter. Now, looking at the ox-headed demon, I guessed that its tines were even larger than the ones I had seen. But the face beneath them was no mild animal countenance. There was a mixture of cunning and ferocity in the red eyes, a manlike glitter that made me shiver.

As I watched this unwelcome doorkeeper, another demon appeared around the corner.

"Any news?" said the first.

"All clear. Did you go in?"

"Too many spell papers. Besides, only her body's left."

My pulse fluttered, a frantic moth. The thought that such creatures were looking for me made me feel faint with terror.

"You stick around for a change. I'm going on patrol."

They switched places with grunts and a clash of armor.

"Don't let her slip by you."

"Speak for yourself! Still, I don't understand how *he* knew she was gone. Never had to post a guard before."

"No idea. Suddenly last night he's in a froth. 'Is she still there?' he says, all mincey and twitchy."

I pressed the knuckles of my hand against my mouth. So Lim Tian Ching had, indeed, heard my cry of surprise last night.

"I almost bit off his head to stop his squealing."

They exchanged a red-eyed look. "Don't bother. If he doesn't complete his task, he's ours anyway, not that he knows anything about it."

The other demon yawned, displaying a gaping maw and a set of razor-sharp teeth. "What should I do if she comes back?"

"Why, make sure she doesn't leave again of course! She'll come back; they all do."

"And her body?"

"The old woman's doing a good job. It should last. Nothing wrong with the body."

"What if she doesn't come back?"

"Gets lost you mean? Then her spirit will shrivel up. Even if she does come back, she won't fit anymore. Be like a dried bean rattling around in a pod."

"Best find her, then."

The first demon strode away as its replacement settled in front of the door. My stomach clenched. I couldn't go back into the house now. Better to remain at large, I thought, as I waited for the demon to relax its guard. It seemed more alert than its predecessor, however, and stood upright, scanning the street and the houses around. I was beginning to wonder what to do when the front door opened.

CHAPTER 15

I WATCHED THE heavy door swing open with dismay, fearing that who-ever came out would fall prey to the waiting demon. I was terrified that it would be Amah, but the figure that emerged was none other than Old Wong, our cook. Despite my anxiety, his intersection with the ox-headed demon was oddly anticlimactic. They avoided each other in a strange little dance, Old Wong obliviously clutching his basket under one arm and the demon stepping aside with bored contempt.

As Old Wong trotted down the street, I wrenched myself loose from the wall, heaving backward into the neighbor's courtyard. In my haste to keep up, I found myself blundering through other people's houses, forcing myself through walls and other obstacles. Old Wong moved onward at a steady clip. From time to time I feared I had lost him, but at last when we had come a fair way from the house, I emerged just in time to see him disappear around a corner.

As I hurried after him I wondered what I meant to do. I had no real plan, no course of action in mind. Yet I remembered that brief instant in the court-yard when he had seemed to recognize me and wished there was some way in which I could increase the visibility of my form. If only it were to rain, the falling drops might show a faint outline. But despite the frequent tropical storms that drenched Malacca, the sky had been clear for the last two days, the huge cumulus clouds, like whipped froth, gliding serenely in the sky like floating islands.

I caught up with Old Wong and called out to him, though with little hope that he would hear me. To my surprise, he turned his head. Astonishment flickered across his face, but he set his gaze forward as though he hadn't heard me at all.

"Old Wong!" I cried again. "It's me! Li Lan!" I darted around, but he studiously ignored me. "Please! If you can see me at all, help me!"

We walked on thus for a little way, I pleading while he paid me no heed. A muscle twitched in the corner of his eye, but otherwise he behaved as though I didn't exist. At last I stood in the street and bawled like a child, the tears leaking through my clenched fists and my nose dribbling unceremoniously onto my blouse.

"Little Miss." Old Wong was looking at me with resignation. "I shouldn't talk to you. Go back to your body."

"You can see me!"

"Of course I can see you! I've seen you wandering around the house the past week. What are you doing here, so far from home?"

"I can't go back. There are ox-headed demons guarding the house." I spilled out the tale of my misadventures, sobbing from sheer relief.

Old Wong broke into my recital. "Don't stand in the middle of the street. People will think I'm mad."

There was an enormous rain tree by the side of the road, its filigreed branches casting a fine network of shade. Old Wong squatted at its foot and said, "Now, what is the matter with you?" As I unburdened myself, he took a twist of newspaper out of his pocket and shook out some toasted melon seeds. "I really shouldn't speak to you," he said from the side of his mouth.

"Why not?"

He made an impatient noise. "Because it's bad! It will tie you to the spirit world. You need to go back to your body. Why else do you think I pretended not to see you before?"

"I've tried," I said. "I've really tried but I can't rejoin my body. And now I can't even go home!"

"You say there's a demon guarding the house?"

"You didn't see him?"

"No, but I sensed something. I can't see demons. That's something I'm grateful for."

"Why is it that you can see me, then?"

"It's a long story. Do you really want to hear? *Aiya*, you were always one for stories even when you were a little girl."

He sighed as he cracked the melon seeds between his teeth and extracted the sweet kernels. Ever since I could remember, he had always had some kind of snack on his person, from shelled peanuts to roasted chickpeas. Despite this he remained as lean and scrawny as a stray dog, his forearms knotted from the efforts of rolling out dough, butchering chickens, and scouring pans.

Old Wong wrinkled his brow. "I can see ghosts. Have been able to since I was a boy. Some people are born with it; others acquire it through spiritual practice. In my case I didn't realize for a long time that many of the people I saw weren't alive. I was born in a small village up north, in Perak. Teluk Anson, where the British have mining concessions. My father was a cobbler; my mother took in sewing. I never told you that, did I? I didn't want people here to know too much about me.

"When I was very young there was a child that I used to play with by the river. Everyday he waited for me and we would busy ourselves playing with sticks and leaves. He never touched anything, just told me what to build. Finally I asked my mother whether I could bring him home for dinner, for he looked thin and hungry. She didn't believe me when I described him, saying there was no such boy in our village, until I took her to the river and pointed him out. It was then that I realized that he was a ghost, for she couldn't see him. In fact, she was quite frightened and I got a real thrashing, I can tell you. I was told never to play with him again. Later, I gathered from the bits and pieces that I overheard from the adults that there had been a child lost years ago. He had wandered away one day and his parents, being migrant workers, had no idea where to find him. Nobody ever heard of the family again and the child was forgotten.

"Because I insisted that he was still by the river, my parents concluded that the child had drowned. One day my father went to the riverbank without me and made a funeral tablet for the child since they knew his name, and burned offerings to him. I never saw the boy again. After that, my parents cautioned me not to talk to ghosts anymore."

"But you did a good thing," I said.

Old Wong spat out the shell of a melon seed. "Yes, but that was an unusual case. They knew his name and his family. Most of the dead are unknown. And none of them since have spoken to me."

"I'm talking to you now."

Old Wong frowned. "You're not dead yet. And you shouldn't talk to just anyone who sees you anyway. There are many evil things abroad, many ghosts who mean harm to the living and will try to trick you."

I shuddered, thinking about Fan and her protestations of love for the old man. "Who taught you that?"

"*Aiya*, after that incident, my mother couldn't sleep for worrying about me. And in a way she was right to be fearful. My eyes had been opened and I realized that many of the people that I had taken for granted were probably ghosts. Every day I saw them; the woman in the deserted fruit stall with nothing to sell or the one-legged man in the back of the *kopi tiam*. He often laughed for no reason, and I had never understood why nobody paid attention to him. Now I realized it was because they couldn't see him.

"One day a traveling fortune-teller came to our village. He performed tricks with the aid of spirits, but it was easy enough for me to see through his effects. When he discovered that I could see ghosts, he wanted to buy me from my parents. My mother refused, but after the fortune-teller left, she was afraid that he might come back and steal me. That was when she sent me to a temple to become a novice."

"And did you stay there?"

Old Wong snorted. "What do you think? I'm sitting here next to you, aren't I? I ran away so many times that in the end the abbot said he wouldn't have me anymore. But while I was there, he gave me private lessons. Maybe he thought he could train me to become an exorcist. He was the one who told me how to deal with ghosts. Much good that did, however. After my experience with the child by the river, I never wanted to have any more to do with them."

"Because it was frightening?"

"No, because it was too sad. Most of them I couldn't help, and I had no interest in making money off them. *Cheh*, you could say I shirked my duty. But I was always in the temple kitchens anyway, so in the end I ran off and became a cook."

"And your family?"

"It was better for me to leave. There was always someone asking me to see ghosts, grant favors, or do mischief for them. I just wanted to be left alone."

I thought about how dismissive Old Wong had always been toward our maid Ah Chun's hysterics and could not help laughing.

"What's so funny?" he asked.

"No wonder you never believed Ah Chun's stories."

Old Wong let a grudging smile escape. "That girl! I could have told her far worse things than she imagined."

"Did you ever see a ghost in our house?"

"Once on the main staircase . . . " He made a face and said abruptly, "But never you mind. The old master had an exorcist brought in."

Only much later would I understand the significance of his words, but at the time I was more anxious to ask, "Did you ever see the ghost of Lim Tian Ching?"

He frowned. "No. But you say he came in your dreams at first. He must have some other link. All I can tell you is that he never bothered to come to the kitchen. Also I don't look for ghosts. I try not to see them or pay attention. It's the only way I can live my life. To see spirits is a taint, not a talent."

He fell silent, while I thought of what a fixture Old Wong was in our household. How strange to think that he had kept this uncanny ability buried beneath the surface of his everyday life.

"Old Wong, can you do something for me?" I asked at last.

"What? I hope that you're planning to come home with me now."

"I can't do that. But can you make me an offering of spirit money or food?"

He sighed. "I don't like to do that. It strengthens the ability of your spirit to stay in the other world. I think you should come back to your body now."

"What good is it if I'm Lim Tian Ching's prisoner? Please—give me a little time to find a way out of this."

"But I have no ancestral tablet to make offerings to you."

"Just write it on some paper."

"Little Miss, I cannot read or write."

I was crestfallen and he saw my disappointment. "I'll buy you some food that you can take directly, since you're here with me. And then later maybe I'll ask your father to write you a funeral tablet, though he won't like it at all. That is, if he's still lucid."

I felt a rush of guilt. "How is my father?"

"Not good. I'm sorry I can't give you better news."

"And Amah?"

"Busy taking care of your body. That's her whole focus these days. She wanted to bring in some medium from the Sam Poh Kong temple, but your father absolutely refused. They had a terrible fight about it. I'm telling you, you better come back soon."

Despite this worrisome news, it was a strangely pleasant occasion. I tagged along beside Old Wong, just as I had done when I was a child and could come and go more freely. We passed an itinerant noodle seller with a pot of steaming soup at one end of a carrying pole and a basket containing a small brazier and various ingredients on the other. Squatting in the street, he set up his portable stove and cooked noodles to order. I had always wanted to try some, but Amah would never let me.

"Can I have noodles?"

Old Wong looked indignant. "Don't you know that they never wash the bowl and chopsticks but simply pass them along to the next customer? I can make you far better noodles than that."

"But I can't go home right now."

"You want to get sick?" I couldn't help smiling at the absurdity of this. "You don't know," he said darkly. "No noodles for you." Then he relented. "Further on there's a *laksa* stall. We'll go there, not this kind of dirty place."

We entered a narrow alley where canvas awnings were stretched against the sun, and hawkers hunched over charcoal braziers. A narrow gutter filled with foul-smelling water ran through it. Amah would have said it was no place for a girl of good family, as the diners consisted of mainly men, both coolies and other townsmen. Old Wong picked his way past the noisy diners packed together at communal tables. Narrow counters were piled high with glossy prawns, tangled noodles, and mounds of red chilies and fresh cilantro. Fried fish, yellow with turmeric, and crispy *begedil*, a meat and potato croquette, were laid out on green banana leaves, while *satay* and stingray rubbed with chili paste were barbecued on charcoal grills. I was so hungry that I felt faint.

Old Wong headed straight to a stall with a line of waiting customers. When his curry *laksa* arrived, Old Wong presented it to me with a mumbled prayer. Then he picked up his chopsticks and began to eat. To my relief, once it had been dedicated, I was able to savor the spicy noodles swimming in their curried broth. Puffs of fried tofu, bean sprouts, and plump cockles were buried beneath like treasure. Once replete, I chattered gaily as I followed him around, forgetting my sorrows for a while. Old Wong bought bananas and bean paste buns, remembering they were my favorites. I told him I wasn't hungry, but he said it didn't matter.

"You may find you can eat them later."

I nodded, remembering the funeral money that had appeared in my pockets.

"I have no more money on me," he said. "Are you sure you can't come back to the house?"

"Not as long as the demons are guarding it."

"But what will you eat in the meantime?"

Touched by his concern, I turned my face away, unable to speak. We were almost home when Old Wong asked me whether the demons were still on guard. I glanced around, annoyed with myself for unthinkingly following him back, but there was no sign of them.

"I'd better go," I said.

He opened his mouth as though to say something, but I left swiftly, afraid to draw attention to him.

CHAPTER 16

A S I WAS now back in familiar territory, my thoughts flew again to the shining thread that I had followed out of my bedroom window and which I had lost while pursued by the hungry ghosts. I searched up and down the street, retracing that earlier route. Just as I was about to give up in despair, I caught its faint gleam with overwhelming relief. Once I had regained it, however, I stood irresolute. If this thread truly led me to Tian Bai, should I seek him out at all? Despite my new suspicions of Yan Hong, it was he that Lim Tian Ching had named as a murderer, and on top of everything, he was preparing to wed another.

Yet I yearned to see him. Foolishly, perhaps, I felt that if I could only look into his eyes again, I would know whether Lim Tian Ching's accusations were false. After all, there was a history of rivalry between them. And if I could only discover Lim Tian Ching's secret task and who was behind it, I might have a better sense of whether his vendetta had just cause. I didn't wish to become like Fan, trapped for decades in the orbit of her lover's life, yet the longing to see Tian Bai one more time, to find out whether this marriage was his own desire, was hard to resist. In the end, I gave in.

As I trotted along, buoyed by a good meal, my spirits began to rise. The thread in my hand led me away from the walled mansions of the wealthy, through the commercial district and out toward the harbor. The distinctive corrugated sails of Chinese junks came into view, mingled with the white sails of European schooners and a low flotilla of Malay *prahus* with painted eyes on their bows. Beyond them lay the Straits of Malacca, the turquoise waters clear as glass and warm as bathwater. From here ships came from Singapore and Penang, unloading their bales of cotton, tin, and spices on the bare backs of coolies like a never-ending procession of ants.

With no one to censure me, I was tempted to dip my toes into the waves, but the thread tugged me to the right. Fine as it was, it had a steely strength and its faint hum grew a little higher, like the hunting call of a female mosquito. The road wound down to a row of warehouses where cargo was stored before it was loaded onto the waiting ships. Our family had once had such a godown when my father still engaged actively in trade. I still remembered the excitement in our household when one of his ships came home with a fine cargo and profit, but those days were now only a distant memory.

The road petered out into a dirt path packed by the feet of coolies and rutted by oxcarts, ending at a large warehouse. The heavy doors were barred but the thread led me to a shipping office to the side. All was quiet and the very air, soft with the smell of the sea, shimmered in the afternoon heat. Inside, it was dim and cool, plainly planked with wood that had weathered gray from the sea air, and empty save for a table with a solitary abacus. I guessed this was where the overseer tallied boxes and paid off coolies, but the thread in my hand began to vibrate insistently, leading me through to an inner office stacked with shelves of ledgers and boxes of shipping records. A long window faced the sea, and ranged upon its sill was a curious collection. Pieces of coral lay next to a dismantled brass clock, the tooth of a whale, and a beautiful little horse carved of sandalwood. At the very end of the ledge the thread terminated at a woman's hair comb. I knew at once that it was mine, the one that I had pressed into Tian Bai's hand.

A flat sense of depression overcame me as I regarded the objects on the windowsill. What had I expected? That Tian Bai would be clutching my comb on his person, just as I had obsessively carried his watch? Fan had said the glittering thread conveyed the strength of feelings, but what if it was only a one-sided attachment? Perhaps it was fitting that my comb lay upon the ledge, the last in a line of trophies. Doubtless the Quah girl had given him something better to remember her by. Tears of disappointment lurked treacherously in my eyes, but I rubbed them away. Turning to the window I sighed and was startled when I heard another sigh close by.

In my haste, I had barely glanced at the other side of the room, which was sectioned off by screens. Now I walked around to discover that they concealed a washstand and a cot bed. On the bed, fast asleep, lay Tian Bai. One arm was thrown carelessly over his head. Even as I watched, he shifted and frowned. The sturdy column of his neck and the flat muscles of his chest gave him a vigor that made me curious about what he did when he wasn't sitting at a desk.

I brushed my hand against his forehead, but there was no response. Fan had said she could enter the dreams of her beloved using her thread. I too had one and wondered whether I dared to use it, but my feet were already crossing the room to retrieve it. Plucking the thread between my fingers, I pressed it into his chest. There was a slight resistance, nothing more. Then the world around me swirled and became gray and cloudy.

I STOOD ON THE edge of a cliff, overlooking a harbor. The sea was a sullen green, the surrounding peaks blue and misty in the fading afternoon light. Wind shredded the clouds and the air was cold and strange. The bay, deep and curving with numerous inlets, held scores of ships far beyond Malacca's capacity. There were tea clippers, steamers, and so many junks that the harbor was dotted with their fierce, finlike sails. As I looked around, marveling at this foreign land, I found that I was standing next to Tian Bai. I must have entered his dream, but what was he dreaming of? The wind blew unceasingly; the shapes of the mountains were new to me. Compared with Lim Tian Ching's flat invasion of my own dreams, there was a vivid clarity to everything. But perhaps that was because he had manufactured a setting. In Tian Bai's case, I was sure that this dream was a memory, and that this could only be Hong Kong's Victoria Harbor.

I had seen black-and-white lithographs of its long channel and the dramatic peaks that sheltered it, but had never imagined I would ever see such a sight myself. For some time I could only stare transfixed, until the sight of Tian Bai's profile recalled me. Tian Bai stood a little apart from a group of sightseers who were dressed in a mixture of Manchu and Western clothing. He himself wore a jacket of gray broadcloth with covered buttons, matching waistcoat, and dark trousers. His hair was already cut short in the Western style. They were speaking Cantonese and English interchangeably, but I could understand every word, perhaps because what he heard and saw, I did too.

One young man seemed particularly close to Tian Bai and I guessed that he must be Yan Hong's husband. He was short, with impish narrow eyes. The others, clearly fellow medical students, laughed at his remarks. The women stood a little apart. I was very interested in their clothes, particularly the boned and waisted walking costumes that nipped in their silhouettes and arched their backs. It was the first time I had seen Chinese women wearing European dress and I supposed that in Hong Kong such attire was fashionable, and the weather cool enough to dress this way without inconvenience. Eagerly, I studied their hairstyles and jewelry, wondering how they pinned their hair up. As I did so, I noticed a girl who did not look quite Chinese. She was about my age, with a distinctive, almost foreign appearance. Her heavy-lidded dark eyes and creamy complexion with olive undertones reminded me of orchids grown in the shade. As she turned to the woman beside her, I noticed three small moles on the pale skin of her neck.

It soon became apparent that Tian Bai was watching this girl. His eye would rest on her, then swiftly glance away. Despite my own fascination with her, I couldn't help feeling the sting of jealousy. Yan Hong's husband came up beside him and laid a hand on his shoulder.

"Is this your first time seeing the beautiful Isabel?" he murmured. "Better not let her brother catch you. He's just over there."

"What was their family name again?" asked Tian Bai.

"Souza. An old Portuguese Eurasian family. But don't even think about it." His grip tightened on Tian Bai's shoulder, then abruptly let go. "Come, we're leaving!" he said.

Absorbed by the events unfolding before me, I now remembered with a start that my purpose was to talk to Tian Bai. I concentrated, telling him urgently, *You can see me. You can.* Obediently, he turned his head with an expression of confusion.

"Li Lan? What are you doing here?"

He stared beyond me at the group of people, now frozen as though time had stopped for them. "I must be dreaming," he said, and in almost perfect accord the world around us began to ripple and dissolve. Realizing that Tian Bai was beginning to wake up, I thought desperately of the office I had found him in. The harder I focused, the clearer the image became. As Tian Bai looked around, adding his belief to it, it solidified until it was indistinguishable from the real room, down to the open window and the faint sound of the sea outside. Tian Bai was lying on the cot and I was standing beside him.

"Li Lan?" he said again. "I heard you were ill. Some said you were on the verge of death." He sat up, rubbing his face. "I must have been asleep. How did you get here?"

I was too happy with this success to speak for a moment. This was far better than I had hoped. I could only stammer, "Y-Yes, I was sick."

"They said you were poisoned. Are you truly better now?"

How could I answer him? Questions flitted through my mind like a swarm of butterflies, but like a fool I could only blurt out, "Are you getting married?"

"What?"

"I heard from my father that your marriage contract had been signed already."

"Is that why you were ill?"

I crossed my arms. "I took some medicine given by a medium."

"Why were you consulting a medium?"

In my daydreams, I had imagined that Tian Bai would understand my situation immediately. That he would instantly grasp my difficulties and somehow deliver me from the peril I was in. But to my dismay, his questions only served to emphasize the gap between us. Watching the frown that flitted across his face, I had no idea how to begin and wished I hadn't blundered onto such topics.

"I was ill, so my amah suggested it. But it didn't seem to help much." That at least was no lie.

"I wouldn't put too much store in mediums," said Tian Bai. "My aunt is overly fond of consulting them."

"Because of her son?" I said.

A shadow passed over his face. "His death was a great shock to her."

"And you—do you miss your cousin too?"

Tian Bai gave me a level look.

"Not in the least," he said.

CHAPTER 17

I STARED AT him, trying to read his expression. I couldn't imagine why he would tell me such a thing, unless he was bent on confessing his misdeeds. Or perhaps he really was as frank and open as his countenance had always suggested. How well did I really know him anyway?

"It's a terrible thing to say," he said, "but we never got along. He was jealous. And I wasn't very kind to him when we were younger. You know my father was the elder brother?"

"I heard. You should have been—well, you are the rightful heir to the Lim family, are you not?" I said. It seemed beyond the bounds of good taste to talk about other people's private family matters, but I had to press on.

"Yes, but I was a child when my parents died and my uncle took over the business."

"Surely it was cruel of your uncle to deprive you of your inheritance?"

"You don't understand. My uncle loves me, you see."

My surprise must have shown on my face. From servants' gossip, as well as his treatment of my father, I had no warm feelings toward his uncle.

Tian Bai cast a swift glance at me. "My uncle can be difficult, but he has his virtues as well. I think Lim Tian Ching always sensed that his father preferred me and resented it bitterly. My uncle was caught between us, as well as the wishes of his wife."

"Madam Lim seems like a complicated person." I chose my words carefully, hoping that he would stay on this topic.

"You can't blame her in some ways. She loved her own son dearly. I often regret I wasn't around when he died and that she was the first one to find him."

"You weren't at home?" Hope was rising in my chest.

"I was up at Port Dickson, inspecting a ship."

I turned away to hide my mounting relief. Lim Tian Ching must have lied to me! I remembered Old Wong's warning not to trust ghosts. Surely, however, I could trust Tian Bai? I wanted to believe him so much.

"Does the prospect of a ship please you so much?" I could hear the smile in his voice without turning around. "If you like, you can see one today."

"Yes," I replied without thinking, forgetting that I would have to conjure up a convincing ship. At the door he paused.

"But I meant to ask, how is it that you're here?" His gaze flickered down the plain house clothes that Amah had dressed my body in.

I hesitated. If I told him the truth, he might shrink from me as a wandering spirit. "My amah is waiting outside," I said. Worse and worse—I couldn't possibly manage an imaginary Amah as well. "Maybe another time."

"Perhaps you're right. After all—" He stopped and had the grace to look awkward.

"The marriage," I said in sudden comprehension. "You're to marry the daughter of the Quah family."

"Li Lan!" Tian Bai reached out and grasped my hand. To my surprise, he caught hold of it instead of slipping right through my immaterial form. I kept forgetting that we were in a dreamworld and in this place he believed that I was just as alive as he was. I felt a tremendous sadness even as the warmth of his hand, the first human touch I had experienced for a long time, seeped into mine.

"Don't be sad," he said, misunderstanding me. "I didn't arrange that marriage and I haven't yet agreed to it."

"But my father said the contracts were signed already."

"Not by my hand. My uncle wishes it, though."

"What will happen if you don't agree?"

"Then he'll disinherit me."

"Is the marriage so important, then?" I said in dismay.

"If Lim Tian Ching had lived, this would have been his match, not mine. The Quah family has certain trading interests that dovetail with ours."

"And if he had lived, would you have married me?" I couldn't keep a note of wistfulness from my voice. Lim Tian Ching seemed to be always between us.

"Do you need to ask?"

"But you hardly know me."

"I knew of the arrangement before I left for Hong Kong."

"Was it made so long ago?" I was surprised, for my father's rambling account had been vague about this "understanding."

Tian Bai drew closer. "They talked about it when we were children. Or perhaps I should say, when you were a child. I must confess that initially I was a little concerned. You were only seven when it was first mentioned." I tried to pull away, but he tugged my hand back. "There I was, almost sixteen, and they said I was betrothed to a little girl in pigtails. But later I did some asking around of my own."

"And who did you ask?"

"That would be revealing my secrets." He smiled at me and I was caught. His eyes darkened, their gaze intensifying. Breathless, I was acutely aware of how close he stood.

Tian Bai tilted my face toward him, running his hand down my neck and shoulders. His hand was warm and dry where it trailed across my skin. I could feel the heat rising from his body through his thin cotton shirt, his arms sliding up to encircle me. He smelled clean, like the sea. The skin of his throat was so near that I could reach out and press my lips against it. His hands, firm and smooth, were sliding up my back. I closed my eyes, feeling his breath hover against my eyelids, his lips barely brushing them so that I could feel their warmth. When they reached the corner of my mouth, he paused for a long moment.

I had been holding my breath and now exhaled, my lips parting involuntarily. Tian Bai pressed his mouth against mine. Amazed, I could feel the warmth of his lips, the moist heat of his tongue. He kissed me, slowly at first and then harder. My heart was pounding, my hands caught in the thin fabric of his shirt. Then he let me go.

"You should go home. It would ruin your reputation if you were discovered here alone with me."

I was overcome with embarrassment, so flustered that I hardly knew where to look.

Tian Bai looked stricken. "It does no good to do this. Not for you, or me."

"I suppose you'd better defer to your uncle's wishes." The words came out more bitterly than I'd meant.

"My uncle has his ideas, but I have no intention of deferring to all of them." For the first time, I heard the flint in his voice. The open expression that gave his face such charm disappeared, and I was surprised at how distant he looked.

"And what do you propose instead?" I knew the weight of family opinion in such matters. It seemed hopeless.

"My aunt, in fact, doesn't support the marriage. She feels it's too painful to see her son's match be given to another."

"He's dead," I said drily.

"Of course." The atmosphere between us was suddenly strained. Tian Bai fingered a small wooden horse, exquisitely carved in every detail. I longed to ask him more questions about the marriage, but had no grounds to object. I couldn't even bring myself to tell him that I was, if not dead, then almost dead myself. I feared he would recoil from me, and I dreaded to lose this moment of physical contact, dream though it might be.

"I should go," I said at last, although I had no wish to do so. It was just that I had no idea of what to do next. How could I ask him to burn hell money for me or buy paper funeral goods? The thought made me feel even more disconsolate.

"There's just one thing," I said. "Please. Promise me you'll do it, even if it makes no sense to you."

"What is it?"

"Can you dedicate a drawing to me? The doctor said that I should have someone draw a picture of a horse or a carriage and burn it in my name."

He frowned, but I hurried onward, unhappy with my own deception. "I know you don't believe in such superstitions, but it would help my situation. Anything you like, just a picture of some kind of conveyance or even a donkey."

"And I'm to write your name on it? What is this supposed to accomplish?"

I heard the skeptical note in his voice again and thought rapidly. "It's supposed to carry off my illness, but my father won't permit it at home."

My halting explanation worked, for his expression softened. "Of course. Why didn't you tell me?" Immediately I felt terrible. Why didn't I tell him the truth anyway? But I feared that he would give up on me, consent to the Quah marriage if there was nobody else to marry—just the shell of a girl lying on a bed in a darkened room. I didn't know it at the time, but I was to bitterly regret this decision.

IT WAS DIFFICULT TO leave Tian Bai, but I told myself that I would return as soon as possible. Far better if this dream ended so that he would believe that it had actually occurred, for I needed him to burn some form of transport for me so that I would be able to journey to the Plains of the Dead. But perhaps at our next meeting. My mind was already leaping ahead, imagining other, less modest, scenarios. I remembered the feel of his hands on me, the heat of his mouth. Once again I thought of Fan and began to understand how she might have frittered years away on this kind of dream life with her lover. As it was, it took a great deal of willpower to sever our connection. I concentrated hard, imagining that Tian Bai saw me into a rickshaw with a silent Amah. Then I left him with the thought that he had lain down on the cot again and fallen asleep.

. . . .

LEAVING THE WAREHOUSES BEHIND, I began to walk desultorily along the shore though my thoughts kept returning to Tian Bai. I couldn't help feeling angry with myself; I had failed to tell him how things really stood. I was a coward, or perhaps my daydreams that he would instantly understand me were simply naive. Still, I was drawn to him. I didn't know if this was love, but it made me tremble, both elated and afraid. I wondered if he felt the same way and how many other women he had kissed. My skin recalled the sensation of his hand as it had slid across my shoulder blades and up my neck, and I had the sudden image of the three small moles on Isabel Souza's pale nape.

The sound of waves and the cries of gulls grew louder as I picked my way through the coarse salt grass. The Straits of Malacca face due west and the sun was beginning to set, hovering over the waters and turning everything to a pure and brilliant gold. A few enormous clouds hung in the sky like the islands of an enchanted land; below on the sands, fishermen dragged their wooden boats in and spread their nets to dry. It struck me: If I could penetrate Tian Bai's dreams with the filament composed of the strength of my feelings, did that mean that Lim Tian Ching had such a thread too? I recalled how Madam Lim had requested the ribbon from my hair when I first visited their house, though it must be a one-way connection. I thought of how weak and unstable the link had always seemed, and was grateful that he didn't seem able to find me anymore.

With a start, I realized that the fishermen were now far behind. Beside me was the fringe of coconut groves and farther ahead, where the sand ended, the dark mass of mangroves that grows its roots into the saltwater. I had never been so isolated from humans in my life. Even wandering the streets of Malacca, I had been aware of other people busy about their own affairs. Now I began to consider what other spirits might emerge with the night. There might be were-tigers in the jungle, and other dark spirits, like the bloodsucking *polong* or the grasshopper-like *pelesit*, who could see me. Fear seeped into my heart and I turned back under the darkening sky.

As I scrambled down a sandbank, I saw a figure standing at the water's edge. It wore a broad-brimmed bamboo hat and a robe with a hem of silver thread. With surprise, I realized it was the young man who had consulted the medium before me, and if I were right, the same man who had been standing outside the Lim mansion the previous evening. There were far too many coincidences about this. Emboldened by my invisibility, I began to make my way down the culvert, sliding in the crumbling sand. Although I was certain that I made no sound, he abruptly strode off at a great pace.

Looking back, I have no good explanation for my actions. I really ought to have retraced my steps, perhaps returning to Tian Bai's office to retrieve the thread that I had forgotten. Foolish! I should have asked him to keep my comb upon his person so that I could easily find him again. These thoughts skittered through my mind like a lizard running through long grass, even as my legs, moving as though they had a will of their own, went stumbling and skipping off after the man in the bamboo hat. He moved away from the shore toward the low mass of mangrove trees. I hoped that he would not go into the mangroves themselves, for they grow in sulfurous mud, their roots raising them above the seawater and providing a buffer between the land and the sea. I had passed a mangrove swamp on one of our childhood drives through the countryside, and I had never forgotten its putrescent smell, nor the strange fruit of the trees precipitously growing a pointed root while still attached to the branch, so that when the fruit fell it would instantly root itself in the mud.

As the man strode along, I openly hurried after him, confident that he couldn't see me. At the edge of the mangroves, he stopped. His head, with its peculiar headgear, swept from side to side as though searching for something, though I still caught no glimpse of his face. Feeling uneasy in the open, I slipped into the shadowy tangle of the mangrove trees. The mud supported my light form so that I could walk on the surface as though upon a thin crust. On an impulse, I climbed a tree. Given my lack of mass, it was surprisingly easy and soon I found myself lying far out upon a branch that would not ordinarily have supported a monkey, gazing down at the stranger.

Now that I had the leisure to examine him, I was struck by the eccentricity of his garb. With the exception of some adoption of Malay clothes, most Straits-born Chinese wore the high-collared costume of China, though strictly speaking this attire wasn't Chinese at all. My father had told me a little of this history, and how the Manchus, a non-Chinese race from the north, had conquered China and forced their new subjects to adopt Manchu clothing, including the male practice of shaving half the head and braiding the rest of the hair in a queue. There had been great resistance to this, for the Chinese men felt it was shameful to shave their heads. Public executions, however, ensured that the antique dress of Han China was now almost never seen.

The man in the bamboo hat was wearing Han clothing. That is to say, he wore a robe tied crossover, the left over the right, and bound by a broad sash. Beneath it he wore loose trousers and boots. I recognized this garb because it was used in books, paintings, and historic plays. In fact, the thought crossed my mind that he was perhaps an actor from some operatic troupe, and if so, I might have wasted my time on a fool's errand.

The sun dipped into the darkening sea like an egg yolk slipping from its shell, and I began to worry about finding my way back to town. But if I stayed with him, I could at least follow him back, for surely he didn't mean to spend the night out here. It was a good thing that I didn't move from my hiding place, for I had hardly come to this conclusion when there was a loud rustling. Branches broke underfoot and I was struck by a burned, carrion smell, as though someone had put spoiled meat upon a brazier. I lifted my head up from where I had pillowed it in my arms, and peered down. There, standing not ten paces away, was an ox-headed demon. I was so startled that I nearly fell out of the tree. Had it tracked me all the way here? But the demon paid no attention to my hiding place and I quickly realized that its business was with the man I had followed.

"So you've come at last," he said. It was a surprisingly pleasant voice—low, yet mellifluous for a man. Certainly, not what I expected from the stranger who had behaved so boorishly at the medium's.

The ox-headed demon inclined its head. I had never been so close to one of them before and was terrified that it would see me through the thin screen of leaves. But it never looked up.

"I was delayed," it said gruffly. "I had a hard time getting away."

"Never mind that. Did you find anything?"

"Plenty of conjecture but no hard evidence."

"That's not good enough."

"Begging your pardon, sir, but I think we can build a case."

"Building a case isn't the same as winning one. There must be records, transactions."

The demon snorted and rolled its dreadful eyes, yet it remained silent. My mind was working feverishly. Who was this man who consorted with demons? My attention was caught by his next words.

"So Lim Tian Ching is proceeding well with his task?"

"If you mean, proceeding as he wishes, then I suppose the answer is yes."

"And with those of the court?"

"The directives were not very clear."

The man paused for a moment. "Much to Lim's advantage, no doubt."

"Yes, but if you check the official records . . ."

"I know what the official records say. There is nothing untoward in them. Anything else?"

"The girl has gone."

The man nodded. "I know. Tell me something else."

"He has given orders to recapture her if possible."

"The girl is a distraction. But she may yet prove to our advantage if he is occupied in that direction."

"Then I should continue with my surveillance?"

"Yes. We'll meet again at the usual place and time."

The demon lowered its great horned head, the wicked tines glinting in the fading light. Then it sprang away at great speed. I heard once again the sound of vegetation being broken and crushed but could no longer see it. Only the faint roasted stench remained.

I remained frozen on my branch, trying to make sense of this peculiar conversation. There was no doubt that my fate was involved, but how? And who were these people? I peered at the man below again but he remained a cipher, his entire head hidden by the wide bamboo hat. With the onset of darkness, however, I began to see a faint glow about him, the slightest shimmer of a spirit light. I hugged the branch tighter, wondering whether I dared follow him to his next destination. After all, he hadn't noticed me earlier. I had just worked up enough courage to begin sliding down the tree when the man spoke again.

"You can come out now."

CHAPTER 18

THERE WAS NO escape for me. Mortified, I jumped the last ten feet, landing softly on the sand. That at least I was thankful for. If I had fallen into the swamp it would have been the final humiliation. The stranger stood with arms folded, his face still shielded by his bamboo hat with its curiously large and turned down brim.

"You knew I was there all the time," I said at last.

He cocked his head to one side. "If you want to follow someone, you ought not to do so at such a pantingly close range."

Stung, I said, "I didn't know you could see me."

"Of course I could see you."

"But you didn't say anything."

"I was wondering what you were planning to do. Beg for clemency perhaps?"

"Why should I beg you for anything?"

"No? That seemed like a logical thing to do."

"I don't even know who you are!" I cried in frustration. "Or what you are, I suppose."

"Ah, the risks of going incognito." The beautiful voice turned ironic. It had a clear, rippling quality that was mesmerizing.

"Never mind," he said. "I suppose I gave you too much credit for discernment. After all, you've been following me. There must have been some reason for that."

"I've seen you before."

"The medium, I suppose. And at the Lim mansion. I wondered whether you remembered."

My annoyance got the better of me. "If you really want to remain incognito, then you ought to change your clothes."

"My clothes?"

"And . . . and that ridiculous hat."

I caught the gleam of teeth from the shadowy recesses of the hat. "The sartorial fault is mine, no doubt. Although I must say that your own taste is also suspect."

Glancing down at the pajamas that Amah had changed my body into, I colored.

"Well, let us begin again, then," he said. "Now that we've introduced ourselves with the requisite compliments."

"I beg your pardon," I said. "You may well know who I am, but I still lack the honor of your name."

"My name is not so important, but very well, I am Er Lang."

Although he said it wasn't significant, there was no doubt that he was expecting some sort of reaction. Unfortunately I was unable to give him any. Er Lang was the plainest sort of name, if you could call it a name. It simply meant Second Son.

"And how do you know about me?" I asked.

"Are you always so impatient?"

"I'm just a little anxious. You would be too if someone was discussing you with a demon." A part of me was warning myself not to antagonize him, but I couldn't bite my tongue. Despite his hidden features, I wasn't as intimidated as I should perhaps have been, accustomed as I was to my father's ruined looks.

THE GHOST BRIDE 157

"So you know about the demons. You've certainly been getting about."

"They were guarding my house; I could hardly go and hide in my room!" Careful, I thought. But he merely shrugged.

"Good. You're more resourceful than I thought."

"And what does that mean?"

"It means that you may be useful to me."

I felt myself bristle, just like the fighting cockerels you see for sale in the market. Although trussed by the legs and wings for transportation, the vendors often shake them a little at one another to demonstrate their fierceness. That was exactly how I felt at that moment. After all, I had very little to lose, having no body anymore. But I told myself not to be foolish. There might be other things, worse still, that could be inflicted upon the spirit. In the meantime, the stranger seemed to have arrived at some sort of decision.

"Come," he said. "Let us walk a little."

The sea was dark and placid, and the moon's faint light was just beginning to silver the sand. The man walked at an easy pace and we fell in step with each other as if we were old friends going for a stroll. After a while I noticed that while I made no footprints in the sand, he left a neat, elegant track behind him. That was why I had mistaken him for an ordinary person. When we had walked for some time in silence, he said to me in an almost companionable manner, "No questions, then?"

"I didn't know that I had leave to ask."

"Self-control is a quality I've always admired. Especially in a woman."

"Well, then," I said. "Who are you really, and why are you interested in Lim Tian Ching? You're not a ghost, are you?"

"As for that, you may think of me as another kind of entity." Amusement tinged his voice. "Perhaps it would be better to describe me as a minor official."

"An official in the afterlife?"

"Of sorts. What do you know about the afterlife?"

Briefly, I recounted what I had discovered from Fan and the other ghosts I had encountered. When I had finished he nodded, the enormous bamboo hat moving like a shadowy bat. "Not bad," he said. "Quite good work for two days."

I might have been more pleased if he hadn't sounded so condescending, but he continued in the same cool tone. "The afterlife, as you've no doubt discovered, is governed fairly strictly. There are rules about the passage of human ghosts through this world and on to their next reincarnations."

The way he said this made me shiver. Suddenly, I was certain that I was in the presence of something completely foreign to me, not human at all, in fact. I wondered uneasily what he was concealing beneath the hat.

"One of the ministries oversees the Courts of Hell. A safeguard, you may say, to ensure the system is not abused. When you have unhappy ghosts and quantities of hell money floating around, you can hardly expect there to be no corruption."

"Are you from heaven, then?" I asked, thinking with chagrin about how I had gone around pretending to be from the peach orchards of paradise myself.

"Not at all. Consider me a mere tool. A special investigator, if you will."

"And are you investigating Lim Tian Ching?"

"I see you've put your eavesdropping to good use. Lim Tian Ching has exhibited some rather suspicious behavior."

"What has he done?"

"His case has certain indicators of bribery and coercion, part of a pattern that has surfaced recently. In other words, one of the Nine Judges of Hell is probably corrupt. Oh, they all are, to some degree," he added. "But it would be well to discover how serious it is, who is raising money and recruiting soldiers. For when the cycle of violence escapes its confines in hell, it causes earthquakes, floods, and other calamities. Don't you remember the eruption of Krakatau?"

Krakatau was the volcano that had erupted in Indonesia in 1883. I remembered my father's accounts of the tremendous sound of the explosion, and how the skies had turned black for days with a rain of bitter ash, even though Malaya was far away from the Sunda Straits. The lava flow was so intense that the entire island was decimated of all living creatures. Passengers on boats and steamships reported seeing human skeletons awash at sea upon pillows of floating pumice stone, even up to a year after the eruption.

"Krakatau was the physical manifestation of a rebellion in hell. Though it was suppressed, not all the conspirators were identified. But if another upris-ing were to upset the spiritual balance of this world, it wouldn't be just natu-ral disasters that occurred. The moral equilibrium will slip and shift so that nations will turn their thoughts to war. The world may yet burn from China to Europe, and even in the jungles of Malaya."

His voice had dropped, as though he were speaking to himself. A cold ten-dril snaked into my heart and I was struck by how insignificant my problems seemed in comparison. I was merely one soul cut adrift from its body. What would it be like if there were thousands, or hundreds of thousands like me? An image of the dead, floating like withered leaves on the surface of the water came to me, and I had the sudden urge to catch hold of Er Lang's sleeve. His presence, strange as it was, was a comfort to me in the darkness.

"Why are you telling me this?" I asked at last.

When he spoke again, his tone was flippant, as though he were embar-rassed at having said too much. "It has very little to do with you; the merest coincidence. It happened that I was interested in Lim Tian Ching's move-ments, and his interest, apparently, also included you."

"If you have any special dispensation," I said hopefully, "perhaps you can return me to my body."

"Unfortunately, that is beyond my powers," he said, and the beautiful voice sounded genuinely regretful. "Your dislocation occurred as a result of something you did yourself."

"But it was an accident!"

"Was it?" he said, and the way he said it made me squirm.

"Well, I didn't mean to. And couldn't you say that Lim Tian Ching drove me to it?"

"It's possible you could make a case for it. But that would have to come up before the Courts of Hell. They may well decide to give you another chance if the ruling goes against Lim Tian Ching."

"But how would I do that?"

"Gather evidence of his wrongdoing. And then, of course, make sure that you don't get assigned to the wrong judge."

"That seems to dovetail rather too well with your own investigation," I said.

"Well, if you can find out what Lim Tian Ching is doing, together with some sort of proof, then perhaps I can also help with the direction of your case."

"He told me that he was murdered, and that he had a task to perform in return for his revenge," I said, unsure about whether to mention the accusation. But if Tian Bai were truly innocent, perhaps we could clear his name.

"Did he now? He's not supposed to be dispensing justice by himself, even if he really was murdered. There's a reason why the courts exist. One assumes that your ghost marriage to him is probably another perk of his obedience. I have my spies, as you've no doubt realized, but they have their limitations."

We had turned inland, the path climbing above the beach and toward the trees. The balmy night was redolent with *champaka* flowers, one or two of whose modest blooms can perfume an entire room. A few stars hung low in the sky. I sighed, wishing Tian Bai was at my side instead of this acerbic, light-footed stranger. I had been studying him covertly and still had no sense of what he looked like. His movements were swift and limber, his form elegant in the old-fashioned clothes that suited him so well. But his face was a mystery to me. Perhaps there were no features beneath his hat at all, merely a skull with loose ivory teeth or a monstrous lizard with baleful eyes.

When we reached the top of the rise, my guide said, "For a young woman, you seem to have a rare gift for silence." This wasn't something I had ever noticed about myself, but I didn't wish to puncture his illusions.

"And are you often surrounded by chattering women?" I ventured.

He shuddered. "I find their attentions very tiresome."

I choked at this display of vanity. Unbidden, the image of shrieking women fleeing from a monster rose in my mind, but he only said, "So, do you think you can discover what Lim Tian Ching has been up to?"

"And how should I do that? Walk up to his house and tell him I'm ready for the wedding?"

"It's not a bad idea at all. Go to his house. See what you can discover."

I stared hard at the darkness beneath the brim of his hat, wondering if he was joking. "But the Lim mansion is probably guarded by demons now."

"True, but that's not what I meant. I was referring to his other house."

I was silent for a moment. "You mean the Plains of the Dead."

"Of course. He won't expect that at all."

"Why don't you go?"

"Because I can't. The Plains of the Dead is for human souls, a transitional place that is a shadow of the real world, for without it the shock from life to death is too great for some."

The Plains of the Dead. From the moment I had heard of it from Fan, I had been drawn to that place. Was it because my spirit was now edging closer to death? But I had very few options left. "I'll go," I said at last. "If it will help my case. But can you give me any aid? Any spirit money or a steed?"

"Those are human goods that I have no traffic in. But I will give you something better."

He slipped his hand into his robe and brought out a shining flat disk, tapering to one end like a flower petal. Grasping it, I was astonished to find that it was a scale, but one so large that I could not imagine what sort of creature had shed it. It was about the size of the palm of my hand, smoothly marked with grooved lines from one direction and culminating in a razor-sharp frill on the other edge. In the moonlight it shone like mother of pearl, so glossy that it looked as though it was wet, though when I drew my finger across it, it was perfectly dry.

"It is a means to call me. Far better than spirit money, don't you think?" He was so pleased with himself that I had to restrain myself from rolling my eyes.

"But you can't go to the Plains of the Dead."

"Well yes, but there are other areas where I may be of help. I'm sure a resourceful girl like you can easily find a way to the plains." His wry tone made me wonder whether he knew about Fan and her offer to me. "You must hold it up and blow upon the rippled edge. Then call my name and, if I can, I will come to you."

To my surprise, we were fast approaching the outskirts of town. Er Lang had led me by a direct route, cutting back like a bird on a wing. When I glanced behind me at the path we had taken, however, I could no longer see it. All that remained was the dark sighing mass of trees and the waist-high spears of *lalang*. I wondered whether I had been dreaming, so clearly could I picture the pale glint of sandy soil upon that winding path, but the route behind us looked impassable.

"Now," he said, pausing before the sea of roofs below us. Oil lamps burned in some windows, and with my sharp vision I could see the faint miasma of green and blue spirit lights in the darkened streets. "Can you manage from here?"

I hesitated. "Yes. As for money and a carriage . . . " I shrugged hopelessly.

"You've already done far better than you can imagine," said Er Lang in a surprisingly kind tone. "There's one thing more to remember. Time in the Plains of the Dead doesn't pass at the same rate as it does here. The rate isn't constant; it ebbs and flows, but in general it will be faster than time here. That is how someone may die one night and be reborn the next day, yet have spent months or even years in the Plains of the Dead. I won't lie to you. There is a certain amount of danger. In fact I'm not even sure you can enter the plains since you're not quite dead yourself."

"And if I can't?"

He shrugged. "Then we must try another tactic. But I shall remember your service to me, regardless." I opened my mouth to ask him another question, but he forestalled me. "If you manage to go to the Plains of the Dead, don't trust anyone. And don't eat anything. You still have a living body, which is a great advantage for it strengthens you beyond what the dead are capable of."

"If I don't eat spirit food, won't I wither away?"

"But if you wish to return to the living, it is better not to dilute your spirit with the food of the dead."

"That's what Old Wong said."

"Who is that?"

"Our cook."

He waved his sleeve in disdain. "Yes, well. Just remember what I said. But I must go now. I have tarried too long and there are other urgent matters at hand."

A dozen more questions sprang to my lips, but at that moment there was a great rushing sound. A strong wind buffeted me, stirring up the leaves and branches in a whirling maelstrom. I closed my eyes against this onslaught and when I opened them again, Er Lang was gone. Far off in the night sky I saw a streak of light undulating like an eel in the ocean, but it passed so swiftly that I wondered whether I had imagined it.

CHAPTER 19

I SPENT THE night on the hillside, not feeling up to the task of going into the town and trying to spend my limited hell money on some kind of conveyance. There was an enormous tree with buttress roots rising like low walls, and I huddled against it like a timid *pelandok*, or mouse deer. We have many local stories of the mouse deer, so tiny that a man could pick one up and stuff it into a bag with ease. It is no bigger than a cat with delicate, twig-like legs. They are reputedly among the easiest game to hunt, for all you have to do is drum upon some dry leaves with a pair of sticks. Eventually a male *pelandok* will appear, thinking it is some rival, and will respond by rapidly drumming its own legs. The hunter then shoots the deer with a blow dart and carries it home for supper. I always felt it was a most unfair way to trap an animal and not at all in keeping with the mouse deer's fabled reputation for cunning.*

As I hugged my knees, I thought that in the grand scheme of things, I was

---

* In Malay tales, Sang Kanchil, the mouse deer, is a brash and clever trickster.

no more effective than a mouse deer, hiding my defenseless self here and there, called out by the drumming of information in dribs and drabs. Was Er Lang to be trusted? While he was with me I hadn't considered it, but now doubt and weariness clouded my mind. In the end I decided that I would trust him, for now. After all, it wasn't as though I had much else to fall back on.

THE NOISE OF BIRDS woke me. It was cold and a pale mist lay heavily upon the grass. From the broken and swaying branches above, a troupe of monkeys had passed overhead. At some point, Amah had changed my pajamas again. Hurriedly, I felt my garments, fearful that the scale that Er Lang had given me might have vanished, but it was still tucked in my pocket. Last night it had shone like mother of pearl, but in the morning light its gloss was even brighter. The creature that had shed it must have been a marvelous sight, and I speculated anew whether Er Lang hid the pouting face of a fish beneath his hat, or more frighteningly, the head of a great serpent. Putting these thoughts aside, I started toward the town below. The huge trees gave way to waist-high undergrowth, dense enough to make passing through it a struggle for me.

The sun was high in the sky, but I was still far from my destination. I groaned inwardly as I gazed at the way before me. Malaya is a land of perpetual green. Under the hot sun and torrential rains, any dwelling that is abandoned is quickly covered with vines; any path untraveled reverts to the jungle. All around me rose the monotonous chirring of cicadas. It was so loud that I didn't hear the clink of a harness until it was almost upon me. Bewildered, I looked around but there was nothing to be seen. At last, I said timidly, "Is there someone here?"

There was no reply, just a soft whicker.

I tried again, feeling even more foolish. "Is there a horse here?"

When I pronounced the word *horse*, I suddenly saw it. It was a small blocky horse the color of sandalwood. Bright dark eyes, like custard apple seeds, peered from under a thick mane that was plaited into bunches. The horse was gaily caparisoned with a blanket and saddle and it was these that I recognized, for it looked exactly the same as the wooden carving Tian Bai had held in his hand. I knew then that Tian Bai had burned it for me. The horses in Lim Tian Ching's grand stables had been static and lifeless, for they were only made of paper. But this horse, carved from a block of wood, moved like a real animal. There were no words for my delight.

"I shall call you Chendana," I decided. It is the Malay word for sandalwood, for the original carving had been done in that fine-grained, fragrant wood. Riding her was easy. Far easier than a real horse, for she stood docilely while I clambered up, and her broad back was as stable as a rocking horse. Chendana didn't tire and she neither ate nor drank. We passed swiftly through the undergrowth; the grass didn't even quiver. It was by these signs that I knew that she was more of the spirit world than I was.

It was afternoon when we entered Malacca. Now that I had found my transport, there was no reason not to find Fan and ask her to show me the way to the Plains of the Dead. Feeling cheerful for the first time in a great while, I found my way to Fan's shop house just as the pigeons were fluttering to their nests. At the front door, I paused, wondering whether to wait until darkness. The family was sitting down to an early dinner and I smelled the tempting aroma of salted fish.

"Fan!" I called.

There was no reply. I squeezed myself through the wooden door with some difficulty. The corridor was lit by the last rays of the afternoon sun and didn't seem as frightening as it had the other night when I had been led blindly through the house by Fan. I walked up and down, calling her name despite the family who was eating dinner. They of course had no idea I was there, though once when I passed close by I thought I saw the old man blink. In the end, having found no trace of her, I made my way back to the front door. While I was contemplating the uncomfortable task of trying to pass through it once again, I heard a faint voice.

"What are you doing here?"

Peering around I found Fan at last. She had been hiding in a shadowy corner, pressed into the door of a cupboard. It was very hard to see her in the last glittering motes of sunset.

"I came back. You said you would take me to the Plains of the Dead."

"Oh, I can't possibly go now," she said weakly.

"Why not?"

"It's not convenient."

"Couldn't you at least point out the way to me?"

She said something unintelligible, then finally, realizing that I could not hear her, she shouted faintly, " ... after dark ... "

Not entirely sure of what she had proposed, I nodded and said, "I'll wait for you outside until nightfall."

To my relief, Chendana was still where I had left her. I was afraid that someone might steal her, so precious had she become to me in a relatively short period of time, but I remembered Fan's words about spirit items needing to be freely given. Otherwise, I supposed, there was nothing to stop hordes of hungry ghosts from pillaging. As it was, I leaned against her side, inhaling the sweet scent of sandalwood, that precious wood from which incense is made. We waited for a long time. The sharp sickle moon rose and still Fan did not appear. I had begun to wonder whether I had mistaken her meaning when she finally materialized through the front door. From her sullen expression, I suspected she had been hiding on the other side. As soon as she saw Chendana, however, her eyes lit up. "You have a steed!"

I couldn't help a tinge of smugness. "Yes. I'm ready to go to the Plains of the Dead."

"But how is it—?" Fan walked around the horse, staring closely. Then she glanced sharply at me. "This is good quality. Very good, indeed. Did you get one for me?"

"I'm afraid that heavenly dispensation only provided transport for me."

"But I'm to be your companion! You should have asked them to provide for me as well."

I hesitated. "I'll pay you when we arrive there. I didn't think you wanted the authorities notified about you."

"Oh." She looked crestfallen. "I suppose you're right."

"And didn't you say you already had transport?"

"I do. But my servants are very shoddy in comparison." She sighed enviously. "Well, when my lover joins me, I'm sure I shall have a grand palanquin at my disposal."

I stifled the urge to roll my eyes, wishing I liked her better. It was difficult to think of enduring a long journey in her company. "Are you ready to leave?" I asked. "If you're not willing, I'll find another guide." Though even as I said this, I wondered how I could possibly manage.

"Whoever said that? Of course I'll go. I have some business there of my own anyway. Still, I need to make preparations." She hemmed and hawed, went back and forth into the house several times but emerged without looking any different. At last, when I was seriously considering riding off on my own, she came out. "Let's go."

I noticed then that her fingers were pinched as though she was clutching something invisible, and guessed that she had gone to retrieve the thread that bound her to the old man. Glancing at me she said almost apologetically, "I dare not go out without it. I would get lost."

Immediately, I felt guilty for harboring such unkind thoughts toward her. She was, after all, a ghost and it was true that she made her way forward with difficulty. She advanced in a mincing manner, subject to sudden gusts of wind and stray shadows. I followed, leading Chendana by the reins. It was not entirely dark yet. The sky was still a deep blue, but already I could see the soft glow of spirit lights. I felt like hurrying Fan along, but she grew increasingly dithery the farther we went from her shop house. At one point she turned round and round as though unable to break out of her perambulation.

"I told you I don't like to go out much," she said petulantly. "It's so much trouble. And it gets worse as the years go by. I'm losing substance, I know I am."

I didn't remind her that it was her own choice to overstay her time in this plane of existence. We crept along at a snail's pace, keeping always to the shadows and avoiding any spirit lights. Fan was terrified of running into border guards and her nervousness was infectious.

"How far away is an entrance to the Plains of the Dead?" I asked.

"I could have sworn there was one right around here," she said. "At least, that was the one I used. Don't tell me that they moved it!"

"The entrances shift?"

"There are many ways to go there," she said irritably. "Sometimes they move for no good reason."

In silence we fumbled around, peering down one dark alleyway after another. I had no idea what Fan was looking for, but when I laid my hand on Chendana's neck, I felt calmer. If I ever returned to my body, I thought, I would ask Father to buy me a horse. Thinking about my father and his troubles, however, made me feel gloomy again. My hand crept toward the pocket in which I had stowed the scale that Er Lang had given me. Its hard edge imbued me with a little more resolve. At that moment, Fan stopped.

"It is here."

I couldn't make out anything except an old doorway in the wall, gaping like a hungry mouth. There was nothing different about it other than the quality of its darkness, which seemed, if possible, even blacker than the gloom around it. Fan passed her hand around the lintel and a faint red light kindled within, as though the door led to some subterranean passage that was fathoms deep. I didn't like it at all, and neither did Chendana. The little mare backed away, prancing hesitantly.

"How do you know?" I asked Fan in a whisper.

"It calls to me," she said, turning to look at me over her shoulder. The crimson light cast a faint glow on her face, accentuating the shriveled, mummified aspect of it. "Can't you feel it?"

"No," I said, not mentioning that it actively repelled me. Well, Er Lang had mentioned something about that. Perhaps I wouldn't be able to pass, and for an instant I hoped that I need not go after all. But Fan was already ducking into the doorway.

"Come!" she hissed. "This is the way to the Plains of the Dead."

PART THREE

The Plains of the Dead

CHAPTER 20

FAN DUCKED HER head and slipped through the door, even as I hesitated. There was no time to say another word. Far down in the depths of the doorway I could see the glow of a crimson light, but there was no sign of Fan. I took a deep breath and tightened my grip on Chendana's reins. As we passed through the doorway, the faint night noises of the street vanished and all that remained was a silence so profound that it felt as though my ears were ringing. It was like entering a tomb.

Holding on to Chendana's mane, I groped my way forward. The ground beneath was smooth and flat, the darkness so thick that it clung like velvet, making it impossible to make out my feet. Far ahead, the red light glowed though it seemed to shed no illumination on anything else. Turning to see if I could find the way back, I was overwhelmed by the sensation of blindness. I was about to panic when I heard Fan's voice close at hand.

"Well?" she said impatiently. "Shall we go?"

"Where are you?" Fan's spirit light, which had announced her presence to me in the shop house, was indiscernible.

"Can't you see me? I can see you quite clearly."

"What does it look like to you?" I asked.

"It's a tunnel. A passageway to the Plains of the Dead."

"Is it lighted?"

"Certainly! There are lanterns hanging from the walls. Do you mean to say that you can't see them at all?"

"No, only a faint red light in the distance."

"How odd," said Fan. "Perhaps it's because you're not a ghost. I suppose few from the heavenly realm come here."

"We're not accustomed to these conditions," I said with some embarrassment at keeping up this pretense.

"Well, at least you can see the end of the passage," she replied. "That light is the entry down to the plains."

To me, the darkness seemed cold and dead, the light less like a welcoming beacon than a warning, a dull red eye staring unwinkingly from some far cavern. I hoped that the rest of our journey wouldn't suffer from this strange dichotomy or I should make a very poor spy for Er Lang.

"Come along, then," said Fan, sounding pleased with her advantage. "Can you follow me?"

By following the sound of Fan's chatter and aligning myself with the faint light, it was easier to advance. I asked her to describe what she saw. "It's very grand," she said. "There are tiles underfoot and the lanterns are of colored silk."

Despite Fan's lyrical description, the ground felt as though it was made of hard-packed dirt and the air was still and breathless. I couldn't shake off the feeling that we were descending into a mausoleum. Only by lacing my hand in Chendana's mane could I force myself onward. She didn't balk again after that first refusal at the doorway but walked quietly by my side. In this manner too, she was unlike a real horse, but I was grateful for her company.

"How do you find your way back?" I asked Fan after a while.

"Oh, from the Plains of the Dead the passage is quite clear. You can't miss it. You just have to remember which door you came in by."

"Did you ever try to go out through the other doors?"

"Once or twice. I know there are a couple of exits in Malacca. One goes to the merchant quarter. I don't know where the others go, though," she said carelessly.

The merchant quarter was where my own home lay. I squirreled this information away with a sinking feeling, as I hadn't realized that getting out would be so difficult. Now it sounded as though I would need Fan's help more than ever, for Er Lang had said he could not come to this place.

"WE'RE ALMOST THERE."

I peered ahead at Fan's words. The light spread like a burning haze to my eyes, which had become accustomed to the dark, and I began to see that the walls of the passage were rough-hewn rock as was the floor, as though some giant creature had wriggled its corkscrew way through the rock. It was nothing like the genteel corridor that Fan described to me. As we walked around the final curving bend of the passage, the light became a blaze that momentarily blinded me. And at last, I saw where the tunnel opened out.

As far as the eye could see was a barren plain. It was so dry that the grass had shriveled into white stalks of dead vegetation, barely covering the crumbling earth, like a thin coarse pelt. Above it rose a burning sky. Accustomed as I was to the lush jungle of Malaya, I stared in wonder and horror at this wasteland.

"You see what I meant by needing transportation?" asked Fan.

Turning, I saw that she now appeared more substantial. Her skin was no longer shriveled and even the details of her dress had taken on the appearance and weight of cloth. She looked out at the grassland with an incongruous expression of pleasure.

"The first time I saw all these flowers, I thought it was paradise," she said. Clearly, things appeared differently to her. I kept my own observations to myself. Next to me, Chendana snorted and stamped a hoof. She didn't seem at all daunted by the endless stretch in front of us.

"We should wait here for my servants to arrive," said Fan. "Whenever I get to this point, they eventually show up to escort me."

"I suppose you could walk," I said.

"Walk? There are settlements across the Plains of the Dead, but they're very far apart."

"And what do they look like?"

"Towns, villages. They roughly correspond to the places above. There is a kind of Malacca, where you find those ghosts who used to live in there, and then there are the outlying villages. But the dwellings come and go as the ghosts move on to the Courts of Judgment. It's always shifting."

"And are there other towns too?"

She shrugged dismissively. "I heard there was a ghostly Penang, and a Singapore too. But I don't know where they are."

We gazed at the endless prairie in silence. Fan scanned the horizon from time to time and frowned. I had expected to find caverns, stalactites, and dungeons; the accoutrements of an underworld such as I had seen illustrated in painted scrolls. Nothing had prepared me for this. Despite the merciless glare, I couldn't see the sun. The sky was evenly lit, which gave it an artificial air. Yet the overall effect was overpowering. With no landmarks, I had no way of knowing how many miles the grassland stretched out for, but it seemed like a great distance. After a time, I became aware of two dark shapes that drew steadily closer. Soon, a pair of coolies emerged from the long grass, carrying between them a shoulder pole with a basket slung under it.

"There they are," said Fan. "My goodness, they look even worse than before."

As they drew nearer I saw what she meant. They reminded me of the servants in Lim Tian Ching's funeral mansions. But unlike Lim Tian Ching's servants, their eyes and noses were roughly shaped, the mouths mere gashes in their lumpy faces. Their general appearance was much faded and worn and the contrivance they carried looked decidedly rickety. When they reached us, they bowed stiffly and dropped the basket to the ground. Fan climbed into it with some reluctance.

"It's such an uncomfortable mode of transportation," she said. "If only my father hadn't been so stingy with me." I refrained from pointing out that she was much luckier than the hungry ghosts, who had nothing at all. "Well, shall we be off, then?" she asked. Her porters picked up the carrying pole and hefted it briskly onto their shoulders. Then without a backward glance, they set off into the burning grassland.

Swinging myself onto Chendana, I followed after. My horse was faster so I held her back, which also relieved me from Fan's constant conversation. Glancing at her swinging awkwardly in the basket, however, I couldn't help feeling sorry for her. It seemed like a most uncomfortable mode of transportation to be tossed to and fro like a load of vegetables. From time to time I caught a glimpse of her white hand as she smoothed her hair, petting it as though it were a live animal.

Turning back, I noted that the passageway we had come from emerged from a range of hills. They were rocky and bare of vegetation, colored a deep oxblood red. It was an awe-inspiring yet dispiriting sight. There was not an insect or a bird that I spied along the way, and no flowers bloomed in the withered grass. It seemed impossible that rain ever fell on this desolate land. If I had been made of flesh and blood, I would surely have been burned in that ferocious light. Still, I wished I had a hat, and I had to improvise by pulling part of my pajama jacket over my head. As I did so, I felt the scale in my pocket that Er Lang had given to me. I was tempted to examine it again, but I didn't wish to draw Fan's attention to it. From time to time she glanced back, and her eyes were hard and bright.

WE TRAVELED FOR WHAT seemed like hours. The glare began to fade from the sky until it was suffused with a curiously beautiful violet color. Urging Chendana forward to draw level with Fan, I asked, "What happens at night?"

"Oh, we just keep going," she said. "I usually try to get this part of the journey over as soon as possible."

It was easier for her, I realized, for despite the jolting motion of the basket, all she had to do was allow her porters to bear her tirelessly along. No doubt my little horse could walk all night, but I was afraid that I might fall off if I fell asleep, and I said as much to Fan. She frowned. "I hadn't thought of that. I suppose we can stop and rest if you like."

We made a makeshift camp in the grass. I had experienced neither thirst nor hunger since we had entered the Plains of the Dead, but despite that, I felt weary with a sense of being stretched ever thinner. Alighting stiffly, I walked around, stretching my arms until I noticed that my feet crunched on the coarse dry earth, and the grasses parted their bleached heads for me. For the first time in a long while, I had a physical impact on the world around me. Instead of relief, however, this discovery filled me with dread. I didn't want to belong to this world. I wanted to go back to Malacca, my living, breathing Malacca, with its humid air and torpid days. Fan watched as I paced up and down. She had climbed out of her basketlike contraption and was now rearranging her hair, which, like the rest of her, seemed to have become more substantial than before.

"What are you looking at?" she asked.

I made a noncommittal noise and she fell silent. After a time, however, she said in a low voice, "I know you see differently than I do. What is it really like?"

In the growing darkness, her face was a pale blur. "Why do you want to know?" I asked.

Her voice faltered. "Sometimes I have a feeling that things aren't what they seem. And I'm frightened of what comes next. If my lover doesn't die with money, or if he doesn't share it with me, then I must pass on to the Courts of Hell."

She seemed so downcast that I couldn't help feeling sympathy for her. "But after the courts is rebirth," I said. "You might find happiness again."

"Oh, rebirth isn't the problem," she said peevishly. "It's what comes before. I'm afraid of the punishment for sins incurred in this life."

"You were young when you died. Surely they won't judge you too harshly."

Fan looked away. "I've overstayed my time in the afterlife. That's why I told you I seldom come to the Plains of the Dead anymore, even though I ought to. I'm not like you." She cast an envious glance at me. "In the shop house I only receive those offerings to the hungry ghosts that my lover puts out. But he burns no clothes, nor shoes. I have to come back here to get what I can."

"Why didn't you ask him to burn funeral goods for you in his dreams?"

"When we're together I don't want to remind him that I'm dead. That would spoil everything."

A pang struck me, for hadn't I made exactly the same decision about Tian Bai? After all, the thought of embracing a corpse was hardly conducive to romance.

"And besides, he might exorcise me." She made an impatient noise. "All these years I've been careful to make him think he's only dreaming when he's with me. I didn't want him to find out that I was really haunting him. How do you think he would react? He's so concerned with his health. A monk would have told him that I was sucking his life force out."

"And were you?"

"Of course not!" she said. "Well, maybe a little here and there to supplement myself. He looks quite good for fifty-seven, don't you think?"

Fifty-seven! I had thought the old man was in his eighties at least. No wonder Fan was in such terror of the authorities. I had thought it a simple case of overstaying, but clearly she had been involved in other trespasses. She turned a guileless face to me.

"That's why I decided to come with you. If you're from the heavenly realm, you should be able to help me with the authorities."

Uneasily, I wondered what else Fan had concealed from me. Just then she gave a cry and flattened herself against the ground. Looking up, I saw swift dark shapes passing overhead. "What is it?"

"Down! Down!" she hissed. I threw myself on the coarse earth beside her. Whatever it was swooped over us, dipping and wheeling with a mewling wail. It was a sound like nothing I had ever heard, piercing and forlorn, yet dreadful in its intensity. Stifling the urge to bury my face in my hands, I glanced up furtively but the creatures were too fast. All I could see was that they flew strangely, as though they sheared the fabric of the air with sharp, triangular wings. They passed ominously low. Squeezing my eyes shut, I flinched as the wind from their passage flattened the grass around us. An instant later, they had lifted off and were gone, flying rapidly into the inky veil of night. After a time, I sat up but Fan remained facedown on the ground, trembling and shaking.

"What were those creatures?" I asked Fan.

She was silent for a while, but at last she said, "Most ghosts ignore them, but I heard that they may be spies for the Courts of Hell."

"I thought this was a place for human ghosts."

"It is, though the border officials sometimes cross into here. But nobody really knows whether these flying creatures belong to them or not."

"The border officials can come here?" Horrified, I'd been under the impression that nonhumans could not.

"Yes, but they seldom do." Fan spoke in a low voice. "There are many things here that I don't understand. That's why I asked you earlier what you saw. Because surely your view of this place is different from mine." Even as Fan pressed me to tell her how things appeared to me, some instinct warned me against it. She was not so easily put off, however. "Why won't you tell me?" she asked, returning to her old petulance. It was as though that moment of vulnerability between us had never been.

At length she gave up and lay down next to her porters. They hadn't flinched when those creatures had swooped down upon us, remaining as inanimate as the basket that lay between them. Chendana had at least snorted once, but she too hadn't seemed unduly troubled. I reminded myself that my little horse was, after all, not a creature of flesh and blood. It was a sobering thought, but did not prevent me from huddling next to her and falling asleep.

CHAPTER 21

I WAS AWOKEN by the gradual lightening of the sky. Just as the day before, there was no sun, merely a slow change in color as though a screened backdrop was rising upon a stage. A breeze rattled through the dry grasses, and once again I was struck by the utter lifelessness of the plain. Not far away, I could see Fan lying on her side, her eyes open. I wondered whether she had slept at all that night. I was glad, however, of the rest, even as I worried about how my physical body fared, far away in the world of the living. If something should happen to it, would there be any sign to warn me? Or perhaps I would be cut off, wandering forever in this sea of endless grass.

As soon as we were ready, Fan gave the order to her porters to start moving. "We're almost there," she called back to me.

I urged Chendana a little forward. "How do you know this?"

"Oh, it's a feeling that I have near the cities and towns. It's like a pull."

"But I don't see anything ahead."

Fan laughed. She seemed to be in a much better mood than the previous day. "It doesn't work like that! The towns appear at their own pace. That's why I need my servants to find them. And that's also why the hungry ghosts could never come here, because they have no funeral offerings to guide them."

Looking back, I could see that we had left the rocky hills where the passageway emerged far behind. Instead of towering in the background, they were now mere bumps on the horizon. I was surprised at how much ground we had covered; in the real world, a journey of six or seven hours could hardly have served to distance ourselves so far. It made me anxious too about how time was passing here.

"There it is!"

Ahead of us was a faint shimmer that became more substantial as we drew nearer. The haze thickened around us until I began to see the outlines of streets and buildings filling in as we went forward, so that the road we were traveling became a broad avenue. There were shops and conjunctions of buildings that looked uncannily familiar. Down a side street I caught a glimpse of what looked like the Stadthuys, and from another, a brief view of a harbor lined with old-fashioned junks and frigates. It was beginning to look like Malacca, but far larger and devoid of the debris that often lined the streets. Some buildings were missing while others were replaced by gaudy monstrosities. The streets were silent and wide; the only people I saw were figures passing at a distance.

"Where is everyone?" I asked.

"There isn't a large population," said Fan. "Ghosts are always leaving when they're called to the Courts of Hell." She turned to me. "What do you mean to do now?"

I told her that I had some tasks to do, keeping the details as vague as possible. I was afraid that Fan would insist on accompanying me, but she seemed disinterested, telling me only that she meant to go to her house. "A shack is more like it," she said. "Can you give me some money now?"

I had prepared myself for a request like this once we had arrived and gave her two strings of cash and some ingots, retaining a little for emergencies. "Is that all?" she asked, wrinkling her nose.

"I'm afraid so."

"Oh, well. Thanks, I suppose. Do you need me to show you the way back afterward?"

"Yes. How long will you stay?"

"I think about ten days. I have some housekeeping matters to attend to."

"If you show me where your house is, I'll come to you at noon on the tenth day, or else send a message."

"If you don't come, I may leave without you. I dare not stay too long here."

I agreed to this, and in surprisingly short order we arrived at her house. The twisting streets loomed out of the haze, winding haphazardly, making me afraid that I would be unable to find my way back. When I expressed this to Fan, she merely laughed. "That's why we have servants. The buildings change when inhabitants leave, and new ones come with their own funeral offerings. Your horse will remember the way." She drew to a halt.

"Well, this is my place," she said. It wasn't as bad as she had made it out to be, though dark and shaped like a box. I guessed that it must have originally been a simple paper model. Fan invited me in, but I declined. Somehow I did not like to pass through that narrow door.

"Why don't you stay with me while you're here?" she pressed.

In the end, I put her off with some vague words. Fan's naked agendas gave me an uneasy feeling, and already I regretted the few pieces of information I had let slip.

After leaving Fan, I let Chendana wander through the streets for a while. As we went along I kept looking for familiar markers. Remembering the glimpse I had seen of the Stadthuys, I thought that if I could find it again I would surely have a better sense of where I was. The map that the Dutchman had drawn for me of the town was still impressed upon my mind, although I didn't know whether that was due to his clarity or some other reason.

At last I saw the Stadthuys but, try as I might, could not approach it. Despite glimpsing it at the end of several streets, as soon as I went down them, it disappeared. Only upon looking back did it reappear like a mirage, around a corner or at the end of an alley. Frustrated, I thought to ask some of the pedestrians I saw at a distance. I drew near an ornate palanquin, but the shutters were drawn and I hesitated, remembering my glimpse of Lim Tian Ching on the street before and how he too had such a conveyance.

While I stood there wavering, the shutters twitched and a shriveled face appeared.

"What do you want?" he said. "A young girl going about alone? What is your family thinking?"

I could only stammer before this onslaught, but the old man pried open the door and climbed out. "Recently dead, are you?" he asked. He was a wizened creature, bent with age. At the end of a scrawny neck, his head bobbed like a fishing weight. Yet he was surprisingly agile, circling me with interest. "Good horse," he said. "They don't make them like that anymore. Now it's only cheap paper, not even cardboard!"

"I beg your pardon," I said. "I just wanted to ask for directions."

"Where do you want to go?"

"I was trying to get to the Stadthuys."

He snorted. "The Stadthuys! It doesn't exist here." At the surprise on my face, he burst out into a cackle of laughter. "You can see it because it exists as a collective memory. All of us here who lived and died in Malacca expect to see the Stadthuys and the clock tower, but you can't visit it because nobody actually burned a funeral copy of it. *Cheh!* I should have told my grandson to burn me one, then I would be the sole proprietor. But you, young lady. What are you doing by yourself without your servants? Who is your family? Where do you live?"

Despite his peculiar behavior, I wondered if he might have some useful information, so I said, "Oh, Grandfather, I was just wondering where everything was. I'm so new here, you see."

"Ask away! But in return you must tell me something about yourself. It's only fair that I get some entertainment out of this."

"So do the areas here correspond to the real Malacca?"

"Of course they do! Or almost nearly. But distances are very deceptive here." He smiled cunningly. "You can spend days getting to some places and only minutes to reach others. It has to do with how things are connected to one another. Everything is relational here. Your house, your servants, your clothes—they all depend on someone else's filial devotion to you. Look at me!

When I died I had nothing to want for. Some of my descendants even went to the temple to pray that I would have a long and extended time to enjoy all these riches. But you see what happened?"

I jumped as his voice rose, and in the distance I saw several passersby quicken their steps to avoid us. Wondering whether I'd had the misfortune to run into a madman, I took a step back.

"I got stuck here for years!" He let out a howl of indignation. "Can you imagine that even my great-grandsons have died and passed on to the Courts of Hell already?" His eyes snapped back to me. "Now, why do you want to go to the Stadthuys?"

"I was just curious," I said. "When I was alive I was never allowed out of the house." He seemed satisfied by this, so I pressed on. "Did you say that the family mansions correspond to the same areas as they did in life?"

"Eh? Yes, by and large. Although there are some who were poor in life but were assiduous about burning funeral offerings, so that they're now rich in the afterlife. But as soon as someone departs for the courts, then their possessions here vanish as well. Were you planning on visiting someone?"

I couldn't resist the temptation. "I had a friend who was married to the Pan family and had a young daughter, but she died soon after."

"*Hm*, an old merchant family. I don't recall anyone from there recently." My face fell, and he gave a dry cackle. "Don't give up hope, the womenfolk are often secluded. She may yet be there. I think they have one or two houses still in the merchant quarter."

I cast my eyes down to hide the sudden beating of my heart. Was it possible that my mother was still here? A shiver ran over me, rendering me deaf to the old man's querulous voice.

"I said, how did you die?" he repeated. "I want to know all about you, so young and pretty." The loose skin on his throat trembled like a turkey's wattle.

"I fell," I said hastily. "It was dark and I slipped on the stairs."

He looked disappointed. "Did anyone push you?"

"Perhaps. My cousin was very jealous of me. We were both interested in the same young man." I hurried on, describing the horse-faced girl to him and the paroxysms of jealousy we had both suffered over an unnamed beau. That at least was true enough. Partway through I paused. "Are all the old Malacca families represented here?"

"Yes, even some whose line has already died out." He named a few and I listened carefully, satisfied when I heard him mention Lim. So it would probably be fairly easy to find Lim Tian Ching's abode.

"Go on, then," said the old man with a leer. "Tell me about your cousin. Did you fight with her?"

I thought quickly, "Oh yes, we really set to it one day. We rolled around on the bed and tore each other's clothes to shreds with our teeth. But tell me, now that we are here in the Plains of the Dead, does anyone have special escorts? I heard that you could bribe the border officials." My voice faltered, fearing I was asking too many questions.

"Nonsense! Nobody can bribe the border officials." He regarded me with suspicion, so much so that I hastily took my leave. Even then, he pursued me down the length of the street before I managed to shake off the lecherous creature. The old man had appeared harmless, almost mad in fact, but I wondered uneasily whether he had merely been toying with me. Well, there was no use fretting over it. At least I had a good idea where Lim Tian Ching might be found.

After backtracking for a while, I headed toward the merchant quarter. That was where the Lim mansion was and, likely, some semblance of my own ancestral home as well. Almost angrily, I debated with myself. Time was short and I really ought to go to the Lim mansion, yet I hesitated, thinking of my mother's face, a face that I had dreamed of often but could never recall. She had never had her portrait painted while she was alive. It had been so long since she had left me that I no longer knew whether the memories I had of her were my own or merely conjured from tales told by Amah. I turned Chendana's head toward my own neighborhood. I would pass by and see what sort of dwelling existed here. It wouldn't take long, I told myself. Just a few moments, that was all.

. . . .

THE STREETS BECAME INCREASINGLY familiar in a strange way. Parts of them looked nothing like what I remembered, yet there was a spatial recognition, some trick of proportion that sang out to me. In some places where there ought to have been buildings, there was nothing but old trees and rocks; in others, there were three or four fine dwellings occupying the same spot. And of course, everything was much farther apart, as though the original streets had been stretched to twice or even thrice their width and length. On one corner, which in the real Malacca held only the shell of a decaying house, there was a grand mansion. From behind the imposing gates came the faint sound of laughter and women's voices. I shuddered as I passed. Despite the gaiety, I couldn't help remembering what that house looked like in the living world, with its roof fallen in and the wild grass breaking up the cracked stone floors. There had been tales about that house ever since I was a child. Some said that a plague had killed all the inhabitants. Others that the last master of the house had gone mad and butchered his wives and concubines, laying their bodies out in the courtyard until the stones ran purple with old blood. As a child I had avoided that house, my head full of frightening tales told by Amah. Now, seeing it as it might have been in its days of glory, I felt terrified yet drawn to it. What would happen if I knocked upon those doors? With an effort I pulled myself away. Curiosity was my besetting sin, I told myself.

As we reached the corner before my house, my throat tightened. Something whispered to me that if I wanted to remain among the living, these things were better left unknown. Yet I pressed onward stubbornly. I wanted to see my mother. How wrong could that be? At first glance, the curving wall that surrounded our house looked exactly the same, but when I reached the front I had a surprise. There were three houses on the site. Each house occupied the same space with no overlap. I stared until my head began to swim. It was some trick that I could not fathom, yet no matter how I peered from the corners of my eyes, I still saw three dwellings.

The first was a grand mansion, somewhat in the style of our home in Malacca, but far more imposing. The ponderous front doors were twice the height they should have been and from behind the serried walled courtyards I could see the upper balconies rising like monoliths. It was as though my home had, in some nightmarish manner, grown like a fungus overnight. Despite the size and splendor, there was an air of decay about it, as though it had begun to crumble from within. The second house was a medium-sized abode in far better condition. It was like a child's drawing of a house, serviceable and sturdy but with no pretensions to grandeur. The third was barely a house. It was very much like Fan's dwelling: a little box, crudely made and roughly finished with a narrow door and mean dark windows. I hesitated before my choices, then dismounted. The second appeared the most welcoming, so I walked up to its front door. As I did so, the other houses melted away into the periphery of my vision. I knocked, but there was no answer. Just as I tried again, I heard a harsh voice call out from the side.

"What do you want? She's gone, and good riddance too!"

CHAPTER 22

I PEERED AT the door and windows, but the voice called out to me again. "Here! On the other side!" Obediently, I retreated until the trio of houses appeared again and then I saw her. Leaning out of the narrow doorway of the smallest house was a frowsy, elderly woman. Like Fan, she too wore funeral attire, though her clothes were faded and worn. Her cheeks, once plump, had fallen into hanging pouches and two lines were etched disagreeably from the corners of her nose to her mouth. Her eyes, however, were sharp, stabbing into me like embroidery needles.

"Are you talking to me, Auntie?" I said politely.

"Whom else would I be talking to? If you're looking for her, she's long gone."

"Who lives in this house?"

"You don't know and yet you go knocking on doors?"

"I was seeking a friend. Someone said she might be living in this quarter."

The woman looked at me contemptuously. "I don't believe you."

My face burned. "If you don't wish to help me, I'll bid you good day, then." I began to retrace my steps, fuming at her rude behavior. Why did ghosts behave like this in the Plains of the Dead? They seemed to have forgotten every civility, the genteel codes of respect that bound our society.

"Huffy, aren't you? I didn't say I wouldn't help you. Just that I don't believe you."

"What don't you believe?"

"That you're looking for a friend. A friend! When you're the spitting image of her!"

I turned in surprise. "Who are you referring to?"

"Why that hussy. That whore!"

The woman disengaged herself from the doorway and took a few steps toward me. Her frame, once large and heavy, now sagged as though it had been stuffed unevenly with lumps of hard cotton. "Surprised?" she asked. "You never would have guessed from the way she looked. Daughter-in-law of the Pan family, indeed!"

I opened my mouth but no sound came out. The woman ignored me, her words spilling from her as though they had been pent up for decades as, indeed, they might have been. "Coming here to look for your precious mother, is that right? I'm sure your father told you nothing but good things about her. He was always a weak, foolish boy." I flinched as though she had slapped me. How quickly she had penetrated my anonymity!

"I know all about you," she said, a thin smile stretching her lips. "Even when you were in her womb. I'm your grandfather's third concubine. You should be addressing me as 'Grandmother,' or haven't you any manners?" She drew closer and I stepped back. "It wasn't easy, being the third concubine, you know! The other women in the household were so jealous of me when he brought me in. Not his wife. She'd given up by then, but the first and second concubines made my life miserable. But all I had to do was get a son by him. His other sons had died except for your father, and I knew what he was— weak!" She stopped for a moment, regarding me with a triumphant air.

I blurted out, "I don't think I've ever heard of you."

It was quite possibly the worst thing I could have said. If she had been irritable before, she was absolutely enraged now. What did I mean, I had never heard of her? How dare I disrespect my ancestors? I retreated down the path, beaten back by her vitriol, but seeing that I was about to leave, she mastered herself into some semblance of reason.

"Oh, but I have so much to tell you," she said. "Don't you want to know more about your mother?" At this I stopped, hating myself at the same time for falling for her tricks. "At least you should have the courtesy to stop a moment instead of running off with no manners."

The problem with the dead was that they all wanted someone to listen to them. Each ghost I had encountered had a story that it was only too ready to share. Maybe it got lonely in the afterlife. Or perhaps those who lingered longest were the ones who could not bear to give up. Something told me that I might regret listening to this woman, but I couldn't help myself. "What is it you want to tell me?"

"Changed your mind, then?" She smiled unpleasantly. "Well, some company is better than none, I suppose! Your family has neglected me shamefully. I still get a little stipend now and then when they burn incense for the ancestors, but it's not very much, is it?" She gestured at the mean little house behind her. "And your grandfather promised to bury me in the family lot. But I showed him. I got my revenge even from beyond the grave."

"What are you talking about?"

"I've been waiting for years for someone else from your family to come along. The last person was your mother. But then she wouldn't talk to me afterward." She darted a swift glance at me.

"I came to see my mother," I said. "If she's gone, there's no reason for me to stay."

"Oh, but she's not gone far. Don't you want to find her?" I had assumed my mother had passed on to the Courts of Hell, but the woman was smiling again. "Sit down," she said. "I want to tell you a story.

"You have to understand that I wasn't always so unpleasant to look at. Once I was a fresh young girl like you. Pretty enough for your grandfather to choose as a concubine, though I was just a servant at the time in his friend's house. Your grandfather didn't know that I already had a secret lover, the second son of the house. When I became pregnant, I thought my lover would surely marry me or take me as a concubine. But he abandoned me. He wanted someone better. Oh, I was filled with grief and jealousy! Who was it, this woman who had stolen him from me? A young lady, he said. Daughter of the Lee family, not a servant like me."

I winced, recognizing my mother's maiden name, and the old woman laughed. "I see you understand where this is going. My lover made me get rid of the baby. He said that *she* would never marry him if he had a bastard. Do you know what it's like to have a child torn from your body? I screamed so much that I couldn't speak for days. After it was over, my lover arranged for me to become your grandfather's concubine. The old man was besotted enough not to notice I wasn't a virgin. I didn't want him, but I had no choice. But my lover didn't get what he wanted either. Your mother turned him down. She wouldn't marry him—oh no! He was only the second son after all, so he married her cousin instead.

"By that time I had other troubles. All I needed was a son to secure my position, but I couldn't get pregnant again. I thought maybe your grandfather was too old, so I decided to get a child by some other means. Your father was a handsome young man then, but no matter what I did, he ignored me. Finally I cornered him, but the fool only stammered and wept. He was in love with someone else. Of course, it was your mother.

"How do you think I felt then? That woman took everyone from me, one after the other." The old concubine's face was raw with emotion. Shame burned my cheeks. I didn't want to hear any more but I was frozen. "She married him—why not? He was the only son of a rich family. That snake pretended she knew nothing of what had happened, but I wasn't fooled. And I still couldn't get a child. I wanted a baby—my baby that I had lost to the abortionist. I couldn't bear it!"

Her voice rose in a howl, so painful that I cringed, but she hissed at me. "One day I brushed past her on the upper landing. She put her hand over her belly and I knew. Your father was behind her and he said with a foolish smile, 'We're having a baby.' I couldn't control myself. I flew at her and we struggled on the stairs. In that instant, your father lunged forward and grabbed her. She was safe. I fell all the way down and broke my neck at the foot of the main staircase.

"Oh, you needn't look so horrified! I'm sure nobody in your household ever mentioned this to you. They said it was an accident. But if your father hadn't brushed past me to snatch her back, maybe I wouldn't have fallen. They made a hasty funeral for me. Your grandfather burned some grave goods, but after a year or so he simply stopped. So you see, I had plenty of reasons to be angry with your family.

"The first few years after I died, I spent all my time spying on the world of the living. I passed through the house so often that in the end they exorcised me. There was a cook who could see ghosts. He was the one who went to the master and said that my unquiet spirit was in the house. So I had to come back here, to this hovel in the Plains of the Dead. And I waited. I was young when my life ended. Only twenty-one, the same age as your mother. I know, I don't look like it anymore. That's because I traded it. There are ways to get around everything. I found a demon who ate the essence out of my spirit body. And in return he sent the smallpox to your house.

"Your mother and grandfather succumbed quickly, though your father survived. Can you imagine the looks on their faces when they arrived here and found me waiting? But they didn't stay. No, they didn't. Your grandfather was only here a few years and then he was called on to the courts for judgment. And your mother? Well, she's still around but can't bear to live in the house your father burned for her. Never accepts her spirit offerings, or anything like that. She's gone to be a whore in someone else's house. Anything to get away from me."

THERE WAS A DULL pain in my chest, a squeezing breathlessness. My head rang with the echoes of her story. I wished I'd never gone to look for my mother. All I had found was a monstrous tale of old sins and deep bitterness. With difficulty, I controlled my voice.

"Why didn't you send the smallpox to your lover, who made you lose your child in the first place?"

She lifted her brows. "It's none of your business what I chose to do. In the end, everyone who's ever crossed me will pay for it. You're upset about your precious mother. Well, let me tell you just where she went and what a good, kind person she is."

Instinctively I shrank back.

"That's right," she said. "When I told her what I'd done, she went straight off to the household of my lover. Oh, he's not dead yet. In fact, he's still in the world of the living. She probably thought I deserved whatever I had suffered at his hands and went to live with his family, no doubt to plot some revenge against me. That's where she is—a kept woman in the Lim family mansion!"

I had thought that nothing she said could shock me more than her earlier revelations, but I was wrong. "The Lim family?"

"That was your mother's revenge on me. Stupid woman! As though I care what she does with herself." She opened her mouth as though to unleash another tirade, and for the second time that day I fled.

The Lim family. All paths led back to their door. Our destinies seemed darkly tangled, and for the first time I considered the burden of the Buddhist Wheel of reincarnation. Groaning beneath its weight, individual lives were forced to play out a farce time and time again. The image of the Anglican church in Malacca rose before my eyes together with its green and quiet graveyard. When I died, I thought, I would rather rest there undisturbed than continue like that old concubine, eaten up by her schemes of vengeance from beyond the grave. But what did I really know about anything? My world had been turned upside down.

CHAPTER 23

FOR SOME TIME I let Chendana wander at will, not caring what path she chose. I clung to her back, hugging my thin pajama top and wondering how this dead version of Malacca had become so cold. A breeze blew unceasingly, at first barely noticeable but over time wearing down my defenses until I shivered uncontrollably. Little things began to fall into place. I remembered Madam Lim telling me in her soft voice, when I first went to her house, that she and my mother were cousins of some sort. The general air of gloom in our family, which I had attributed solely to my mother's death, must have held lingering echoes of the death of the Third Concubine, Old Wong and Amah's dislike of our main staircase, and everyone's reluctance to speak of the past. I remembered the pitying glances of other amahs when Amah took me out as a child. Now it occurred to me that they might have seen me as an unlucky creature, born of a household plagued by ill fortune. As for the Third Concubine's lover, I had little doubt as to who that might be. Lim Teck Kiong, father of my tormentor Lim Tian Ching and false friend to my father. It seemed that he had never ceased meddling in our affairs.

Tears streamed from my eyes and dried in the wind. I didn't know what I felt sorrier for—my father's years of grief, the unmasking of my childish fancies, or even the Third Concubine's wasted life and her wicked schemes. All I could fix upon now was to go to the Lim family mansion in this ghostly world. There, I must surely find some of the answers to my questions. And I might see my mother, although I had begun to dread that meeting. The kind, gentle mother that Amah had fostered in my blurred memories might turn out to be another virago.

My visit to the Third Concubine had consumed almost all the daylight, and the drop in temperature seemed to correspond with the number of figures of the dead that I glimpsed, hurrying here and there on the gloomy streets. These bleak emanations might have stemmed from the ghosts themselves, for there had been little evidence of such a chill upon the grasslands the night before. It was as though with the dimming of the light, the icy breath of the grave grew stronger.

I now had a good sense of where the Lim mansion might be and Chendana set off at a brisk trot. We passed through endless streets and wide boulevards, far more than the real Malacca ever possessed. The distance was interminable, the rows of darkened houses eerily expectant. At last we drew up in front of an imposing gate. If I had thought that any of the homes in my family's ghostly neighborhood were grand, this put them all to shame. A great wall, almost ten feet high, surrounded it. The doors alone were massive, yawing upward into dark shadows that were barely pierced by a pair of gate lanterns. This was no mansion. It was an estate. For long moments I hesitated, struck by the sudden fear that the gates would be manned by more ox-headed demons, but then I remembered that Fan said they rarely came here, and I plucked up my courage. At worst, it might be no more than one of those silent automatons. I slid off Chendana's back and let the great iron door knocker fall with a clatter.

There was a long silence as the echoes died away, then slowly, the great gates opened. A pale face peered out. It was a manservant, dressed in old-fashioned livery. I was surprised to see that he was a human ghost and not one of those puppetlike servants. His eyes swiveled around the empty street, then rested upon me.

"What do you want?" he asked.

"I—I'm looking for . . . " I stammered. Fool that I was, I had been so intent on the revelations of the day and the pressing need to get to the Lim mansion that I had completely forgotten to think of some pretext for entry.

"For work?" he barked. "You're late. Didn't they tell you to go to the side entrance, not the main door?" Then he paused. "Or perhaps you mean the other kind of work." Leaning forward, he brought a lantern up to my face and examined it closely.

"I heard you needed a kitchen maid," I said quickly.

He gave me a long leer. "If you ask me, you'd be wasted there. The master's been looking for new concubines. They don't need you in the kitchen with so many puppet servants."

"You mean, those manikins burned as funeral offerings?"

"Hush your mouth! We don't talk about funerals here. Nobody wants to be reminded about his death. We call them puppet-men. And to the master, don't refer to them at all. He doesn't like them. Any pauper can have a puppet servant or two. Even I have one! That's why at the great houses they hire human ghosts as staff."

"If you have your own servant, why are you working here?" I asked.

"Same reason as you, sweetheart. Not enough funeral money burned for me. But why waste yourself in the kitchen?" His eyes fastened on me greedily and I began to feel afraid. "I could use a wife myself."

I shrank back, glancing into the shadows where I had left Chendana out of sight. If I had to, I would rather pretend to be a candidate for Lim Tian Ching's harem than be accosted by this gatekeeper. At least I would stand a better chance of getting farther into the house. But another voice rang out from within.

"Who's there? Why have you left the gate open?"

The gatekeeper turned sullenly to face another retainer who had appeared at the entrance. "I was just giving her directions. She wanted to go to the kitchen."

"The wrong door, eh?" The second man, older and more heavyset, turned to me. "Now then, who are you?"

I cast my eyes down, mumbling that I had heard there was an opening for a kitchen maid.

"You can do better than that," he said. "In fact, the master will be pleased to see one like you."

I began a tale about having pledged true love to my fiancé, but he sighed and cut me off. "Never mind. I've heard this kind of thing before. I'm sure you'll change your mind after twenty years in the kitchen. If you have a change of heart, let me know. I'm the steward here. Make sure to address me politely when you see me."

I trailed after him, avoiding the baleful glare of the gatekeeper. "Sir, I have a few possessions still outside."

He barely turned his head. "I'm sure you do. Some grave goods and such. You can collect them later." And so, thankful that I had told Chendana to hide until I came back for her, I crossed the threshold of the Lim mansion.

WE WALKED A LONG way, down endless corridors and through count-less courtyards. I glimpsed echoing expanses of silent banquet halls and felt a shiver course down my spine. I had been here before in my dreams, those suffocating nightmares when I had been forced to wander these halls night after night and admire Lim Tian Ching's wealth. Though puppet servants still stood blankly at attention, there were also a number of human ghosts. Some were dressed as servants, but others appeared to be guests or residents of the house. They wore the same kind of stiff, gaudy attire that I had seen Lim Tian Ching wear, which gave the whole scene an antique air. Feeling like a complete nonentity, I scurried behind the steward with a lowered head.

After a while, the surroundings became more utilitarian. "Don't expect to come in through the main gate again," the steward said curtly without break-ing his stride. "You're lucky I happened to pass by when I did."

We were now rapidly approaching an outbuilding from which the clang of pots and sounds of shouted orders became discernible. It was a homely cacophony, so unexpectedly like the world of the living that I was surprised to find a lump in my throat. It had been only two days since I had passed into the realm of the dead, but already I longed for the noise and clatter, the living air of my own Malacca. The kitchen was a vast hall filled with servants and steam. Rows of dishes were laid out, many arranged elaborately like spirit offerings. There were a number of puppet servants, all busy chopping, frying, and steaming this bounty. If this had been a real kitchen, the smell of oil heating, garlic and ginger being pounded, and fish frying would have assailed my nostrils, but the smells here were muted. I had to sniff hard to tease them out. The steward spoke to a large, paunchy human ghost who was in charge. After a brief conversation, he beckoned me over.

"This is the new girl."

"Too dainty. I can't use her. Send her upstairs."

"She doesn't want to do that kind of work," said the steward significantly.

"I don't need another kitchen maid."

"If you please, sir," I ventured. "I can also serve and wait."

"There you go," said the steward. "Use her as waitstaff. They can always do with more humans on show."

The cook looked at me skeptically. "I have enough puppet waiters. At least they don't spill soup on people. I can't afford another mistake like that again."

The steward rolled his eyes. "Do as you will. If you can't use her, send her to housekeeping, then."

When he had left, the cook regarded me with a raised brow. He had small cunning eyes above a broad, squashed nose with flaring nostrils. It was unfortunate that he was so fat. His corpulence only served to accentuate his resemblance to a pig, especially when he sank his jowly chin into his neck to regard me.

"All right," he said after an awkward silence. "I'll give you a trial. But don't come crying to me if it doesn't work out. You shouldn't be here at all and you know it."

I blanched, wondering if my covert mission was so easily discerned. But he went on to say, "The steward talks tough but has a soft heart for young girls like you. He left a daughter behind, about your age, I think. Otherwise you really should be auditioning for the master's bedchamber." He laughed coarsely and I shrank even further into myself. "Nah, don't worry. I said you can have a trial here. But if you don't suit, then it's off with you. Plenty of ghosts wanting work nowadays, especially since this household is doing so well."

I bobbed my head, thinking of an alias. "Thank you. My name is—"

He cut me off with a dismissive gesture. "Don't bother. We don't use names here." Seeing my eyes widen, he shook his head. "You must have just died. Listen, all of us here came because we had descendants or some family member who bothered to burn offerings to us. We're technically the privileged ones, who can spend some time enjoying the fruits of filial piety before going on to judgment at the courts. But some of us end up working as servants out of boredom or necessity. Still, we don't use our true names, understand? My grandchildren want to think that I'm enjoying an afterlife of leisure here and I want to preserve that illusion. So no names."

"But how would they know what you were doing here anyway?"

"*Cheh!* Of course they don't know, but we don't like to think about them getting wind of it through some spiritualist or medium. You never know what sort of information leaks out. Anyway, for our own pride, we don't mention it."

I nodded obediently, wondering again at this ghost world, which seemed to have so many of the vices and failings of life.

"So you can be girl number six."

"Number six?"

"Yes, there were five before you. Don't ask me what happened to them. Now, go over there and start preparing that fish. I want to see you clean and steam it Teochew-style. Understand?"

He gestured to a shining pile of pomfret, their silvery bellies slick and plump. I often helped Old Wong in the kitchen, though I was mostly relegated to menial tasks like pinching the roots off bean sprouts and cleaning squid. Occasionally, however, he let me prepare dishes. Now I carefully slit a fish open to remove the guts. To my surprise, however, there was nothing inside at all—only a hollow space. Setting the knife down, I examined it thoroughly. It looked like a fish, and felt like one, right down to the slippery flesh, but when I brought it to my nose there was no smell at all, not even the clean salt tang of the ocean. Over my shoulder I heard a burst of laughter.

"Never seen a fish like this before, have you?" said the cook. "They're pretend fish, just like all this food isn't real food either. There's very little taste, so that's why the kitchen is so important. We have to do our best to make it palatable."

"But I thought that offerings had flavor," I said.

"Oh, they taste fine when they're fresh and received when you're in the world of the living," said the cook. "But when you cross over into the plains they seem to lose all savor. That's why a lot of the dead like to go visit their old haunts from time to time. Ah, it's been a long time since I had some freshly made *pie tee*, or a bowl of *assam laksa*." He stared off into the distance for a moment. "The *pie tee* my mother made was so delicious. The outside was crisp and the turnip-and-prawn filling sweet yet toothsome. She used to arrange them on a plate so that they looked just like tiny, crunchy top hats. And the chili sauce! My mother was famous for her chili sauce, which she pounded every morning and mixed with vinegar, garlic, and sugar."

Listening to him reminisce made my mouth water. I had to close it to prevent myself from drooling, and for the first time since I had arrived in the Plains of the Dead, I became aware of a dull hunger. This was not good. Er Lang had specifically warned me against eating spirit food. I bent over the fish and rinsed it in a clean bowl of water. Then I selected a shallow metal pan from a large stack of pans while the cook watched me expressionlessly with his small piggy eyes. I broke off a knob of ginger, peeled, sliced, and arranged it on the dish. After placing the cleaned pomfret on top, I added sliced tomatoes, then looked around.

"The sour plums are over there," he said flatly.

Under his watchful eye, I fished out four or five plums preserved in brine and laid them on the fish. Using my fingers, I mashed them to spread their soft flesh like a paste.

"Why so many? What a waste!" he barked at me.

"I thought I should add more because there's so little taste," I said.

He nodded in satisfaction. "At least you have some brains. Remember, everything here has to be highly spiced, sometimes even double or triple what you used to use before you passed over. Otherwise the guests will complain. All right. You can stop now."

My arms were leaden and my shoulders ached with weariness. The cook was still talking and I had to concentrate to follow his rapid instructions.

"—so get your things. You can sleep in the servants' quarters tonight. There are no other serving girls right now, so you'll have your own room for the moment. Now hurry up. I want you in here early tomorrow morning when the fires are lit."

I looked up at him, dazed. "How will I find my way?"

"Didn't you hear me? I'll send a puppet servant out with you. You can get your grave goods and other belongings. Store them in your own room and don't bring them into the main house. They don't need your cheap clutter here. Tired, are you? It's the air of the plains. It takes some getting used to when you first get here. Go on with you, then," he said.

An expressionless manikin had glided up beside him and now it took off swiftly. I supposed it was to be my guide and hurried to catch up. Lit only by dim sconces, the low, narrow passages closed in upon me like a nightmare. My guide was also horribly familiar. I had seen that bland face repeated twenty times over on various puppet servitors around the house. It walked with no need for light, silent except for the occasional loud, papery rustle. I did not speak to it—though it was formed in the semblance of a man, I could not think of it as having a gender—and it paid no more mind to me than if I had been a stray dog. Soon we arrived at a walled garden with a small bolted gate. This, presumably, was one of the back doors that the gatekeeper had mentioned. I had little time to wonder at my surroundings, however, for my guide trotted rapidly along the outer rim of the wall until we approached the main gate from the outside. Then it stopped.

"I'll just get my things, then," I said.

The creature gave no sign of comprehension, but since it was clearly waiting, I hastened to find Chendana. To my relief, she was still concealed in the shadows. I had asked her to hide when I had first approached the gate hours ago, and part of my anxiety since then had been over her safety, even though I remembered Fan's words about how no one else could tamper with your grave goods unless you gave them away. Aware of my silent guide, I took her bridle and led her back with me.

Our reentry into the Lim mansion was surprisingly easy. Perhaps it was because we came through the servants' entrance, but there was no one around to comment on my horse. The puppet servant led me to a series of low out-buildings that stood behind the kitchens. These were obviously the servants' quarters for human ghosts like myself, for piles of bedding and other sundries were laid out. Across the way I could see lights and hear men's voices, but the women's quarters were silent and dark. Leading me to a small room at the end, my guide opened the door and with a stiff jerk of its head, motioned me in.

"Where are the kitchens?" I asked, anxious that I should find my way in the morning. Another swivel and it pointed to the bulk of a building, just visible in the gloom. Then it walked off. I was so tired that I stumbled into the low-ceilinged, dark room. Obviously intended as dormitory housing for three or four servants, it was now empty and lit only by the fitful flicker of an oil lamp left by the puppet servant. I'd meant to leave Chendana outside, but the room depressed me, so not caring about propriety, I led my little horse inside. She had to duck to fit through the doorway, but her neat familiar form made me feel much better. Dragging a pallet out, I threw myself down into oblivion.

CHAPTER 24

I WOKE TO the sounds of clanging and scraping. It was still dark, but from the narrow window I could see a faint lightening of the sky. Recalling the cook's injunction to go to the kitchen when the fires were lit, I jumped up hastily. I patted Chendana's nose, grateful again that she was not a real horse and could be left waiting indefinitely for me. Not wishing to draw attention to her, however, I backed her into the darkest corner of the room and pulled a bamboo screen, meant to divide the servants' sleeping quarters, in front of her.

The sounds I heard turned out to be two puppet servants who stood outside the back door of the kitchen sluicing down large cooking pots with buckets of water. They ignored me, so I brushed past them into the large kitchen. The fires in the numerous charcoal stoves were already lit, and I had barely time to take note of my surroundings before the cook pounced on me. "You're still here."

"You told me to come in the morning," I said.

"So I did. Didn't really expect you, though."

"Why not?"

"Ah, girls, you know. Flighty. Didn't think you'd care much for the lodging."

I blinked, realizing that most ghosts who had funeral offerings probably had their own houses and might well turn up their noses at such shabby accommodations. "It's all right," I said cautiously.

"Then get started."

I SOON REALIZED THAT the cook didn't need my help for any of the menial tasks such as plucking chickens, washing vegetables, or scouring pots. He had plenty of puppet servants to do that. Instead, he used me to relay orders, keep an eye on the puppet servants, and most important, help him taste and season the dishes. Breakfast was being prepared for an unnamed number of guests, and we were busy with cauldrons of rice congee laced with sliced raw fish, fried fritters, and scores of soft-boiled eggs nestled in little bowls with soy sauce and pepper. It was when I was directing a puppet servant to make *kaya* toast that I really felt tempted to eat. The thick slices of bread were toasted over a bed of charcoal on a wire net until they turned crisply golden. When done, they were smeared lavishly with butter and *kaya*, a custard-like jam made from caramelized eggs, sugar, and *pandan* leaves. Unthinkingly, I brought a smeared finger to my lips, then stopped, reminded of Er Lang's injunction. With a stab of panic, I realized that I had no way of knowing how long I'd have to stay here or how much time had passed in the real world. Er Lang had said that time often passed at a different rate in the Plains of the Dead, and my anxious thoughts flew back to my comatose body, so far away from me.

"You don't have to frown so much. Breakfast is almost done." The cook's voice made me jump. "*Aiya*, such a pampered miss like you. Just give up. Go home."

"I'm fine."

He gave me a skeptical glance. "Anyway, my other helper should be back tomorrow."

"Your other helper?"

"You don't think I do this by myself all the time, do you? She's the one who usually helps supervise the puppets, but she ran afoul of the Second Wife and got boiling soup thrown on her. That woman is really a piece of work. Pretty as they come, but a bitch when she opens her mouth."

"Who is she?"

"The Second Wife? She's the old master's bit of skirt."

"I thought the master of this house was quite young."

"The old master was seventy-two when he died. You must be talking about the young master."

"How can there be two masters here? I thought that each home was burned as a funeral offering for an individual."

"Sure. But it doesn't mean they can't combine them. It's true that most of the wealth came with the young master when he passed over. But this was already a great house before. The old master is Lim Tian Ching's great-uncle. I don't know what happened to the grandfather. Probably already went on to the Courts of Hell. The Lim family's seat was represented by the great-uncle until the young man died. And what a fortune he brought! His parents spared no expense on his funeral, I tell you. In any case, his great-uncle and he joined households. More convenient, I suppose. But the young master is hardly here anyway."

Now that the breakfast rush was over, the cook ladled himself a steaming bowl of rice congee. He sprinkled cilantro and shredded ginger on top, and doused it with soy sauce and sesame oil. "What?" he said, catching my gaze. "You can eat too if you want. No shortage of food here."

I drew a stool up near him and pretended to pick at a fritter. "Is he here now?"

"Why do you want to know?"

"I'm just curious. I heard he's young, about my age."

"Want to marry him?"

"What? Oh no!"

The cook laughed coarsely. "Come off it. There are marriages arranged in the spirit world everyday. And your fiancé won't even have to know about it."

I shook my head vigorously, but the cook mistook my agitation for shyness. "You might change your mind. He's quite a catch."

"Isn't he married already?"

"Who? The young master? Not yet, though they were making arrangements just the other day. A whole banquet hall done up with red lanterns and lots of food."

I blanched, remembering the dream in which I had found myself alone with Lim Tian Ching in that spectral hall of red lanterns. That was where he had pressed me about the marriage and I had fled, forcing myself awake through the coiling mists of his dreamworld. But the cook was chattering away.

"It was supposed to be an engagement party. He was in a terrible temper after that, though. I think the bride didn't show up."

"She didn't?" I asked faintly.

"If you ask me, I heard she was still alive. Can you imagine the cheek of that fellow? Even the Judges of Hell don't take too kindly to such marriages. Oh, they might make an exception if the deceased and the living were in love, but in general it just proved to everyone how much favor Lim Tian Ching has curried with them."

I pricked my ears up at this. "How is he on such good terms with them?"

"Beats me." He placed one finger on the side of his nose and gave me a sly grin. "I'll say no more, though, if I want to keep my place. Ah, the rich get richer and the poor get trampled down. It was the same when I was alive." The cook had emptied his bowl of porridge and pushed himself away from the table. "Since you're here, go and take some breakfast to my assistant. I'd send a puppet but they're busy right now."

He glanced at the courtyard where three puppet servants were busily butchering an enormous pig. Unlike a real pig, however, it stood motionless while the manikins dismembered it. Even as they carved off hams and shoulders, the pig showed no reaction. Neither did it bleed. As I watched, one of the servants whacked off the heavy head, leaving it blinking placidly on the flagstones. Suppressing a shudder, I picked up a tray with a bowl of congee and a teapot.

"Her room is close to yours, but it's a single, not a dormitory," said the cook. "Hurry up! I want you back here so that we can start lunch."

I made my way out through the courtyard, averting my eyes from the bloodless porcine slaughter that was still going on. Even if Er Lang hadn't warned me against eating food here, this would have permanently put me off. Unlike the food that Old Wong had offered me, this pig must have been a paper funeral effigy. No wonder the cook here complained constantly about tastelessness. As I wended my way to the servants' quarters, I concentrated on not spilling the scalding porridge. My wrists began to ache and I began to understand why the cook had been so dismissive of me initially. No doubt it took strength to carry the food such great distances to the banquet halls. When I reached my quarters, I glanced around. Last night it had been so dark that I hadn't noticed any other inhabitants, but spotting another door, I made my way toward it.

It was silent in the courtyard, and the light had a blank brightness so that the shadows lay on the paving stones like crisp paper cutouts. Setting the tray down, I knocked cautiously. The stillness convinced me that no one was there, so I was startled to hear a voice call out.

"Who are you?"

I sighed. In my brief existence parted from my flesh, I was invariably greeted with a lack of ceremony. Perhaps it was less a function of this ghost world than that I was now a wandering spirit, no better than a beggar, really.

"I'm the new girl," I said. "I've brought your breakfast."

The door opened and a tiny old woman came out. At first glance I was startled, so striking was her resemblance to Amah. She too had a birdlike figure, bright dark eyes, and gray hair scraped into a bun. A closer look, however, revealed that her features were different. The eyes larger, the nose a little higher. Still, like Amah, she was dressed in the ubiquitous black-and-white uniform and the general impression, coupled with age, was remarkably similar. She could have been Amah's older sister. As I got over my shock, I realized that the old woman was also staring at me.

"What's your name?" she asked.

"I'm girl number six," I said, remembering the cook's injunction against names.

"But who is your family?"

"My surname is Chen," I said, cursing the perpetual nosiness of old ladies. The last thing I wanted was for rumors of my background to get around to the owner of this house.

"Chen . . ." she said. "I wonder whether you're related to any of my friends?"

"Oh, probably not, Auntie," I said, addressing her politely. "My family was from Negri Sembilan. We just moved to Malacca before I died."

She nodded absently. "There's a folding table inside. Can you bring it out for me?"

I glanced down, registering that her forearms were wrapped in bandages. "What happened to you, Auntie?"

"It's nothing. Just some burns." Catching my eye, her mouth quirked. "Injuries heal here faster than in the living world."

"Does it hurt?"

"Yes, but as there's no infection here, there's no risk of gangrene. After all, we're already dead."

This was the second time she had alluded to death in our brief conversation, and it seemed contrary to the general aversion to talking about one's demise among the ghosts.

"It must have been a bad accident," I said.

She snorted. "Accident? The Second Wife threw soup at me. She was in one of her moods the other day. You'd do well to stay away from her."

I went inside and brought out a rickety folding table and stool. It was a room far smaller than mine, though my quarters were, of course, designed as a dormitory for multiple servants. Though threadbare, it was scrupulously clean. There was nothing but a sleeping pallet, a wooden chest, and a few neatly folded clothes. Outside, I set up the table and stool with her breakfast.

"You don't have to wait on me," she said.

"I don't mind," I said truthfully. There was something about this old woman that made me feel comfortable. It might have been her resemblance to Amah, or simply that despite her initial wariness, she seemed friendly.

"The cook isn't too bad," she said as she began to eat. "He's a bit coarse, but he won't try to use you, unlike some others."

"How long have you been here?"

"A long time. It's hard to tell in this place. And you?"

I spun her the same story that I had given the cook about needing work and not having any place to stay. She nodded briefly. "If you want to stay in the kitchens and out of the master's bedchamber, you'd better run along now. The cook gets impatient. But don't worry, tell him that I'll be back at work soon."

I HASTENED BACK TO the kitchen, suddenly anxious about having been away for so long. I wanted to ask the old woman more about this mysterious Second Wife who had scalded her. In my heart, however, I had a sinking feeling that I knew who she was. Back in the kitchen, the carcass of the pig had already been disposed of into neatly butchered chunks. The head, thankfully, was nowhere to be seen; though, gazing at a few enormous pots, I hoped that the cook wouldn't ask me to lift their lids to stir. Fortunately, he was otherwise occupied. The lunch rush had already begun and he was shouting at the puppet servants who were washing, chopping, and stir-frying vigorously. I made my way timidly over to him and apologized for being late.

"Next time don't get lost," he said without glancing at me. Then, "How is she?"

"The old lady?"

"You can call her Auntie Three. Everyone does. She's the third one we've had, at least that I know of."

"She said she'd be able to work soon."

He turned. "At least she didn't go blind. I thought for sure the soup would scald her face."

"Why did she do it?"

"The Second Wife? No reason. Boredom maybe. She's like that. If she wasn't so beautiful I think the old master would have got rid of her a long time ago. But there's something about her. Maybe because I'm a man, but even I feel like I couldn't refuse her anything if she jumped into my bed." He gave a coarse laugh and told me to start checking the dishes. "That's usually Auntie Three's job. Let's see how well you do."

The next few days passed in a blur of activity. Though each morning I donned an amah's uniform of plain white blouse and black cotton trousers, I discovered that by evening I would be wearing my own clothes again. Perhaps this was because the uniform was only borrowed, unlike my pajamas that renewed themselves and reminded me that Amah was still caring for my body somewhere in the real Malacca. Nevertheless, I slipped Er Lang's scale into the pocket of whatever I wore. It was of no practical use here, but its cool weight gave me some comfort. The work in the kitchen was unendingly monotonous in the absence of smell. Without aroma, the food passed before me like wax models. I tried to press the cook for more information about the family, but he gave me only dribs and drabs. The steward would probably have been a better source, but he was always in a hurry when he came to the kitchen and ignored me. With only a few days left until I had promised to meet Fan, I regretted not taking some other job within the Lim household. If I were a waiter or a cleaner instead, I would have an excuse to eavesdrop in the main house. As it was, I felt a gnawing sense of frustration and anxiety with each passing day.

On the third day, Auntie Three came back to work despite the bandages on her hands. The cook was quite astonished to see her.

"Why so surprised?" she asked. "I told you I'd be back soon."

"Ya, well I didn't think you really meant it."

"What did you expect me to do? Sit in my room and look at the wall?"

He shrugged but insisted on seeing her arms.

"It's all healed, I tell you," she said, but when the cook peeled back one corner of the bandages, I winced at the sight. Her skin was flayed where she had been scalded, though the wounds were bloodless and absent any color or pus.

"I don't think you should be working yet," he said.

"If you're worried about *her*, I know how to keep out of her way," she said, turning away. I watched her birdlike movements with a mixture of pity and curiosity. That small, stubborn figure clad in black and white reminded me of Amah in so many ways that my homesickness was almost palpable.

MY CHANCE CAME TWO days later. During the evening meal, the steward suddenly appeared in the kitchen. "Another steamed fish, quick!" he hissed.

"What happened?"

"Puppet servant collided with another. Now we're missing a course, and the master has guests."

"Guests?" asked Auntie Three, coming up behind the cook.

The steward started at this interruption. "Oh, it's you. I'd ask you to serve but you know what happened last time. And she's not in a good mood tonight."

"What kind of guests?" asked Auntie Three again.

"You know," he said. A glance flickered between the three of them.

"None of the puppets here have been trained to wait on guests. Aren't there any others outside?" asked the cook.

"We're low on servers. Some of them were damaged during the last banquet and haven't been replaced yet."

"I'll do it," I said.

They turned to look at me. "No!" said Auntie Three, but she was interrupted by the steward.

"I forgot about you." He gave me a measured look. "Yes, you might do."

"She has no idea how to behave!"

"It's not so formal tonight. Only the old master is present. The young master is still away."

Pulse racing, I smoothed my apron and reiterated my willingness to serve.

"All right," said the steward at last. "But be quick! We're between courses and I asked the musicians to play first." Grasping my elbow, he propelled me out of the kitchen, muttering instructions. "The puppet servants will bring the food from the kitchen to the sideboard. I'll present the main dishes at the tables. You stand on the side to arrange individual portions and keep an eye on the puppet servants for me. This batch is unreliable. Hopefully, it won't be necessary for you to approach the tables. Understand?"

I nodded, then, fearing he could not see me in the dim corridor, added "Yes, sir" for good measure. I was itching to ask him who the guests were, but he looked so preoccupied that I held my tongue. The saving grace was that Lim Tian Ching, the young master, was not here, though by this point I was so desperate to do some spying that I might have braved his presence anyway. As we walked swiftly down the corridors, I kept my eyes open for possible hiding places. I had tried to sneak into the main house before, but the cook always locked the great kitchen door at night. Now that I was on the other side, perhaps I could find a place to conceal myself before he did so.

The banquet room was lit with dozens of oil lamps. A trio of puppet musicians was performing—two *er hu* players and one *yang qin* player accompanying them. The sight set a shiver through me. The last time I had seen live musicians had been at the Double Seventh Festival at the real Lim mansion in Malacca, and there we had been entertained by such a trio as well. As I well remembered, Tian Bai had been one of the musicians. What was it about this ghost world that seemed to create uncanny parallels with the living? I thought of Auntie Three in the kitchen and how much she reminded me of Amah, and wondered whether these coincidences were intentional or merely part of a peculiar synchronicity between the two places.

I had little time to reflect upon this before I was hustled to a serving station by the steward. The guests were in the midst of eating and I could see by the stacks of dishes on the sideboards that it was a lengthy feast. Hissing some final instructions to me, the steward hastily made his way to the largest table with a steamed fish. He set it upon the table with a flourish and deftly deboned it for the waiting diners with much smiling and bowing. This must be the head table, I decided, for him to serve them first, and I craned my head to see its occupants. There were ten figures seated there: two of them enormous enough to dwarf the other diners. With a sinking sensation, I recognized the humped, hulking form and sweeping tines of an ox-headed demon.

CHAPTER 25

I TOLD MYSELF it didn't matter. They wouldn't notice me, hidden as I was at the back and dressed in a drab uniform. Still, my hands trembled as I carried out my tasks. I didn't think that they were the same creatures that I had seen stationed outside my house. Those had been lowly foot soldiers, while these two had an air of command. I hoped they might not know me by sight. Preoccupied with my racing thoughts, I suddenly realized that I had allowed a couple of puppet servers to wander aimlessly around the room.

The steward shot daggers at me with his eyes but it was too late. One of the puppet servers stumbled against the nearest ox-headed demon. With a snarl, it turned and bit off the server's arm, spitting it out on the floor. It happened so fast that I had barely time to blink. There was a moment's hush in the room, then conversation resumed as though nothing had happened. The puppet server was now aimlessly rotating on the spot while its severed arm twitched spasmodically like an insect on the marble floor. The steward, still in the midst of serving the steamed fish, cast an agonized glance at me. I thought about sending another puppet to fetch it back, but dared not do so. Keeping my head down, I made my way swiftly around the room and steered the damaged server back to the side.

"Stay there," I whispered and, miraculously, it obeyed me. Now there remained only the problem of the arm. I crept toward it, trying to remain below eye level of the guests. At last, with a shudder, I seized it. It jumped and spasmed like a live thing although it was cool, with no trace of warmth. The flesh had an unpleasant yielding consistency, like wax. Gritting my teeth as I tucked it firmly under my arm, I was about to retreat when a foot trod heavily on my hand.

It was a wide foot with a bony ankle, shod in an old-fashioned man's court shoe with upturned toes. Everything in this realm of ghosts was grotesquely and ornately old-fashioned. It was as though the funeral goods burned for the dead had marked no changes in vogue, no passage of time. I wriggled my hand experimentally, trying to remove it from under the foot, but it merely pressed down harder. For a moment I crouched there, wondering what to do. Then I gave a sharp tug. The foot came off with a jerk and its owner made a sound of indignation. I couldn't help glancing up.

"What a surprise," said a familiar voice. "What are you doing here?"

It was the shriveled old man whom I had first met when I had come to this ghostly Malacca, fresh from the Plains of the Dead. He was the last person I expected to see supping at the Lim family mansion, and my shock must have shown on my face.

"I thought you were going to see your friend," he said. Desperately, I pleaded with my eyes for him not to draw attention to me, but the wretch merely gave a cackle that cut through the buzz of conversation. "Why are you dressed like a servant?"

"Is something the matter, Master Awyoung?" A woman's voice broke in. The silvery sound of it made the hairs on my neck stand up.

"I've caught a little chicken," he said gleefully. "Someone who shouldn't be here."

Chairs scraped as the guests peered around and down. I cowered, wondering if, in a mad moment, I could dash across the floor to the passageway. But the same female voice was speaking again. "Really, Master Awyoung. It's just a servant."

"Ah, Madam. I don't know whether this is really one of your servants," he said. I felt an overwhelming urge to kick the evil old man in the shins.

"Why do you say that? Stand up, girl."

Reluctantly I stood, dropping my head and hunching my shoulders. Faces turned expectantly toward me. Thankfully, I was far away from the two ox-headed demons, a sentiment seemingly shared by the other guests who had moved their chairs slightly away from them. The rest were human ghosts, all elaborately turned out in the stiff costumes that I had come to hate. My eye went to a gaunt old man, very yellow and wrinkled, with eyes that glittered like paring knives. A single wart with two long hairs sprouted from his cheek. This must be Lim Tian Ching's great-uncle, whom the servants referred to as Lao Ye, the Old Master. Next to him sat the source of the female voice.

She was young. Not much older than me and strikingly beautiful. Her classically oval face was as smooth and white as a powdered rice biscuit, the sloe eyes long and tilted. Her nose was a trifle too long and the tip drooped; in old age it might become unsightly. But she would never grow old. She was already dead, after all. Numerous jade ornaments hung from her headdress and dangled from her ears and neck. When she moved, they gave off a faint ringing sound. Her delicately painted eyebrows were knitted together in a frown.

"Who are you?" she asked.

I ducked my head respectfully, "I'm a new servant, Madam."

"I can see that," she said. "But exactly who are you?"

The yellow-faced old man made a dismissive gesture. "My dear, do we need to trouble our guests with domestic issues? Question her later if you want."

At this point, the steward broke in. "Lao Ye," he said, addressing him respectfully, "I hired her a few days ago because we were short of staff."

"Oh, is that so? I seem to recall a problem with the kitchen staff. Something about soup." He raised his eyebrows at the woman but she turned away from him, pouting prettily. I could hardly breathe. Although I knew I shouldn't, I couldn't stop staring at her. Was this my mother? I searched her features for any sign of familiarity. Did I look at all like her? Was my forehead like hers, my eyes, the shape of my ears? I couldn't remember any specific details that Amah had told me, only that my mother was very lovely. Look at me! I willed her to gaze upon me with some spark of recognition. Can't you see that I'm your child? I'd heard that even animals could recognize their young, but she gave no sign of it. Her bored glance slid across my face and drifted across the table to rest upon the ox-headed demons opposite.

"Your Excellencies," she said. "I hope you're finding the food to your satisfaction."

Taking this as my cue to be dismissed, I backed away only to be arrested by a thin, grasping hand at my wrist. "Not so fast," said Master Awyoung. Inwardly, I cursed the accidental meeting that had thrown me into his path earlier. "I spoke with this girl just a few days ago. She was asking questions about demons and the corruption of border officials."

"How do you know this?" asked the Old Master.

"I stationed myself near the entrance as is my usual custom to check out any newcomers. She spun me a tale about looking for a friend, but now she turns up here. There can't be any such coincidence. She must be a spy."

I blanched. Fool, fool! I'd dismissed him as a mad old man, but now I bit my lips and tried to keep my eyes on the floor. "If you please, sir," I said in a trembling voice, "there must be some mistake."

"Take her away and lock her up," said the Old Master. "We'll question her later." He glanced at an ox-headed demon, and it grunted in assent. The steward made an involuntary move, his face filled with consternation, but the Old Master waved over a puppet servant dressed in dark livery, which had been leaning against the wall. I guessed it was part of his personal bodyguard. Seizing my arms with an iron grasp, it propelled me from the room. I cast a despairing glance at my mother, but she was lifting a morsel to her exquisitely rouged lips with a pair of ivory chopsticks. She didn't even turn her head at my exit.

I WAS FROG-MARCHED SWIFTLY down endless dim passages. Gone were the suites of splendid rooms, the grand reception halls. This was a place

I had never been to, far away from the kitchen and all that was familiar to me. As soon as we were out of sight, I struggled to free myself, but my attempts were only met by a tightening of the viselike grip. I had no illusions that the puppet servant would crush my bones with no qualms. And then what would happen to me? My spirit form might be injured, just as Auntie Three had been scalded. The thought made me shudder and any resistance I had melted away. At last we stopped before a plain door. The servant opened it with one hand and thrust me unceremoniously in with the other. "Wait!" I cried. "Leave me a light!" But it was no use talking to the creature. With a bang, the door closed upon me and I could hear its footsteps, rapid and impersonal, receding into the distance. I sank to the floor in despair.

After a time, my eyes became accustomed to the darkness. A dim, barred shape resolved itself into a shuttered window. Faint gleams of light came through the slats, but they were fastened so tightly that I couldn't pry them apart. The room itself was barely ten paces across and smelled musty. It was dry, however, and on ground level. I guessed it was a disused storeroom, which seemed infinitely better than being cast into a dungeon. Though perhaps they were only holding me here temporarily. I remembered the ox-headed demon's casual assumption about interrogation and began to panic again. If it didn't like my answers, it might well decapitate me on the spot and then what would happen to my soul?

I had cried before when I felt sorry for myself, but now I found I was weeping silent tears of pure terror. After some time, however, I gave myself a fierce shake. If I died here, truly died with no hope of an afterlife or rebirth, then it would be my own fault for getting into this. So I might as well try to get out by myself. I searched the room several times, fumbling around in the darkness. The door was solid and would not yield to my attempts. There was not even a stick of furniture, nor a weapon of any kind. I sat down heavily on the floor and felt the familiar shape of Er Lang's scale. With trembling fingers, I drew it from my pocket and immediately it began to glow with a pearly radiance.

Carefully, I examined Er Lang's gift again. He had said that I could call him by blowing upon the fluted edge of the scale, although he warned that he couldn't come to the Plains of the Dead. Still, I picked it up and blew gently across the edge, much as one might blow across the mouth of an empty glass bottle. A faint, musical sound emerged, like the wind catching the last notes played on a faraway hillside. Nothing happened. I blew again a few more times, then ran my fingers across it. It held a razor-sharp edge and, with growing hope, I dug it into the doorjamb. It was sharp enough to bite into the wood, but progress was painstakingly slow. I turned my attention to the thinner window slats instead, hoping they would give more readily. As I worked, I began to wonder whether anyone would come for me at all. The banquet must be long over. Perhaps they had forgotten about me. My heart leaped absurdly at this hope, then sank again. I heard the distant sound of footsteps.

Quickly, I thrust the scale deep into my pocket, then hesitated. What if they searched me? In the end I tucked it into the waistband of my trousers in the small of my back. The footsteps grew steadily louder. There were at least two or three of them, but though I listened hard, none sounded as heavy as the footfall of an ox-headed demon. There was the jangle of something metallic, then the Old Master's voice. "You put her here?"

There was no reply, so I assumed the puppet servant must have merely nodded. I had never heard any of them speak, and the thought of a voice emanating from such a lifeless mockery made me shiver with revulsion.

Master Awyoung asked, "Is it secure?" I'd hoped he would leave after the banquet, but obviously he was much in the Lim family's counsel. Why had I ever spoken to him?

"She won't get out." The cold, silvery voice was my mother's. Then the door swung open.

THEY WERE HOLDING OIL lamps, or at least the servants were holding them. Accustomed as my eyes had become to the dark, the light was blinding.

"Get up!" said the Old Master. "Who are you, girl? And what are you doing in my house?" A puppet servant seized me by the arms. It wasn't difficult to drop my head and mumble.

"Please, sir. I don't know what you're talking about!"

"Who is your family?"

"They're from Negri Sembilan. We moved to Malacca shortly before I died."

"What about that story that you told me about your cousin?" Master Awyoung interjected.

"It's partly true. But I was afraid to talk to you because you're a stranger."

"She's lying," he said contemptuously, but the Old Master stooped over me for a closer look, forcing my face up under the oil lamp with his cold bony hands.

"Well, it might be true I suppose," he said sourly. "I can see why a young girl might not want to tell you everything."

"Nonsense! She knows something, I'm sure of it."

"It's too bad our guests had to leave." It was the first time that my mother had spoken since she had entered the room. She hung back, watching the proceedings with a bored look. "They would have had the truth out of her quickly."

"Well, they're gone," snapped the Old Master. "And I hope this isn't a waste of time."

"Give her to me," said Master Awyoung. "I'm sure I can make her talk."

My mother merely raised an eyebrow. "As if we didn't know that you just wanted another plaything."

"I don't need any more trouble," said the Old Master. "Give her to the demons. They'll look into her soul and if she doesn't know anything, then my grand-nephew can have her. So don't cripple her."

"But what about me?" Master Awyoung said.

"You can have her if he doesn't want her." My mother's light laugh echoed through the room. "But I'm sure he will. There's been a shortage of concubines lately."

The puppet servant abruptly released my arms and I collapsed onto the floor. My interrogators began to exit, taking the oil lamp with them. "Please!" I begged. "At least leave me a light."

"A light?" asked Master Awyoung, lingering. "No such thing. In fact, you don't need food or water either. That's one of the beautiful things about this world. I can shut you in this room for months, even years. You'll be like a doll in a cupboard. And by the time I take you out again, you'll be begging to do whatever I tell you to." The door swung shut. Outside, I heard him address the puppet servant. "Stay here. Whatever happens, don't let her out of this door." Then his footsteps died away.

I LAY ON THE floor for a long time after they had left, not daring to breathe. The faint gleam of light from beneath the door revealed the shadow of the servant outside. It was a silent guard that would never sleep, never eat, and never succumb to weariness. I supposed I was fortunate that they hadn't maimed or tortured me. But if I ever fell into the hands of Master Awyoung, I didn't think I would remain unscathed for long. That is, if I survived an interrogation by the ox-headed demons. Where they had been suddenly called to, and when they might reappear, was an alarming prospect. And my mother. The sting of her betrayal cut deep, even though I tried to tell myself she had no idea who I was. But the faint, sweet image I had long treasured of the gentle mother of Amah's stories and my father's sighs was shattered. The worst part was that there was nothing in her demeanor or speech that drew me to her. She was calculating and sly, exactly as the Third Concubine had depicted her. I told myself that it was an act, and she would surely return to rescue me. My ears twitched in the silence, waiting for the sound of light footsteps, but they never came.

WHEN I OPENED MY eyes again, it was still dark behind the nailed-down shutters of the window. I must have slept a little, for my bones ached from lying on the cold floor. Strange that one could suffer physically even in this world of the dead, a thought that didn't bode well for the prospect of torture. Master Awyoung's threat of walling me up like a doll in a box filled me with dread. The one solace I had was that I wasn't hungry, at least not yet. Anxiously, I sprang up. The clatter triggered a sharp rustle from the puppet servant stationed outside the door. I froze, hardly daring to breathe. It took many false starts before I made my way over to the window and began to work on the shutters again with the scale. The small, regular noises appeared to soothe the puppet servant, for after a while the shadow that I could see under the door fell back into a trance. Still, I feared that any sudden sound would propel it out of its stupor.

I began to scrape harder, feeling a dull pain in my wrist and shoulder, my mind wandering to Tian Bai. Where was he, and what was he doing? How many days had elapsed in the world of the living? Why had I been in such a hurry to reach this wretched place? I wished I had lingered to share his dreams further. Remembering the firm pressure of his hands upon me, I blushed in the darkness. I replayed our conversation endlessly, trying to recall his exact words and tone of voice. My fancies ran on, imagining what it would be like to marry Tian Bai, sit by his side, and slide my arms around him at night. A dark thought crossed my mind, however. Such a marriage would make me a member of the Lim family, dooming me to reenter this house if I ever truly died and passed on to the Plains of the Dead. It had a deflating effect on my fantasies.

I don't know how long I stood there in the darkness, sawing at the slats with Er Lang's scale. It seemed ages before I managed to pull out first one, then another. My hands and neck ached from the tension. Through the gap that I had made I could see the dim outlines of trees and guessed I was facing part of the estate grounds. There were no fine gardens there, only a bleak slope of dry grass and, in the distance, a high wall topped with tiles. Despite the pall of night, my eye was caught by a flickering movement, a cloud of swift wings that dipped and wheeled. It passed so quickly that I wondered if I had been mistaken, but then I remembered that I had seen no wild birds in this world of the dead.

The window slats were made out of some kind of hard timber, perhaps the legendary *belian*, or Borneo ironwood, which is said to be as hard as metal. From time to time I checked the edge of Er Lang's scale, fearing that I had blunted it, but to my surprise it was as sharp as ever. I tested it against my finger and a few drops of blood welled up. The sight relieved me, for though I had no physical body here, I was glad that, unlike the carcass of the pig that had been butchered in the courtyard, I could still bleed. Exhausted, I sat down and blew tentatively across the fluted edge of the scale. Again, I heard the faint musical sound of a distant wind whistling across vast empty spaces. It called to me, like a flautist playing a lonely melody on a moonlit mountainside.

THE SKY WAS INFUSED with the gray colorlessness before dawn. I had dozed off again for a few minutes and, with a sense of panic, I jumped up and ran to the window, wondering if the ox-headed demons had returned. Peering out, I was startled by a dark shape, like a grotesque mushroom, that rose up abruptly outside the window. I stifled a scream.

"I was waiting for you to wake up. Goodness knows, it took you long enough."

I knew that voice; those bored, aristocratic tones so at odds with the attractive timbre. "Er Lang?" I whispered.

"You're lucky I got here."

"But I thought you couldn't come."

"Technically I shouldn't be able to. As I mentioned before, this is a place for human ghosts. But I had a little help."

"From whom?"

"Don't you remember when we first met?"

I thought wildly at first of the mangrove swamp, but as though he could read my thoughts he cut in impatiently. "No, the medium by the temple wall. That's right," he continued, "You were there to get some spell against Lim Tian Ching (much good that it did you), but I was there to talk to her about the Plains of the Dead." There was a certain smugness in his tone.

"So you managed after all," I said.

"Well, it was a little difficult. And as you can see, I'm not here in my physical body."

I glanced out of the window. The dark mass that I had mistaken for a mushroom was none other than Er Lang's ubiquitous basket hat. "You look the same to me."

"Of course I do. It's just not my physical body. But it's good enough for spying."

"Then what did you need me for?" I was beginning to feel indignant. "Why did you send me here to find out about Lim Tian Ching when you were planning to come by yourself all the time?"

"You were a bonus, so to say. And it wasn't as though I was entirely sure that I could come here anyway."

"Do you know I'm supposed to be interrogated by demons?"

"Yes, well, it's not my fault that you proved to be such an inept spy."

"Inept!" I inadvertently raised my voice and the puppet servant outside my door stirred suddenly. Hurriedly, I began to hum and after a breathless moment, the shadow behind the door lapsed back into stillness.

"Why are you humming?"

"Because there's a puppet servant guarding me," I hissed. "It responds to strange noises."

"Oh, is that so?" I hated the way Er Lang sounded so amused. "Actually I ought to thank you," he continued. "If it hadn't been for you I probably couldn't have reached this place, despite the medium's help."

"How so?"

"Why, you called me of course. If you hadn't, I might not have made it."

I turned over the scale in my hand. It had a soft radiance, like a pearl. "When did you get here?"

"Yesterday evening, in the reckoning of this place. I spent some time finding my way around the estate. It really is terribly ostentatious."

"Why didn't you come and let me out then?"

"I couldn't locate you until you called me again. Besides, there were a number of interesting things going on. But first, I want an update."

In a low voice, I hurriedly recounted all that I had observed, including the presence of the ox-headed demons. I left out the part about my mother, however, feeling ashamed for having gone to seek her in the first place. Er Lang listened with no comment, merely nodding his head from time to time so that the enormous hat bobbed like a boat upon the water.

"Is that all?" he said when I had fallen silent.

I flushed. "Yes. It's not very much, is it?"

"Well, at least we've discovered that Lim Tian Ching's great-uncle is also implicated in whatever is going on. Do you remember any of the other guests?"

"There was an old man, Master Awyoung. He was the one I met when I first arrived."

"It's too bad you weren't able to remain incognito longer," said Er Lang coolly. "But I suppose we shall have to make do with what we have. Master Awyoung is an interesting development. He's been in the Plains of the Dead for a suspiciously long time."

"He said he was tired of it and wanted to go on to the Courts of Hell, but his descendants prayed for him to have more time to enjoy their funeral offerings."

Er Lang gave a sharp laugh. "Did he tell you that? Just between us, I don't think that Master Awyoung is in any rush to go to the courts for judgment. In fact, his name came up precisely because he has stayed almost two hundred years here."

"How did he manage it?"

"The official record is the same as what you have told me—namely, that due to the filial piety of his descendants, his term was extended. But I have my doubts that he really wants to go. In the first place, he has plenty of sins awaiting retribution in the courts, which he's in no hurry to face. No doubt he has made a deal with someone, possibly even one of the Nine Judges of Hell, for his cooperation. Secondly, having an agent like him is useful because the Plains of the Dead is an interim place. From here it's easy to coordinate movements between planes of existence, or even return to the world of the living as a shade. For what could be more incognito than a ghost?"

"But he said he never went anywhere."

"You really are naive. It's rather sweet, in a way. Besides, he could easily send a spy or a courier. Someone like Lim Tian Ching, for example. I'd like to know who is pulling the strings behind Master Awyoung."

"I thought he was mad."

"Yes, well, that would be a rather convenient persona to cultivate."

I was crestfallen.

"In any case," said Er Lang, "that's certainly a useful piece of information. Let's see what else we can sniff out."

"If you pull out the bars, I think I can climb out," I said.

"I'm beginning to wonder whether it might be better to leave you where you are."

"What?" My voice emerged in a squeak.

"Think of what would happen if they should find you gone. And also, what else you might glean from Master Awyoung if he thinks you're his prisoner. In fact, I don't see why you shouldn't be questioned by the ox-headed demons as well. I'd like to know which guard company they come from."

"If they read my soul, it would mean the end of your undercover investigation."

There was a gleam of teeth from within the shadows of his hat. "Well, that would be a problem, wouldn't it? I suppose I had better let you out."

I stared hard at Er Lang, wondering whether he really would have left me behind if it suited his purpose.

"Oh, don't look so hostile," he said lightly. "It's not becoming."

I watched in fascination as he began to break the window slats. His hands were long and slender and, in the pale dusky light, looked entirely human. Yet they possessed a strength beyond their refined appearance as he snapped off the ironwood slats with ease. He made hardly any noise, but I glanced nervously at the shadow of the puppet servant under the door.

"What about my guard?" I whispered. "It was under strict orders not to let me out."

"Of the window?"

"Oh. I see. They said the door."

"That's the problem with these automatons," said Er Lang cheerily. "Quite brainless, though utterly devoted and completely trustworthy. No wonder my investigation was stalled until I could find a way to come here myself."

"Couldn't you have asked some other ghost to help you?"

Er Lang paused. "What makes you think you were the first?"

While I considered this uncomfortable thought, he removed the last barrier. I scrabbled to lever myself over the high window ledge. After a few minutes of this, Er Lang reached over and pulled me out. I had been afraid that his hands would be chill and inert, like the puppet servant, but to my surprise they were warm, with a firm grip. Despite myself, I blushed. I was not used to being touched by a man, and this contact, brief though it was, made me uncomfortably conscious of Er Lang's tapering, elegant fingers, so different from Tian Bai's square hands. Embarrassed, I turned my face aside, focusing instead on wriggling through the narrow window. My hips and legs scraped against the frame and actually became stuck at one point.

"Please stop!" I gasped.

Er Lang tilted his head as though he were listening to some far-off noise. Then ignoring my protests, he braced himself against the wall and simply pulled harder. With a creak, the window frame bowed and gave an extra inch, allowing me to slide out like a crab from an upturned pot.

"Didn't you hear me?" I said. "That hurt!"

"It would have been worse to be stuck," he said. "Quick! There are gardeners coming."

With little ceremony, we scuttled into some nearby bushes, Er Lang half dragging me along. "Keep down!" he hissed. From my crouched vantage point, I could see a pair of feet walking with the monotonously jerky gait of a puppet servant. It was followed by two more sets of footwear. Wordlessly, they moved in tandem, clipping and trimming the shrubbery. I shrank back against Er Lang as they approached us. A faint fragrance of incense clung to his clothes, surprising in that dead world. Closing my eyes, I breathed in the refined, courtly aroma of aloeswood. It made me think of hushed voices and poems read by candlelight, the time measured out by the elegant practice of burning a stick of costly incense. I could not imagine Er Lang taking part in poetry competitions; he would probably say something perverse. Still, who had scented his robes for him? I wrenched my thoughts away. It really didn't matter what Er Lang did in his spare time, which might be devouring maidens or diving for catfish, for all I knew. I shouldn't be too curious about him. Yet, I was exquisitely aware of our proximity and how my back was pressed against the warmth of his chest.

His left arm, resting on his knee, almost encircled me—and I felt his muscles flex, then tense, as though he was anticipating something. I tried not to think of how close he was, but could only hear the distracting rhythm of my own pulse. A burning flush crept up my neck. Afraid that Er Lang would notice, I stiffened, but he paid no attention to me, other than to tighten his grip on my shoulder warningly.

The feet of the puppet gardeners drew ever closer until I realized with dread that they meant to prune the very hedge that we were hiding in. At the last moment, Er Lang rose abruptly. He waded out of the bushes and began to busy himself with the greenery, rocking his heels in imitation of their movements. His large bamboo hat was not quite like their pointed coolie hats, but I hoped desperately that such details wouldn't matter to them. They stopped and huddled together, then to my great relief, moved on to another stand of trees.

It was some time before he motioned for me to come out, and when I did so, I couldn't help glancing around nervously. The gardeners were now mere specks in the distance.

"Do they work at night as well?" I asked, looking at the dusky pall that still thankfully covered the sky.

"It will be morning soon," said Er Lang. "But they seem to go around at all hours. You look dreadful, by the way," he remarked conversationally.

I glared at him, conscious of the way my hair had straggled out of its plaits, the dirt that encrusted my clothing, not to mention the tear stains on my grimy face. "Why does it matter?"

"Well, if you were caught spying on Master Awyoung, it would help to look a little more alluring."

"Are you planning for me to be interrogated by him as well?"

"It might be quite useful."

"I hate you," I said before I could stop myself.

He seemed genuinely surprised. "Most women say they love me."

I turned away to hide my irritation. Er Lang's high-handedness and egotism constantly amazed me, despite any gratitude that I ought to have felt for his rescue of me. But then he was the one who had instructed me to come here in the first place, I thought angrily, conveniently forgetting that I had had no other options at the time. Before, I had speculated whether Er Lang was hiding the head of a cold-blooded fish beneath his impenetrable hat brim, but now I decided that he must be the Pig Marshal—a monstrous hog who was the companion to the Monkey King of Chinese mythology. Formerly a marshal of the Heavenly Hosts, he had accidentally been reborn into a sow's litter, and spent most of the time chasing women in the mistaken belief that he was irresistible. That, I thought sourly, was probably Er Lang's true form.

"Of course, I would endeavor to rescue you," said Er Lang, rather pompously, I thought. "I wouldn't leave you here."

"Wasn't that what you were just planning to do?" I asked.

"You'll have to trust me. Besides, I don't see that you have many other options. If you don't find a way to rejoin your body soon, you might lose it forever."

"How many days has it been in the real world since I left?" I asked, suddenly anxious.

He paused. "Almost three weeks."

"But I thought you said time tended to run faster in the Plains of the Dead than in the world of the living!"

"That doesn't mean it always does. If we're lucky, it might reverse itself and run slower."

Fear closed my throat. "How much time do you think I have left?"

"At best, a few weeks."

"And worst case?"

"The deterioration in fit between your spirit and body might have already begun."

. . . .

"I'M SORRY," SAID ER Lang after a long and awkward silence.

I felt like crying but there was no help for it. Tears would do me no good, even if I withered away into a wraith. "Very well," I said with forced cheer. "I'll go and find Master Awyoung."

"He must have a powerful sponsor in the Courts of Hell if he's organizing a rebellion. Try to find out who is pulling the strings, although I'm afraid your disappearance from the storeroom may soon be discovered. Which means we have very little time."

That reminded me. "I was supposed to meet Fan tomorrow. She said she would show me the way back—or can I go with you?"

"Out of the question. The way that I took to enter this world is not one that you can follow." Er Lang shook his head decisively, making the broad-brimmed hat wobble. It was on the tip of my tongue to ask him why he wore it, but I thought again about what sort of monstrosity it might conceal and bit back the question.

PROGRESS BACK TOWARD THE mansion was slow. Er Lang moved quietly, pausing to freeze into the shadows or against walls. I had merely to follow his lead as we made a series of hurried sorties, always keeping a lookout for the ever-present household staff. The whole place was burdened with an outdated Chinese ambience that I barely saw in Malaya. I wondered what the afterlives of Sikhs, Tamils, Malays, and Arab traders were like. Indeed, what was the Catholic paradise? For some reason, Tian Bai's dream of the Portuguese girl Isabel Souza crossed my mind. If she died, I thought, did she have to scuttle around the grounds of a hostile mansion like this? I had my doubts.

In another time and place I would have liked to examine a few of these designs and structures, some of which I had only seen illustrated in books and scrolled paintings. The small pavilions, the little crooked trees, and occasional pagodas were all strangely familiar to me. But there was an eerie chill about the place, a deadness in the colors and the blank light that made me feel as though I were passing through a paper landscape, myself no more than another cutout upon a *wayang kulit*, or shadow puppet stage. As much as I disliked the place, however, I had to admit there was a certain thrill in sneaking around Lim Tian Ching's property. After all, how many times had he entered my own dreams without permission? At last we came to a small door in a wall. Er Lang laid a hand on the wooden surface and it gave slightly.

"Good," he said with some satisfaction. "No one has bolted this yet."

"Where are we?" I whispered.

"Behind the private apartments of the family. I did some reconnaissance yesterday and left this door open."

I felt some shame at my earlier indignation over his belated rescue of me.

"Beyond lays a series of small courtyards. If there are any important guests staying with the family, they ought to be lodged somewhere around here. I leave it up to you to find Master Awyoung's chambers. Do whatever you need to, but return by dusk."

"Here?" I said.

"Do you see that pavilion in the distance?" Turning, I could just make out a tiled roof and red-lacquered pillars. "Wait there. If for some reason I don't show up by next morning, I suggest that you find your way out and contact your friend Fan."

"And just leave you?"

"I can take care of myself," he said. "It is you who may have difficulties leaving the Plains of the Dead."

He slipped through the gate like a drop of spilled ink and vanished.

CHAPTER 26

I PUSHED THE gate open. Inside was a private courtyard; a neat yet lifeless enclosure consisting of potted plants arranged in rigid ranks. Every plant was identical, down to the number of flowers and the angle of the leaves. I couldn't help thinking that they must have been printed on a card and burned, for the pleasure of some long-dead Lim. Three doors opened onto this space from the enclosing walls. I hesitated again, wondering which path I should take. Guessing that the plainest door might be a servant egress, I tugged on it. It opened suddenly and noiselessly into a hallway.

It was soon apparent that this was a private wing in which I had never been. The corridor was narrower, yet more sumptuous than the open passageways of the main house. There were silk hangings on the wall, and as I glanced at them I saw they were part of a private art collection. Strange beasts rolled their ink-dark eyes at me from the scrolls; and as I walked farther along, the paintings became more and more curious, some of them embarrassingly so, as they depicted couples writhing in sexual congress, women transforming into animals, and hollow-eyed ghouls gnawing on bones. I averted my eyes from the most terrifying ones, for the painted images seemed to have a life of their own.

The sound of light footsteps, tripping quickly across the cold tiled floors, reminded me of where I was and the task at hand. I searched wildly for a bolt-hole. There was a door nearby, but it was so grand and ornate that I wouldn't have dared enter it save for the fear of discovery. I tried it and surprisingly, it swung open. Fortunately the room was empty, although it looked as though it was someone's private quarters. I glimpsed a writing desk and, in the far corner, a traditional bedstead fashioned like a box. Books and papers lay about in disarray, but I had no time to examine my surroundings. The single large armoire that might have concealed me was locked. I tugged on it futilely, then slipped into the box bed. The brocade curtains were half drawn and I crouched behind one of these, my heart beating uncomfortably. No doubt the footsteps would pass, I told myself, but they stopped right outside the room.

"Awyoung! Master Awyoung! Where are you?"

It was my mother's voice. To my horror, I realized that I hadn't quite closed the room door and it swung, reproachfully, ajar. There was a moment's hesitation, then a slim white hand, laden with heavy rings, pushed it open. Hastily, I ducked behind the bed curtains.

"Are you here?" she called out.

I could hear her walking around the room, flicking through the open books and pushing aside piles of papers. What was she looking at? And why was she here? Realizing that the slightest twitch might betray my presence, I crouched in my corner, hoping that she wouldn't think to examine the bed. The bedstead had been built like a three-walled curtained box with low sides that one could recline against. Traditional romances often featured such beds, along with descriptions of beautiful heroines languishing helplessly within. I had never dreamed that one day I might find refuge in one of these beds, hiding in a ghost world from my dead mother as she rifled through the secrets of an unpleasant old man. I bit my cheek as inappropriate laughter threatened to choke me. What a joke! I had longed for my mother, dreamed of her, antici-pated and imagined our reunion, and this was the result of it.

There were scratching noises and holding my breath, I inched my face behind the curtains until I could see. Her back was toward me but she was using a brush to write something on a scrap of paper. The scratching sound was the hasty noise of an ink stick being ground with little water on a dry ink slab. In Malaya, I had had slate pencils and even wooden graphite ones. Presumably, no one had bothered to burn any such modern replicas for the dead, as my mother was reduced to brush and ink. She was so absorbed in her task that she hardly noticed the approaching footsteps until it was almost too late. The door creaked in protest, and with a start, she pocketed whatever she had been writing and hastily shuffled the papers.

"Ah, madam! What brings you here?" It was the voice of Master Awyoung.

"You, of course." I had to hand it to her. The woman had nerves of iron.

"What are you doing in my humble room?"

"But Master Awyoung, you have your own house. Your own mansions and villas, which make this place look quite provincial." Her voice dropped to a purr.

"You know my stupid descendants. They would never let me carry on my research there."

"Oh? No doubt that's why you brought your paintings here."

His laugh was a rattle of small stones. "You like them? I instructed my grandson to burn my entire collection after my death so that I could receive them here. They cost a lot, too! My son was against it—wanted to sell them off, but my grandson complied. *Hmph!* It was worth it to indulge that boy while I was alive. But what are you here for? Surely not to admire my paintings?"

"I was examining them in the hallway when I noticed that your door was ajar."

"You're too kind. What can I do for you?"

Her tone changed. "Has my husband's good-for-nothing grandnephew accomplished anything?"

"Lim Tian Ching? I thought you would know more about the matter than me."

"He doesn't trust me. But I know what you've been up to. Flattering and cultivating that young fool." Though her words were harsh, the cadence of her voice was strangely seductive. I wriggled uncomfortably in my hiding place, my ears tingling.

"As long as he remains a fool, it suits my purpose. Otherwise he wouldn't dare relay such treasonous messages and packages."

She laughed, a high tinkling sound that was surprisingly youthful. I hadn't thought it possible to dislike my mother any further, but her laughter made me grit my teeth. "Remind me never to underestimate you."

Master Awyoung said, "As soon as he died, I knew I had my tool. Do you know how many years I've been waiting for such a courier to come by? Lim Tian Ching has just the right connections for this task. A rich family, a doting mother in the world of the living, and too much self-absorption to blind him to all but his own concerns."

"And what do you get out of this?" I heard a strange rustling sound.

"What do you think? Having my stay in the Plains of the Dead extended indefinitely."

"But you complain so much about it." The slippery sound of satin again.

"That is only more of my cleverness." He gave a grunt and made a horrible slurping noise. I peered through my inadequate peephole and blushed furiously. From what I could see, the wretched old man was pawing my mother, and she, shameless creature that she was, had already slid one alabaster shoulder out of her gown. I turned away, my cheeks flaming. How could she! They were each as dreadful as the other. Another, more pressing thought struck me, however. Sooner or later they might move to the bed and my hiding place would be discovered. Panicked, I glanced around. There was a small space between the bed and the wall, so unbearably narrow that I got stuck halfway. The heavy brocade curtains twitched, as though tugged by an unseen hand. In a frenzy of fear, I forced myself through. No sooner had I managed to slide down behind the back of the bed and onto the floor when there was a loud thump and a squeal of laughter. Master Awyoung and my mother had thrown themselves upon the bed.

For several minutes I lay there, my face pressed against the cold stone floor like a gecko, listening to the sounds above me. There was no bed skirt hiding the space beneath the bed and if anyone entered the room, I could easily be seen. I was wriggling my way forward when I heard my mother speak again.

"I really shouldn't be here at all." She pouted.

"Nobody will find out." He sounded muffled. "I love calling you 'madam' and the icy look in your eyes."

"If my husband should ever suspect!"

"You know he's not really your husband."

"How dare you say that!" There was a rustling sound, as though she had gathered her garments together.

"Come, come. There's no need to pretend with me. You know as well as I do that you were never formally married to him. The title Second Wife is merely a courtesy. You just showed up one day, looking so beautiful that he couldn't resist you. *I* can't resist you myself, even though you probably plan to discard me."

My mother laughed uncomfortably. "As long as you treat me well, I shall always be with you."

"Well, how does another hundred years of happiness sound to you?"

"Really?" she cooed. "Tell me, who's really behind all these secret meetings and money transfers? It's one of the Nine Judges of Hell, isn't it?"

He sat up suddenly. "Who told you that?"

"Am I right?"

Master Awyoung was silent for a while, then he began to laugh. It was a dry, malicious cackle. "My dear, dear madam. If heaven should get wind that you know even this much, your existence would be as brief as a candle flame on a stormy night."

She shrugged him off. "As long as I'm with you I know I'll be all right. Now, what would you like me to do?"

"Well, I was thinking about the girl."

"Girl? You mean the servant we locked up?"

I had begun to creep toward the front of the bed, but froze at this change in subject.

"Pretty, wasn't she?"

"Are you still thinking about her? Personally, I didn't find her very appealing."

"That's too bad. I would have liked to see the two of you together."

She snorted. "In your bed, no doubt."

The frost in her voice was enough to chill the atmosphere, but Master Awyoung only laughed. "Ah, that's why I have such a soft spot for you. You're the only one who dares tell me off. Come now, don't be so angry." With these and other endearments he was able to entice her back into the bed, causing me to heave a sigh of relief. I had been terrified that she would see me if she stood up to leave.

Glancing up, I was encouraged by the sight of the drawn bed curtains. No doubt they wished to shield themselves from prying eyes, but it was to my advantage as well. Silently, I began to creep across the floor, expecting to hear a cry of discovery at any moment. The heavy armoire was placed such that the view of the door was obscured, and this was my goal. Pulse racing, I set off in an ungainly scramble and miraculously reached it. The door now stood directly in front of me, but I was faced with a dilemma. Since the armoire only partially blocked it, any movement of the door could be seen from the bed. If only the door were still ajar! But it was firmly shut. My hand crept toward it and pushed the latch down. It made a loud clack.

"What was that?" It was my mother's voice.

I heard the bed curtains pulled back and then Master Awyoung said, "There's nothing. See for yourself." While I was steeling myself for a quick dash, I heard him chastising her. "You're too jumpy. Nobody ever comes to my apartments."

"What if Lim Tian Ching discovers what he's actually doing?" she said urgently.

"Nonsense! He's so consumed by his own grievances that the thought has never crossed his mind. He wants to drag down his cousin and marry some girl. Ridiculous demands!"

"You're sure of this?"

"My dear, why do you bother yourself with such details? Or are you planning to sell me out?"

. . . .

SHE HAD JUST BEGUN to protest when there was a rap on the door. I froze, as did the couple on the bed. There was no escape this time.

"Who is it?" hissed my mother.

"Ah, I forgot. A servant with a message."

"Why didn't you ensure there were no interruptions?"

"But how was I to know that you would be here today?" he said. "Never mind. Keep the curtains drawn." Raising his voice, he called out, "Who is it?"

The door opened and directly in front of me stood Auntie Three. Her eyes widened when she saw me, but her face remained impassive.

"Master Awyoung, the messenger delivered something to you."

"I'm taking a nap," he said. "Just put it on the writing desk."

Auntie Three walked around me and past the armoire, as though I did not exist. She put a small package on the writing desk and looked inquiringly toward the box bed with its drawn curtains. "Is there anything else you need, sir?"

"No. Don't disturb me anymore."

"Very well, sir."

As she walked back toward the door, she paused and gestured quickly with her hand. I suddenly understood that by standing there, she blocked the view of the door from the bed, allowing me to escape. Once we were in the corridor, she seized me by the wrist. "Quick!" she whispered.

She led me swiftly down the winding corridor. Mortified at what she must think of me, I started to stammer out an explanation, but she put her finger to her lips. I followed her, feeling as though we were mice creeping past the lair of a *musang*, or civet cat. The Malays like to tame them for they are supposed to be ferocious mousers. I had always wanted one, but had only seen them, stiff and cold, their beautiful fur bristling, brought to market by hunters who sold them for medicinal soups. What would it be like to be so tiny and snapped up by such wicked jaws? Those of an ox-headed demon were large enough to sever my head with a single bite. I shuddered and Auntie Three turned to look at me.

"We'll rest for a moment," she said.

She pushed open a door to a storeroom filled with stacks of stiffly folded funeral clothes. A pyramid of antiquated embroidered shoes rose in one corner, looking for all the world like a heap of discarded hooves. Closing the door behind her, she asked, "What happened to you?"

I told her how Master Awyoung had locked me up for interrogation.

"I heard about that from the steward," she said. "I went to look for you this morning but there was a guard at the door, so I didn't dare approach it. How did you get out?"

Deciding it would be better not to mention Er Lang, I mumbled something about climbing out of the window.

"The window! That was clever of you." She looked at me with a curious sort of pride. "But what do they want with you anyway?"

It was too difficult to prevaricate further, so I gave her the bare bones of my story; how I was almost dead, or dying in the world of the living, and had come here because Lim Tian Ching was haunting me.

"Why did you come here?" she asked. "It was far too risky!"

"What choice did I have?" I said. "I could have wandered around Malacca until my spirit faded, or returned to my room to be captured by Lim Tian Ching's demons."

"And you came straight here?"

"Well, I stopped by my family home on the way. I heard my mother was here."

"Your mother?"

"And I found her too! She's the Second Wife."

The effect on Auntie Three was surprising. She turned as white as a piece of rice paper and sank down on the pile of shoes. "That woman! What makes you think she's your mother?"

"I was told she came to this house by a former concubine. And she's the right age and personality."

"I see." Auntie Three looked down. "What do you think of her?"

Since Auntie Three had little reason to like my mother, I felt there was no reason to hold back. "She's perfectly horrible! I can't understand why my father and Amah were so enamored of her."

"What did your father say about her?"

"That she was kind and gentle. But mostly that she was beautiful. Now I see that he must have been as blind as Master Awyoung."

"Did you miss your mother so much?"

"I did. But now I wish I'd never met her."

Auntie Three seemed agitated. She stood up and opened the door a fraction in order to peek out. "You should leave this place," she said. "It's only a matter of time before they discover your escape. Besides, I heard that the ox-headed demons were returning tonight."

"Tonight! They're planning on interrogating me." An uncontrollable shudder ran up my spine until even my hair lifted at the roots.

"How will you get out?"

"I have a horse," I said. "It's still in my quarters."

"Why don't you come back with me now? I'll hide you in my room."

It was a tempting offer and I paused—to hide in her room, to burrow down behind a mattress and cover myself with blankets until the danger had passed—these were all things I longed for. Besides, Auntie Three was the first person in a long time who had offered to take care of me. Well, if one discounted Er Lang. Although his help appeared to be more along the lines of steering me into various situations, like an expert kite flyer in high winds. Still, I remembered Er Lang's injunction to meet him at the pavilion; and despite the lure of a safe haven, I couldn't help but feel a frisson of excitement at all that I had accomplished already.

I hesitated, not wanting to tell her that I wished to spy into Lim Tian Ching's room. How many times had he invaded my own room, my own dreams in the world of the living? Besides, something was nagging at me.

"You go first," I said. "I'll meet you in your room after I check something."

"But can you find your way back?" The wrinkles in her aged face creased like spiderwebs; her forearms were dappled with age spots and the skin hung soft and loose from them. She was so old—far more ancient than Amah, I thought. Yet there was a decisiveness about her that was different from Amah.

"Tell me how to get back," I said.

She tore off a piece of wrapping paper, and pulling a hairpin from her bun, used it to score the paper with a map. "The outer garden is less frequented by guests, but is a much longer route. In the house, this passage is a service corridor."

"I'll be very careful," I said. "Which one is Lim Tian Ching's room?"

She looked horrified. "The young master is not at home."

"Exactly! Please, if you want to help me at all, I need to find out something. Otherwise my spirit will shrivel up so I can never rejoin my body." Faced with this argument, she could only acquiesce reluctantly.

"I'll come to your quarters as soon as I can," I said. "Can you look in on my horse for me? Her name is Chendana."

"I'll wait for you by the kitchen gate at the hour of the dog this evening," said Auntie Three. "I don't think the demons will arrive any earlier than that, and you must be gone before they set foot in this house." She opened the door of the storeroom and cast a furtive eye outside. "I must go, or this area will be full of puppet servants searching for me soon. Li Lan—" she was about to say something, then stopped. "Come back quickly!"

CHAPTER 27

I WAITED UNTIL the patter of Auntie Three's footsteps receded. There was no sense in waiting around too long. Master Awyoung and my mother might finish their rendezvous at any moment. Armed with the map that Auntie Three had scratched out for me, however, I felt far more confident in my errand. The paintings on the walls began to decrease and their subject matter became more mundane. I wondered whether my mother had really been examining them as she claimed, or if she had deliberately gone to search his room. Thinking about her caused an ache in my chest. Why had I ever listened to Amah, or my addled father? The woman I had spied upon was no better than any common prostitute.

There was only one place on the map that looked like it might present difficulties: a large open atrium between Master Awyoung's wing and that of Lim Tian Ching. Auntie Three had said that when the family was in residence they might often be found there. When I reached it, I saw that it was furnished with a selection of rosewood chairs. At the edge of a low table rested a single teacup, from which a thin curl of steam emerged. I stopped short with an unwelcome realization. If the tea was still hot, then someone must be there to drink it.

I had no sooner thought this when I heard the sharp nasal tones of the Old Master. "Take this away and bring me Pu'er tea instead!"

Startled, I thought he must have taken me for a servant. To my horror, however, a figure detached itself from the wall barely an arm's length away from me. It was a puppet servant, but thankfully it ignored me. And what I had taken to be a cushion was actually the back of the Old Master's head as he reclined on a stiff daybed. Standing where I was, he had merely to turn his head to see me. The puppet servant was busy clearing the tea tray when I bolted behind a pierced lacquer screen. This was a much better hiding place, though there was a large gap between the screen and the floor, which meant that anyone could see my feet.

The servant shuffled off and I turned my attention back to the Old Master. To my dismay, he remained sitting upright, his gaze fixed upon a sheet of handwritten paper. Long minutes passed while I fidgeted uneasily. The servant was bound to return soon and I wasn't sure that it would ignore me a second time. I stared intently at the paper he was holding, but he held it such that I couldn't see the writing. It wasn't a long missive, and the way that he studied it gave the impression that he was rereading parts of it. I speculated whether it had anything to do with the papers in Master Awyoung's study that my mother had copied, and if it was possible that the Old Master truly had no idea of my mother's extracurricular activities.

As I gazed upon his sour, sallow features, I tried to discern whether there was any resemblance between him and Tian Bai or, for that matter, Lim Tian Ching. There was some similarity in the shape of the forehead and the slightly flattened ridge of the nose. But Tian Bai's eyes tilted upward at the corners, which was his chief charm, whereas this man's turned down, matching the ill-tempered grooves between his nose and lips. Tian Bai was better than all of them, I told myself.

The Old Master's head jerked up. I heard a footfall and wondered whether the puppet servant had returned. The angle of the pierced holes in the screen was such, however, that I could see in only one direction. A thin smile appeared on his face. "You're back early."

"What else was there to do, Great-Uncle?" Those petulant tones were horribly familiar to me. It was none other than Lim Tian Ching.

I BROKE INTO A cold sweat. If he were to glance this way he would surely see my feet. There was a window behind, with a narrow ledge only a hand span wide and I crouched on this, teetering on my narrow perch. Only by bracing my arms against the sides of the window could I keep my balance, but it was better than leaving my feet exposed.

"Did you do everything I asked you to do?" asked the Old Master, quickly folding the letter into his hand.

"Yes, yes, I delivered all the packages. They said to expect a large shipment next week." There was a heavy flop, as though Lim Tian Ching had flung himself onto a chair. "I don't know why I have to be the one to do this. Can't you send a servant?"

"I told you before, these are delicate business deals. And it's a good way to introduce you, my descendant and heir, to various important personages."

"Well, some of them hardly qualify as people."

His great-uncle made a sharp sound. "Don't ever say such a thing again! You can't afford to offend them. After all, they may help you in your quest."

"You would think my own parents would aid me. But they won't."

"What have you been up to now? Wheedling your mother in her dreams?"

"Oh, dreams! At first I thought it was so much fun to manipulate them, but it's boring now. My mother is so terrified, she just weeps whenever I appear. What kind of mother is that? She should be glad to see me, even if it's only in her dreams."

"And your father? Is he well?"

"Well enough," Lim Tian Ching replied sulkily. "It's harder to get through to him. The thread isn't strong. And I can't get through to my cousin at all. If I could only give him a few night terrors that would be well worth it."

"You just have to keep trying. Very soon this matter will be resolved."

"Why do I have to wait anyway? They're supposed to help me collect evidence for my court case. Instead, I seem to be running errands for all these other people."

"Patience is a virtue you seem sadly lacking in, Grand-nephew. It's a matter of bringing your case to the right authorities. And I don't mind telling you that we have a powerful advocate on our side." He dropped his voice to a murmur; as he did so, I noticed that he unobtrusively put the folded letter in his hand, away from Lim Tian Ching, on the other side of the daybed. It was now closer to me, and I held my breath as I saw the stiff sheet of paper pop open slightly. Blessing the preternatural sharpness of my vision, I squinted, deciphering some of the characters.

—your good work . . . last shipment of weapons received on . . . His Honor the Sixth Judge of Hell is most pleas—

Heart pounding, I stared at the inked characters until the words were burned into my memory. I was sure Er Lang would be extremely interested in such a letter, which appeared to link the conspirators of a rebellion with corruption in the Courts of Hell.

It was madness, I knew. But I had to get that letter. Frantically, I searched for a distraction and spied a stiff arrangement of fruit on the sideboard. The only problem was that a puppet servant stood in between. Inching forward on my hands and knees, I crept past it, praying that it would ignore me as it had before.

The men were still talking. "—still missing!" That was Lim Tian Ching in a louder tone. "Where can she possibly have gone?"

"That reminds me. We caught a girl last night."

"A girl? Here?"

"Yes. Master Awyoung said she seemed suspicious."

"And you think that was Li Lan?"

"The thought never crossed my mind," said his great-uncle blandly. "But now that you mention it, I wonder whether it is the same girl."

I reached up and grasped an orange. It was hard and perfectly spherical. I stuffed it in my pocket. Then another.

"But how would she get here? She had nothing, no funeral goods, no carriage."

"That's why I didn't consider the possibility earlier. But you may see her if you like. In fact, you can have her after the demons are done interrogating her."

"Can it really be her? Is this girl pretty?"

"Oh, tolerable. Enough to make your aunt here jealous." The two men laughed, while I felt another sting at the thought of my mother, who had now rejected me in more ways than I could count. Silently, I wriggled until I was just behind the Old Master's daybed.

"Well, I'll take a look at her, but what if it isn't Li Lan?" asked Lim Tian Ching.

"A man can have concubines. In fact, it is his duty and his reward."

I felt my ears burn with rage at these pronouncements. My neck was beginning to ache from crouching awkwardly, but I dared not move. The letter was so close now that I could almost touch it. But the Old Master's hand, dangling over the side of the daybed, was only inches away.

"When are the ox-headed demons coming?" asked Lim Tian Ching.

"Tonight. Be prepared to inform them of your progress."

With agonizing slowness, I eased the letter out, but even as I thrust it into my clothes, I saw the Old Master's hand descend as if to pick it up. Taking a deep breath, I hurled the orange at a spindly table on the other side of the atrium. The throw was hard and low, and though it missed the table, it hit the side of the wall with a dull thunk. They both started, heads swiveling. I rolled my second orange after the first. As they stood up to peer at the noise, I slithered frantically backward. But in my haste, I tripped over the puppet servant. A hard hand shot out and seized my arm. As we struggled in desperate silence, the heavy wooden screen teetered, then fell with a tremendous bang, smashing into a curio cabinet and sending shards of porcelain flying everywhere.

I had a second's glimpse of Lim Tian Ching and his great-uncle staring at me in shock. Their mouths hung open and the family likeness was absurdly pronounced. Then I was racing wildly down the corridor. Behind me I heard shouts of confusion. My heart was hammering, my legs sliding on the tiled floors. The sound of running footsteps came to my ears, a monotonous gait as though a number of people were moving in unison. It could only be puppet servants, fanning their way through the mansion. Panicked, I searched for an exit but there was only a single window, its bars too narrow to fit a cat through. At its foot was a vase as high as a man, filled with a stiff arrangement of white chrysanthemums and spider lilies. There was no water in this bouquet for the dead; the flowers needed none and would last forever. Frantically, I pushed them aside and rattled the window bars. The running steps drew ever nearer, chilling in their utter absence of other noises. Then the puppet servants fell upon me.

Later I would be grateful for my terror, for when they seized me, clamping their hard, cold hands over my mouth, I was so petrified that I fainted. In this manner I was spared the consciousness of being carried by them, not to the storeroom where I had first been imprisoned, but somewhere else entirely.

CHAPTER 28

S OMEONE WAS STROKING my hair. At first I thought that I was a
child again and Amah was soothing me after a bad dream. The relief
of waking up was so great that tears streamed from my closed eyes. Then I
opened them. Lim Tian Ching was bending over me. It was his hand that was
tangled in my hair, and his face that lingered so solicitously next to mine. I
began to scream.

"Stop it!" he said, but I couldn't. Lim Tian Ching tried to stifle my cries
with a meaty hand, but it only made me more hysterical. He shook me roughly
and, reflexively, I slapped him. The sting of my hand upon his face was the best
feeling I had experienced since I had lost my body. We stared at each other in
shock.

"What did you do that for?" he said.

"How dare you touch me!" I said. "You kidnapper! You fiend!"

His thick lips loosened in surprise as he quailed momentarily before this
barrage. "What are you talking about? You're the one who came here. How did
you get here?"

I looked around. From the size of the room and the men's clothes strewn upon the ground, I had the sinking feeling that it was Lim Tian Ching's bedroom. Crossing my arms, I was relieved at the stiff rustle of the letter hidden in my clothes. So they hadn't searched me yet. In the chaos of broken furniture, the Old Master must have momentarily forgotten his letter, but inevitably he would realize his loss.

Stalling, I said, "I was lost." Lim Tian Ching's small eyes stared hard at me, flicking across my disheveled clothes and wild hair. "I followed some ghosts and they took me down a tunnel across a plain until we reached this place."

"You crossed the Plains of the Dead? How did you do that?"

The last thing I wanted was for him to know about my little horse. "I walked. It took a long, long time. Months," I said, remembering Er Lang's discussion of how time moved erratically here.

"So that's where you were!" he said, half to himself. "No wonder you look terrible." For some reason, his words enraged me and I flew at him with my nails. He blanched for a moment, then caught me by the wrists.

"My, my," he said. "I see your temper hasn't improved." He brought his face close to mine, even as I struggled futilely. Despite his soft and pudgy appearance, he was far stronger than me. He was a man, even in this world of deathly make-believe, and I was only a weak girl. The same thought must have occurred to him, for his expression changed.

"Li Lan, I can't tell you how happy I am that you are safe." The moony shine had returned to his eyes. I struggled in silence. "My people were looking for you everywhere."

"Who told you to send demons to my house? I was frightened out of my wits!"

"You were frightened?" he cooed. "Of course, I should have thought of that. My poor dear. You had no need to be afraid of them. They are merely my minions." At this I almost snorted, but his solicitous gaze was making me feel increasingly uncomfortable, especially since he still had me by the wrists.

"You know, I was wrong to say you look terrible." His large face loomed ever closer, so that I could see every shiny pore. It was a shame that death hadn't improved him. I thought illogically that it must have been difficult for him to grow up in the shadow of Tian Bai's pleasant features.

"In fact, you look quite . . . fetching. I like your hair loose like this." He touched a strand of my hair, and any pity I felt for him vanished. I jerked abruptly away from him.

"Don't touch me! You have no right to touch me."

"How can you say that? You were promised to me."

"I did no such thing."

"Well, it doesn't matter what you want." He turned away with a wounded air. "The border officials have already approved our marriage."

"Do you mean those ox-headed demons?"

"Be careful of what you say! Some of them are of very high rank." The smirk on his face was a pale imitation of his great-uncle's. Lim Tian Ching walked toward the far end of the room and picked up a cup. "Some tea?" he asked. I sat down heavily, relieved by the physical distance between us.

"I can't imagine why you had to run off like that," he said. "You must know I only had your best interests at heart." The hurt look reappeared on his face. "Why are you always so stubborn? Isn't it better for a young maiden to marry someone who cherishes her? I hadn't intended for you to reach the Plains of the Dead so soon. Indeed, I hoped you would enjoy many more years of a long life."

His words reminded me of Fan and her prematurely aged lover. "So you could feed off my *qi*?"

Lim Tian Ching's denial was a shade too vehement. "I don't need to resort to such cheap tricks! I'm not some hungry ghost. Look around you." He drew himself up. "I'm an important man, Li Lan. If you're lucky, you can be a great *tai tai* here."

"What makes you think you're such a great man?" I asked. "Just because your family humors you?"

His expression darkened. "I'm the one who humors them! It's because of the special status of my case that we have a relationship with the border officials. And when I've gathered enough evidence, I'll prove to everyone what happened."

"How do you even know whether you were murdered?"

"Don't be ridiculous! It's true I had a fever that day, but it wasn't until I drank that tea before bedtime that my pulse began to race. I couldn't breathe or even call out. And in the night, my heart stopped." He glared at me.

"It could have been a seizure from the fever," I said, thinking rapidly of all the illnesses Amah had ever warned me about.

"There was a thick residue in the cup. You know he was once a medical student—who else in the house would know about drugs and dosages? And who profited from my death but Tian Bai?"

I swallowed, wondering whether to say anything. "There might have been other people who didn't like you. Or your mother," I said, hurrying on in spite of his outrage. "Tian Bai wasn't even at home when you died. And Yan Hong still has your teacup hidden away. Did you ever consider her instead?"

"She hid it?" He had an odd expression on his face. "How do you know?"

Not wanting to mention that I had gone spying into the real Lim mansion, I dropped my eyes. But Lim Tian Ching said angrily, "So what if she kept the teacup? That doesn't mean anything. It was Tian Bai who gave me a present of rare tea!"

My tongue was thick and numb, as though it was two sizes too large for my mouth. Lim Tian Ching began to pace, picking at his trailing robes.

"He could have slipped something into the leaves earlier. He didn't need to be around when I died. In fact, he would probably ensure he was away at such a time. Yan Hong must have been protecting him. The two of them were always close, always against me. When she wanted help arranging her marriage to that penniless husband of hers, who did she go running to, Tian Bai or me?" He paused, controlling his voice with difficulty.

"My cousin always got what he wanted. The servants cosseted him, even my father had a soft spot for him. The only one who saw through him was my mother. She urged my father to send him abroad to study. I hoped he would never come back." The pupils of his eyes contracted until they were no more than specks.

"Did you know he had a mistress in Hong Kong?" Seeing my reaction, he pursued his advantage relentlessly. "She was some half-caste Portuguese girl.

There was a huge scandal and he was forced to leave school. My father had to pay an enormous sum of money to get rid of her. Some people said there was even a child. So don't believe him if he says you're the only one he loves. In the end he would have abandoned you, just as he cast that woman off."

A terrible silence descended upon the room. Lim Tian Ching wiped his mouth with the edge of his sleeve. I couldn't utter a word. At length, he gathered himself. "I'll leave you to think about this. It has no doubt been a shock to your delicate sensibilities." He clapped his hands and the door opened. A female puppet servant appeared. "See that she's given every consideration," he said. Glancing at me, he added, "The demons will question you tonight. Perhaps then you'll revise your opinion of me."

FOR A LONG TIME after he left, I didn't move. The puppet servant waited, its patience unrelenting until, at last, I roused myself to follow its bidding. Dazed, I washed and combed my hair. Clothes had been laid out for me—heavy, stiff garments of an antique cut. Burial clothes. I put them on numbly, slipping the letter and the scale in unobserved. The female puppet servant dressed my hair, pinning it elaborately with jeweled ornaments. With impersonal movements, it powdered my face with rice powder and rouged my lips and cheeks. Then it lit a candle and blackened a pin with soot. It mixed this with a little wax paste and used it to darken my eyelashes. I didn't flinch, even when the pin was brought close to my eyes.

I didn't cry. Since the Lim family had approached my father about a ghost marriage, I had shed tears at every juncture. When Lim Tian Ching had begun haunting me, when I learned of Tian Bai's arranged marriage, and later, when I was disembodied and wandering the streets of Malacca. This time, however, there were no tears. My heart felt as hard and dry as a salted apricot.

Lim Tian Ching might be lying to me. Nothing would please him more than to destroy any relationship I had with his cousin. And the symptoms of his death could apply just as well to a fevered seizure as to an overdose of a stimulating herb like ma huang. But there was no denying that he had constructed a plausible case. It would have been easy, very easy to do just as he suggested and include a poisoned decoction among the rest. I thought with despair of Tian Bai and realized that I didn't know whether he was capable of such a deliberate risk.

But the most damning evidence was what I had seen when I entered Tian Bai's dreams and memories. There on a high cliff, I had seen him stare longingly at a Eurasian girl. Isabel Souza, I remembered her name well. Surely this was the mistress that Lim Tian Ching had alluded to. To think that he might have had a child by her! If I survived all this and managed to return to my body, what future would I have? To be held in Tian Bai's arms in the flesh, I had thought, would make all this worthwhile. But even if he were innocent and such a thing came to pass, I would never be first in his heart.

DUSK DESCENDED LIKE A curtain in this staged world. My face in the mirror was a pale oval in the dimness of the room. I looked thinner, more mature. The angles of my cheekbones frightened me, and I wondered if they heralded the beginning of my starvation as a hungry ghost. Perhaps it was the clothes or the elaborate makeup; but the girl in the mirror, with her slender neck and shadowed eyes, looked like all the romantic heroines I used to pore over in books. I felt sick. Whatever charms I possessed were destined for Lim Tian Ching's bedchamber. It was he who would lift the red bridal veil, and his sweating palms that would seize hold of me. I thought about snatching up a hairpin to disfigure myself, but I was reminded of my mother and her status in this household. It would be foolish to throw away any leverage I had.

Glancing out of the window, I was struck by an unwelcome realization. The ten days that I had asked Fan to wait for me were up. She must have already started the journey across the Plains of the Dead. Even if I survived my interrogation by demons, I might be walled up in this mansion for centuries as Lim Tian Ching's bride. And what of Er Lang? Perhaps he too had gone, since I had missed our rendezvous at the red pavilion. In my anguish, I gave an involuntary cry. "Er Lang!"

There was a clatter as an empty basin fell off the washstand. I froze, fearing the appearance of a puppet servant, but long minutes passed without interruption. Yet something strange was occurring. The air near the washstand twisted and darkened like smoke, then condensed abruptly into a familiar, mushroom-brimmed form.

"I thought you would never call me." Er Lang's voice was the sweetest sound I had heard.

"What—where were you?" I asked. In my eagerness, I grasped his sleeve. It disappeared between my fingers and I gave a faint cry of surprise.

"It seems I'm having some difficulties maintaining a form in this world."

"Er Lang!"

"Call me again!" he said urgently.

I repeated his name, and to my amazement his figure solidified until I could feel the weight of the cloth in my hand. "What happened to you?"

"Well, it was harder than I thought to stay in the Plains of the Dead. This spirit form proved to be quite unstable. It has taken me all this time to break through again, and if you hadn't called me, I probably wouldn't have been able to return."

"So you didn't do any spying after all," I said. It was a childish thing to point out, but he made a mock bow.

"No, I didn't. In fact, I'm in your debt. And by the way, you look lovely tonight. Much improved from last time."

Despite myself, I colored. When Lim Tian Ching had complimented me, I had merely felt revulsion, but praise from Er Lang made my chest flutter unexpectedly. That fascinating voice was an unfair advantage, I thought. One that made even his offhanded remarks beguiling. But it didn't rule out the possibility that he might use me as some other sort of bait.

"Can you get me out of here?" I asked, ignoring his last comment. "The demons are coming to interrogate me soon. Or were you planning to wait until they were done with me?"

"What a scold you are!" he said. "How can you possibly expect to catch a husband like this? It wasn't as though I was exactly sitting on my hands."

Despite his complaints, I could hear the amusement in his tone, or perhaps it was just that I had become accustomed to him.

"If you didn't insist on wearing that ridiculous hat, you might have better luck materializing here."

"It's purely for self-protection. I would be far too recognizable without it."

"Who would recognize you?"

He shrugged. "I can't help that I was born with such remarkable looks. But enough about me. What has happened here?"

HASTILY, I RECOUNTED ALL that had happened, including the conversations between my mother and Master Awyoung. Lastly, I produced the crumpled letter I had stolen from the Old Master with a feeling of triumph.

"It has meeting dates and names the Sixth Judge of Hell," I said. "Is that evidence enough for your case?"

Though I couldn't see his face, Er Lang seemed extremely pleased.

"Very good," he said at length. "I must congratulate myself."

"Yourself?" I spluttered.

"Why, yes. For recruiting you as a spy. From the moment I saw you, tracking me so diligently through a mangrove swamp, I thought that this was a girl who could certainly be counted on to dig around the underworld."

"Why . . . you!" I said indignantly, until I realized that he wasn't serious. "You owe me a favor, then. I need to return to my body."

"As for that, I promised you my help. But shouldn't you be concerned about getting out of this place first?"

"Can't you help me?"

He spread his hands regretfully. "Much of my strength is gone, for I expended too much *qi* trying to get here. To reach the realm of the dead, I had to empty myself of it."

Despite my disappointment, I could scarcely resist the urge to cling to him. I'd come to rely too much on him, I thought. "Then find Auntie Three!" I burst out. "The little old woman from the kitchens. She said she would help me. Also, can you catch up with Fan?" Hurriedly, I gave him a brief description of her. "By this time she should be somewhere on the plains; but if you can travel fast, tell her to wait for me at the entrance to the tunnel, for without her I don't think I can find the right door. Or can you show me the way out?"

"I told you, the way I came is not possible for you. This tunnel you speak of—I doubt that I could help you see in it. Remember, you and I are the only living creatures in this world." His words, though softly spoken, brought a chill to my heart. And I was all but half dead already.

"I must get out!"

Even as I said these words, doubt filled my heart. Now that I had handed him the letter, what was to stop Er Lang from simply abandoning me here? His very features, under the ubiquitous bamboo hat, remained a cipher to me. My fears must have shown in my face, for he laid one hand lightly on mine. Without thinking, I clutched it. Er Lang didn't say a word, but his grip tightened. I could trace the warm width of his palm, the length of his fingers. Yet it was indisputably a man's hand: beautifully boned, larger, and far stronger than mine. The tightness in my chest eased. A peculiar comfort seeped into my skin as I considered his words, *The only living creatures in this world*. I had been too long in this negative realm, surrounded by the dead and their facsimiles of life. But I wasn't dead yet.

Er Lang turned. "Prepare yourself, then. If I can, I will find this Auntie Three. The ox-headed demons are coming."

"How do you know?" I ran after him, suddenly fearful of being left again.

"It's better if you don't know. Now, the door will open shortly. If I were you, I would take off some of that unsuitable jewelry."

With that, he was gone. Hastily, I plucked the pins from my hair, braiding it again into my usual schoolgirl plaits. The formal robes I wore were completely unsuitable for running, let alone riding, and I cast around frantically for my servant's clothes. They were gone, however, and my own pajamas had not reappeared as they used to. A new fear seized me. Had Amah stopped taking care of my body? Whatever it was, there was no time to waste. I stripped off the outer robes, thankful at least that I had a pair of loose trousers under the

trailing garments. The shoes were impossible: thick heeled and clumsy with
ornate toes. I would have to go barefoot.

Sooner than I had expected, I heard a shout outside. There were thumps
and movement, as though people were milling around beyond the door. Then
silence. Suddenly the door opened with a quiet click, as though someone had
unlatched it. I bolted into the corridor. It was empty except for Er Lang.

"Go that way," he said. "I'll delay them."

"What did you do?"

"Set some fires," he said laconically. "Paper houses burn well, if you know
the right way to go about it. I'll try to find your friend Fan on the plains. Now,
run!"

CHAPTER 29

I THINK I shall always remember that mad journey. The twisting corridors, the endless suites of empty rooms. It was well that I had memorized Auntie Three's map, otherwise I would surely have been lost. Indeed, sometimes I still see that house in my dreams and fear that I shall never leave it. At one point I ran through the very banquet hall that Lim Tian Ching had decked out for our engagement, so long ago it seemed. The same crimson banners and lanterns still hung there; the long tables still piled with festive platters of fruits and flowers that did not decay. When I passed the spot where he had toasted our impending nuptials, my heart shied like a nervous horse, but there was no one there. In that, Er Lang had been as good as his word. I didn't know how he had accomplished it, but there was not a soul in that part of the mansion.

When I reached the banquet hall, I threw open the sliding doors and ran out into the night. I knew from Auntie Three's map that if I could get out into the grounds, there was a good chance I could follow the outer wall and reach the kitchen quarters. Outside, the ground was rough and uneven. I slipped several times and wished heartily for shoes, but it was too late. I would have to run on, even if my soles were shredded to the bone.

There was no moon and no stars in that dead world, just the deepening of the sky as though the curtain was coming down on a play. At last I reached the outer courtyard of the kitchens. Whatever had stricken the rest of the mansion, the kitchen at least seemed immune. I could hear the clang of pots and even the barks of the cook as he presided over his puppet servants. I strained to hear whether Auntie Three was with him. Could she have gone to look for me? Slipping through the gate, I dashed across to the servants' quarters and fumbled my way into my room, not daring to light the oil lamp. I called out softly to my little horse, but there was no response. In growing dismay, I pushed aside the barrier of screens to find that she was gone.

I choked. How could I possibly traverse the plains without my steed? Perhaps Auntie Three had taken her. She'd said she would wait for me near the back gate, although it was long past the time we had agreed on. I ran, my breaths coming as heaving sobs. When I reached the gate, a small figure detached itself from the shadows. It was Auntie Three.

"Li Lan! Are you all right?" she asked.

I nodded, barely able to speak. Something was wrong, however.

"You must go!" said Auntie Three. "Your horse is here outside the gate." Then she asked, "Why do you look at me so strangely?"

"How do you know my name?" I asked.

"Your name?"

"I never told you my name. I said I was girl number six when I arrived."

In the faint light, Auntie Three looked stricken. Pressing a hand to my aching side, I continued, "You called me by my name earlier as well, when you found me in Master Awyoung's quarters. I didn't think about it at the time."

"Does it matter? You don't have time for this."

"Of course it matters! How do I know if I can trust you?"

She was silent for a moment, then she lifted her eyes. "I lied to you."

I shrank away from her outstretched hand.

"But I did it for your own good."

"My own good!" I said bitterly. "It's surprising how many people know what's best for me."

"How can I explain? You should go now, before the demons come."

"So what are you really?" I asked. "Another spy? One of Master Awyoung's minions, or do you belong to Lim Tian Ching? It was really very clever. I actually liked you."

"You liked me?" For some reason, this seemed to affect her.

"What does it matter? No doubt you're here to lock me up again."

"How can I convince you?" she asked, wringing her hands.

"Then tell me the truth!"

"Listen then, Li Lan, although I am afraid this will only delay you. I am your mother."

MY MOTHER! HOW COULD this ancient creature be my mother? I had been so sure that Second Wife, in all her lissome beauty, was she. My disbelief must have shown in my face. "You must find me disgusting," said Auntie Three. "I know that I look nothing like what you expected. Believe me, it has been difficult to hide this from you."

"But how is this possible?"

"You were right that I came to this household. You met the Third Concubine at our old house? I guessed as much when you spoke to me earlier. Truly, your grandfather was wrong to take her as a concubine. She was young and full of life; she was sorely disappointed in him. I didn't know then about her connection to the Lim family or to my cousin, who later married Lim Tian Ching's father. He's still alive, is he not?"

I nodded, speechless momentarily.

"Still, when I died, I was surprised to see her here and also at the extent of her bitterness. Did she tell you about the smallpox?"

"She said she sent it." I faltered.

Auntie Three, or my mother, as I supposed I ought to think of her, sighed. I took the chance to study her. Her wrinkled face, scored with a thousand lines, looked weary and frighteningly ancient.

"She did send it. When I died, your father was very ill, and so were many members of our household. What a waste!"

"But you still haven't explained! Why are you so old now? Did you trade something, just as the Third Concubine did when she caused the smallpox?"

"Yes, I too traded the youth of my spirit body, or part of the essence of my soul. I did what she boasted of doing. I sought out the same creature."

"How could you do such a thing? And why?"

"Do you not know why? I wish you wouldn't ask me."

"But I want to know! You owe me this, at least!"

"I left you alone, motherless. But I traded my youth for your recovery from the smallpox."

My hand fingered the small scar behind my left ear. That was all that remained of the disease that had ravaged our household. At the time, a fortune-teller had said I was extremely lucky.

"She meant to do as much damage as possible. If you hadn't died, you would have survived like your father, permanently scarred. Then who would marry you? You would have had no future."

"You did that for me?"

"It was my fault. Why should you suffer her wrath?"

"How can you say that it was your fault?"

"Because I saw she was unhappy and I did little to befriend her. We were young women living in the same household, except I was married to a man I loved and she was the concubine of an old man. And she wanted a baby desperately. I've often thought that if only I had been a little kinder to her, then maybe none of this would have transpired."

"But she was so horrible about everything!"

"Child, what does it matter now? When you came here, to the Lim household, I could hardly believe it."

"You recognized me?"

"You looked familiar to me. Your voice and your mannerisms. The stories you told about your amah. She was my amah too, you know."

My heart was beating with a strange kind of happiness. She had recognized me! My mother had known me!

"I was so shocked that you were here. I was afraid you were dead, but your name hadn't come up on the lists of the deceased yet."

"I thought I could find out something about Lim Tian Ching," I said. "But why are you here in the Lim mansion?"

Auntie Three shrugged. "I was afraid if I went back to the house your father burned for me, looking the way I do now, the Third Concubine would know that I too had made a bargain with a demon. It wasn't cheap. It cost me more than it cost her simply to save you. If she knew that I'd tried to help you, she might well try something else. So I wandered around, waiting for my time in the Plains of the Dead to be up. I worked in a few great houses in return for room and board."

"Why didn't you travel to the world of the living to see me?" I asked.

"I did. A few times only, until the journey became too difficult for me. Because I didn't return to the house, I couldn't accept any funeral offerings, which might have made it easier." The matter of fact way in which my mother said this pierced me to the heart. "Eventually, either she or I would go on to the Courts of Judgment. And you were alive and doing well. Amah was taking good care of you. Can you believe that I'm now older than Amah is?" She gave me a watery smile.

"But how did you come to the Lim mansion?"

"I heard rumors about the young master and his obsession with the daughter of the Pan family."

"But you said you had been here for years!"

"It has been years. Time passes strangely in this place."

I clasped her hands in mine.

"Don't be sad, Li Lan," she said. "To see you, and speak to you, has been more than I could ever expect. But the night is passing. You must be on your way. I didn't wish to burden you with this sad family history. I wanted you to live your life free from these old feuds."

"Come with me!" I said. "My horse can carry us both."

She shook her head. "I would slow you down. And it would be suspicious if I disappeared as well, especially if they started to dig further. Right now, they think you're merely a distraction, the object of Lim Tian Ching's desire."

"But I need you!" The words burst out before I even realized it.

"You don't need me, Li Lan," she said. "You're no longer a child. But you must go now. If they catch you it will be all for naught. Don't let them capture you!" She grasped my hand, her grip surprisingly strong. I gazed into her rheumy eyes, the irises clouded with the bloom of old age, and understood with a shudder that she, more so than others, realized what it meant to be in the clutches of a demon.

We hurried through the small back gate. Outside, all was dark and still. The road winding around the estate was deserted, a pale ribbon in the gathering dusk. My little horse stood outside, already caparisoned with saddlebags. When she saw me, she gave a soft whicker. "What's this?" I asked as I touched the bags. They were stiff and bulky, bound with rope.

"It's meat. Not real meat, but the food of the dead," said Auntie Three. "You may need it if they send pursuers. I pray that you will not."

"How did you know I would need it? Did Er Lang find you?"

She nodded. "I was frightened when he appeared. But he said he was your friend. Otherwise I would never have known to get ready. That man—" Her voice trailed off.

"He's not human, I know that."

She looked relieved that I was at least aware of who I was consorting with. As I clambered onto Chendana, my mother fussed over the bags, tightening a girth here and repacking them. Her movements were so precise that I felt a tightness in my throat. How I had missed her! And yet, her method of packing and checking was familiar. We had both been raised by Amah, after all.

"Mother!" I said. She looked up. "Come with me," I entreated again.

She shook her head. "When all this is over, I'll try to cross the plains and see you again." I bent my head in sorrow, but she reached up and planted a dry, whispery kiss on my forehead. Her thin hand caressed my hair for a brief second, then Chendana leaped away, her hooves devouring the surface of the road. I turned behind me. My mother was a tiny figure standing in the road. Her stooped form, with one hand raised, receded rapidly into the gloaming until I could see her no more.

CHAPTER 30

I GAVE CHENDANA her head, telling her only to take me to the mouth of the tunnel. The streets of ghostly Malacca appeared and disappeared before my eyes; the houses faded in and out of one another like wraiths. At this time of night, some were darkened shells while others were lit with a blaze of lamps, as though grand parties were celebrated within. One house was on fire, but though flames licked the rafters, the framework of the house never collapsed. At one point, I could have sworn we galloped right by the Stadthuys, then turned a corner only to find ourselves advancing on it again. There was little traffic on the roads. The faces of the dead glanced at me as we passed them, some surprised, others bored and incurious. When we had passed the harbor, where ghost ships bobbed on a sea of grass, I became afraid that we would never be able to leave, but suddenly we were out on the endless plains again.

A strong wind blew, chilling me through my inadequate clothing. How I wished now for some of the bulky garments that I had discarded! But Chendana was running like a horse that scents freedom. Her sturdy legs pounded the ground and the stiff grass flew by below us. Above was the dark vault of the sky. I could neither see nor hear any signs of pursuit, but a heavy dread lay upon my heart. Something was coming; it was only a matter of time before it found me. As we galloped tirelessly, I was aware of how easily we could be seen among the silvery dried grass. My thoughts flickered back to Tian Bai. I felt if only I could look into his eyes again, I would know what sort of person he was. It was no use telling myself I was being ridiculous; my heart refused to obey my mind. Indeed, the desire to see him seemed to grow in proportion with the suspicion that lay coiled within me.

After a time I grew weary. Terrified of falling off, I wound my arms and legs through Chendana's harness. I had been afraid that the weight of the bags would slow my little horse, but she didn't seem to notice. I compared her speed with the sedate pace of Fan's rickety bearers. Surely we were going twice, no, thrice as fast! At this rate, I might well catch up with her before she disappeared into the mouth of that tunnel. At some point I must have fallen asleep, for I was dimly aware of lying across Chendana's back, my face buried in her sweetly scented mane.

I was woken by a sudden jolt. Dazed, I raised my head, wondering whether we had arrived at our destination. A fine line of gray light showed on the horizon, like the embroidered border on a sleeve. The sea of brittle grass stalks moved restlessly in the wind. Ahead lay the mountains I remembered, where the passageway to the world of the living was. The dark jagged maw was visible, yet it was still so far away! I couldn't understand why we had halted until I noticed the shimmering air in front. It thickened and curdled, just as it had in the Lim mansion. "Er Lang!" I cried. The air quivered, but nothing happened. I pulled out the scale and blew against its fluted edge. This time the vapors condensed into the familiar, bamboo-hatted figure. It stood for an instant, then crumpled forward.

With a cry, I scrambled down from Chendana's back. Up close, his clothing was scorched and the hem of his robe had been ripped away.

"What happened to you?" I asked.

"It appears that I overexerted myself," he said.

Despite his cool tone, he doubled over, pressing a hand to his side. There were ominous stains on his clothes and his forearms were scored with welts. As I stared at them, it occurred to me that his was the first blood that I had seen besides my own in the Plains of the Dead. Even Auntie Three (for I couldn't help thinking of my mother by this name) had only pale, bloodless wounds when her arms had been burned.

"Let me see," I said, but he avoided me with a slight movement.

"There's nothing you can do," he said sharply. "These are wounds of the spirit. I must get back to my body in order to heal them, and so should you. But that's beside the point. You have very little time left. I delayed them as long as possible, but they are coming now."

"What does that mean?"

"It means," he said with irritation, "that you should get on that horse and ride as fast as possible. I managed to find your friend. She was about to enter the passageway, but I persuaded her to wait. She's there now, can you see?"

I squinted into the distance and saw, by the dark opening, a white speck that could have been Fan's dress. "You went there and came back just to tell me that?"

"Stop asking foolish questions and go!"

"But what about you?"

"I'll stay in case they come."

"You can't possibly stay here! You're too weak."

"Don't be ridiculous," he said.

Ignoring him, I glanced back at my little horse. "Help me!" I said to her. She came and knelt so that I could drag Er Lang across her back.

"It will slow you down," his voice was growing faint.

"Then I'll just get rid of this meat," I said. Quickly, I dragged the saddlebags off, slashing at the knots with Er Lang's scale. The sacks tumbled onto the ground and I began to shake them out, wincing at the bloodless joints of meat, offal, and flaps of skin that my mother had packed. I scattered them haphazardly, throwing some of the smaller pieces farther away. It occurred to me that I should keep a few of them with me just in case. Er Lang hadn't said what was pursuing me, but I had an uneasy feeling that it might be carnivorous. Hastily, I scrambled onto Chendana's back but as I did so, Er Lang began to slide off. I realized then that he had lost consciousness.

"Get up!" I shrieked, dragging at his arms. "Hurry!"

He grimaced but managed to hold on to the girths. Chendana began to gallop in earnest. I was thankful again that she was not a real horse. Her gait was steady enough so that I could just hang on to Er Lang as he slumped behind me. It was far more difficult than I had thought. He was heavier than me and kept sliding backward. I wound my arms around him, feeling the muscles of his lean torso tense in pain. It was then that I remembered the cords that had tied the saddlebags. Using a few lengths, I tied him as best as I could to myself, the ropes cutting in across my shoulders as we were bound back to back. Several times, I was sure that we would both fall off, but miraculously we remained seated.

The mountains in front were clearer, but I realized that it was also because it was getting brighter. The cover of darkness that had felt so comforting was beginning to dissipate. It was hard to describe the agony of that ride. Er Lang must have fainted again, for he began to slip. With every jolt, I felt his limp body shift away and I strained to counterbalance his heavier weight. After a while, I felt a warm trickle on my neck and putting my hands up, found them stained with blood. For a moment I thought that the ropes had cut into my flesh, but it soon became apparent that it wasn't my blood. He must have been more seriously wounded than I had thought. I reached behind me to grasp his waist and he came to with a cry of agony.

"We must stop! You can't travel like this!"

"I told you to leave me," he said.

"Can you go back? Can you disappear through the air again?" I shouted at him, against the rushing wind.

"Not enough *qi*," he mumbled. "Just dump me here."

"I won't!"

"You fool."

"Who's the fool?" I said angrily. "You should just have gone away."

"Then you would have missed your friend Fan."

"Who cares?" I shrieked. "And take that stupid hat off! It's cutting into my neck."

He began to laugh weakly. "What a harridan you are. How could I let you be devoured when there's still so much scolding left in you?"

"How dare you say that!" But I was secretly relieved that he could speak again. "Now take that hat off."

"If I remove it, you will never treat me the same way again." His tone was so serious that I was afraid that I had offended him. My father too was wary of displaying his ruined face before strangers. Of all people, I should have been more sensitive to that. Er Lang seemed to have read my mind, for he didn't speak again for a long time.

The sky grew ever brighter as we rushed toward the cliffs ahead. "Hold on," I said, "we're nearly there."

"No." Er Lang's voice was dull. "It's too late."

In terror, I twisted around. He was facing backward and I could see in the distance a dark cloud flying swiftly across the land. "What is it?" I asked.

"They sent the birds. The flying beasts."

FAR AWAY I COULD see them gathering, those strange creatures that had flown over our camp that first night on the Plains of the Dead. I remembered how Fan had fallen to the ground, trembling and weeping at their approach, their swift flight slicing the air with triangular wings. At first they were no more than a faint cloud in the distance, but with frightening rapidity they began to advance, their forms becoming crisper and darker in the morning light.

"Run! Run as fast as you can!" I cried to my horse.

In response, Chendana sprang away at an even greater pace. I could barely hold on to the pommel of the saddle and would surely have fallen if Er Lang had not gripped me from behind.

"Cut the ropes!" he hissed.

"You'll fall off!"

"I won't!"

Indeed, he seemed much stronger than before and I was amazed at his stamina. Now the mountains were racing to meet us. With every moment that passed they loomed larger. I could clearly pick out Fan's tiny figure, like a paper doll at the entrance to the tunnel. She turned as if to go in, but hesitated. I was terrified that she would leave without me. Twisting round, I glanced again at the birds, expecting them to be almost upon us, but to my surprise they had halted. They wheeled around, swooping and diving in confusion.

"The meat," said Er Lang. "It was a good idea."

I opened my mouth to say that it was my mother's foresight, not mine, when I remembered the last saddlebag that I had kept. Leaning over, I pulled the cord open with my teeth, scattering the stiff gobbets of flesh as we rode. I hoped this would delay them enough for us to reach the tunnel, but when I looked back, only a few stragglers remained behind. The main body of the flock was flying rapidly now, streaming toward us with every flick of those unnatural wings. I could not imagine their speed, for they must be many times faster than Chendana to gain on us like this.

"Let me loose!" Er Lang was struggling again, and his attempts to free himself from the ropes that bound us together threatened to plunge both of us from the horse. I tugged the scale he had given me out of my pocket, then paused.

"Why?" I screamed.

"Just do it!" He grabbed my hand and with a swift movement, sliced away the ropes.

"What are you doing?" I cried, but in an instant he was free. I thought he said something, but I barely heard it because the birds broke upon us like a storm.

WITH PIERCING, MEWLING CRIES, they fell on us like starving creatures. There was nothing but leathery wings, staring eyes, and sharply serrated beaks. They were like no birds I had ever seen before, with scythe-like claws. The sky was blotted out. I couldn't even cry out with the fierceness of their onslaught. A talon raked across my face as I cowered behind Er Lang, clinging to his body instinctively as a barrier against them. Then he was changing, his form writhing and contorting even within my astonished grasp. I couldn't hold him anymore. Smooth scales slid beyond my hands, his body too large to be encompassed. I caught glimpses of a pearl-like sheen, a thousand slippery plates sliding past one another in an endless loop, then an enormous head, the eyes shining like lamps and the teeth gleaming in a whiskered jaw. He rose up into the sky, shaking and snapping at the flock, curling back on his snakelike length and slashing with his claws. A great dragon, a *loong*, lord of the water and air. I watched in bewilderment as Chendana carried me away at a frantic gallop, staring up at the battle that now raged high above me.

The birds mobbed him, diving and tearing rapaciously. At first I thought he had the advantage, for several fell, broken-winged and crippled, but there were so many more of them. I could hardly see him for the black shapes that ravaged him, ripping mercilessly until gouts of dark blood stained the pearl white sides. I cried out in horror, but even as I did so the struggle moved ever farther from my sight, so that I could hardly make out the details anymore. I realized then that even as I rode toward the cliffs, he must have been flying in the opposite direction. "Stop!" I screamed, but for once my little horse ignored me, bearing me swiftly out of danger. They were now so far I could barely spy them, a smudged cloud on the horizon. Suddenly, the mass of wings dropped from the sky. It was no longer a battle. It was carnage. I covered my face and wept.

WE REACHED THE MOUTH of the cavern without further incident. My face was covered in blood and tears, my clothing torn and shredded. The gash over my forehead had bled copiously and I had done little to stanch the flow. More than once I had tried to turn back, but it was to no avail. Chendana would not heed me; I wondered whether it was a natural instinct to preserve her mistress, or whether Er Lang had said something to her so that his sacrifice wouldn't be in vain. I would never know.

When I dismounted, Fan was standing there waiting for me. She was one of the last people I wished to see, but there was no hope for it. Staring at my bedraggled appearance, she said, "You lied to me."

I barely had the heart to nod at her.

"You said you were from heaven."

"I never said that. You just assumed it."

She sighed. "I thought you wouldn't make it. Come, we must hurry."

Once inside the tunnel, the familiar gloom descended upon us. Soon, I could see less and less, relying on my hand entwined in Chendana's mane to keep me from stumbling.

"So," said Fan conversationally, after we had walked some time in the darkness. "You're just a ghost like me after all."

I felt a great weariness, but she went on. "That man told me. He appeared out of the air, just as I had reached the cliffs. I was so surprised! He asked me if I was the one who had brought a human to the Plains of the Dead, and he told me to wait for you."

"That's right," I said at last. I had no wish to talk to her, but she kept pestering me with questions. It was easier to give her desultory answers while my mind, in shock, was still fixed upon Er Lang. Had he survived? It seemed impossible.

"So all this about a mission was also untrue?" she asked.

"No, I was helping him, in return for my body."

"Your body?" She seemed much interested in the fact that I still had a living body in Malacca. "What a waste!" she said. "How could you abandon it? If I were you I would have stuck close by."

"If I had, perhaps he wouldn't have died."

"Who was he, after all? I couldn't really see what happened, only that the birds stopped chasing you and started flying the other way."

Surprised, I realized that with the whitening sky and the great distance,

Fan might not have been able to see Er Lang's pearl bright form against the horizon.

"He was a minor government official," I said.

THE REST OF THE journey through the tunnel, shut in on all sides by enclosed rock, passed in a numbed daze for me. Fan kept chattering, but I had little stomach to answer her. The air grew close and suffocating. The silence pressed on me like a stone.

"Well, I had a wonderful time in the Plains of the Dead," she said at length. "It was so nice to go back to my house. I changed my clothes and everything. Do you want to see what I bought with the money you gave me?"

I heard the swish of cloth, but by this time the darkness was complete to me. On the way in, we had had the faraway glow from the mouth of the tunnel to guide us, but going in the opposite direction there was no relief from the shadows.

"Oh, I forgot. You can't see anything here, can you? It must be because you're only half dead. That also explains why you looked so different to me." Fan continued to prattle on about her visit, her glowing account completely different from the glum and dismissive behavior she had displayed before. "Really, I don't know why I don't visit more often. It's such a pleasant place. I can't wait until my lover and I can build our own mansion there."

It's because you were afraid of the authorities, I thought, but didn't voice it.

"And socially—well! It was far better than my last visit. I met a number of high-ranking people who were very kind to me." Fan's light voice tinkled off the walls. At length she turned solicitously to me. "We're almost there. Do you need to rest?"

"So soon?" I asked. In my mind, the outward journey had taken a far longer time, but maybe that was the way with all unknown ventures.

"Yes," she said. "What will you do when you get back to Malacca?"

I hung my head. With Er Lang gone, I had no idea of what to do. If he were, indeed, dead. Even now, I wanted to turn back to search for his body, though it was madness. What if he was lying wounded somewhere in the grass? The thought distressed me so much that I could hardly breathe. But Fan was repeating her query.

"Go home, I suppose," I said, wishing she would stop asking me questions. I could barely even think of what to do if my house was still under guard.

"Oh, me too! I can't wait to see my lover again."

My own thoughts turned to Tian Bai. Perhaps I should find him as well, question him in his dreams and find out the truth behind Lim Tian Ching's accusations. But I didn't have the heart to think about it right now, overwhelmed as I was.

I was roused by Fan. "Here we are," she said.

I could see nothing at all, but I was conscious of her movements in front of me. There was a sudden rush of fresh air, as though the pressure had changed, and the faint gleam of stars in a night sky. I stepped forward, then stopped for a moment.

"Are you sure this is right?"

My words died in my mouth as I turned. Behind me I saw a door vanishing slowly, its edges fading into darkness. I caught a glimpse of Fan's pale face, illumined once again with the hazy green corpse glow she had lost in the Plains of the Dead. She was smiling, a faint, wicked smirk that winked out abruptly as the door closed. I stared around frantically. I was lost.

PART FOUR

Malacca

CHAPTER 31

I T WAS DARK outside, far darker than I would have expected in the immediate environs of Malacca. Shadowy trees loomed overhead and the stars were brilliant through the punctuated jungle canopy. In the Plains of the Dead, there had been no scent in that dry world, but here the air was green and intensely alive. I drank it in tremendous draughts, even as I felt like crying. Fan had betrayed me. This was nowhere near my home.

She had spoken of different doors in that passageway to the world of the dead, and had been surprised when I admitted that I couldn't see them. Any door might lead to a different place. What if this were somewhere far away, such as Johore, or even Kelantan on the east coast? Or an island across the Straits such as Bali or Kalimantan? There was no one to save me now. Er Lang was gone, Tian Bai a possible murderer, my mother a servant in the Plains of the Dead. I ran my fingers through Chendana's mane, thankful that she, at least, was still with me. It was true I could be anywhere, but I had the feeling that I wasn't too far from Malacca.

The smell of the vegetation and the faint tang of the sea were familiar. And I doubted Fan's capacity to thoroughly lose me. Fan was lazy; she would probably shove me out of a door fairly close to the one that we had entered from. Besides, she herself had admitted that she'd explored almost none of these alternate exits, fearing her incapacity as a ghost to find her way home. I wasn't like her, I told myself. I was only half dead, though the thought made me grimace. It didn't seem like something to be proud of. One of the few advantages of the Plains of the Dead was that I had been corporeal again there. But now as I gazed down at my feet and the dead leaves that were faintly visible through them, I was gripped by fear that my form was even more tenuous than it had been before. Er Lang had warned me about the long separation from my body. How many days, even weeks, had it been since I had left the world of the living? I felt so agitated that I almost started off into the jungle, wishing only to find some familiar landmark, but I stopped myself. It was dark and I was at the end of my strength. My eyes were swollen from crying. In the morning I might be able to take better bearings.

WHEN I WOKE, THE sun was shining. There had been no sun in the Plains of the Dead, but now shafts of warm light caught the tops of the jungle giants though their feet were still shrouded in gloom. I had never been so glad to be back, yet so downhearted as I surveyed the thick tropical undergrowth. It reminded me of how close I was to never returning to this world again. My path was as narrow as the blade of a knife. One false step, and I would be permanently severed from my body. I looked around to see if I could discern any sign of the door through which I had passed last night, but there was nothing. With each passing moment, I felt a pressing urge to return to Malacca. To find out if my body was still preserved. To see Amah, and my father. And Tian Bai. I was sure, perhaps naively so, that if I confronted him I would be able to tell if he was a liar. Or a murderer. I wondered too whether Fan's betrayal was purely spite or if someone put her up to it. Or if Lim Tian Ching and his demons were even now searching for me. But overshadowing these anxieties was the loss of Er Lang.

The chances of his survival were bleak. With a shudder, I recalled how he had joked about being devoured in the Plains of the Dead. I did not know what that meant, only that it had a dreadful finality. Since losing my own body, Er Lang had been the only one with whom I could speak freely about my fears and concerns. But I had never thanked him properly for coming to my aid, even when he could have saved himself and left without me. I missed his odd companionship desperately; it seemed impossible that I would never see him again. My chest constricted as I recalled how pleased he had been when I gave him the letter. And now that evidence too was destroyed.

I had often heard tales of *loong* during my childhood: great lords who controlled the rain and the seas. Sometimes they appeared as magnificent beasts, other times as kingly men or beautiful women. Occasionally, they took human wives or lovers; the emperor of China himself claimed descent from dragons and embroidered them on his robes. Five claws for royal garments, three for common folk. Recalling the tale of the scholar who visited the wonders of the Dragon King's palace underneath the sea, I could certainly understand now why Er Lang had felt entitled to patronize me. To see a dragon was considered lucky, but what if one were complicit in the death of one? The thought plunged me into greater depression.

Taking the scale out of my pocket, I examined it carefully. To my dismay, the color was flat and the shining luster dulled. I fought back the unhappy suspicion that the life had gone out of it and blew tentatively on the fluted edge. The sound was faint and choked. After a while, I put it away and buried my face in my hands.

With Er Lang gone, whom could I go to with my tale of rebellion and conspiracy in hell? And who would intervene in Lim Tian Ching's schemes to marry me? My hopes of regaining my body seemed doomed. I leaned back against the rough bark of a tree. The jungle around was thick and filled with the sound of insects. I heard a grunting sound as a wild pig ran through a clearing and, later, the curious coughing bark of a tiger. But there were no people or spirits. This door might once have opened onto an ancient settlement, though long ago, the last hungry ghost in this vicinity must have withered and vanished away. It was no use staying here, but the trees were so close that I had no sense of my surroundings beyond thirty feet. Gazing up at the forest canopy, I was struck by the idea of climbing to get my bearings.

It was far easier than I imagined. My light body needed scarcely any effort to pull up. Again, I tried to suppress the terrible suspicion that I had lost substance. Gritting my teeth, I set my gaze higher. When I broke through at last, I was dazzled by the brilliant sunlight. All around was an unbroken sea of green, an undulating ocean of thousands of leaves. The sky was a pure cerulean, as blue as the finest Ming porcelain. Butterflies the size of my hand fluttered slowly past, their wings glittering. In the bright sunshine and wind, I couldn't help heaving a sigh of relief.

From my perch I could see the distant sparkle of the sea and the curve of a bay. I could even, with my preternatural eyesight, spy the smudge of low red rooftops. I was right, Fan had discarded me just a few doors down from the correct exit. For most ghosts, a journey of this length would be impossible given their frail natures and difficulties walking straight. But I wasn't a ghost yet, and I still had my horse.

Though I rode as fast as I could, Chendana still had to pick her way between trees and over rocks as it was exhausting to pass through solid objects. I suspected that every time I did so, I lost more substance. To make matters worse, I frequently lost my way among the massive trunks and was forced to climb again to get my bearings. From time to time, I blew on Er Lang's scale. There was never any response, but I continued in the vain hope that it could call him back. The hours dragged on till nightfall while the distance to the sea decreased in agonizingly slow increments. Naively, I'd thought I might get there by the next day at least, or even the day after—but to my dismay it took me almost a week to reach the outskirts of the port.

WE APPROACHED MALACCA FROM the north, coming up along the bay. Once we were clear of the trees, Chendana cantered freely and the miles of sand were eaten up under her hooves. We passed fishermen's settlements with wooden stilt houses standing over the water, boats drawn up on the beach.

Fish smoked over fires, and naked children played in the shallows. I passed them in a blur, unseen and unnoticed. Even the hungry ghosts stayed out of my way. The urge to return home was reeling me in like a fish on a line. I felt frantic with anxiety, for something strange was happening to me.

Sharp pains had begun to assail my body, followed by interims of numbing weakness, as though someone had sucked the marrow from my bones. Examining myself, I saw no visible wound, but I couldn't deny it. I had suffered some kind of harm. If it hadn't been for my little horse I would never have made it back, but she bore me onward when I was too weak to lift my head. These exhausting episodes came and went, though they weren't the only thing that worried me. My clothes had begun to change as well.

Instead of the usual pajamas that Amah used to dress my inert body in, I began to notice *sam foo*, and loose cotton dresses that I used to wear around the house. At times the garments became even more formal. *Baju* that I rarely used, even my mother's *kebaya* once. When that happened I was terrified. Were they preparing me for burial? But the clothes continued to change and I still remained in this world of the living. Still, I was anxious, very anxious.

As we drew nearer, warehouses began to appear and I realized that we were very close to Tian Bai's office in the Lim family godown. The temptation to stop and see him was irresistible, so I turned aside. When I'd last seen him, it had been a slow, torpid afternoon, but now it was midday and the fierce tropical light beat down. The warehouse was swarming with coolies laden with crates and sacks. I stopped in the narrow pathway outside, invisible to the gaunt men who, half naked, toiled under the burning sun. Their rib cages stood out in stark relief, their toenails were black and broken. Some had cut their hair in the new Western style, just as Tian Bai did, but the majority still bore long greasy pigtails, the front of their skulls shaven like a new moon. A rank smell of sweat rose from their bodies as they passed close to me.

Slipping off Chendana's back, I made my way through the stream of people, shuddering at how they avoided me instinctively like a plague-ridden dog. At the doorway, I was struck by another bout of weakness. Reeling, I crossed the lintel and knelt on the floor. I heard orders being barked and the heavy tread of feet. Despite my lack of substance, I had an instinctive fear of being trampled and tried to rise. It was then that I heard Tian Bai's quiet, steady voice.

He looked thin and there were shadows under his eyes that I didn't remember. Still, he passed through to the rear office with the easy gait that I remembered. I stumbled after him. Tian Bai seemed graver, not so quick to smile as I remembered. The conversations he had were all business related. I was impressed that he could speak so many different dialects of Chinese: Hokkien, Cantonese, and Hainanese, as well as Malay and even a little Tamil. But why should I be surprised? Most people could speak at least two or three languages here. My estimation probably stemmed from the fact that it was Tian Bai, and I was inclined to admire all things that he could do.

Midday turned into afternoon and I told myself that now that I had seen him, I should go home. Still, I lingered. I watched him anxiously, wondering if there was any deceit in that open face. Tian Bai had tiffin delivered to his desk as he pored over paperwork. He negotiated contracts and made abacus calculations with swift flicks of his wrist. Observing his competence, I could easily imagine how his uncle would favor him over his own spoiled son. Surely Lim Tian Ching's accusations were pure jealousy, although my doubts remained. Now that I had journeyed to the land of the dead and had seen that desires and feuds lingered even after death, I couldn't say such things were impossible.

Late in the day, an older man came in with a stack of papers.

"Not done yet?" he asked Tian Bai. He shook his head. "Your uncle works you too hard." The other man had a sly manner that I distrusted, and hearing the turn of the conversation, I drew closer until I stood at Tian Bai's shoulder. "I'm sure he's glad you came back from Hong Kong," he said. Many people said you would never return."

Tian Bai frowned. "Who said so?"

"They said you liked it better there."

"They were wrong."

"Really?"

Tian Bai lifted his eyebrows. "A Chinaman is still a second-class citizen there, even if he's a member of the Commonwealth."

His interlocutor raised his hands and laughed. "Ah, why so serious? Anyway . . ." He paused. "I wanted to congratulate you on your upcoming marriage. When is it?"

"In two months' time."

"I'm sure your uncle is anxious for you to be married, now that you're the only heir."

"He's been good enough to agree to it. Officially, the family is still in mourning."

Marriage! So he had agreed to the marriage, I thought. Miserably, I paced up and down after the man had left, passing so close to Tian Bai that I brushed his jacket with my sleeve. He didn't look up. It could only be to that horse-faced girl. Who else would be so acceptable to his uncle? I leaned over in front of him; I plucked at his sleeves with my insubstantial fingers, but to no avail.

"Tian Bai!" I cried. "Can you hear me?"

There was no response, but after a while he pushed his chair back with a sigh. In repose, his face was closed, the expression distant. I looked at the windowsill where his collection of curiosities was still arranged. Among the carved wooden animals, I noticed that the horse was missing and my mouth quirked. I knew where she had gone. And there was my comb at the very end of the row, almost like an afterthought.

A thin silvery line still ran from it, that insubstantial filament that had originally led me to Tian Bai. I walked over and plucked it between my fingers. Perhaps it was a trick of the light, but it seemed darker and less translucent than before. Still, it hummed to my touch like a live thing. I glanced over at Tian Bai who was still deep in thought. *Sleep*, I thought. *Sleep, so I can talk to you.* My will carried through the line, or it might simply have been the effects of a long day, for soon Tian Bai's eyes closed. When I was sure that he was asleep, I pressed the thread lightly into his chest, just as I had done before.

I WAS STANDING IN the front hall of the Lim mansion in Malacca. Long shadows stretched over the black-and-white tiled floor, and the house had a gloomy, watchful air. Tian Bai was walking away from me and as he turned down one passageway after another, I hastened to keep up with him in this dreamworld of his making. At length he reached the room with the clocks and began to wind them. He did this with great precision, yet as fast as he wound, he never finished the task. The clocks appeared to multiply under his fingers. I stole a glance at his face. It was set in concentration.

"Tian Bai!" I said. At this, he looked up.

He seemed utterly unsurprised, even pleased. "Ah, Li Lan. Give me a hand here."

Obediently, I began to wind the clocks. "What are we doing?" I asked.

"Making sure they don't run down."

"Why does it matter?"

"Of course it matters." A shadow creased his brow. "We don't want time to stop."

"What would happen if it did?"

Perplexed, he looked up. "It won't stop. It mustn't."

I couldn't understand him, but I had a terrible feeling that my own time was running out. Concentrating, I changed the scene to the courtyard with the lotus pond where we had first met.

"Tian Bai!" I said urgently. "I need to talk to you."

With the disappearance of the clocks, the tightness left his shoulders and he finally looked up at me. The warmth in his regard made me color.

"I haven't seen you for a long time," I said after a pause. "I'd like to know how you've been."

Tian Bai shook his head, amused. "What do you want to know?"

I opened my mouth, wondering whether I should ask him whether he had murdered his cousin. The question rolled back and forth on my tongue, like a weighty glass marble. And yet, I felt reluctant to waste this moment with him. The languid sunlight, the soft gleam of the lotus pond. I could have cried with the relief of it, even if it was only the figment of a dream.

"I heard you were going to be married," I said at last.

He took a step toward me, then another. "Yes, that's right."

"Oh." I was crestfallen. "Congratulations, then."

"Thank you." There was a glint in his eye, as though he was enjoying a private joke. Then he slipped his arms around me, drawing me against him. "I think there are better ways you can congratulate me, don't you?"

Dazed, I couldn't resist. I lifted my face to him and felt the touch of his breath, then his lips as he brushed them against my neck. At the very last instant, I twisted away. "But your fiancée!"

"What about her?" He buried his face in my hair and ran his hands through it, discarding the few hairpins that were left. My hands slid across his chest, then stopped.

"Wait," I said breathlessly. "Don't you care what she thinks?"

"Of course I care."

"Then why are you doing this?" I pushed him away with an effort, but he was still smiling. It was beginning to make me angry. "You're just like your cousin!" I said. "I suppose it doesn't matter how many concubines you have."

"What are you talking about?" He looked surprised.

"I mean, what do you think your fiancée would say if she saw you?"

"I don't think she would mind."

"Well, I mind," I said angrily. How could he behave like this? As though I were a mere side dish for the main event of his wedding. Tian Bai tried to take me in his arms again, but I stiffened despite the temptation to forget my sorrows in his embrace. No wonder Fan had chosen to continue her ghostly existence for years, if this was what it meant to enter a lover's dreams. But I wasn't Fan.

"Let me go!" I said through gritted teeth, though it took all my willpower to disengage myself.

"What's the matter with you?" he said.

"I don't even know who you're marrying."

A strange look appeared on Tian Bai's face. "You know who I'm marrying."

"Then say it! Just say it!"

"I'm marrying you, Li Lan."

. . . .

DUMBFOUNDED, I COULD ONLY stare at him. Tian Bai pulled me close and caressed my hair, murmuring endearments. "How is that possible?"

"I told my uncle he should honor the agreement he made with your father. And he finally acquiesced. But you know all this." He glanced sharply at me.

"When did this happen?"

"About a week ago."

"A week ago? And did I talk to you?" I asked, stupidly.

"I went over to your house as soon as I got his permission. They said you were sick, but you came down to see me. Don't you remember?"

"No. It's just not possible," I said. Anxiously, I shook him. "Are you sure?"

"Of course! We started planning the wedding right away."

"What did I look like?"

"Why, you looked like yourself. A bit pale, perhaps. And you were a little confused in the beginning. But no more than right now. Are you not well?" he asked.

"You don't understand," I said. "You can't have talked to me last week. I was very sick."

"I know," he said patiently, as though humoring a child.

I bit my lips. "Listen," I said, "whoever you spoke to last week wasn't me." But even as I spoke, I could see it was a lost cause. I entreated him to take me seriously and told him that he must only trust what I said to him now. He nodded, but as I could scarcely believe such a tale myself, I could hardly expect him to either. Panic threatened to engulf me. I had to get back to my body as soon as possible.

"I have to go," I said.

"So soon?"

"Yes, I really must. But I have one more question for you."

He smiled. "Oh? You're really in an odd mood today."

"Did you murder your cousin?"

The light went out of his eyes. "Why do you ask me this?"

"I just wanted to know," I said desperately. "I'm sorry." I hadn't meant to be so blunt, but anxiety made me stumble onward. "He died so suddenly, people said it was the tea you gave him."

"That? I gave it to him before he died. I also gave some to my uncle at the time."

"Then why does Yan Hong have Lim Tian Ching's teacup? She kept it after his death."

Tian Bai looked bewildered. "I don't understand you," he said. "And how do you know all this anyway?"

My pulse was racing irregularly. There was a buzzing in my head. His surprise seemed utterly natural; I wanted to believe him so badly. As if in response to my agitation, the world around us began to crumble and dissolve. The lotus pond shattered like a glass plate, and the courtyard around us wavered as though a wind had blown through it. Tian Bai had been studying me with a strange look, but now he glanced around. "What's happening?"

I could no longer hold on to the pretence of reality. The very flagstones beneath our feet were melting away into nothingness. "Is this a dream?" Tian Bai asked. I wanted to say something, to question him further about Yan Hong. But as soon as he uttered those words, the dream broke and I was falling, twisting, despite my best attempts, until I found myself staring down at Tian Bai's sleeping face once more.

CHAPTER 32

I HAD TO get back home. I didn't know why I was unable to sustain the dream conversation with Tian Bai. It could have been due to my exhaustion, or that our spirits had become too troubled. Whatever it was, I didn't have the luxury to speculate right now. Chendana needed no guidance as I told her to go home. Quickly, very quickly, indeed, we passed the Stadthuys and the town square. The sun had almost set, but though I looked for my friend the Dutchman, we cantered by so swiftly that I could not see if he was still there. Oil lamps were already being lit by the time I reached our house, their warm glow so different from the cold lights of the dead. Our street looked almost shockingly normal, after the winding, shifting distances in the Plains of the Dead. Standing in the white dusty road before our heavy wooden door, I felt a shiver of relief as though I had never left it.

I had been afraid that an ox-headed demon would still be standing guard, but the quiet street was empty. Perhaps it was merely out on patrol, but another detail arrested me. The yellow strips of spell paper that Amah and I had painstakingly pasted over every door and window were gone. I could hardly imagine that Amah would do such a thing, or that my father would rouse himself to remove them. Perhaps it was a good thing, for it now meant that I could enter freely into the house, something I had feared would hinder me. Yet, my hands trembled as I loosed Chendana's reins and slid down.

I passed easily through our front door. Too easily, to my dismay. It seemed that I had woefully little substance left in this world since my return from the Plains of the Dead. The hallway of our house was oddly small to my eyes, yet achingly familiar. I started up the stairs, my heart hammering in my chest. I could find no sign of Amah, but I almost ran down the corridor toward my room, so great was my anxiety. The door was ajar, and I considered for a brief moment if Amah was inside, but when I entered, there was nobody there. The bed where my body had lain was empty; the sheets smooth and unwrinkled as though no one had ever slept in it.

Gasping, I sank to the floor. A wave of weakness rolled over me and I silently cursed it. Now was not the time to be incapacitated. With an effort, I forced myself to look around. Nothing appeared particularly out of place. A few trinkets stood on the dresser; and when I peered under the *almirah*, Tian Bai's brass watch still winked in a dark corner. Presumably, no one had discovered it yet, which didn't say much for Ah Chun, our maid, and her housekeeping skills. Even as I thought this, Ah Chun herself appeared in the hallway outside with a bundle of laundry. I ran out after her. She didn't see me, of course, but so strong was the urge to speak to her that I had to clasp my hands together to prevent myself from grasping her shoulder. She walked downstairs, muttering under her breath, "Wash the clothes at night? I never heard of such a thing. Really, she's too much!" As she passed by the atrium, then the dining room downstairs, I heard voices. The family was sitting down to dinner, and to my horror, I heard among my father's measured tones, the familiar sound of a girl's voice.

The round marble-topped table was laden with food. Bowls of rice, platters of vegetables, even a steamed fish. Gathered around it was my father, a familiar-looking older woman with a plump face, and myself. At least, the physical form was mine. I stared at her disbelievingly, this stranger wearing my face. She was dressed in rather gaudy clothing, garments that I didn't recognize at all, and demurely picking at her food. From time to time she tilted her head to one side and, when spoken to, let out a fatuous little laugh. I would never have giggled in that way, I thought angrily. Yet no one seemed to notice. My father had lost a great deal of weight and his pockmarked skin was chalky and uneven. Still, he was in good spirits, glancing at his false daughter and smiling weakly from time to time. The other woman was speaking.

"So, Li Lan, we were happy to find out that you recovered. What a fright you gave your father!"

My impostor simpered and cast her lashes down.

"She was very confused when she came to," said my father. "She didn't even recognize me for a while."

"Let alone me!" laughed the woman. "Well, I haven't seen you for quite a few years, Li Lan, but I thought you might remember your own aunt."

No wonder she looked familiar. This aunt was one of my father's sisters who had moved away with her husband to Penang. Her daughter had been my dearest childhood friend. I hadn't seen her for years, but life in Penang must have suited her, for she had put on a great deal of weight.

"I came when I heard you were sick, but what a surprise to find you up and about, and engaged to be married, no less!"

"Yes, it was quite a shock to me as well," said my father. "The young man had been coming round, even though I told him she was sick and couldn't see him, but suddenly last week he barged in and said he had permission to marry her. Luckily, Li Lan had just started sitting up the day before, otherwise I don't know what we would have said to him!"

His smile was genuinely happy. I was surprised at the lump in my throat.

"It's a good marriage, then," said my aunt, approvingly.

"Yes, very good." My father helped himself to some stir-fried *kai lan*. "It's that boy from the Lim family. Do you remember him?"

My aunt frowned. "You mean the one—"

"The one who was originally betrothed to Li Lan."

"Oh, I thought they had broken it off!"

"Isn't it lucky that they changed their minds?" The girl at the table—that other me—gave a little laugh and reached for the steamed fish. Avidly, she scooped out the succulent cheeks, the best part, for herself, with no thought of offering them to her elders. I was consumed with icy rage. I knew that laugh.

Advancing toward the table, I shouted, "So this is how you repay me, you wretch!" But no one paid any attention to me. They continued to eat and talk calmly, as though I didn't exist. She did, however, lift her head from her plate momentarily, and that was when her eyes widened. The color briefly drained from her face, then a small, secretive smile appeared. From within the eyes I could see Fan's spirit peeking out at me. And clearly, she could see me too.

Dinner was a torment. In agony, I stalked round and round the table, shouting and pleading with her, but she paid me no heed. It became apparent that although she could see me, she couldn't hear my voice. Fan sat smugly, clad in my physical body, eating like an ox and giggling like a fool whenever anyone spoke to her. After dinner she went upstairs, pleading indisposition. I went after her, trailing angrily in her wake and berating her until my voice was hoarse. She went into my bedroom and shut the door in my face. When I forced myself through the door, I found her sitting at the mirror, combing her hair and staring dreamily at her reflection. After studiously ignoring me for a while, she turned around at last.

"So you found your way back here. I'm surprised." She yawned. "Oh, there's no point in shouting. I can't hear you anyway. I'm sure you want to know how I managed this. Well, it was very simple. I was always very curious about you, you know. Why you were so different. And of course, I didn't really swallow that story about you coming from heaven."

I ground my teeth in rage.

"Well, maybe in the beginning," she conceded. "But when we got to the Plains of the Dead, I followed you and found your ancestral home. Afterward, I talked to the old concubine, the one who was screaming about your family and your mother. I found out all about your situation, although I still didn't understand how you were so different from the rest of the ghosts. But I lost you then; I had no idea where you went, but while I was wandering around town a few days later I met this awful old man. He called himself Master Awyoung and he was very interested in what I had to say about you."

The hairpins she was playing with had been my mother's, and it stung me to see her casually toying with them.

"Anyway, Master Awyoung didn't tell me much, other than the fact that he suspected you were half dead. I had the feeling that he dismissed me. Most people do, you know. But I had my own ideas. You really are stupid," said Fan. "I would never have left my body alone like that. Especially such a young, beautiful body. Don't you know anything about spirit possession? I hate to say this, but you're far better looking than I ever was. It's a pity that I won't see my lover anymore, but physically he's too old for me now. I'm going to have such fun with this body."

I stood before her, so angry that tears streamed down my face. Fan grimaced. It was strange to see my own features move in unfamiliar ways, but I could clearly discern Fan's spirit behind my face. It was utterly infuriating.

"Oh, don't look like that! I have to admit, I almost lost my nerve at one point. When that man with the bamboo hat appeared right when I was about to enter the tunnel. If it hadn't been for him, I would have left without you, but he frightened me. But then you said that he was devoured by the birds. So everything worked out well for me, even the exits from the tunnel. When I told you there was a door to the merchant quarter, you looked far too interested and of course, once I knew where your house was in the Plains of the Dead, it was easy to find it here." She turned dismissively away from me. "Now I think you'd better go. There's nothing you can do here. And your spirit is only going to get weaker and weaker until you fade away. I'm not going to talk to you anymore."

I lunged at her, hoping that I could somehow dislodge her alien spirit from my flesh, but nothing happened. Fan merely closed her eyes—*my* eyes—and lay down on the bed. After a while, I realized that she had fallen asleep.

THAT NIGHT I STAYED by my body for hours, watching Fan sleep the untroubled sleep of those with no conscience. I tried again and again to sink into my body, to lie cradled within that comforting flesh that had, even after my dislocation, still welcomed my weary spirit and given me respite. But it was not to be. My body now behaved like any other live person's body. It repelled me. I paced round and round until I grew so exhausted that I collapsed on the floor, filled with grief and self-recriminations. Why, why had I ever left my body alone? Fan was right; it had been stupid of me. I had thought I could solve my own problems; I had never even considered the possibility that another spirit might possess it.

I couldn't understand how Fan had managed to take over my body when I myself could not. And how too did she enter our household, which had been shielded with spell papers against spiritual intrusions? Did she know some arcane art that I did not? A thought jolted me upright. I should have gone to the medium. The medium at the Sam Poh Kong temple who had given me the spell papers in the beginning. She had said she could see ghosts. Maybe she could help me. I had been so distracted when I was first severed from my body that I hadn't considered her, thinking only of following the thread that led me to Tian Bai, and one thing had led to another. I ought to see her as soon as possible. After all, even Er Lang had had need of her services. Thinking about Er Lang plunged me into fresh misery. Fan said he had frightened her in the Plains of the Dead, and I wished with all my heart that he were still with me. If he were, I thought bitterly, she would never have dared to do such a thing. But he was gone, and it was my own carelessness, my own stupidity in leading Fan to my house. Er Lang would no doubt have pointed that out, though if I could only hear his voice again, I would gladly welcome even the most caustic comments. Pulling out his scale, I blew on it but as usual there was no answer. My eyelids drooped inexorably; I was so tired that I curled up in the corner like a dog and fell asleep.

When I woke up, the room was empty. Fan had left but there were traces of her presence. Face powder was spilled carelessly, and the clothes she had worn the night before lay strewn around the room. I would never have done that. Amah had trained me since young to be neat and tidy. Even as I thought this, Amah herself came trotting into the room. The sight of her, so tiny and withered, gladdened me more than I could express. I had missed her more than I could have imagined. Even her grumbling and nagging were dear to me now that I was so far removed from her. Like my father, she looked more careworn, shrunken as though she was steadily progressing toward dollhood.

"Amah!" I said, following her around. But she paid me no heed, merely picking up the clothes and straightening the bed. She wiped the dressing table clean of face powder and put away the pots of rouge and hairpins that Fan had left. The corners of her mouth turned down disapprovingly, but she made no comment aloud. Did she know that there was an impostor? I hoped fervently that she did. Then I remembered someone else who might help me. Quickly, I started down the hallway after Amah's retreating form, but I had scarcely taken two steps before another bout of weakness overcame me. With trembling hands, I forced myself to stand up, only to be transfixed by the sunlight streaming in from the window. My fingers were now completely transparent. I gave a cry of despair.

How long I stood there, clutching my hands, I do not know. The sun moved overhead but time stopped for me. My existence had been brought to a single point, a mote of dust glimpsed through the unraveling substance of my hand. At that moment, it didn't matter whether or not I had a past, or who had wronged me. All that consumed me was that I had no more future; my spirit was dissipating like vapor. It was a long time before I returned to my senses, and when I did, retching and shuddering, I was terrified by the loss of time. It reminded me of the hungry ghosts and how they stood motionless for hours, even days. Alone, unburied, with no funeral rites because no one knew my spirit was wandering. I would be lost forever, doomed to drift unanchored until the end of time.

At last I stirred myself. The very thought cost me a great deal of effort, but I finally shuffled along the corridor. As I passed the living room, I saw Fan sitting with her back to the door in a rattan chair. Amah sat nearby, sewing something with a mouth that was pursed over her thread. With a shock, I saw that it was the piece of batik that Yan Hong had sent me after I had won the needle-threading competition at the Lim mansion, so long ago it seemed. Now it looked as though Amah was making it up into a sarong to match a *kebaya*. I caught the tail end of Fan's conversation.

"I asked you to get it ready by today, and it's still not done."

"What's the hurry?" said Amah dourly. "You're not in any fit state to go out."

"Yes, but he might come again. In fact, I'm sure he'll come today."

I froze, a horrid suspicion forming. Fan sighed and stroked her hair (*my* hair) obsessively, like a woman caressing the pelt of a cat. "Really, I was surprised at how attractive he was."

"Surprised?" said Amah. "And hadn't you been mooning over him for weeks before you took sick?"

"Oh . . . yes, I suppose so. Fetch me a cup of water, will you?"

Amah got up obediently. I was surprised at this meek acquiescence, but at the door, she stopped. "Do you want hot water or cold?"

"Hot of course. I have to take good care of myself." I couldn't see Fan's face, but I could guess at her smug expression.

A muscle in Amah's cheek twitched. "That's right," she said. "You always like your water hot."

I had no idea what prompted Amah to say this. She knew perfectly well that I hated hot drinks and had often scolded me as a child for chilling the humors in my body with cool water from the well in our backyard, or chipping away at the bits of ice that my father bought on rare occasions. Amah went down the passageway to the kitchen and I followed. There was someone else I was hoping to see.

IN THE FAMILIAR DIM kitchen with its windows obscured by the star fruit tree outside, Old Wong was seated at the rough wooden table peeling water chestnuts. Amah reached for the kettle by the side of the stove and felt it with the back of her hand. With a grunt, she poured some warm water into a teacup. "Wrong cup," said Old Wong. It was true. That was not the cup I was accustomed to using, but Amah merely shrugged and carried it out on a small tray. Old Wong raised his head as she went by, and it was then that he caught sight of me. At first he looked astonished, then he squinted as though he wasn't entirely certain of what he was looking at.

"Old Wong, it's me!" I cried. Still, he continued to stare as though he was befuddled. "Can't you see me?"

"What happened?" he asked at last. Then in alarm, "Did you die?"

"No, I'm not dead. But that's not me! You have to tell everyone!"

"What are you talking about?"

I was babbling, the words spilling out in my eagerness. Old Wong furrowed his brow as he tried to follow me, his paring knife suspended in midair. "Wait, wait," he said. "Do you mean to say that some other spirit has possessed your body?"

When I nodded, he dropped his knife with a clatter and slammed his hand on the kitchen table. "*Aiya!* Little Miss, I told you not to go wandering! How could this happen? And we were all so happy you recovered. *Sum liao!* This is a terrible thing." He rubbed his face vigorously, still muttering to himself, then scolded me until I burst into tears. "I told you! I warned you not to go away and leave your body!"

"I know. I'm sorry. I'm really sorry." All the fine ambitions I had had about saving myself came crashing down.

Old Wong sighed. "I don't know what to do, frankly. I could tell your father."

"Father doesn't want to believe in ghosts," I said wretchedly.

"Your amah now, she might believe me."

"Do you think so?"

"She's been acting strange ever since you recovered. Not that I got to see you much the past week. I thought you were sick, so you didn't come to the kitchen. But now that I think about it, perhaps she suspects."

Hope burgeoned in my heart. "Can you tell her?"

"I'll do my best. But that doesn't solve your problem."

"Can't we find an exorcist?"

"We can try. But you don't look like your spirit is in good shape."

I nodded wordlessly. Was it so apparent even to Old Wong that I had lost substance? And now that I could no longer rest in my body, my deterioration in this half-dead state was accelerated. Even if Old Wong hadn't been illiterate, I doubted that food offerings made to a soul tablet could halt it.

"That's why I thought you'd died just now," he said bluntly.

"I went to the Plains of the Dead," I said. "I saw my mother."

His eyes widened. "You went? What was it like?" Then he raised his hand. "No, don't tell me. It's not good for the living to find out too much about the dead. How did this spirit find you anyway?"

Miserably, I explained how I had inadvertently led Fan here.

"I thought it was strange that the first thing you did when you recovered was to ask for all the yellow spell papers to be removed from the windows. Well, I'm probably also guilty." He sighed and rubbed his grizzled head. "When you left, I was afraid you couldn't return, so I removed one paper from the pantry window, hoping that you could find a way in. That was my mistake, as I see. I thought I could watch that window since it's in the kitchen, but clearly I failed." Tears welled up in his eyes. Suddenly Old Wong banged his forehead on the table. "I'm also at fault for this situation!"

"What's going on?" It was Ah Chun, our maid. She must have been out on some errand, for in one hand she carried an enamel bowl filled with blue pea flowers. Seeing Old Wong glower at her, she stammered, "I—I didn't mean to be late. I went over to the Chans' to pick *bunga telang*. I know you wanted to make *pulut tai tai* for the young mistress, but I heard the most amazing story!" Old Wong continued to glare at her, nonplussed, but she went on. "They said this house is haunted! I always knew it!"

The Chans were our neighbors three houses down. Their backyard wall was covered with the trailing blue flowers of a type of pea plant. These were much in demand for making glutinous rice cakes laced with *kaya*. Ah Chun loved to go over, as their cook was a great gossip.

"*Cheh!*" said Old Wong. "You should stop listening to such nonsense."

But Ah Chun had noticed the red mark on Old Wong's forehead. "Why were you hitting your head on the table?" she asked.

"It was an accident," he replied angrily.

"But you were talking to someone. I heard you in the passageway."

He scowled so hideously that she blinked, then continued, "Anyway, they said someone had seen spirits entering and leaving our house!"

"What kind of spirits?"

"Horrible things with cows' heads and dogs' teeth. And also a wicked-looking woman. I don't want to stay here anymore!"

"Ask her who the woman was!" I said to Old Wong. In my heart, I had the terrible fear that it was myself.

"They weren't talking about our Little Miss, were they?" said Old Wong.

"Oh no! Somebody else, they said. With a pinched face, like a corpse. The cook heard it from a traveling peddler who claims to see spirits."

I remembered the mummified look that Fan had had when I first met her, as though the skin had shrunk away from her bones. "That's her!" I said to Old Wong.

"What are you talking about?" he muttered.

"I'm just telling you what I heard," said Ah Chun with a martyred air. "But of course you don't believe me. I want to go home."

"Wait," Old Wong said. "Maybe you're right. You should tell Amah. Also the master."

Ah Chun stared at him as though he had sprouted a tail. "Tell the master?"

"I'll tell him too," said Old Wong. "If we're going to have a wedding, maybe we should have an exorcism first."

"Are you mad?" she said. "That's the last thing anybody wants to hear before a wedding!"

"So what? Just tell them."

"And lose my job?"

"I thought you said you wanted to go back to your village."

Ah Chun glared at him. "Don't put words in my mouth." She stalked off down the corridor, her bowl of flowers forgotten on the table.

"Well, she has a point," said Old Wong. "Nobody is going to want to do an exorcism so close to a wedding."

"What does it matter?" I asked. "Call off the wedding."

"Is that what you want?" Old Wong fixed me with a curiously pitying look.

"I don't want her to marry him!"

Old Wong sighed. "Little Miss, even if the wedding is canceled, do you still think you can marry him yourself?"

His words seared me like a hot iron. I bent my head in shame. It was true that I kept this childish dream of Tian Bai in my heart. And I still didn't even know whether he was a murderer. Sometimes I wondered why he occupied my thoughts so; I couldn't even say if this was love. For some reason, the image of Er Lang sprang to mind. Lately, I often found myself keeping up an imaginary commentary with him. Such thoughts comforted me in my loneliness, though perhaps this was only further proof that my frail spirit was unraveling. In this case, the Er Lang in my mind merely raised an unseen eyebrow and turned away. He was of no help at all. But Old Wong was speaking again.

"I know it sounds harsh," he said, "but how will you claim your body back? I never heard of a case like yours where the spirit was separated unwillingly from the flesh. Usually it's because the spirit doesn't wish to return."

"Do you think there's a curse on me?"

"I told you, I don't know much about this kind of thing. I've tried to avoid it my whole life."

"I'm sorry." I caused nothing but trouble to the people around me. Even Er Lang had perished for my sake. With every moment that passed, I despised myself more.

"Don't look so unhappy," said Old Wong gruffly. "I just don't want you to be unrealistic." I looked down, blinking back tears. "I'll tell your amah myself."

"Tell her to contact the medium! The one at the Sam Poh Kong temple."

"Are you sure you want to do that? If a medium comes, we may not have much of a say in what she decides to do."

"Can't you tell her?"

"But a medium plays by different rules. We ordinary people don't know what kind of spiritual balance she may choose to maintain. Ah well, it may all be for the best, in the end."

"What do you mean?" I said slowly.

"Little Miss, the medium may decide to exorcise you as well."

CHAPTER 33

OLD WONG'S WORDS haunted me as I drifted around, numbly noting the various household activities that continued as though I had never left. In a sense, I hadn't. My body was still there, inhabited by Fan. She spent an inordinate amount of time choosing clothes, applying powder and rouge, and making demands of the servants. There was no doubt that she was naturally inclined to be a rich man's wife. I tried talking to her, begging, bargaining, and pleading, but she ignored me. It was easy enough as she couldn't hear my voice.

Nothing further happened during the daytime other than the fact that I suffered another painful and debilitating attack, which left me so weak that I could only huddle in a corner. Old Wong was right; my spirit body was fading fast. I didn't know whether he had found the time to speak to Amah and I brooded over his words. Deep in my heart, had I truly not wished to return to my physical self and was thus sundered? The thought filled me with unease, as did the disappearance of the ox-headed demons, though Lim Tian Ching might have called them off when he had held me captive in the Plains of the Dead.

At sunset, I slipped out of the house again. I couldn't bear to remain near

Fan. I realized now how little I'd appreciated my body while I had it, seldom thinking about it other than to braid my hair or change my clothes hastily. Fan, on the other hand, spent hours rouging her lips and staring at her reflection, pouting and trying out various seductive poses. Despite my disdain, I couldn't help noticing how attractive she looked. Maybe I too should have spent more time applying rice powder in thin sheets to my complexion. But then I hadn't yet known Tian Bai. Thinking of him, of Fan pressing those lips to his, made my blood boil. I was so angry that I almost wished that he were, indeed, a murderer. Serve her right if he strangled her! But such thoughts filled me with guilt. Amah was always wary of voicing misfortunes, fearing that to do so would only make them come true. I told myself that I didn't believe such superstitions, though in any case, almost everything that could have gone wrong with my situation had already happened. I pressed my hands into my eye sockets, noting dispiritedly that the faint glow my spirit form emitted in the dusk had brightened. Surely I could trust Tian Bai. His surprise had been so reasonable, so plausible, that I should stop doubting him. Lim Tian Ching could simply have died of a fever. And even if he hadn't, Yan Hong had just as much motive and opportunity. In fact, if she were guilty, I suspected Tian Bai would protect her as they seemed so close.

Even as I considered this, I was startled by the arrival of a rickshaw. I couldn't imagine who could be calling at this time when I saw that it was none other than Tian Bai himself. Amah opened the door and, pursing her lips, pointed to the front room. I almost followed him in but, realizing that Fan could see me, thought better of it. My hands trembled as I pressed myself against the window, concealing myself in the substance of the wall. Of all people, he must realize she was an impostor. If he knew me at all, he must. I couldn't bear it if he didn't suspect a thing. Very soon Fan came tripping in. She gave a coy smile and to my horror, ran straight into Tian Bai's arms with an air of familiarity. At the sight of Amah still standing in the corner of the room, she frowned and told her to go away.

"Li Lan," said Tian Bai with some embarrassment. "You mustn't be so impatient."

"That nosy old woman!"

"She's your amah, didn't you tell me she raised you?"

Fan turned her face aside and pouted, so that her lips resembled a flower bud. Only I knew how long she had taken to perfect this expression. "Did you bring me a present?"

Tian Bai produced a pink paper packet from his pocket with an indulgent smile. She tore it open, squealing, "A gold necklace!"

I was so overcome with jealousy that my vision clouded. Didn't Tian Bai notice that she wasn't me? How could he be such a fool! Even as I watched, she turned and exposed the nape of her neck.

"Put it on!" she said.

Tian Bai's hands slipped the necklace around her throat, lingering on the creamy skin. I couldn't read his expression, for his face was turned away, but his fingers traced the curve of her neck. She wore her hair piled up elaborately, unlike the schoolgirl plaits I was accustomed to. Now she lifted it with her fingers, loosening the tendrils so that they spilled over. Tian Bai buried his face in her hair, just as he had done to me in his dream. I covered my eyes in anguish. There was a fierce pain in my chest. I wanted to cry out, to pull him out of her arms. To look was a torment to me, worse than the tortures of hell. But even as I rubbed my eyes, I heard him speaking softly.

"I had a dream about you yesterday."

As Fan twined her arms around him, I froze. She of all people would understand what it meant to be visited by a spirit in dreams. "What happened?" she cooed.

"You said some strange things."

"Oh?" Her tone was sharper. "What sort of things?"

Tian Bai twined a strand of her hair around his finger. "Just some odd things. About my cousin."

Fan narrowed her eyes. "Did I act differently? Did I tell you not to trust me?"

"What a strange thing to say," said Tian Bai. "Why would you think that might happen?" His tone sounded strained to me, although it was hard to tell without seeing his face.

Fan's eyes darted accusingly around the room, searching for my spirit form. I was glad that I had concealed myself well. "I don't know," she said. "You seem disturbed. Tell me." She stroked his arm. "I want to hear all about it."

"And why is that?" Perhaps it was my imagination, but Tian Bai sounded cold.

"Because dreams can trick you. They can be the work of evil spirits that lie to you."

"Do you really believe that?"

"You mustn't underestimate such creatures. Now, won't you tell me what your dream was about?"

"In my dream you asked me a strange question."

Fan was alert now, her body tense rather than seductive. "Oh?"

"You asked me," said Tian Bai slowly, "whether I was a murderer."

Whatever she'd been expecting, it wasn't this. Fan gaped at him but he held her gaze intently. I felt like bursting into hysterical laughter.

Fan recovered first. "Well!" she said. "I'm glad it was only a dream." She rubbed her face against his shoulder like a cat. "It's probably an evil spirit. I'll give you a charm to keep it away."

Tian Bai's expression was inscrutable. "You know I don't believe in charms."

"Don't be silly! We'll go to the temple together and get one. And maybe we can cast a fortune for a lucky wedding day."

I held my breath. She didn't know that he was Catholic, but even as I considered this, she smiled winsomely. How was it that I'd never realized what a weapon a smile could be? But the way he was looking at her, almost appraisingly, made me uncomfortable. After all, for all he knew, she was me. He tilted her face up with one hand and examined it.

"Li Lan, if you marry me, I want you to know that I expect my wife to stand by me."

"Of course I trust you!" She laughed uncomfortably.

He said nothing, but after a while he dropped his hand. She continued to fawn over him, but the fleeting look I'd caught in his eyes made me uneasy. I had always associated Tian Bai with good humor. Indeed, that open, pleasant countenance was one of his chief charms. But in repose, his face was like a closed book.

I COULDN'T STAY LONG after that. They sat together in the front room like any courting couple, talking about inconsequential things. Perhaps they couldn't say much because Amah silently reappeared, standing just inside the door. Fan made sure to lean against him, stroking his arm at every opportunity, and by this and many admiring questions, teased from him an indulgent smile. Expertly, she showed off the curves of the body I had underappreciated. I would have sat, stiff as a schoolgirl at his proximity, but she had no such inhibitions. At one point, when Amah turned away, Fan brought her upturned face close to his, her parted lips an invitation he couldn't resist. I saw Tian Bai steal a kiss from her and how she smiled at him then, passing her tongue swiftly over her lips. She was far more experienced than me. I was so distressed that I could no longer tell whether I was imagining innuendos and undercurrents. In the end, I forced myself to turn away. Once out in the street, I called Chendana, feeling a pang of remorse for having left her outside so long. My little horse touched my hand with her soft nose, and for a while I clung to her.

I had meant to wait and follow Tian Bai until he fell asleep. But as I sat miserably on the doorstep, I wondered whether it was right to keep following him, to invade and alter his dreams. If I did, I would be no better than Lim Tian Ching. If only I had told Tian Bai about my condition when I had the chance. Explaining things now was awkward, especially since I had accused him of murder the last time.

Instead, I decided to seek out the medium at the Sam Poh Kong temple. I couldn't bear to wait outside while Fan pressed her thigh against his. Even though Old Wong's words about exorcism troubled me, anything was better than this half-existence. Hugging my knees, I thought of how Er Lang had silently held my hand in the Plains of the Dead and how his grip had alleviated the terror I had felt at the time. Dying now seemed unutterably lonely.

Would I ever see him again or my mother, or would I lose my wits along with my substance, an unburied wraith like the hungry ghosts? I wondered whether my recent fits of distraction were symptoms of this change, and if in the end, I would be reduced to nothing more than a swirl of residual emotions. Still, I quailed at the thought of leaving this world. I had too much left unfinished—my soul was full of unfulfilled desires and yearnings.

The night was growing darker and spirit lights began to appear. One by one they lit their pale ghostly fire. Some were white, others red or orange, and many were the same eerie green that had characterized Fan. Their silent advent, like a spectral display of fireworks, raised the hair on my neck even though I had but recently returned from the Plains of the Dead. I could see that these spirits were different from those I had encountered there. True, there were human ghosts wandering among them, but others were strange creatures I had never seen before. There were tree and plant forms, tiny flitting creatures, and disembodied heads trailing long strands of hair. There were some with horns and protruding eyes, and others that were simply mist or vapors. They paid me no heed, but I was afraid that soon, very soon, they would notice me.

We left the town without incident and began to pick our way through the cemeteries toward Bukit China and the Sam Poh Kong temple. In the darkness, the graves rose around us like small empty houses. Terrified of meeting hungry ghosts or something worse, I regretted my haste in leaving home. If something should come upon me, weakened as I was, I would be completely defenseless. Still, I saw no trace of spirit lights among the silent mounds. It was too far from town and all who were buried with such ceremony had long since gone on to the Plains of the Dead. Yet this very solitude chilled me to the bone. Alone in the dark, I wandered for an eternity among the graves. Bitterly, I thought of my grievances and how Fan and I had changed places. There were so many peculiar parallels between the world of the living and the dead. How many ghosts had felt the same way before? I shuddered to think that I had joined their ranks.

The moon rose. Its wavering, silver light shone on the silent tombs, picking out the names of the long dead. Better to be exorcised, I thought. Fan and

I must both sever our ties to this life. But I was afraid, despite my resolve. Chendana walked steadily onward, following the narrow road that unfurled like a ribbon of moonlight. Pain engulfed me then, that same agony that had pierced me before. The attacks were becoming more frequent, their duration longer. Never before, however, had one been so merciless. I could barely think. A paralyzing weakness seized me so that I slid off Chendana's back and collapsed in the long grass by the path. As I lay there, something sharp dug into my side. After a long time, I summoned the strength to pull it out. Er Lang's scale. It glimmered in the moonlight, though whether it was merely a reflection, I could not tell. I put it to my lips and with a faint breath, blew hopelessly.

CHAPTER 34

A BREEZE WAS blowing. A rushing wind that rattled the leaves and made the elephant grass stream like ghostly banners. Raindrops fell in a spatter. I wondered dully if a monsoon was coming, and whether I was now so ephemeral that I would be blown into the South China Sea.

"If you don't get up, you'll be blown away."

I opened my eyes to a pair of elegant feet. "Er Lang?"

He bent down, the enormous bamboo hat almost blotting out the night sky. I was so happy to see him that I couldn't speak.

"Are you glad to see me, or terrified?" The beautiful voice sounded genuinely curious.

"Of course I'm glad to see you!" I said weakly. "You fool! I thought you died."

He laughed. "I am not so easy to kill. Though it was a close thing."

"You look well." I struggled to sit up. Indeed, he did. He was just the same as when I had first met him; even his clothes were no longer torn and scorched as they had been in the Plains of the Dead.

"This is my physical body," he said. "But you are in very bad shape."

I lifted my hands up. They were now completely transparent. "I'm dying."

"Yes." His voice was calm.

A curious peace filled me now that I had come to the end of things. I wondered whether it was a side effect of dying, or because Er Lang was here and I no longer felt anxious.

"Where did you go?" I whispered. "I called you, but you didn't come."

"It took some time to recover. Then of course, I went to make my report."

"What did they say?"

"The case is pending but we have a chain of evidence now, thanks to the letter you acquired. Proceedings have begun against Master Awyoung and the Lim family."

"I'm glad, though I was sorry for Lim Tian Ching in the end. They were just using him as a cat's-paw for their dirty work."

"That's very good of you, considering you were to be his compensation." I heard the irony in Er Lang's voice, but was too weak to retort. Besides, I had other things on my mind.

"He said something about bringing murder charges against Tian Bai. Is it a legitimate case?"

Er Lang paused. "It's not under my jurisdiction. Do you wish me to find out?"

"Please."

"Why are you so meek all of a sudden?" he asked.

"I'm dying, of course!" I opened my eyes again in irritation. "Can't you let me die with some dignity?"

"I don't understand why you're not back resting in your body, instead of traipsing around the middle of a cemetery."

"Oh. I didn't tell you. Someone else has possessed my body."

"What?" There was nothing for it but to tell him the whole sorry tale. I could see him shaking his head before I finished.

"Unbelievably stupid," he murmured.

"You were the one who told me to go to the Plains of the Dead!" I had no strength to shout at him anymore.

"Not you, me."

"Why?" I had slipped down, unable to sit up. My head was pillowed on his knee. Strange that he could support my spirit form, but there were a lot of odd things about Er Lang.

He made a sound of annoyance. "I should have considered the possibility. But I thought the ox-headed demons were guarding your body."

"Well, it's too late now."

"Yes, it is."

We didn't speak for a while. It was a balmy night, redolent with the sweet breath of trees. The long grass rose around us, and the faint trails of fireflies mingled with the low-hanging stars. Though I couldn't see his face, he appeared to be deep in thought.

"Will you do something for me?" I said at last. "After I die, please take care of my family. Make sure that Fan doesn't cause any trouble. Maybe exorcise her, if you can."

I saw the gleam of teeth beneath his hat. "Why not?"

"And one more thing."

"You seem to have a lot of requests for a dying person." He didn't seem to take my demise seriously at all, which pained me. After all, I had missed him desperately, shedding tears and suffering agonies of guilt when I thought he had died. If I had been stronger, I would have pointed it out but it was too late to argue with him.

"Take off your hat."

"Why?"

"I want to see a dragon face-to-face."

"Are you afraid?"

"It's supposed to be lucky to see a dragon. I'd like some luck for my next life."

He was silent for some time. Then he removed the hat.

MOONLIGHT SHONE ON HIS face. I don't know what I had been expecting—perhaps the head of the great beast I had glimpsed on the Plains of the Dead—but I should have considered that he had a human form as well. For he was handsome beyond belief. Beautiful, even. Gazing at the pure, keen countenance, I was so flustered that I couldn't stop staring. The long aristocratic eyes, the sharp brows like swords. My vision was filled with the fine planes of his face and the light and shadow of his pale skin and dark hair. But it was his gaze that captured me. Those eyes, which beneath the slant of his lashes, were both fierce and tender, searing in their clarity. For an instant, I understood the depths of his inhumanity, that monstrous nobility that placed him far above me. I could not hide before it. I was entranced, like a moth drawn to the moon.

Then he spoiled it all by saying, "Well, can you die happy now?"

Abruptly reminded of his flippancy, I couldn't bite my tongue. "Is this why you think you're irresistible to women?"

Er Lang smiled. It was a dazzling smile that made me feel faint. "I always tell the truth."

I turned my face away. The last thing I wished was to give him the same reaction that every other woman must have done when they saw his face. No wonder he had such an opinion of himself, I thought, even as my own treacherous heart raced like a runaway horse. This was not how I'd been planning to die, but so be it. I couldn't expect to win every round. I had, in fact, already lost in this life. But Er Lang was shaking me.

"Are you really dead?"

"How is it that you can touch me?"

"You're a spirit. I have jurisdiction over spirits in my official capacity," he said.

"I thought you were just a minor government official."

"Not after this case is settled."

"Good for you." I closed my eyes. The strength was draining out of me, like water running through my fingers, but he was shaking me again.

"What is it?"

"You can't die. Yet. I may need you as a witness."

"It's too late for me." An overwhelming weakness ate away at my limbs. My form was visibly fading. Er Lang looked at me sharply.

"There is another way. You're almost a hungry ghost now. Don't you know that you can sustain yourself with the *qi* of another?"

I shuddered. That was what Fan had done for years, sapping the life of her lover. "I couldn't do that to Tian Bai. I would rather die."

Er Lang's glance was unreadable. "Do you love him so much? In any case, that's not what I was proposing. It would be illegal."

I couldn't look too long at him. His beauty was unnerving, almost unnatural. "What do you suggest, then?"

"Something that emperors have killed for."

I was too weak to roll my eyes. "And what would that be?"

"Why, my life force of course."

I COULD BARELY COMPREHEND what he was talking about. Something about procedural irregularities, documentation, and sustaining a witness. I faded in and out of consciousness briefly, though I had the odd feeling that he was trying to convince himself as much as me.

". . . would change you, of course."

"What?" I said weakly.

"You are dying," he said suddenly. "Quick! Choose!"

I struggled to regain myself. "Choose what?"

The corner of his mouth twitched. "Whether you want my breath or my blood."

Sorcerers were said to feed their familiars through a hole in the foot, but even in my debilitated state, I could not conceive of drinking his blood. To do so would be no better than some evil revenant, or *pontianak*—a wraith with all its attendant horrors.

"Breath," I said at last.

"Then hurry!" he said.

Too proud to show my fears, I fell into his arms. He was close, too close. I clenched my eyes. His lips brushed mine, briefly at first, as though he was considering it. A shiver traced its way between my shoulder blades. I thought he was about to say something. Then he exhaled.

· · · ·

HIS BREATH WAS HOT and clean, a wind that pierced and melted me in an instant. The world spun, the stars in the sky guttered like candles. I knew nothing but the grip of his arm and the heat of his mouth. There was a burning sensation wherever his skin touched me, against my cheek, my neck. Forcing my lips open wider, he pressed his mouth hard against mine. His breath penetrated me, permeating every fiber of my being until I couldn't contain it. I wanted to bite him, to scream. His tongue darted into my mouth, swift and slippery as an eel. Shaking, I dug my fingers into his back until he gasped in pain. My chest squeezed, a shudder racked my body. From far away, I heard him groan deeply, but I would not let go. This, then, was how a ghost could steal the life out of someone. I felt feverish and a strange languor overcame me. Then he was gently shaking me. "Enough."

I OPENED MY EYES reluctantly. We had fallen together into a tangle. For a dreadful moment, I thought he was dead. Then I felt his chest rise and fall beneath me. The moon had turned everything to silver, as though we inhabited a world of grays and blacks. I pressed my face into his chest. His curious Han clothes couldn't hide the lithe grace of his body, nor the taut planes of his abdomen. I could hear the beating of his heart, the slow coursing of the blood in his veins. I felt intensely alive, as though I could flit to the moon or plumb the depths of the ocean. But he didn't move for so long that fear seeped into me. In the moonlight, his face was drawn and exhausted. As I watched, he opened his eyes.

The pale light had stolen all colors, so that they were unfathomable, like the sea at night. I was afraid he had forgotten where he was, or regretted his decision. Then Er Lang was looking at me ruefully. "You have taken at least fifty years of my life!"

I was stricken. "Take it back!"

"I can't. But fortunately, my life span is many times yours."

"How long can a dragon live?"

"A thousand years, if he is lucky. Not all of us are, of course." He raised an eyebrow.

"I'm sorry." I couldn't look him in the eye. Instead, my gaze was drawn to the strong line of his throat. If he had given me blood, I would surely have killed him. But Er Lang was struggling to sit up.

"I should have stopped you sooner. Though I now understand why men succumb to ghosts." He spoke lightly, but my ears blazed with mortification.

"You were the one who put your tongue in my mouth!" I blurted out, regretting it instantly. To talk about other people's tongues was the worst, revealing the depths of my inexperience. And yet, the memory of his made me shiver and burn, as though I had a fever. It hadn't been like this with Tian Bai; it was easy to understand where I stood with him. But he had been courting me, whereas Er Lang was an entirely different commodity. We did not have that sort of relationship, I reminded myself.

But he merely gave me a wry glance. "I was a little carried away."

"Thank you," I said at last. I realized it was the first time I had thanked him formally.

"I fear you may be changed in more ways than one."

"How so?"

"I can't tell right now. I don't usually go around offering *qi* to people."

I looked down at myself. The translucency that had affected me had disappeared. I seemed solid, almost alive except for the faint spirit light around me. That itself had faded until it was no more than a pale glow. Er Lang put his hand on my face. I flinched as though he had burned me.

"There is earth on your cheek," he said coolly. I rubbed my face, embarrassed, but he didn't say anything. Clouds scudded over the moon, so that the night lost its luminosity. The weather was changing, the air thickening as though before a storm.

"What will you do now?" I asked.

"I was on my way to a council, in fact, when you called me. No doubt they shall be quite put out, for the warrants will be delayed."

"So Lim Tian Ching is still loose?"

"Yes, but I would worry more about Master Awyoung." Er Lang lifted his head sharply, his expression alert. "I must go."

"Why?"

"There are ox-headed demons on the move. I cannot tell which guard company."

"Take me with you!"

"Certainly not! I don't want my witness damaged."

I tried to shout at him, but a gale blew my words back into my face. Sticks and leaves scattered like a whirlwind, and then he was gone. I stood alone on the deserted road.

CHAPTER 35

DESPITE MY EARLIER resolution to seek out the medium, a mounting anxiety drove me to turn Chendana's head toward home. Something was happening in the spirit world, and I feared for my family. Er Lang would no doubt disapprove, but I didn't care. My body felt strong, the blood singing in my veins. Chendana raced through the graveyard, her mane whipping back into my face. The night sky, so clear earlier, was now shrouded with clouds. The moon had hidden her face.

We were at the outskirts of Malacca before the exultation that had filled me drained away, like a wave that crashes on the shore. I was overcome by a sense of desolation. Er Lang had left so abruptly that it felt as though part of myself had been ripped loose. I wrenched my thoughts away, wondering instead what had happened to the ox-headed demons. They had been absent for so long that I didn't know whether Fan was even aware that they had guarded my house. Otherwise she might not have removed all the spell papers from the windows. In all likelihood, she had done so for her own benefit, thinking it would be easier for her to come and go if she needed to. As we entered the town, the sky took on a brooding look. Even the spirit lights on the streets were diminished and scattered. Scarcely anyone or anything was abroad, yet my skin prickled. When we reached the house, I saw at once that something was wrong.

Although the hour was fairly late, lights blazed from all the windows. I slid off Chendana's back, telling her to wait for me. It was surprisingly difficult to pass through the front door. A good sign, but I had no time to appreciate it. I ran through room after room looking for Amah or my father. It wasn't difficult to find them. All I had to do was follow the sound of screaming.

Fan was standing in the dining room, clutching my father as a shield. The whites of her eyes showed all around so that she looked like a madwoman. The object that she shrank away from was nothing more than an infusion of herbs on a serving tray.

"Take it away!" she screamed.

Amah picked up the glazed pot and moved toward her. "What's wrong?" she asked. But Fan let out a shriek, as though she had been offered a scorpion.

"Tell her to leave this house!"

"Li Lan, what's the matter with you?" asked my father. Bewildered, his pupils were unnaturally dilated. I knew he had been smoking opium again.

"She's taken leave of her senses," said Amah. She took another step toward Fan. "You're still sick," she said soothingly. "This will make you feel better."

About to dart forward, I stopped, remembering that no one besides Fan could see me. Instead, I concealed myself in the wall. With a swiftness that surprised me, Fan dashed the pot from Amah's hand. It shattered on the tiled floor and my father gave a cry of distress. It was part of a set from my mother's dowry.

Fan jumped away, avoiding any of the liquid in it. "This old woman means to poison me!" she said to my father. "She's the one who caused my illness. She put a curse on me!"

"Is this true?" my father asked.

Amah shook her head, but her distress merely made her look like an old woman in her dotage. "I would never—"

But Fan cut her off. "Ask her to turn out her pockets," she said. "Then you'll see what charms she's been carrying against me."

My father set his mouth. I knew how much he abhorred superstition and his recent disagreements with Amah over my illness. "Show me!"

Amah was crying. With trembling hands she pulled out several packets of herbs, as well as some yellow spell papers.

"How dare you bring such things into my house!" said my father. "I won't have you upsetting Li Lan like this! I should have stopped you years ago."

"They're not against Li Lan!" said Amah. "They're to ward off demons and evil spirits. Old Wong said—"

But my father had cut her off. "What rubbish are you talking about?"

Scooping up the pathetic little pile of charms, he opened the courtyard door and cast them out into the night. I longed to leap forward and defend Amah, but dared not let Fan see me. For all she knew, I had already faded into a wraith.

Fan folded her arms. "Out!" she said. "I want her out of this house tonight!" She pointed at the open door with a glint of triumph. Then her features crumpled.

I smelled it before I saw it; that burned carrion scent that I could never forget. The skin on my back seized up. Not daring to turn my head, I stared fixedly down at a monstrous shadow that inched its way across the floor. Whatever caused it was entering from the open door. Closer and closer it loomed, the wicked tines casting their own curved shapes on the tiled floor. Fan's eyes were wide and glassy. Despite my hiding place in the wall, a sick fear gripped me. At last, unable to endure it, I turned. It was an ox-headed demon.

"Are you Li Lan, of the Pan family?" The guttural voice shook the walls. Rank stench filled the air; in these enclosed quarters, it induced an animallike panic. I barely controlled the urge to bolt. Fan could only gibber in terror. My father and Amah stared at her in astonishment and I realized that they could not see it.

"I asked, are you Li Lan?"

Fan blinked frantically. "What do you want?"

"She's gone mad!" said my father.

Amah ran to her side, but Fan's eyes were fixed on the demon.

"I have been sent to fetch the daughter of this house," it said.

"No—oh no! I'm not Li Lan!"

"You match the description I was given."

"There's been a mistake!" Fan gabbled. "I'm not her. I'm just . . . taking care of her body."

My father and Amah were distraught now, thinking that she had lost her mind. The demon narrowed its eyes at her. The cavernous mouth, bristling with teeth, dropped open. I could almost feel the heat of its fetid breath.

"My orders were to bring you back to the Lim mansion," it said.

"No!" Fan was backing away. "I know the laws of the afterworld. You're not allowed to take a living person!"

There was a pause, as though it was pondering this. It occurred to me that she might be right. A gleam of defiance shone in her eye. "This is my body now."

Amah lunged forward as though she had suddenly made up her mind. With her right hand, she slapped a spell paper onto Fan's forehead. The effect was instantaneous. Fan's eyes rolled up and she crumpled like a paper doll. My father gave a cry of despair. But I could see what they could not. Fan's spirit was abruptly cast out of my body. Shocked, she stumbled forward. At that instant, the demon leaped forward and snatched her. I saw her white, terrified face, the mouth opened in a silent scream. Then with a single bound, it carried her off into the night.

Amah and my father gathered around my fallen body. Amah was wailing, "I shouldn't have done it! The medium said not to use it. It might sever all bonds." But I felt an intense pain in my chest. It was pulling me, like a rope that was tightening and squeezing. Gasping, I ran toward my body and collapsed on it.

CHAPTER 36

A LONE SUNBEAM illuminated the foot of my bed. The burble of pigeons and the rhythmic scrapes of Old Wong sweeping the courtyard rose through the open window. It was an utterly ordinary morning, except that I was back in my body. Amah was kneeling at my bedside again, where she had fallen asleep at her post. Gently, I touched her sparse gray hair.

"Amah," I said.

"Is it really you?" She had aged, though she was still younger than my mother had appeared in the Plains of the Dead.

"Yes."

"Oh, Li Lan! My little girl!" She stroked my face. "Where did you go?"

"Someone else took my body," I said.

"I know. I knew she wasn't you."

We held on to each other for a long time. Later I would tell her a little about my wanderings. But not too much. I was mindful of Old Wong's injunctions. I didn't want to trouble Amah, superstitious as she was. Of my mother, I said little other than I had seen her and she had helped me. Amah was tearful. I didn't tell her about how my mother had aged, nor the life she led as a servant in the Plains of the Dead. To my father, we said nothing other than I had recovered from a brain fever. He seemed to accept it, just as he accepted the odd events of the night before. No doubt the opium affected his perceptions.

It was strange to be back in my body. I spent some time examining my fingernails, the blue pulse in my wrists, and the crisp ligaments of my knees and ankles. They were a wonder to me, yet also completely undistinguished. Within a few days, I would forget about them completely. Yet I was grateful. In the end my body had, indeed, called to me, just as the doctor had said it should. Uneasily, I considered whether it was only until Fan had taken it, and showed me how charming and seductive my body could be, that I had wanted it back so fiercely. Or maybe it was some quality of Er Lang's shape-changing *qi.* Once or twice I caught myself pouting or glancing sideways from lowered lashes in the mirror, and recoiled. If these were habits my body had acquired, I would have to be careful.

There was some weakness in my legs and arms caused by the weeks of lying in bed. Amah had massaged my limbs daily, which had helped, but Fan had done nothing to improve their condition. She had only been interested in looking beautiful. As much as I disliked her, however, even she didn't deserve such a fate. I couldn't forget the sheer terror in her face in those last moments. It frightened me, to think that such creatures had been looking for me. I could only guess that it was some last, desperate plan of Lim Tian Ching's, or Master Awyoung's before his arrest, and I wondered again what had happened in the world of the spirits. For I missed it. Although I had spent so much time trying to get back into my body, I felt restless and anxious, longing for the freedom to wander to unknown places. Being half-dead, despite its drawbacks, had been far more interesting than being constrained to my limited social circle. Guiltily, I tried to put such thoughts from my mind. I was grateful, very grateful to be back. Still, I chafed at my restrictions. Perhaps this contact with the spirit world had, indeed, spoiled me, as Old Wong had warned. He had said it was a taint, not a talent, and a dark melancholy filled me as I considered how similar his words were to the medium's at the Sam Poh Kong temple. My skin prickled at odd moments and I started at shadows, though I could no longer see anything. Yet I felt the presence of the unknown, the filmy touch of vapors that eddied in dark corners. It crossed my mind that these sensations were caused by spirits and that they hung, translucent as jellyfish, in the very air that I passed through. I had experienced a hidden realm, which though terrifying, had also been a source of pure wonder. Lying in my familiar bed, I recalled the spirit lights as they bloomed in the darkness like cold and silent fireworks; the mystical creatures that gathered in the streets of Malacca, that perhaps even now still conducted their odd business every night. And I remembered an impossibly handsome face, once seen by moonlight.

NOTHING PLEASED ME AS it had before, not even Tian Bai. He came to see me almost every day, just as charming and pleasant as before. But I was no longer the same girl who had been so impressed by his worldliness and his travels. One afternoon we sat together in the front room, just as he had sat with Fan. She was like a shadow between us. Although she was gone, I still found evidence of her at every turn: the hairpins she had discarded, the new dresses she had ordered to be tailored. Fan had accumulated quite a collection of jewelry in the short time she had possessed my body, most of it gifts from Tian Bai, no doubt. Strangely, she had hidden it all over the house, as though she didn't quite trust her good fortune and was squirreling it away in case of an emergency. I felt sorry for her every time I came across one of these caches, even though she had quite willingly consigned me to the fate of a hungry ghost.

"What are you thinking?" asked Tian Bai. He had brought me a slim jade bangle that day, mottled green and white like the bark of a jungle tree. I resented the fact that he didn't seem to realize I wasn't the same girl who had coveted such presents. But Tian Bai had brought it out so hopefully, the dimple in his left cheek appearing as he slipped it onto my wrist, that I couldn't hold a grudge against him.

"I don't feel very well," I said.

Once again, I regretted never telling him that I had been dispossessed from my body. If I had told him from the beginning, perhaps things would have been different. Yet, he had helped me even without knowing it. He had given me Chendana, whom I could no longer see or find. I worried about her, anxious if she still stood patiently in the street outside our house.

"You haven't seemed like yourself recently," he said. "Is something troubling you?"

Sometimes I wondered why I didn't tell him, but I was afraid he would think me mad. There was some stigma over my purported brain fever. He didn't say it, but I heard from the servants that the Lim family still thought to cancel the marriage if I proved incompetent. If that should occur, what would happen to my father's debts? And I loved Tian Bai, didn't I? Still, there was no denying I was cooler toward him. I let him caress my hair and embrace me. He even kissed me, gently and with great tenderness. But Fan was always there between us. I couldn't forget how free she had been with my body, and in some ways, I felt violated. I wished I knew whether he noticed we had changed places, or worse still, preferred her to me. She had been far more affectionate, coquettishly hanging on his every word. In contrast, I was melancholy and often withdrawn.

My thoughts turned endlessly to Lim Tian Ching's accusations of murder. Despite Tian Bai's explanations, I felt the stain of suspicion in my heart, like a fungus that would spread swiftly if unchecked. Tian Bai was patient. He didn't comment on my reserve, nor did he ask for more than I would give. I wished that I could lift this doubt, which was Lim Tian Ching's dark wedding gift to me.

"I heard something about you," I said at last.

"Oh?" His eyes creased at the corners.

"Perhaps it was only a rumor. But I wanted to ask you myself."

He ran his finger down the nape of my neck, the same gesture he had used with Fan. "Is this what's been troubling you?" he said. "I suppose it's only fair that you should know, since we're to be married."

I waited, my heart in my mouth. He walked over to the front window.

"I'm older than you, Li Lan. I won't deny that I've had other relationships. There was a woman that I loved in Hong Kong."

"Isabel," I said, before I could stop myself. He looked surprised.

"So you heard the gossip. But it was impossible from both sides."

"Was there a child?" I asked, hating myself for being so intrusive.

"No. There was no child. She married someone else, and that is also why I didn't seek you out and marry you when I first returned from Hong Kong. You must have been surprised that we were betrothed for so long, even before my cousin died. But I think it was better this way. I didn't know you then, you see."

He smiled at me, that slow beguiling smile that had captivated me from the beginning. I couldn't help myself. I went over and put my arms around him. He kissed me then, a lingering kiss that made my cheeks grow hot.

"You look like a schoolgirl," Tian Bai said, tugging on my braids. "You must put your hair up when we get married."

LATER, I CHIDED MYSELF for not pressing him about his cousin's death. When we were together it felt like a foolish suspicion, but when I was alone it returned to haunt me. Just as I wondered what his expression was when I couldn't see his face. I couldn't forget that cold, almost appraising look with which Tian Bai had fleetingly regarded Fan when she was still in my body, and I wondered again if he had truly not noticed we had switched places.

I was searching the house, as was my custom now. I had been searching it ever since I returned and that was how I had discovered Fan's little hoards. But I wasn't interested in jewelry. I was looking for Er Lang's scale. Like Chendana, it too had disappeared once I returned to my body; and try as I might, I could not find it. I was afraid that I had left it on Bukit China among the graves, and even persuaded Amah to return with me to the Sam Poh Kong temple—to pay my respects, I said. All the way there and back, I scanned the road anxiously from the rickshaw, but there was nothing to be seen. I couldn't even be sure of the spot where I had fallen from Chendana and where Er Lang had given me part of his life.

For more than anything else, I wanted to see Er Lang again. To see his oversize hat, hear his irreverent remarks. To scold him for leaving me for so long, with no further word. I told myself that he had always come back for me, even from the brink of death. Surely he would return, though I feared there might be no more reason to do so. I still had questions. Whether Lim Tian Ching had really filed a suit against Tian Bai in the spirit world for murder, as he had boasted he would. And if I was needed as a witness against Master Awyoung and the Old Master. Only Er Lang could tell me those things. But his last words had merely underscored the fact that he wanted to preserve me for his records. An inexpressible sadness haunted me. I wished that I had never seen his face, yet it was seared into my memory. He had warned me not to look at him. Why had I not listened?

In the tales I had read from China, the interactions between spirits and humans were often tantalizingly unresolved. The chrysanthemum nymph's plant was cut down, the bee princess returned to her hive, and even the cowherd's happiness with his celestial bride was short-lived. Yet every time the wind blew hard enough to rattle the shutters or heavy rain lashed the house, I ran to the windows. But Er Lang did not come.

CHAPTER 37

TIAN BAI AND I were to be married in two months' time. I sought to delay the wedding, pleading illness and the fact that the year of mourning for Lim Tian Ching was not yet up. Tian Bai said he would consider it. In the meantime, Amah and I were sewing my trousseau. Amah was happy. At last I was to be married, though my eighteenth birthday had passed unnoticed during my supposed illness. It was the culmination of her ambitions to see me as the first wife in a great household. My father wandered around as though a great weight had been lifted off his shoulders. Even Old Wong was pleased with me, though he couldn't help scolding me from time to time. But sometimes, when the moonlight stole through my bedroom window, I felt tears sting my eyes. And sometimes, when Tian Bai was sitting with me, I found I could barely meet his gaze.

The rains were very heavy that year. The monsoon came early and the streets turned to mud. Clothes hung out to dry remained damp from the humidity. Amah sighed and said we would never get my trousseau done in time. Other girls had spent most of their childhoods preparing a chest of elaborately embroidered materials, from napkins to bed curtains, but I had little to show in that department. She finally gave up the faint hope that we would be able to sew my trousseau before the wedding and decided to hire a seamstress instead. Still, Amah felt terribly ashamed that it wouldn't be my own handiwork on show that day.

"Your mother did everything herself," she said. "She even made five pairs of beaded slippers!"

I had seen those slippers, embroidered in eye-wateringly tiny beads. It was hopeless to think I could replicate them, even if Amah complained that my father had wasted my time with studies. Secretly, I thought that if he hadn't taught me to read, I would never have been able to decipher the letter that Lim Tian Ching's great-uncle had held in the Plains of the Dead. But that was not the world I lived in, though I sometimes quailed at the thought that if I married Tian Bai, I would be doomed to reenter the ghostly halls of the Lim mansion after my death. In any case, there were other things that demanded my attention. I was to be married, a wife and hopefully a mother. Friends and neighbors congratulated my father on such a fortunate match. I was very lucky, they said. The luckiest girl in Malacca.

I hoped that these preparations would give me an opportunity to see Yan Hong. There were many things I wanted to ask her, most pressingly about the teacup she had hidden in her room. Tian Bai seemed pleased that I had taken such a fancy to his cousin, yet he was disinclined to arrange a visit to the Lim mansion.

"After we're married, it will be your home," he said. "There's no need to rush. My aunt is not well."

I wondered, disloyally, whether he was trying to shield me from his aunt's disapproval, or prevent me from finding out more about his family. Or even, more ominously, whether the spirit of Lim Tian Ching still lingered in their household, despite Er Lang's promises of arrest. But the more gently he dissuaded me, the more determined I was to talk to Yan Hong.

And so, when Old Wong mentioned he meant to return some cake molds borrowed from the Lim household, I said I would go with him. Of all people, he was the one who most understood my concerns, although I dared not tell him all the details. He blew out his cheeks.

"Little Miss, things are finally going well. Must you dig further?"

Not meeting his eyes, I nodded.

"Well, you seem to know what you're doing lately," he remarked, and surprisingly, said no more about it.

We entered the Lim household through the servants' quarters. The household staff paid me little heed, taking me for Old Wong's assistant in my plain *sam foo*. I was glad of it. The last thing I wanted was to sit in some front parlor, fielding polite chatter with various relatives of the Lim family and losing my chance to speak privately with Yan Hong. In other ways too, the anonymity was comforting, reminding me of the time I had spent in the kitchens of that other, ghostly Lim mansion. For the hundredth time, I wondered how my mother fared and if we would ever meet again in this life.

"Is Yan Hong here?" I asked a servant.

"She's in the garden."

I had never walked through the outer garden before and couldn't possibly have found her if the servant had not guided me. It seemed a long way as we wended through walkways and arbors and traversed wide lawns. These were laid out in the English fashion, the grass pressed by heavy rollers and trimmed so that it resembled the short fur on a cat's back. Like the other great mansions along Klebang Road, the extensive grounds backed onto the sea. A low wall covered with a fiery tangle of bougainvillea was all that separated it from the steep drop below. Yan Hong seemed pleased, albeit surprised, to see me, although her complexion was puffy and dull.

"I meant to call on you," she said, "but my stepmother has been ill."

"What are you doing here?" I asked. It was a remote spot, far from the main house and hidden by drifts of trees.

"Inspecting the wall. The rains have been so heavy lately that there've been several landslides. And look what has happened here."

Coming up beside her, I saw how a yawing fissure had opened up in the loose earth. It terminated in a narrow shaft, so deep that I could not see the bottom from my vantage point. The sides were oddly regular and I realized that it was a disused well. The landslide had destroyed the upper portion so that it resembled nothing less than a lopsided funnel that dropped sharply into the old well.

"Long ago there was a house here, half a mile from the coast in my grand-father's time. But the sea has eaten in until nothing is left," said Yan Hong. "Soon this too will disappear."

I was surprised that there should be a well so close to the sea, but our climate was so wet and torrid that there were numerous underground springs that ran to the ocean. It was not difficult to sink a well anywhere, though this one had long since gone dry. I wondered where the old house had stood and what had happened to its inhabitants. Had they passed on to rebirth, or was it possible that in the Plains of the Dead, there was still such a house by the seafront? My skin prickled, and once again I was reminded of how I would dwell on such thoughts for the rest of my life.

YAN HONG DISMISSED THE servant with some instructions while I gazed at the view. The contrast between the crumbling earth and the mani-cured lawns beyond the drifts of trees was stark.

"We used to play games here when we were children," said Yan Hong, her eyes fixed on some distant memory. "It was our secret place. Of course, the well wasn't like this then. It had a proper top and a cover. We said it was haunted and that a woman had thrown herself down it."

"Was that true?" I asked. Now that I had seen the spirits of the dead, I could easily imagine a hungry ghost, lank-haired and gaunt, tethered to the old well.

"Of course not. But we liked to frighten one another. I said the woman had died for love, but Tian Bai said she was a witch who still lived at the bottom."

"And Lim Tian Ching?" I asked, eager to discover more about their rela-tionships.

"Oh, he was a crybaby and a tattletale! He was much younger than us, though. Once we tricked him. We told him there was a secret passage here and if he waited, we would show him where it was. But we ran back to the house instead. Tian Bai wanted to go back and fetch him, but it was dinnertime and we forgot."

I pictured Lim Tian Ching as a fat and frightened child, shivering beside the old well in the gathering darkness. Perhaps this was just one of the many grievances he held against Yan Hong and Tian Bai.

"That was rather cruel," I said.

"I suppose so. We were sorry about it, but he told on us and we were punished by my father. It wasn't so bad for me, but Tian Bai was beaten so badly that he couldn't sit down for two days." She spoke matter-of-factly, far more frankly than I had expected. But perhaps it was because I was now Tian Bai's fiancée and she considered me an ally. She had no idea that I had entered this house as a spirit, drifting around and spying on her. Ashamed, I felt even more reluctant to question her about Lim Tian Ching's death.

"What will you do with this well?"

"Now that it's been destroyed like this, we'll have to wall this area off. I must tell Tian Bai about it. He's out right now, but he ought to be back very soon. Why don't you wait for him?"

Secretly, I was relieved he wasn't around. It was awkward enough to question her; several times I began to say something but stopped myself. But I was acutely aware that time was passing. It might be my last chance to speak with her before the wedding. My last chance before embarking on a lifetime of suspicion. And so, holding my breath, I plunged into a tale of how I had been troubled by a dream. A dream of Lim Tian Ching, who said he had been murdered. It was suitably vague and mostly true anyway. I watched Yan Hong carefully, but though she turned a trifle pale, there was little change in her expression.

"Do you believe in such things?" she asked, fingering a papery bougainvillea blossom.

"I don't know," I said. "He was upset, though. And very angry with Tian Bai."

She frowned. "If it truly was his spirit, I wouldn't be surprised if he meant to make trouble. He was always like that."

"But he said you kept his teacup."

She looked startled, then oddly defiant. "Did he accuse me too?"

"Do you have the cup?" My pulse quickened. If she lied to me, I would know not to trust her.

"Yes. I have it." She gave me an appraising look. "It was part of my mother's dowry. He took a fancy to it so she gave it to him. When he died, I took it back. He should never have had it in the first place." There was a wealth of bitterness in her voice and I remembered the look of resentment she had given Madam Lim on the staircase.

"Did Tian Bai put anything in it?" The words hung between us like poisonous flowers. Once said, I could never take them back.

Scornfully, she said, "Tian Bai would never do anything like that! Do you even know everything he's done for you? He's already repaid your father's debts. If you can accuse him like this, you don't deserve to marry him!"

"Then did you put anything in it?" I pressed on, aware that I was burning all my bridges. After this, she would never look on me as a friend again. The thought was painful, yet I wanted, desperately, to know the truth.

Her gaze was bright and sharp. "If I said yes, would anyone believe you? But let's suppose I really had a grudge against him. That from childhood, my mother and I had to serve him and put up with his demands and humiliations, because he was the son of the first wife. And just suppose one day he was malingering and I wanted to punish him. I might well have put something in his tea. But those are purely suppositions, of course."

She brushed past me then paused. "If you see the ghost of Lim Tian Ching again, you can tell him that I'm glad he's dead."

SPEECHLESS, I COULD ONLY watch as Yan Hong walked on without another word, but she had gone no more than ten paces when a figure appeared from among the trees. Yan Hong stopped short, even though the creature ignored her. I caught my breath for an instant, convinced it was a hungry ghost. The ghost of the woman Yan Hong said had died in the well. Then I realized that the gaunt features and sparse, wild hair belonged to Madam Lim.

Her once plump cheeks had fallen in and her neat figure had shrunk until it was little more than bones rattling in a bag of skin. The expensive *kebaya* had been replaced by a shapeless shift, the collar stained with food. I had heard she was ill, but it was a terrible change from the self-possessed woman who had invited me to play mahjong a scant few months ago. She shuffled forward and seized my wrist with a grip that was surprisingly strong. I flinched, but dared not shake it off.

"So, you're going to marry into this house after all." Her eyes wandered past me. "It's the wrong one," she said. "The wrong one."

"What do you mean, Auntie?" In this state, I no longer wondered that Tian Bai had tried to keep me away from the house.

"I said you're marrying the wrong one! You were supposed to marry my son. But my son is gone." The wail she let out had an eldritch, unnerving quality. "He's really gone. He doesn't come to me in dreams anymore."

I stared at her, recalling how Lim Tian Ching had boasted of his influence over his mother. No doubt that had ended when Er Lang had instigated the arrests in the spirit world.

"It's better this way," I said as gently as I could. "Let him pass on."

"How can I, when he was murdered? I heard you talking to Yan Hong just now. You said you saw him as well!"

Alarmed, I glanced at Yan Hong, who stood frozen behind her. "It was just a dream. We were only talking about dreams."

But Madam Lim was muttering and shaking her head. "She said it! She killed him and Tian Bai must have helped her."

"Didn't you hear Yan Hong? Tian Bai had nothing to do with it."

"Lies! All lies!" She released my hand and lurched forward, dangerously close to the crumbling edge of the disused well. Instinctively, Yan Hong stretched out a hand toward her and she grasped it. Too late, I caught the glint in her eye. With surprising strength, Madam Lim shoved Yan Hong. Uttering a cry, she lost her balance and as I grabbed for her, we teetered crazily and fell over the edge.

CHAPTER 38

I WAS SLIDING, falling. Desperately, I clung with my fingers to halt my descent but the loose earth broke away beneath my hands. Small stones rattled and cut my face. My hands were bloodied and raw as I snatched at the sides, gasping with relief as I found a foothold. Above me, Yan Hong shuddered to a halt as well. Like two geckos, we pressed ourselves against the steep slope while below, the dark shaft of the well gaped like a wound. Looking up, I saw Madam Lim's white face as she peered over.

"You stupid girls!" she said. "If it hadn't been for you, my son would still be here. Both of you caused him so much grief."

A stone hit me, and then another one. I heard Yan Hong give a sharp cry.

"Mother!" she said. "Please!"

"Don't you dare call me Mother! Your real mother was a suicide. I'll tell everyone you did the same thing and dragged Li Lan over. And now, I'm going to do what I should have done a long time ago." Her face vanished, and though we screamed and shouted, it did not reappear.

· · · ·

FROM THE ECHO OF falling stones, the well wasn't very deep. Just enough to break our necks if we fell. Though I fumbled blindly with my feet, I dared not climb farther down. I closed my eyes in sheer terror. Above me, I could hear Yan Hong sobbing.

"Can you climb up?" I called.

"I can't. I'm afraid of heights."

Peering up, I saw that we weren't that far from the edge, although the slope of the funnel was perilously steep. If she could climb a few feet she might make it. "Feel with your hands!" I said. "Try to pull yourself up. I'll help you fit your feet." I found a rocky foothold and supporting her ankle, guided her to it. In this manner, trembling and halting frequently, Yan Hong managed to climb higher. Grimly, I pulled myself up after her. My heart was racing, my palms slick with sweat and blood. If I looked down into the darkness, I was lost.

When she was almost at the top, Yan Hong began to cry again. "I can't! I just can't! The stone comes out here."

I saw that she was right. A large rock, displaced by the landslide, bulged outward above her. It would be very difficult for her to make the final ascent. Ignoring the pain in my arms, I forced myself a little higher until I found a narrow shelf to wedge my feet on.

"Step on my shoulders," I called.

Sobbing, Yan Hong put one hand out and grasped the rock. I placed her foot on my shoulder and braced myself as she put her weight on me. As she scrabbled for another handhold, I extended my arm. "Put your other foot on my palm!" The effort of supporting her made me gasp. "Hurry!"

Yan Hong was almost over the bulge when she slipped. Her feet flailed wildly as she grabbed for a foothold. With all my strength, I shoved her up. She made it over, but I lost my balance and slid helplessly down, so terrified that I couldn't even scream. I was going to die now, my neck broken at the bottom. Above me, I heard Yan Hong's despairing shriek. "Li Lan!"

My slithering fall was broken by a ledge to which I clung. It was dressed stone, the remains of the well shaft that had broken off in the landslide. My feet kicked desperately in the air, then I lost my grip and dropped into the darkness. I landed on soft dampness, the bottom of the well. When I looked up, I saw Yan Hong's frightened face far above me.

"I'm all right!" I shouted at her. "Go and stop Madam Lim! I can wait!"

Yan Hong nodded frantically, then disappeared.

FOR SOME MINUTES AFTER she had gone, I could only think of how long it had taken me to walk from the main house through the extensive grounds. Had it taken a quarter of an hour, or even more? Either way, I would have to wait for a while. And what if Madam Lim had planned something else for Tian Bai? Yan Hong had said he would be back at any moment, though she might simply abandon me. After all, if she had really poisoned Lim Tian Ching, she had every reason to silence me as well. Perhaps it had been foolish to help her, but there was no other option. As my eyes became accustomed to the dimness, I explored the bottom of the well. Mud had cushioned my fall and spared me serious injury, but the walls of dressed stone rose sharply on all sides. They were damp and slippery with moss, and try as I might, I could not scale them.

AS I SQUELCHED AROUND, ankle deep in mud, I stepped on something hard and long, about the length of a human thighbone. A dreadful suspicion made me freeze, thinking of the woman Yan Hong said had committed suicide. But those were only children's stories, I told myself, not wanting to think that if Yan Hong abandoned me, I would become the hungry ghost in this well. Reaching down, I was relieved to fish out the broken handle of a broom. There was other debris as well: an old ax head, the rusted-out bottom of a pot. But nothing that would help me climb out. I stared up, seeing that the sky had turned an ominous gray as another storm threatened to sweep in off the coast. The air smelled wet and cold.

A heavy spatter of raindrops hit me. I wished for my light spirit body, which could easily have scaled the walls. I wished for the company of my sweet horse. But most of all, I wished for Er Lang. If I had still had the scale, I could have called for him. But there was a vast gulf between his position and mine; I had no right to expect anything further. Gritting my teeth, I told myself that I wouldn't call him even if I could. I was too proud to do so; I would rescue myself.

Again and again, I tried to scale my prison. Several times, I gained a few agonizing feet only to lose my grip on the slick dressed stone. My nails were broken and bleeding, my breath coming in gasps. As I leaned against the wall, I thought bitterly of how weak this physical body was. Death was always near and despite my brief break from its clutches, it would soon claim me again. I had escaped once, from the Plains of the Dead, but I had not been alone—and perhaps in the end, it was hubris for me to claim I needed no one.

"Er Lang!" I shouted. "Er Lang! Where are you?"

My arms ached as I leaned against the shaft; my legs trembled with weakness. The light was fading. Tears ran down my face, mingling with the downpour that had started in earnest. Exhausted, I felt my strength seep away with the cold rain that stripped the warmth from my body. Though I longed to sit down, I shrank from the mud and its unknown contents. I shouted for help intermittently, but the estate grounds were so extensive that I despaired of anyone hearing me, especially in this deluge. It was laughable, even hysterical, that I should die now after having gone through so much effort to reclaim my body. Old Wong was right, I was a meddlesome fool who was throwing away my chance at happiness, my chance to marry Tian Bai and be a wife and mother. How long had it been now? Hours, or merely minutes? My teeth chattered; my thoughts became increasingly disjointed. I prayed to Zheng He, the admiral who had sailed these waters almost five hundred years ago, and to my mother, wherever she was in the Plains of the Dead. Gabbled prayers, with promises to be good, to never do anything like this again if only Er Lang would come. Just one more time.

"Er Lang!" I cried again. My voice had grown hoarse. "Er Lang, you fool! You promise breaker!"

"Is this your way of asking for help?" And then he was there, looking down at me. The rain streamed off his bamboo hat in a sheet of silver needles. "What on earth are you doing?"

The relief of seeing him made my knees buckle. I wondered briefly whether he was a mirage drawn from the shimmering curtain of rain, but the exasperation in his voice was too convincing. Incoherently, I began to explain my predicament, but he shook his head. "Tell me later."

To my horror, he jumped down the well shaft.

"What have you done?" I said. "Why didn't you get a rope?" Overwrought, I almost burst into tears. "You . . . you insane creature! How will we ever get out again?"

Er Lang examined his shoes in dismay. "You should have told me there was mud down here."

"Is that all you can say?" But I was glad, so glad to see him that I hugged him tightly. Despite his concern about his shoes, he didn't seem to mind as I pressed my grimy face against his shoulder.

"Last time it was a cemetery, and now the bottom of a well," he remarked. "What were you doing anyway?"

As I explained, his tone became icy. "So, you saved a murderer and let yourself be abandoned. Do you have some sort of death wish?"

"Why are you angry?" Pushing back his hat, I searched his face. It was a mistake, for faced with his unnerving good looks, I could only drop my eyes.

"You might have broken your neck. Why can't you leave these things to the proper authorities?"

"I didn't do it on purpose." Incredibly, we were arguing again. "And where were you all this time? You could have sent me a message!"

"How was I supposed to do that when you never left the house alone?"

"But you could have come at any time. I was waiting for you!"

Er Lang was incensed. "Is this the thanks I get?"

If I had thought it through, I would never have done it. But I grasped the collar of his robe and pulled his face to mine. "Thank you," I said, and kissed him.

I meant to break away at once, but he caught me, his hand behind my head.

"Are you going to complain about this?" he demanded.

Wordlessly, I shook my head. My face reddened, remembering my awkward remarks about tongues last time. He must have recalled them as well, for he gave me an inscrutable look.

"Open your mouth, then."

"Why?"

"I'm going to put my tongue in."

That he could joke at a time like this was really unbelievable. Despite my outrage, however, I flung myself into his arms. Half laughing, half furious, I pressed my mouth fiercely against his. He pinned me against the well shaft. The stone chilled my back through my wet clothes, but my skin burned where he held my wrists. Gasping, I could feel the heat of him as his tongue slipped inside. My pulse raced; my body trembled uncontrollably. There was only the hard pressure of his mouth, the slick thrust of his tongue. I wanted to cry, but no tears came. A river was melting in me, my core dissolving like wax in his arms. My ears hummed, I could only hear the rasping of our breaths, the hammering of my heart. A stifled moan escaped my lips. He gave a long sigh and broke away.

"Aren't you getting married next month?"

My face was red, my hands shaking. "I'm sorry. I shouldn't have done that."

"Congratulations, then. You must be very happy."

I SCARCELY KNEW WHERE to turn in that confined space. Er Lang wouldn't look at me either. Instead, he glanced up at the narrow slice of sky, heavy with rain clouds.

"We should get out of here." His tone was sober. I had no words left.

With little effort, he slung me over his shoulder and began to climb. I didn't know how he found foot- and handholds in the slippery shaft, but he ascended with ease. His body was light and strong, far stronger than any normal man, as I had long suspected. Dizzy, I clung to him, feeling like a sack of rice. If I opened my eyes, there was only the darkness below. The pulse in my neck was throbbing. With each movement, I could feel the muscles of his back contracting and relaxing beneath my fingers. When we reached the top, he set me down. I cradled my cut hands, exhausted. I was terrified that he would leave me again.

"What happened to Lim Tian Ching and Master Awyoung?" I asked, after a strained silence.

"Well," he said, "thanks in part to your evidence, a number of arrests were made, including your erstwhile suitor. They've been sent on to the courts for judgment."

"What about Fan? An ox-headed demon said it was taking her to the Lim mansion."

"She never arrived. I'm afraid there's no trace of her."

I was silent, digesting this. It was a terrible end for Fan. Er Lang made no comment, but he studied me intently.

"I've done you a disservice," he said at last. "It's only fair to let you know, but you won't have a normal life span."

I bit my lip. "Have you come to take my soul, then?"

"I told you that's not my jurisdiction. But you're not going to die soon. In fact, you won't die for a long time, far longer than I initially thought, I'm afraid. Nor will you age normally."

"Because I took your *qi*?"

He inclined his head. "I should have stopped you sooner."

I thought of the empty years that stretched ahead of me, years of solitude long after everyone I loved had died. Though I might have children or grandchildren. But perhaps they might comment on my strange youthfulness and shun me as unnatural. Whisper of sorcery, like those Javanese women who inserted gold needles in their faces and ate children. In the Chinese tradition, nothing was better than dying old and full of years, a treasure in the bosom of one's family. To outlive descendants and endure a long span of widowhood could hardly be construed as lucky. Tears filled my eyes, and for some reason this seemed to agitate Er Lang, for he turned away. In profile, he was even more handsome, if that was possible, though I was quite sure he was aware of it.

"It isn't necessarily a good thing, but you'll see all of the next century, and I think it will be an interesting one."

"That's what Tian Bai said," I said bitterly. "How long will I outlive him?"

"Long enough," he said. Then more gently, "You may have a happy marriage, though."

"I wasn't thinking about him," I said. "I was thinking about my mother. By the time I die, she'll have long since gone on to the courts for reincarnation. I shall never see her again." I burst into sobs, realizing how much I'd clung to that hope, despite the fact that it might be better for my mother to leave the Plains of the Dead. But then we would never meet in this lifetime. Her memories would be erased and her spirit lost to me in this form.

"Don't cry." I felt his arms around me, and I buried my face in his chest. The rain began to fall again, so dense it was like a curtain around us. Yet I did not get wet.

"Listen," he said. "When everyone around you has died and it becomes too hard to go on pretending, I shall come for you."

"Do you mean that?" A strange happiness was beginning to grow, twining and tightening around my heart.

"I've never lied to you."

"Can't I go with you now?"

He shook his head. "Aren't you getting married? Besides, I've always preferred older women. In about fifty years' time, you should be just right."

I glared at him. "What if I'd rather not wait?"

He narrowed his eyes. "Do you mean that you don't want to marry Tian Bai?"

I dropped my gaze.

"If you go with me, it won't be easy for you," he said warningly. "It will bring you closer to the spirit world and you won't be able to lead a normal life. My work is incognito, so I can't keep you in style. It will be a little house in some strange town. I shan't be available most of the time, and you'd have to be ready to move at a moment's notice."

I listened with increasing bewilderment. "Are you asking me to be your mistress or an indentured servant?"

His mouth twitched. "I don't keep mistresses; it's far too much trouble.

I'm offering to marry you, although I might regret it. And if you think the Lim family disapproved of your marriage, wait until you meet mine."

I tightened my arms around him.

"Speechless at last," Er Lang said. "Think about your options. Frankly, if I were a woman, I'd take the first one. I wouldn't underestimate the importance of family."

"But what would you do for fifty years?"

He was about to speak when I heard a faint call, and through the heavy downpour, saw Yan Hong's blurred figure emerge between the trees, Tian Bai running beside her. "Give me your answer in a fortnight," said Er Lang. Then he was gone.

CHAPTER 39

TIAN BAI TOOK me home in a rickshaw that day. He was pale and didn't speak much, other than to ask if I was all right. I had shivered in my wet clothes, having refused all offers of entering the house to change. My heart was too full, my thoughts a storm of paper fragments. The Lim mansion seemed to frown on me even more than usual that day, the eaves weeping as the rain ran ceaselessly off its roof. The whole household was in an uproar. No one inquired too deeply as to how I had got out of the well. I supposed my scratched arms and cut hands led them to presume I had crawled out by myself. There was no one to insist that I change my clothes, or berate me for catching a chill as Amah surely would have. It was only Tian Bai who, in the midst of it all, quietly slipped his cotton jacket around my shoulders. Later I found out that Madam Lim had attacked him when he had returned home, though I only learned the full story when Old Wong came home that evening.

"She was waiting for him with a kitchen knife," he told us later. "I don't know how she got hold of it, but she tried to stab him."

Fortunately, her frailness betrayed her and Tian Bai had escaped with no more than an ugly cut on the arm. It was this that I saw, bandaged loosely with gauze, when he took me home that day. Alarmed, I had protested he need not accompany me, but Tian Bai merely shook his head. He looked drained, utterly weary, and I wondered whether sending me home was an excuse to escape the hysteria in that house. During our brief ride home, I stole occasional glances at him. The sinister inflections I had previously ascribed to him seemed to have evaporated with my suspicions of murder. There were lines under his eyes, and a smudge of ink on the cuff of his left sleeve. He was just a man whose family was falling apart. A good man, if Yan Hong could be believed. An unexpected tenderness filled me, even as my swollen mouth recalled me to another.

The last subject Tian Bai broached as he handed me out of the rickshaw was a request to keep things quiet about the situation with Madam Lim. I nodded, knowing that duty called and no breath of scandal must touch the Lim family. They were contemplating sending her to a madhouse, although the shame of it would reflect badly on them.

"It would be better to keep her at home, but she needs constant supervision." Tian Bai glanced guiltily at me. "Would you mind if we postpone the wedding?"

I didn't mind at all, though I could hardly express it to him. He held my hand.

"Li Lan, I'm glad you're here."

Afraid that he might kiss me, I half turned my face away. As soon as I had done so, I was filled with guilt, but he merely tightened his grip.

"I'm sorry," I said, hardly knowing what I was apologizing for.

"What for?" he said. "Yan Hong told me that you saved her."

Tian Bai touched my hair briefly. His calm demeanor, his ability to handle difficult situations; these were all qualities that I admired. He would be a good husband, levelheaded and dependable. Amid the frenzy, he had still thought to cover my wet shoulders with his jacket. Remembering this small kindness, I could not help but place my other hand on his face. If I belonged to him, my family and I would surely have a good life.

· · · ·

TO MY SURPRISE, WE received a constant stream of visitors and gifts from the Lim family over the next few days. I would have thought that I was the last person they wanted to see, since I was privy to how Madam Lim had tried to kill first Yan Hong and me, and then Tian Bai. On the third day, Tian Bai's uncle, Lim Teck Kiong himself, came expressly to see me. Amah rushed to tell me of his arrival, seizing me by the arm and hastily fastening up my hair.

"Your clothes!" she hissed. "You can't receive him like that."

She frowned at my plain *baju panjang*, but it was too late for such niceties. Besides, I had the suspicion that he had other things in mind than his future niece-in-law's dress. When I entered the front parlor, he was sitting down with my father as though their friendship had never suffered a rupture. I studied him with new eyes, thinking of the Third Concubine in the Plains of the Dead and wondering how he could have been the lover who had driven her to so much bitterness and damage. But he was still the same, portly and complacent, the image of a wealthy businessman.

His small glittering eyes, so like Lim Tian Ching's, rested on me, and after inquiring in a roundabout manner after my health, he began to talk of my father's debts. These, as I knew from Yan Hong, had already been settled by Tian Bai, but now his uncle put a fresh gloss on them, saying that as we were to be relatives soon, he had reinvested the remainder of my father's capital to secure a modest but stable income for him. He then went on to say that he admired me immensely and had heard a great deal about my scholarship. At this, my father was flattered enough, despite my protests, to retrieve a sample of my calligraphy from his study to show him. While he was gone, Lim Teck Kiong asked me whether I had ever thought to study abroad.

"A girl like you would benefit from a formal education," he said. "Especially in England, where they have colleges for young ladies. What do you think?"

In another time and place, I would have leaped at this suggestion, but now my stomach clenched. "What about the marriage?" I asked.

"Tian Bai would wait until you came back. There's no hurry, you're both young."

I heard a faint snort from Amah, who had hidden behind the door. Young, indeed! In her mind I should long have been married off, but I could not afford to offend this man. "Uncle, England seems very far and I think I would miss my family and Tian Bai."

"To be sure! Well, if that is the way you feel, then perhaps we had better have the wedding sooner, then. But remember, if you ever wish to study or travel, you need not worry about the well-being of your family. I would be happy to sponsor you."

I looked at him, thinking of Yan Hong's tale of how this man had once beaten Tian Bai until he could not sit down for two days. Yet in the end, Tian Bai had turned out far better than his own spoiled son. But I understood him very well. He would prefer not to have me marry into his family, knowing all the sordid details as I did. If the British authorities should find out about the attempted murders, they might well use them as an excuse to make an example of his household. At the very least, there would be scandal to be explained away. If he could not get rid of me, however, the next best thing would be to have me under his continual scrutiny. But two could play at that game, I thought, completely forgetting my own hesitation about marrying Tian Bai. I leaned forward and gave him an enchanting smile, one that I had learned from observing Fan.

"You are very kind to me, Uncle. And to my father. I'm so grateful to you."

Although he continued to study me, I noticed a subtle change. His eyes widened and a bemused smile flickered across his face. Fan had once said I did not know how to use my face and body, that they were wasted on me, and now I realized she had been right. It was strange to think that power in this world belonged to old men and young women. Still, I had mixed emotions of shame and triumph after he left. It would be a difficult road, but I thought I could manage marrying into the Lim family.

IT WAS HARD TO believe that I had gone from having no marriage prospects to two, although you could hardly call either of them ideal. I was happy—that is, I felt that objectively I ought to be happy—but in truth I was quite miserable. Amah had drilled me well. In our community of Straits-born Chinese, marriage was a weighty proposition, a transaction that sought to balance filial duty and economic worth. In that sense, Er Lang's proposal was quite out of the question. In fact, I was still in shock over it.

I knew very little about him. Far less than the Lim family, with all its intrigue, though Er Lang had warned me that his family would be worse. How much worse, I could not imagine. But he had never lied to me. That was certainly one of his inhuman qualities. To follow Er Lang would be a leap into the unknown, the culmination of all my desires and terrors. I wasn't sure that I was brave enough to act with the same impulsive certainty that he had when he had risked his life for me on the Plains of the Dead. We were too different; it was impossible.

My mind wandered off in tangents, I could barely sew a seam straight. I wished I could speak to my mother again. Of all people, I missed her counsel, experienced as she was with the ways of the living and the dead. I was on my own, however, with no one to confide in. Whatever I chose, there was a heavy price to pay. If I went with Er Lang, I would lead a curious half-life, wandering the fringes of a hinterland peopled with ghosts and spirits, though I clung to the hope that I might meet my mother again. But it wasn't even clear whether I would have children myself, though I remembered how the Chinese emperors had claimed descent from dragons and wondered if I might bear such an honor, or give birth to a monstrosity.

If I stayed with Tian Bai, I would gain the security of a good marriage and the familiar comfort of my family. It also, however, meant living with the Lim legacy of madness and murder. Besides Tian Bai's uncle, there were the other wives and concubines to contend with. I must steel myself, learn to manage them the way that Madam Lim, or even Yan Hong, had. In some ways, I was surprised that Yan Hong had even returned for me. It would have been far more convenient for her if I had perished in that well. But she called on me a few days after Lim Teck Kiong's visit.

. . . .

WHEN YAN HONG CAME, I was in the back courtyard raking out the chicken coop. Old Wong always kept a few chickens, which he fattened for a month before slaughter, not permitting them to leave their pen until they were plump and succulent. In a great household like the Lim's, a daughter of the house would not be doing such a task, but Ah Chun claimed the feathers made her sneeze so Old Wong had handed me the rake that morning with a grunt. I started guiltily when I saw Yan Hong appear with Amah, as though our positions were reversed. Strangely, Amah did not press me to change my clothes. She merely looked satisfied and I suddenly understood that this was because, unlike Tian Bai's uncle who valued pretty women, it was important to impress upon the women of the Lim household what a virtuous and hard-working daughter-in-law I would make. Amah announced she would go and serve the many-layered *kuih lapis* cake that I had made (a complete fabrication) and that we ladies should come in for tea.

"I owe you," said Yan Hong as soon as we were alone together. "For saving me."

Not knowing what to say, I kept quiet.

"I didn't mean to kill him," she went on. "It was an accident, whether you believe it or not." She twisted her hands together. "He was always malingering; he used it to punish us if he felt neglected. That evening I was at the end of my patience. I had some ma huang prescribed to me before. I heard a larger dose would give him a headache and make him vomit, but I didn't think he would actually have a seizure."

Ma huang was the stimulant herb derived from the jointed stems of ephedra. Steeped into a tea, it gave relief to coughs and loosened phlegm from the lungs, but even I had some idea of its dangerous properties and could not quite believe that Yan Hong had been so ignorant of its side effects.

"Are you going to tell anyone?" she asked, biting her lips. It was the same nervous gesture I had witnessed when I had wandered through the Lim mansion as a disembodied spirit.

I shook my head. Who was I to judge her, or know exactly what had happened that evening? Yan Hong glanced away with a mingled look of shame and relief.

"I'm glad you're marrying Tian Bai," she said at last. "He's lucky to have you. Because someone has to take charge of the Lim household."

"Why can't it be you?"

"My husband has family and business interests in Singapore. I've told him that I'd prefer to move there." She straightened her back, avoiding my eyes. "It will be better for you and Tian Bai without so much baggage. Take care of him, will you? It hasn't been easy for him in our family."

"Does he know about Lim Tian Ching's death?" I asked.

"No, though he might have suspected. I almost told him at the time, I was so terrified at what happened. Sometimes I wish I had."

"Don't," I said. We both knew that Tian Bai would only try to protect her. It was better for me to bear the burden of this knowledge than him.

"Thank you," she said.

We walked back to the house in silence. I couldn't help wishing that matters had turned out differently. For despite everything she had done, I still liked her.

CHAPTER 40

A ND NOW THE days are passing too quickly, one following the other. My fortnight is almost up. I can hardly sleep; my thoughts and regrets weigh so heavily on me. I laugh too much at Old Wong's jokes and weep in secret over the slippers Amah is painstakingly embroidering for me. The easy thing to do is to marry Tian Bai and spin out my years with him and my family, hiding my strange youthfulness. And at the end of it, wait for Er Lang if he still remembers his promise. But that is the coward's way.

I think I already knew what I wanted a long time ago. Perhaps it began when he held my hand in the Plains of the Dead, where there were no other living creatures but the two of us. Or, if I am honest, when I first saw his face. It is possible that the seeds were set even further back, when the medium at the Sam Poh Kong temple told me to burn funeral money for myself. Did she know already that I would half-sever my thread with this world and never truly fit in again? Perhaps I really should have died then.

For all who have seen ghosts and spirits are marked with a stain, and far more than Old Wong, I have trespassed where no living person ought to have. I have spoken with the dead, served in their houses, and eaten spirit offerings.

My two worlds overlap like distorted panes of glass. Haunted, I chafe at the tight orbit of mahjong parties that I once thought so glamorous, and glance over my shoulder for wind and shadows, yearning for the forbidden.

Tian Bai's uncle has promised that my father, Amah, and Old Wong will be well taken care of, should I depart on a long journey. He won't care where I go, as long as it is far away from the Lim family's good name. I will have to bind him to such an agreement and check on them from time to time, if it is permitted, though I'm not sure where or even when I will go. Perhaps they will think that I have gone away to study, or maybe I will simply vanish one moonlit night, like those tales of ghosts and spirits. I only hope that I may return to visit them, even if it is only as a shiver on the wind. And if they should die before me, as they surely must, I will be waiting to escort them to the Plains of the Dead.

As for Tian Bai, I don't know how to face him. He will be disappointed in me. Though when it comes down to it, I'm afraid that I will falter and take the easy way out. It has happened before, when I stood tongue-tied in front of him and could not tell him the truth. For all his kindness, he has never really understood me, nor I him. If anyone had said that the opera I heard at the Lim mansion, so long ago, should express my feelings for him, I would have laughed, thinking that we were meant to be lovers. There is a river between us, however, like the Milky Way that separates the Cowherd and the Weaving Maid. And no matter how much I shout and call, I will never cross it. He will smile at my foibles and comfort me with gifts. His eyes are fixed on someone else, not me.

But I want to see Er Lang. I don't want to wait fifty years, or cheat Tian Bai out of a love that he will never have. In the darkness of a thousand withered souls, it was Er Lang's hand that I sought, and his voice that I longed to hear. Perhaps it is selfish of me, but an uncertain future with him, in all its laughter and quarrels, is better than being left behind. Though given how much I resisted becoming Lim Tian Ching's ghost wife, it's not even funny that I'm willing to leave my family for a man who isn't human. When Er Lang comes for his answer, I will tell him that I've always thought he was a monster. And that I want to be his bride.

NOTES

GHOST MARRIAGES

The folk tradition of marriages to ghosts or between ghosts usually occurred in order to placate spirits or allay a haunting. There are a number of allusions to it in Chinese literature, but its roots seem to lie in ancestor worship. Matches were sometimes made between two deceased persons, with the families on both sides recognizing the marriage as a tie between them. However, there were other cases in which a living person was married to the dead. These primarily took the form of a living person fulfilling the wish of a dying sweetheart, or to give the rank of a wife to a mistress or concubine who had produced an heir. Sometimes an impoverished girl was taken into a household as a widow to perform the ancestral rites for a man who died without a wife or descendants, which was Li Lan's situation. In such a case, an actual marriage ceremony would be performed with a rooster standing in for the dead bridegroom.

Occasionally the living were duped as well. If a family heard from an exorcist or a fortune-teller that a deceased member wanted to get married, they would sometimes place a red envelope (*hong bao*), commonly used for cash gifts, on the road. Whoever was unlucky enough to pick it up on the mistaken assumption that it contained money was designated as the husband or wife of the ghost. It is interesting to note that such tales of ghost marriages seem to be mostly confined to the overseas Chinese communities, particularly those of Southeast Asia and Taiwan, and even then they are not very common. I was surprised to find that many mainland Chinese had never heard of such practices, and I could only assume that it was due to the Communist influence that discouraged superstitious behavior for decades.

CHINESE NOTIONS OF THE AFTERLIFE

Chinese notions of the afterlife often seem to be a mixture of Buddhism, Taoism, ancestor worship, and folk beliefs. Despite borrowing the Buddhist concept of reincarnation in which souls seek to escape the endless cycle by giving up all desires to enter a state of nothingness, they also maintain the existence of several paradises ruled over by various guardians and deities. This contradiction is further complicated by Taoist beliefs such as attaining eternal life, magic, levitation, martial arts, etc.

There is also a Chinese literary tradition of supernatural stories that describe a bureaucratic afterlife closely modeled upon the traditional official bureaucracy. Thus, in many tales, hell is governed by corrupt and inept officials who commit crimes and take bribes. Various heavenly deities are then charged with solving the cases and dispensing justice. Er Lang is one such minor deity who appears in a number of different stories. In some cases, he is a human who became a deity because of his filial virtue. In *Journey to the West*, Wu Cheng En's classic story of the Monkey King, he is the Jade Emperor's nephew charged with restraining the reckless monkey. Er Lang is also associated with water as an engineer who defeated a dragon to prevent flooding. I took the liberty of making him a dragon himself, as they were known for their shape-changing and rainmaking abilities.

The Plains of the Dead specifically is also my invention, although it reflects a common Chinese belief in an afterlife peopled by ghosts and their burned paper funeral offerings. It was not entirely clear how this idea connected to Buddhist concepts of reincarnation, so for the purposes of this book, I created a more substantive link between them.

MALAYA

Malaya is the historic name of Malaysia before independence. British Malaya was a loose set of states, including Singapore, that was under varying degrees of British control from 1771 to 1948. Malaya was extremely profitable for the British Empire as the world's largest tin and rubber producer, and the Straits Settlements of Penang, Malacca, and Singapore were its principal ports of commerce.

STRAITS-BORN CHINESE

Early Chinese migrants to Southeast Asia from the fifteenth to eighteenth centuries were overwhelmingly single men who intermarried with local women and whose descendants formed unique communities of overseas Chinese known as Peranakan Chinese. Strictly speaking, the term refers to the children of intermarriage between natives and foreigners. A Peranakan was not necessarily Chinese; there were also Peranakan Dutch, Peranakan Arab, Peranakan Indian, etc., but the largest community in Malaya was the Peranakan Chinese. They incorporated a number of Malay cultural practices, such as speaking creolized Malay, dressing in Malay clothing, and eating the local cuisine. Sons born of such unions were often sent back to China to receive a Chinese upbringing, whereas daughters remained in Malaya but were only allowed to marry Chinese men. In this manner, the community retained a strong Chinese character.

From the 1800s onward, there was a sharp rise in the number of Chinese women emigrating, and the communities became almost wholly Chinese, although they retained a great deal of local culture and later Chinese who emigrated also adopted these customs. Li Lan's family would be an example of this, having come from China more recently but assimilating local customs such as dress and food. Within the community, there were finer distinctions between those who had older roots and those more-recent arrivals. Still, if they were born in the Straits Settlements of Penang, Malacca, or Singapore, they were British subjects who self-identified as Straits-born Chinese.

In Malacca in the nineteenth and twentieth centuries, they emerged as the dominant business elite who were quick to learn English and were anglicized in many respects. Quite a few young men, like Tian Bai, studied in Britain or the Crown Colony of Hong Kong.

MALAY SPELLING

This book uses colonial spellings of Malay words to reflect the time period and to make it easier to pronounce for people unfamiliar with the romanized Malay spelling reforms of 1972. Thus *Melaka* has retained its historic spelling of *Malacca*, as have other words such as *Bukit China* and *chendana*, which, despite no change in pronunciation, would be written as *Bukit Cina* and *cendana* today.

CHINESE DIALECTS

A broad variety of Chinese dialects was and still is spoken in Malaysia, though the majority of them were from southern China, which saw the greatest number of immigrants to Southeast Asia. Overseas Chinese had strong ties to their ancestral clans and villages, and distinguished between themselves even after settling in Malaya for several generations. The most common dialects include Cantonese, Hokkien, Teochew, Hakka, and Hainanese. The wide variation in spoken dialect meant that many Chinese could not understand one another, although the written language, for those who were literate, remained the same.

Many professions often followed clan lines, as people tended to bring relatives into the same industry. For example, there were a number of Cantonese amahs, as well as Hainanese cooks, which is what I had in mind for the characters of Amah and Old Wong.

CHINESE NAMES

For the purposes of this book, I debated standardizing the names to Pinyin but chose not to do so in order to reflect the diversity of the time. The pronunciation of a particular name would have varied depending on the dialect and clan of the person. For example, the surname "Lin" in Mandarin can be pronounced as "Lim" in Hokkien or "Lum" in Cantonese. Even within a dialect, odd and arbitrary spellings were applied, depending on who was recording the name and how they decided to spell it. There are many examples of Chinese names that were butchered by a recording clerk to end up with inadvertently peculiar meanings.

Traditionally the family name is given first, such as in Lim Tian Ching's case. I've referred to him by his full name throughout the book to make it easier to differentiate between Tian Bai and him. Tian Bai and Tian Ching have similar names because they are both males from the same generation. Typically, there is a generational name dictated by the family poem. Each generation takes one successive character from the poem as part of their name, so that by reciting the poem, you can immediately tell whether someone is from an older or younger generation of the family.

Meanings of Names

Li Lan—Beautiful Orchid
Tian Bai—Bright Sky
Lim—A family name meaning "a grove of trees"
Lim Tian Ching—Eternal Sky
Fan—Fragrance
Yan Hong—Red Swallow

Lim Teck Kiong—Strong Morals

Er Lang—Second Son. As can be guessed, this is probably not his true name. The Chinese have a tradition of taking many different names to correspond with various stages in life. For example, a scholar might have a childhood name, an official name, and later a literary name if he became famous. In his old age he might choose another name to signify his retirement from the world.

ACKNOWLEDGMENTS

I T WOULD HAVE been impossible to write this book without the many wonderful people who supported me in this. I'm deeply indebted to:

Jenny Bent, my amazing agent, whose vision for this novel has guided and inspired me. Rachel Kahan, my editor, whose discerning eye and enthusiasm for this book spurred me on to richer depths. Trish Daly, Lynn Grady, Mumtaz Mustafa, Doug Jones, Camille Collins, Kimberly Chocolaad, and the Harper-Collins sales force. It's been a pleasure and an honor to work with all of you.

My wonderful and long-suffering family, including: my parents, S. K. Choo and Lilee Woo, whose love instilled in me a great wonder and curiosity about the world; Chuin Ru Choo; Kuok Ming Lee; and Jennifer and Spencer Cham, for their love and support over the years.

Sue and Danny Yee, Li Lian Tan, Abigail Hing Wen, and Kathy and Larry Kwan, dear friends who championed this book from the start, encouraged me to submit it, and remained enthusiastic despite having to read endless drafts and analyze imaginary characters. Without you this book would never have been published.

Readers Carmen Cham, Suelika Chial, Beti Cung, Christine Folch, Paul

Griffiths, Diane Levitan, and Rebecca Tulsi, who provided fearless and invaluable feedback from the first page to the many alternate endings.

Dr. Teow See Heng, my resident Hainanese expert; Alison Klein, my Dutch adviser; and Mr. and Mrs. Tham Siew Inn, who so kindly showed me around their hometown of Malacca and helped me find a site for the fictional Lim mansion near Klebang.

Most of all, my husband, James, whose patience, love, and wise discernment make my world anew every day, and my children, Colin and Mika, who are my joy.

And to the one who has led me through the valley of the shadow of death. (Psalm 23:4)

About the author

About the book

Read on

Insights,
Interviews
& More...

Meet Yangsze Choo

James Cham

YANGSZE CHOO is a fourth-generation Malaysian of Chinese descent. Due to a childhood spent in various countries, she can eavesdrop (badly) in several languages. After graduating from Harvard, she worked in the corporate sector before writing her first novel. She lives in California with her husband and children and a potential rabbit. Yangsze loves to eat and read, and often does both at the same time. You can follow her blog at yschoo.com and on Twitter @yangszechoo.

Reading Group Guide

1. Perplexed by her father's absences and worried by finances and marriage negotiations, Li Lan wonders, "What was happening out in the world of men? . . . Despite the fact that my feet were not bound, I was confined to domestic quarters as though a rope tethered my ankle to our front door." How does Li Lan chafe against notions of femininity, and in what ways does she rebel?

2. Malacca is a city settled by various ethnic groups over the centuries, with a long colonial history as well. The Chinese in Malaya, like Li Lan's family, keep their own practices and dress, but don't follow tradition as rigidly as the Chinese in China. How does Li Lan benefit from this blending of tradition?

3. After Li Lan gives in to Amah's superstition and visits a medium at the temple, she observes a Chinese cemetery that has been neglected due to fear of ghosts: "How different it was from the quiet Malay cemeteries, whose pawn-shaped Islamic tombstones are shaded by the frangipani tree, which the Malays call the graveyard flower. Amah would never let me pluck the fragrant, creamy blossoms when I was a child. It seemed to me that in this confluence of cultures, we had acquired one another's superstitions without necessarily ▶

any of their comforts." What do you think the comforts of superstition are? As Li Lan interacts with the spirit world, does her perspective on superstition change?

4. Why is Li Lan drawn to Tian Bai when they meet? How do her feelings for him change over the course of the novel, and why?

5. The ghost world Li Lan enters is a richly imagined place governed by complicated bureaucracy. How does the parallel city reflect the world of the living, and in what ways is it different?

6. When Li Lan thinks that she has found her mother—a second wife in the ancestral Lim household—she is shaken by how horrible she is. How does meeting her real mother, Auntie Three, help Li Lan understand her own family?

7. When Li Lan is a wandering spirit, able to observe from another perspective, what does she realize about herself and her world? Are there positive aspects to her time spent outside her body?

8. Li Lan thinks, "All who have seen ghosts and spirits are marked with a stain, and far more than Old Wong, I have trespassed where no living person ought to have." How has Li Lan's time spent in the realm of the ghost world—speaking with

the dead, eating spirit offerings, seeing Er Lang's true identity— changed her? Is it possible for her to go back to normal life?

9. When Er Lang proposes to Li Lan, he warns her, "I wouldn't underestimate the importance of family." Were you surprised by Li Lan's decision at the end of the novel? If you were in her shoes, do you think you would have chosen the same route, with its sacrifices?

10. Did you know anything about traditional Chinese folklore before reading *The Ghost Bride*? What did you find fascinating or strange about the mythology woven throughout the novel, and the Chinese notions of the afterlife? ᕗ

Why You Should Write That Book. Anyway.

I MUST CONFESS that when my mother found out that I was writing a book about dead people and ghost marriages, she said plaintively, "Why . . . why can't you write something *nice*?" I could tell her only that I thought it was an interesting story. Then I went away (rather guiltily) and continued writing whenever I could sneak some free time. Now, as much as I still listen to my mum, despite the fact that I'm quite middle-aged, I'm very glad that I didn't heed her. Because if I had, it would be the second time that this book, *The Ghost Bride*, did not get written.

In fact, when I was still a university student struggling over what to do with my senior thesis, I'd wanted to write about the historical role of female ghosts in Asian culture. Thanks to a childhood spent reading far too many strange Chinese tales, I had always wondered: (1.) Why is it that by and large, Asian ghosts seem so much more terrifying than Western ones and (2.) why are the worst ones all female? Clearly, it must be some sort of subconscious recognition that women were traditionally disempowered in Asian society, and perhaps this reflected their frustrations.

Unfortunately, I never did write that thesis because I chickened out, thinking that no one would ever employ me if they saw that on my resume (more fool me, because I later realized that nobody really cares what you write about for your thesis unless you're going into academia)! Instead, I ended up writing a terrible dissertation about the economics of Chinese industrial townships, which was so mind-numbingly boring that even I could hardly read it without feeling the urge to rush out of the library and buy myself a bag of Cheetos. Needless to say, I didn't find any extra inspiration, besides gaining several pounds and permanently orange-stained hands.

However, I kept the idea of women and ghosts rattling around in the back of my head and they showed up in a number of short stories that I wrote. Years later, I started a novel about an elephant who was a detective. There were many reasons why this (though marginally better than industrial townships) was also not a good subject, but in the meantime, while I was doggedly researching my elephant book in the archives of our local Malaysian newspaper, I came across a sentence that alluded to the decline of spirit marriages amongst the Chinese.

"What is this?" was my first reaction. Never mind that there wasn't anything about elephants in the article. Then I realized that this must refer to the marriage of the dead. I'd vaguely heard of this before, since ghost stories are the weapon of choice for Chinese grandmothers, but this matter-of-fact reference was so intriguing that what began as a subplot for my elephant book took on a life of its own.

There's actually a long Chinese

Why You Should Write That Book. Anyway.
(continued)

literary tradition of strange tales set in the blurred borderline between spirits and humans, where beautiful women turn out to be shape-shifting foxes, and the afterlife is run like a monstrous parody of Imperial Chinese bureaucracy. It's a very rich and curious mythology that I'd love to introduce readers to, especially since I think the prospect of being married off to a dead man touches on all sorts of fears for women—in addition to an arranged marriage, there's family pressure and, worse still, a bridegroom who's actually dead.

My mother has now come around to the idea of the book. In fact, she read and loved it, which made me ridiculously happy. (I need to figure out the secret behind maternal approval and apply it to my own children.) But most important, though it was sometimes a struggle, I enjoyed writing this novel. Far more than I ever connected with the economics of Chinese industrial townships. So whether you're writing or reading, I'd like to encourage you to pursue what you find deeply interesting. And don't eat too many Cheetos.

Thank you so much for reading this book. For further suggestions about what to eat while you read, come visit my blog at http://yschoo.com! 〜